Beginning Acting

The illusion
of natural behavior

Beginning Acting
The illusion of natural behavior

Richard H. Felnagle

PRENTICE-HALL, INC., Englewood Cliffs, New Jersey 07632

Library of Congress Cataloging-in-Publication Data

FELNAGLE, RICHARD H., (date)
  Beginning acting.

  Includes bibliographies.
  1. Acting. I. Title.
PN2061.F4 1987   792'.028   86–15159
ISBN 0–13–071631–6

Editorial/production supervision and
  interior design: Marianne Peters
Manufacturing buyer: Harry P. Baisley
Cover design: Diane Saxe
Cover photos: Richard H. Felnagle

© 1987 by Prentice-Hall, Inc.
A Division cf Simon & Schuster
Englewood Cliffs, New Jersey 07632

Printed in the United States of America
10 9 8 7 6 5 4 3 2 1

ISBN 0-13-071631-6 01

Prentice-Hall International (UK) Limited, *London*
Prentice-Hall of Australia Pty. Limited, *Sydney*
Prentice-Hall Canada Inc., *Toronto*
Prentice-Hall Hispanoamericana, S.A., *Mexico*
Prentice-Hall of India Private Limited, *New Delhi*
Prentice-Hall of Japan, Inc., *Tokyo*
Prentice-Hall of Southeast Asia Pte. Ltd., *Singapore*
Editora Prentice-Hall do Brasil, Ltda., *Rio de Janeiro*

Contents

Preface

This book is organized in a series of ten "lessons," one of which appears before each chapter. Lesson One defines the *illusion of natural behavior*—the goal of all realistic acting, and the following chapter explains how this kind of acting evolved and how it is perceived by an audience. Lesson Two introduces the principle of *playing with conviction*—a principle that applies to all of the following lessons. The chapter that follows describes this concept in detail and explains how it links acting on the stage with the kind of acting found in everyday life.

The next five lessons deal with the real "meat" of the book. Lesson Three describes the way in which the actor relates to the setting of the play. Lesson Four explains how the actor establishes a character's relationship to the other characters in the play. Lesson Five discusses motivation and how it is communicated to the audience through character objectives. Lesson Six describes how actors derive character objectives from a close reading of the script. Lesson Seven covers the all-important process of playing beat changes.

The next two lessons deal primarily with important supplementary concerns. Lesson Eight describes how characterization is an essential function of playing beats and objectives. Lesson Nine addresses the subject of emotion and suggests some guidelines for beginning actors to follow in the use of emotion in their acting.

Lesson Ten summarizes the component parts of the *illusion of natural behavior,* and Chapter Ten presents an actor's checklist for the ten qualities that define good realistic acting.

At the end of each of the chapters (except the last), there are suggested exercises. If at all possible, students should do these exercises after having studied each lesson and the material in the following chapter. Also, several of the chapters present scenes for analysis. To gain the maximum benefit from the discussions attending these scenes, students should act the scenes in order to demonstrate for themselves the techniques described in the analysis.

Through reading the lessons, studying the supporting material in the chapters, attempting the exercises, and performing the scenes presented for analysis, students should be able to gain a solid understanding of the principles of realistic acting for the stage.

Acknowledgments

Many people have assisted me in the preparation of this book, and I would like to express my appreciation to them at this time: Dr. Leonard Pronko, head of the Department of Theatre at Pomona College; Dr. West T. Hill, Centre College professor emeritus and former head of the Dramatic Arts Program; and Mrs. Johnette Hoop, a professional actor and a great friend. They all agreed to critique the manuscript at my request, and their comments and suggestions have been invaluable. I would also like to thank Dr. Betty Bernhard of Pomona College for her comments as well.

Many of my former students have contributed to the work on this book in various ways, but I would particularly like to express my appreciation to the students of my Drama 30C Acting Techniques class at Centre College who were the guinea pigs on whom I tried out an early draft of this text. I would particularly like to thank the students who posed for the photographs that accompany this text: Catherine Stork, David DeWitt, Helen Layne, Lynnell Major, Martha Nichols, Susanne Sing, and Randall Harmon.

I also owe a debt of gratitude to Centre College for considerable material assistance with the typing, duplicating, mailing, and other costs associated with the process of writing a book. In particular, I would like to express my gratitude to President Richard Morrill and Professor Milton Reigelman for their support and encouragement. I am especially grateful to Mr. Jack

Kineke, whose infinite patience helped me to master the wonders of word processing.

I would also like to acknowledge a longstanding debt to Mrs. Dulce Odriozola, Miss Elizabeth Talbot-Martin, and Mr. Robert F. Denniston of the Pasadena Youth Theatre Workshop for having given me my first opportunity to try out some of my theories of teaching acting. I am particularly grateful to Mr. Denniston for having given me my first roles as an actor and for having instilled in me a sense of the integrity and worthiness of the theatre as an institution.

Finally, I am grateful to my family for their understanding and support through the long process of writing this book, and particularly to my wife for her assistance with proofreading, her suggestions, and her willingness to listen to my ideas until the late hours of the night.

Beginning Acting

The illusion
of natural behavior

Lesson One

Introduction

In life, our behavior automatically reflects the nature of where we are, who is there with us, and what we are doing. When any of those things change—when we go to another place, work with different people, change our actions—our behavior automatically adjusts to reflect those changes. And these adjustments occur spontaneously, without our having to initiate or direct them consciously.

As actors onstage, we pretend that we are somewhere other than where we really are, that we are with people other than the people who are really there with us, and that we are doing something other than what we are really doing. The truth is that we are on a stage, we are with our fellow actors, we are reciting words we have memorized, and we are walking through movements we have rehearsed. And our behavior will reflect this truth automatically unless we think to do something about it. On the stage, we must consciously and deliberately create the adjustments to our behavior that would occur spontaneously if we were really where we pretend to be, really with whom we pretend to be, and really doing what we pretend to be doing.

When an actor on a stage can create all of these adjustments effectively, the result is a convincing illusion of natural behavior, that is to say behavior that is natural to the place where the play is supposed to take place, to the nature of the relationships among the people who are supposed to be there, and to the actions which the actor's character is supposed to perform.

Creating all these adjustments is what the process of realistic acting is all about.

Chapter One

Realistic Acting

The purpose of this book is to help beginning actors master the principles of realistic acting for the stage.

Modern realistic acting emerged as a distinct type in the late nineteenth and early twentieth centuries. It evolved in response to certain innovations in the way that plays were being written and produced. Today, it is the most popular type of acting all over the world. Even though other types of acting have come along since, realistic acting continues to eclipse all other kinds in popularity, particularly in the United States.

One reason realistic acting has become so popular is the influence of movies and television. In fact, because of this influence, realistic acting has become the first truly international type of acting. Evidence of this fact can be seen in the movies and television shows that are produced in countries with their own unique theatrical traditions that are older than realistic acting. In India, for example, the tradition of the Kathakali dancers goes back more than 300 years: in Japan, the complex tradition of the Noh drama goes back for more than 600 years; in China, the tradition of the Peking Opera is older still. And yet, when movies are made in India, Japan, or China, they usually feature realistic acting. And when these films are dubbed into other languages, they can be understood by audiences anywhere in the world.

Because of the popularity of realistic acting, we rarely have the opportunity to see any other type. As a result, we tend to take the principles of realistic acting completely for granted. We assume that we know what realistic acting is all about—but do we really? Many people believe that realistic acting simply requires actors to act "naturally" and nothing more. However, realistic acting on the stage involves many strange theatrical conventions that are, in their way, fully as artificial and unnatural as the conventions of Kathakali, Noh, or Peking Opera. When the behavior of a realistic actor on the stage is compared with the natural behavior of a person off the stage, the actor's behavior doesn't seem natural at all. To be sure, the principles of realistic acting are based on the principles of natural behavior, and realistic actors must become observers of the human race in order to become successful as actors. But realistic acting also involves certain purely theatrical conventions that must be mastered as well.

In essence, realistic actors create the illusion of natural behavior, not the thing itself. How actors create this illusion and what theatrical conventions are involved in the process is the subject of this book.

By way of introduction to this study, this chapter examines the following topics:

How and why realistic acting evolved as a distinct type of acting
What the unique qualities of realistic acting are that set it apart from other types of acting
Why realistic acting is international
Why realistic acting on film is perceived differently from that on the stage

Since realistic acting is the only type that most people ever see, we need to talk about other types of acting first. By comparing realistic acting with other types, we can better understand the qualities that make realistic acting unique.

EVOLUTION OF REALISTIC ACTING

The oldest type of acting is what we might call conventionalized acting. This type uses sign language and other conventions of movement, gesture, or costume that are symbolic and not derived directly from natural human behavior. Examples of this kind of acting include the previously mentioned Kathakali dancers of India, who have to learn the hundreds of hand gestures that are used to tell the stories. Also belonging in this category are the shadow puppet theatres of Southeast Asia, Balinese temple dancers, mummers' plays, and all other forms of primitive ritual that portray mythological events. While watching performances of this kind, a person who does not know the meaning of the gestures or the other conventions is usually not able to follow the story being dramatized. Also, in this type of acting, the performers often do not impersonate their characters. Instead, through costume and gesture, they *represent* gods and demons and the like. As a result, more than one performer may even play the same character at the same time. Therefore, the emphasis is less on the illusion of the presence of the character and more on the perfection with which the actors are able to perform the intricate movements that tell the story.

Probably just as old, but more characteristic of advanced societies, is what we might call stylized acting. Examples include Japanese Kabuki, Peking Opera, commedia dell'arte (in its pure form and not in the literary versions of playwrights such as Carlo Goldoni and Carlo Gozzi), modern mime, and the kind of acting that is often seen in story ballets, such as *Sleeping Beauty* and *Swan Lake*. The performers in this type of drama usually impersonate their characters, but their movements and speech are exaggerated and stylized versions of natural behavior. The chief difference between conventionalized acting and stylized acting is that a person watching a stylized performance does not need to know a specialized vocabulary of gestures in order to follow the story. Because the performance is based on natural behavior, anyone should be able to understand some or all of the play through observation alone. However, the emphasis is more on the aesthetic beauty of the movements and the singing (when present) than on the illusion of impersonation.

Of more recent origin is the immediate predecessor of realistic acting. This type is usually called presentational acting, and it gets its name from the way in which the performers tend to face the audience (that is, the way they "present" themselves) throughout the performance. Examples of this kind of acting include various historical European styles (particularly French classical tragedy) and the kind of acting that is usually seen today in opera and some children's theatre.

Possibly this type of acting originated with the Greeks. The use of full-face masks has a tendency to force actors to turn out toward the audience. If you have ever done any work with masks yourself or watched masked actors performing, you may have noticed that when a masked actor turns away from the audience, the actor's character almost seems to disappear from the stage. Masks are also used in conventionalized and stylized acting, but Greek drama put a new emphasis on the recitation of the spoken text. In conventionalized and stylized performances, the texts are often traditional and are already familiar to the audience; therefore, the performers chant and sing the texts with elaborate vocal ornamentations that render the words almost impossible to understand. But the Greek plays (in their original productions) featured texts that audiences were hearing for the first time. The playwrights wanted the audiences to hear and understand the poetry, and therefore, the use of gesture had to be restrained. The singing and the chanting had to enhance the meaning of the text, whereas the chanting and singing often

heard in conventionalized and stylized performances are usually independent of the meaning of the words.

Therefore, the emphasis in presentational acting tends to be more on
voice and speech than on movement. Actors face out toward the audience
as much as possible in order to be heard and to be understood. Movement
and gesture must be graceful and must not distract from the meaning of the
text. The resulting behavior of presentational actors can seem very affected,
particularly in the case of nineteenth-century melodrama. A scene from such
a play appears as Figure 1–1. Note particularly the man with his hand on his
forehead; the gesture is symbolic of grief or despair, not an actual attempt
to create the illusion of the emotion realistically.

Until the nineteenth century, the most popular type of acting found in
the European and American theatres was presentational acting. Beautiful
voices and graceful gestures were the most emphasized qualities of the presentational actor's art. History tells us, for example, that Molière (in the sev-

FIGURE 1–1.   An Advertising Woodcut for the Play *Progress* by Thomas William Robertson.   *The scene
is supposed to represent a drawing room, but the actors' body positions appear to be opened
up toward the audience in a way more appropriate to presentational acting. Also, the actors
are not really relating to each other, and their emotional expressions are very conventional.*
(From Stanley Applebaum's *Scenes from the Nineteenth-Century Stage in Advertising
Woodcuts,* Dover Publications, 1977.)

enteenth century) never mastered tragedy because he did not posses a tragic voice. On the other hand, Charles Kemble (in the nineteenth century) was much admired for his measured and mannered diction.

But in the early nineteenth century, the Romantic movement in art and literature created an interest in historical plays that featured accurate period costumes and settings. Also, the popularity of melodrama increased the audience's desire for more realistic settings. As this kind of scenery began to be provided, actors had to adjust their performances accordingly. In other words, if the scenery realistically depicted a drawing room, the actors were expected to act as if they were in a drawing room and not just as if they were merely on a stage. In order to achieve this effect, they began to turn away from the audience and to relate more to the scenery. In the case of indoor settings, actors actually began to use the furniture; bold experimentors even tried playing whole speeches while sitting down.

Today, it is difficult for us to appreciate what an innovation it was for the actors to start using the scenery because we take this characteristic of realistic acting so much for granted. Even when the scenery for a play is abstract or nonrealistic or just a bare stage, realistic actors are supposed to behave as if they were in a particular place at a particular time. No other type of acting had ever before required actors to create the illusion of time and place in this way.

In Germany, one theatre company particularly became famous for the photographic realism of its scenes: the Meinigen Company (1866–1890), so named for its benefactor and chief costumer, the Duke of Saxe-Meinigen. The visual integration of the actors and the scenery was nearly perfect in their productions. Even so, the acting was still presentational. André Antoine, a famous director and innovator of the late nineteenth and early twentieth centuries, reviewed the Meinigen's production of Friedrich Schiller's *William Tell* in 1888. He admired the naturalness of the crowd scenes in particular, but nevertheless, he observed:

> The only objection I have to their technique is this: in *William Tell*, for example, Schiller having written a part for the crowd, all the supernumeraries recited the same phrase in unison. The result was heavy and artificial. Could not the cues of the crowd be handled by means of a cleverly conducted uproar?[1]

The idea of a whole crowd of people reciting the same phrases in unison is characteristic of a Greek chorus, clearly a presentational technique. This kind of unnatural behavior on the part of the chorus would have been perfectly acceptable in a presentational staging of the play. But when the illusion of time and place was otherwise so natural, the unnaturalness of the chorus' behavior was especially noticeable.

Therefore, when the actors started relating realistically to the scenery, they also had to start relating realistically to each other. But the principles of presentational acting didn't tell them how to do that. The stylized and symbolic gestures of presentational acting didn't work with the realistic illusion of the new stagecraft. Furthermore, playwrights were abandoning the set speeches and overblown rhetoric that presentational actors loved to perform. The dialogue was becoming increasingly realistic as well. The old ways didn't work well with the new drama either.

An incident from the history of the Russian theatre helps to illustrate this problem and its eventual solution. When Anton Chekhov's naturalistic play *The Seagull* was first produced in Russia in 1896, it was a complete failure. *The Seagull* is a complex play that realistically portrays a delicate network of human relationships. The actors in the first production in St. Petersberg were essentially presentational actors. When they tried to read Chekhov's sensitive and often fragmentary dialogue with the same bombast and posturing usually reserved for Romantic drama and verse tragedy, the results were very unsatisfactory. At that time, many people felt that the play had been at fault. Two years later, Constantin Stanislavski and his associate, Vladimir Nemirovich-Danchenko, persuaded Chekhov to let them produce the play at their newly formed Moscow Art Theatre, and this production was a resounding success—both for the Moscow Art Theatre and for Chekhov. Trying to explain how they had solved the acting problem, Nemirovich-Danchenko wrote,

> The actor of the old theatre acts either *emotion:* love, jealousy, hatred, joy, etc.; or *words*, underlining them, stressing each significant one; or a *situation*, laughable or dramatic; or a *mood*, or *physical self-consciousness*. In a word, inevitably during every instance of his presence on the stage he is *acting* something, representing something. Our demands on the actor *are* that he should not act anything; decidedly not a *thing*; neither feelings, nor moods, nor situations, nor words, nor style, nor images. [2]

In this passage, Nemirovich-Danchenko defines precisely the boundary between presentational acting and realistic acting. The presentational actor plays *things*. What the realistic actor had to learn to do is to play *actions*. When Stanislavski produced *The Seagull*, he got his actors to concentrate on playing the actions of the characters, not their moods or their words or their emotions. Subsequently, other innovators repeated Stanislavski's discovery, and the concept of playing actions became widely accepted in the European and American theatre.

Even so, once the principles of realistic acting had evolved, they were not universally accepted. In Russia, Vsevelod Meyerhold, who had been an actor with Stanislavski and the Moscow Art Theatre, started his own theatre, in which acrobatics and broad pantomime replaced realistic acting completely. In Germany, Bertolt Brecht, an important playwright and director, condemned realistic acting. He did not want his actors to try to create an illusion of natural behavior for the audience. He advocated the need for a "distancing effect" that would constantly remind the spectators that they were watching a play. In more recent times in America, such groups as The Living Theatre, the Open Theatre, Mabou Mines, and others have produced distinctly nonrealistic plays that use the techniques of conventionalized, stylized, and even presentational acting. Therefore, beginning actors need to realize that no matter how popular realistic acting has become, it is still only one of many possible types of acting required by the modern theatre. And a mastery of the principles of realistic acting does not guarantee that an actor is ready for other types of acting as well. However, realistic acting is unquestionably the dominant type found in the modern theatre (not to mention film and television), and a mastery of the principles of realistic acting is vital for anyone who wishes to make a living as an actor today. (In May 1985, even Julian Beck, the founder of The Living Theatre, appeared in a cameo role in the television soap opera *All My Children.*)

In summary, then, the two qualities that define realistic acting as a distinct type and set it apart from all other types of acting are the way in which the actors are expected to relate realistically to the scenery, as if they were in the place being represented, and the way in which actors relate realistically to each other through playing actions. Realistic acting places much more emphasis on the way actors use their bodies than does presentational acting. In presentational acting, speaking the text with a beautiful voice and precise diction is the most important element. An occasional graceful, refined gesture is also desirable, as long as such things do not distract from the recitation of the text. In realistic acting, however, everything the actor does is supposed to fit into the sense of the whole stage illusion; voice and gesture must be subordinated to the nature of the action that the actor is trying to play.

GIVING THE MEANING TO THE WORDS

Everywhere in the world that a play is to be produced with realistic acting, rehearsals usually begin the same way: the scripts are handed out and the actors are assigned their roles. Thereafter, the actors' first task is to read the play and to learn the lines. What happens next will vary from production to production, but in virtually every case, learning the lines comes first. In other words, the playscript is the starting point for every production.

But the words in the script are indeed just that: the starting point only, not the end itself. Many amateur actors seem to think that when they have learned their lines, their work is over. To them, bringing the playwright's work to life means just memorizing and saying aloud the playwright's words.

That attitude reflects the commonly held assumption that a playwright's words retain some kind of absolute meaning. But written words are symbols, ink smears on paper that have only the meaning they have been assigned by the person who put them there. We know the particular meaning of any written word only by looking at the other words around it, that is, the *context* in which that word has been used. For example, the simple banal word *cat* may denote a small domesticated pet, and then again it may denote a huge, carnivorous jungle animal or a kind of fish or a type of boat or a whip or even a human being, an afficianado of jazz. (Equally possible meanings, according to the dictionary, include a Medieval shelter, a double tripod, and a tractor.) To know which meaning is the one that a given author has intended, a reader must look at the context in which that word is used. Words alone simply do not possess absolute meanings; the meaning of every word is a function of how it is used.

And just as written words derive their meanings from the context in which they appear, spoken words derive their meanings from the physical, interpersonal situation in which they are used. When one person says "I love you" to another person, the specific meaning of those words can only be understood by carefully observing what the speaker is doing at the time: standing or sitting, smiling or scowling, looking at the other person or looking away, and so on. How close is the speaker to the listener? Are they touching? Where is all of this happening? What is their relationship to each other? How quickly are the words being spoken? What sort of vocal inflections are being used? Only after all these factors have been considered will the listener be able to know what the speaker meant by saying "I love you." The speaker might be proposing marriage or merely saying good-bye. The speaker might be trying to beg forgiveness or just expressing simple endearment, as one might remark about a good wine or a favorite book. The speaker might be pledging a long-term commitment or just trying to proposition a one-night stand. In summary, when words are exchanged between people, the meaning of those words is always a product of the situation in which they are spoken, just as the meaning of each written word is a function of the context in which it is used.

Nowhere else is this fact more true than in the theatre. Actors should never assume that because they know what the playwright's words mean, that meaning will automatically be communicated to the audience. The actors must give the meaning to the playwright's words by creating the right physical context.

But how do actors know what context to create? The answer is that they have to look for certain clues in the dialogue. In this sense, dialogue is actually a kind of code which actors must learn to decipher in order to determine the correct physical context in which the words are to be spoken. Once the code has been broken, then the actors should be able to figure out how to move and gesture in a way that will give the spoken words the meaning the playwright intended. In other words, the practice of realistic acting is made up of two separate processes: first, studying the script to find the right clues for action, and second, putting those clues to work.

The point may be obvious, but it is so important it deserves to be stated again. Actors must learn to do more than just memorize their lines. Once the actors have learned their lines, the real work is only just beginning: they must then take the words they have been given to say and turn them into things to do.

Doing is what realistic acting is all about, not reciting. And this characteristic is also true of acting in general. Otherwise, acting would be called *speaking*. But it isn't; it's called *acting*. To act means to do; to do, one must move. There is no acting without moving. If actors are not using their bodies, they are not acting—regardless of what they may be saying or how well. Acting is movement; movement is acting. Movement, after all, is the most basic sign of life; things that don't move are dead—including actors.

To return to the point with which this section began, the playwright's words may be the starting point of every production, but in performance, the actor's movements are what counts. *Plays* may be verbal, but theatre is physical, and therefore, primarily a visual medium. Particularly in the case of realistic acting, what an audience sees gives the meaning to what it hears.

So important is this relationship between the text and the physical performance that it forms the basis of one of the most important aesthetic principles of realistic acting: An audience might not be able to understand every word spoken on stage, but the audience should be able to understand the meaning of the words anyway by watching what the actors are doing. Consider the fact that Stanislavski and the Moscow Art Theatre toured the United States for a period of over twelve months during 1923 and 1924. They were warmly received by adoring audiences everywhere they played. And after the tour, Stanislavski was so moved by the enthusiasm of the American audiences that he dedicated his memoirs, *My Life in Art,* to the American people. *And yet, the Moscow Art Theatre performed throughout the United States, not in English, but in Russian!* Commenting on Stanislavski's American tour in her book *The Stanislavski Heritage,* Christine Edwards affirms,

> As for the language acting as a barrier, while a few found it an impediment to a full appreciation of the plays, the majority felt that the acting of the Moscow Art Theatre surmounted even that obstacle.[3]

Furthermore, she cites a comment made by John Corbin writing in the *New York Times* for January 14, 1923: "Many of us forgot through long stretches that we understood no word of the text."[4]

Stanislavski was not the only non-English-speaking actor to conquer the English-speaking world. Eleanor Duse (1859–1924) was similarly adored by audiences throughout the United States, and she performed primarily in Italian. There is an anecdote which, I believe, is attributed to Eleanor Duse. Supposedly, she was asked to perform a short speech at a private party given in her honor during one of her American tours. After a moment's thought, she began a rambling monologue in Italian that soon had the English-speaking listeners in tears. Later, when asked to name the play from which the beautiful speech had been performed, she confessed through an interpreter that she had merely been reciting the alphabet.

To state the principle as strongly as possible, the goal of realistic acting is to communicate as much information as possible about the characters, the situation, and the story itself through physical action.

Two other points need to be made about realistic acting before going on to the next part of this discussion. The first is that realistic acting embraces many different *styles* of acting. The full spectrum of these styles ranges from the neo-presentationalism associated with modern musical comedy and opera to the scratching, mumbling naturalism associated with the American Method. Each of these various styles has its own special conventions and unique problems for the actor. The spectrum is so vast that some actors have difficulty in recognizing all these different styles as belonging to the same family. However, as long as a given style demands that the actors relate realistically to each other and to the setting of the play through the playing of actions, the type of acting is properly identified as realistic. Therefore, the guidelines and techniques discussed in the following pages are understood to apply to all the various styles of realistic acting.

In addition to the modern performing styles already referred to, realistic acting also embraces many hybrid styles that result from modern attempts to re-create period acting styles. Today, most productions of Greek tragedies, commedia dell'arte farces, classical French comedy, and the like are usually performed in styles that are combinations of period conventions and realistic acting techniques. The reason is that if these period styles were reproduced as authentically as possible, they would seem strange and daunting to modern audiences. Greek tragedy, for example, was performed by masked men who danced and sang the text to music improvised on the flute and harp; modern scholars think such performances may have resembled a cross between primitive ritual and grand opera. Such carryings-on today would be almost incomprehensible to a modern audience. Authentic commedia dell'arte was mostly nonverbal slapstick and obscene gesture. The written scenarios that survive today are mostly attempts by playwrights, such as Gozzi and Goldoni, to sanitize real commedia and make it literary. Classical French tragedy was performed in a singsong chant with very little movement. And there are other examples as well. Today, only nineteenth-century melodrama is performed in anything like the authentic style of period presentational acting—and then only for laughs. Thus it is that most so-called period acting styles that we see today are really variations on the techniques of modern realistic acting.

In light of that last observation, the second point about realistic acting that needs to be made is that it is essentially a type of performance, not a type of drama. Although it is true that realistic acting was perfected essentially to serve the needs of realistic drama, it is not true that it is an exclusive function of such drama. Virtually any type or style of play can be performed realistically if a particular group of actors wishes to do so. Any play—from

Greek tragedy to Restoration comedies of manners to expressionistic learning plays—all can be performed realistically. (Whether or not they *should* be is another matter.) The reason is that in any piece of realistic acting, the actors create most of the details of the physical performance from their own imaginations. No playwright, not even strictly naturalistic ones, can supply all the information in the text that an actor needs to create the physical performance. Therefore, the process of inferring, supplying, creating, and devising the physical performance is essentially independent of the type of play on which that performance is based.

In light of that last observation, students will note that example scenes for this book have been chosen from several different types and styles of drama. For example, a scene from *Macbeth* is discussed in great detail in Chapter Five from the point of view of a realistic actor. Today, Shakespeare is usually performed in some kind of quasi-Elizabethan/realistic hybrid style. As already stated, if the actors were to pose and posture and rant and declaim in the authentic style of presentational acting, most audiences would be horrified. In contemporary theatrical practice, realistic actors are frequently called upon to act in realistic as well as nonrealistic dramas; therefore, scenes from nonrealistic as well as realistic plays are discussed in this book.

THE STAGE VERSUS THE SCREEN

As stated at the beginning of this chapter, the purpose of this book is to help beginning actors master the principles of realistic acting *for the stage.* The italicized words were included in that statement deliberately.

Any student who seriously wants to learn realistic acting for the stage or the screen needs to get into the habit of going to the live theatre on a regular basis—the *professional* theatre, and often. Only by watching trained, professional actors at work in person will students be able to understand what acting in general, and realistic acting in particular, is all about.

Of course, it is difficult for many students of acting to attend live, professional theatre on a regular basis. So what about studying the performances of great actors on film and videotape? Doesn't that count for something?

The answer is yes and no. Yes, there is a lot of great acting that has been captured on film and videotape, but no, it isn't very useful to students of acting as an object of study. The camera (both film and video) inevitably causes certain distortions in the way we perceive actors on a screen. Watching actors perform on a movie or television screen, we see them very differently from the way we see them on stage.

Since most of us in the United States have seen more film and television than live theatre, the differences between how stage acting and film acting are perceived need to be examined. As we will see, these distortions have a major effect on how we perceive what acting is all about.

One obvious example of the way the camera distorts our perception of acting is through the use of the close-up. Early silent movies were photographed like stage plays; the camera would rest in a single position for long sequences of action, during which time the film frame was treated like a proscenium arch. Then some early film makers began to experiment with the startling device of changing the camera's point of view during a given sequence of action, something an audience watching a play is never permitted to do. These film makers soon noticed that certain changes in point of view, particularly the sudden shift to a close-up view of actors' faces, could have considerable impact. Some film historians credit the pioneer director D. W. Griffith with popularizing the close-up in the United States, particularly in such films as his 1915 epic *The Birth of a Nation*. Even in this epic film with huge vistas of battle action, the intimate close-ups of actors' faces at appropriate moments have the greater impact on the audience's emotions. The close-up is now an accepted, even overused, element of film grammar. The camera prefers to watch actors mostly from the waist up, or in the case of films made for television, from the neck up. The result is a greater emphasis on what the actor does with the face than with the whole body. On the sound stage, the actor uses the whole body just as much as in the live theatre, but the camera dwells primarily on the face. As a result, many beginning actors seem virtually lifeless from the neck down. They are not aware of how their favorite actors use their whole bodies on camera, and therefore these beginners often don't think to use their whole bodies on stage.

This is only one distortion resulting from the way that movies are perceived. On the screen, actors often appear to be speaking in soft, conversational tones. On the stage, many beginners try to do the same and wonder why it doesn't work. What they forget is that in a movie theatre, the actors' soft, conversational tones are amplified through great big speakers that render soft, breathy voices audible. Another perceptual distortion is caused by the way that the camera usually dwells only on the actor who is speaking at any given moment. When it's someone else's line, the camera cuts to a view of that actor, and everyone else disappears for a while. On the stage, an actor is present throughout the scene, and what the actors do while they are not speaking is often just as important as what they do when they are. Stage actors must retain the illusion of character at all times, but many beginners drift off into space when they're not speaking, almost as if they think the audience, like the camera, cannot see them.

The camera not only shows film actors using their bodies less than stage actors, it often *makes* them use their bodies less. On stage, actors are expected to move around a lot; acting is moving, as has been already stated. But on a sound stage, depending on the type of film being made, the camera often demands that actors stay in one place throughout the shot. Anytime the actor moves, the camera has to follow, and there are technical problems to be considered, not the least of which is simply deciding what kind of camera movement is to be used: a panning shot, a tracking shot, a hand-held shot, a crane shot, and so on, each of which requires its own special preparation and execution. Also to be considered are the problems of keeping the image in focus throughout the shot, keeping light on the subject throughout the movement, and following the subject with a microphone if synchronized sound is being recorded. These problems are particularly acute in television soap operas; so much dialogue must be videotaped during each working day that there usually isn't time to plan for as many camera setups as can be used in the shooting of a motion picture. Actors in daytime dramas frequently make their entrances and stand on their marks throughout whole scenes. The scene is not perceived on the home screen as being static because several cameras are used at once, and the director in the control booth can change the view by switching from camera to camera as desired, thus eliminating much of the need for movement by the actors. No wonder so many beginners tend to stand around on stage like sticks!

When actors are allowed to move and the camera does follow the movement, yet another perceptual distortion is created. The camera's point of view adjusts automatically to the actors' new positions as needed to view the action. Many beginners often forget this fact; they cover their business and upstage themselves almost as if they expect the audience to get up out of their seats and walk around to see what is going on. Part of learning to act on stage is learning to move so that the audience can always see whatever needs to be seen. A student actor can learn nothing about this kind of movement from watching motion pictures.

A thoughtful student may be able to compensate for some of these distortions while studying a given piece of film acting. But no amount of compensation can alter the fact that the total impact of a motion picture is more than just the sum of the actors' performances. The audience responds to the editing and the photography and the musical score and the special effects as well. While watching a stage play, the audience also responds to the scenery and the other elements, but the actors relate to the audience *directly* and are never obscured by the other elements of the production. As the reader probably knows, an actor in a film usually plays a given sequence of dialogue several times for the motion picture camera to photograph from different angles. What the audience sees in the finished film is a compilation of different views of the performance taken at different times on different pieces of film and assembled by the film editor; the result is not even a continuous performance as an audience sees on a stage. Thus, when an audience responds to a particular scene on film, they are responding to the editing and the lighting and the camera angles and the special lenses and the sound mix and all the other elements of modern film production as much as they are responding to the actors' performances alone.

The following example should make the implications of this point even clearer. The late film director Alfred Hitchcock on several occasions explained the power of the editor in the following way: A shot of children at play, followed by a shot of a man smiling, has the effect of making the man seem warm and friendly. But the same piece of film of the man smiling when preceded by a shot of a woman undressing makes the man seem to be a lecher. The same performance when manipulated by the editor in this way has two completely different meanings. And when the film of the man smiling was originally shot, the man was probably looking at nothing more than the film crew standing around behind the camera! The audience's understanding of the performance in this example is entirely a creation of the editor.

No thoughtful viewer, no matter how well informed, may separate all the elements of film production from each other in this way. And why should anyone want to? Movies are not intended to be picked apart in this way. Part of the whole aesthetic of the motion picture is the way that different elements can be blended and juxtaposed to achieve different effects. This principle was exploited in the Woody Allen film *Zelig*; actual documentary footage of celebrities of the 1920s was doctored to make it appear that Allen's character, Leonard Zelig, had actually been photographed with these celebrities. Through careful editing in one sequence, Allen made it appear as though Ziegfeld Follies star Fannie Brice was actually singing a song to him.

Audiences watching Woody Allen in *Zelig* knew that what they were watching was the result of a clever special effect. But movie audiences are often fooled in other ways. For example, Dustin Hoffman first came to national prominence through his role as Benjamin in *The Graduate,* in which he played a bumbling, mealy-mouthed "lost" youth typical of the late 1960s. Many people who saw that film assumed that they were seeing the real Dustin Hoffman in that role. Later, Hoffman presented a totally different identity and personality in his role as the street bum Ratso Rizzo in *Midnight Cowboy.* The transformation was so effective that many people who had seen both films had to be reminded that both Benjamin and Ratso had been played by the same actor. When it was announced that Hoffman was to play Willy Loman in a Broadway revival of Arthur Miller's *Death of a Salesman,* the role was so unlike anything he had done previously, many people could not even imagine him in the part.

This example points to another fact of life about the movies. Moviegoing audiences become familiar with the appearance and personality of certain actors to the extent that they become willing to pay money to see more films starring those actors. In the Hollywood system of motion picture production, films are often financed and promoted on the strength of audience identification with the stars. There is, therefore, a tendency to think of "movie stars" primarily as actors who do not change their identities from film role to film role. But in the theatre, the expectations of the audience are exactly the opposite. A role is an illusion created by the actor, not an inseparable function of the actor's own personality. Ideally, an actor ought to be able to create any kind of illusion the script demands regardless of how like or unlike the actor personally is to the role. Mary Martin enjoyed one of the most memorable successes of her stage career at the age of forty by playing an adolescent boy in a musical version of *Peter Pan*. (Needless to say, no film director today would cast a forty-year old woman in the same role, although to be fair, she did perform the role to great acclaim on network television.) *The most fundamental difference between stage acting and movie acting is that stage actors are expected to change their appearances from role to role, and movie actors are not.*

There are prominent film actors who have challenged the Hollywood "star" system and won. Actors such as Albert Finney, Ellen Burstyn, Jon Voight, and Peter Sellers have changed their appearances when they have played before the cameras. Finney, who has been known for classic leading-man-type roles in such films as *Two for the Road* and *Tom Jones*, transformed himself totally into a dumpy, middle-aged Belgian detective for his role as Hercule Poirot in *Murder on the Orient Express*. Also, he reversed the usual method of casting for the musical film *Scrooge*; previously only venerable character actors had been chosen to play Ebeneezer Scrooge on film, actors such as Alistair Sim and Basil Rathbone. Finney made himself over into Scrooge as an old man and then, without the age makeup, also played Scrooge as a young man in the ghost-of-Christmas-past sequences. Ellen Burstyn affected a Texas dialect and flamboyant mannerisms for her role in the film *The Last Picture Show*; audiences who were otherwise not familiar with her work did not immediately recognize her as the same actor in her highly acclaimed performance as a waitress in the film *Alice Doesn't Live Here Anymore*. Jon Voight without the aid of character makeup transformed himself totally from the would-be country stud of *Midnight Cowboy* to the young German journalist of *The Odessa File*. Peter Sellers was one of the few actors whom audiences came to expect to see in a variety of guises. He became strongly identified with his hilarious creation of Inspector Clouseau in *The Pink Panther* and the several sequels. But audiences also applauded his appearances as the Indian doctor in *The Road to Hong Kong*, the American concert pianist in *The World of Henry Orient*, and the disoriented gardener in *Being There*. However, these actors are more the exception than the rule.

It is not so surprising then that students who know only film and television acting don't really understand how the stage demands a complete characterization. Beginning actors seldom attempt the physical transformation that should be required for every stage role. They seldom do it because they've so seldom **seen** it! As a result, many beginning actors routinely audition only for roles that are consistent with their self-image. But <u>learning to</u> <u>be an actor means</u> learning to deal with any kind of role that is offered.

Therefore, student actors really do need to get into the habit of going to the *professional* theatre on a frequent basis. Really. There is nothing inherently wrong with acting on film or television, but there are too many ways in which the actors' images are manipulated on the screen for beginning actors to use those images as reliable objects of study. If you are a serious student of acting, you will gain much from reading this book, but you will gain much more if you will also go to the theatre and watch professional actors at work.

SUMMARY

The two qualities that distinguish realistic acting from other types are the way actors are required to create a sense of time and place and the way actors are required to play actions. Since actions are essentially nonverbal, realistic acting communicates with audiences primarily through movement. The way an actor uses the whole body gives meaning to the words being spoken in such a way that audiences shouldn't have to understand the language in order to grasp the meaning. The highest goal of realistic acting is to communicate as much information as possible through the body alone.

This second goal of realistic acting is readily apparent to audiences watching a live performance by professional stage actors, but is less clear to audiences watching motion pictures and television. The camera causes certain distortions in the perception of actors' performances. Among the causes of these distortions are the use of the close-up, the way actors' movements are limited by the needs of the camera, and the conventions of film editing. Also, film actors are required to change their identities to fit their roles much less than stage actors. As a result, acting on film is not reliable as an object of study by beginning actors. Only by observing professional actors at work in live stage performances can beginners really learn the conventions of realistic acting.

EXERCISES FOR CHAPTER ONE

The most important principle illustrated in Chapter One is how the actors give the meaning to the author's text through movement and gesture. The following exercises are intended to help students see this principle at work.

1. Try watching a television drama with the sound turned off, ideally a program you have never watched before. Try to observe how much information the actors are able to communicate by physical means alone. For best results, select

a program that was produced on video tape or one that was filmed before a live audience. In these programs, the actors' performances are most like stage performances, not compilations of various film clips. Pay particular attention to everything the actors do from the neck down. Ask yourself, how much and how well are they using their whole bodies to communicate the meaning of what they are saying? How much does the camera allow you to see?

When the program is over, try to write down the story of the drama you have watched and any other information about the story that you have observed. Ask yourself if the actors could have done other things to make the story clearer. Were the actors just reciting their lines or were they really acting with their whole bodies? If possible, compare your notes later with someone else who watched the same program with the sound turned on and see if you have correctly understood everything that happened. If not, try to identify what the actors did (or didn't do) that caused you to misunderstand what was happening.

2. Try to re-create Eleanor Duse's recitation of the alphabet. Using the letters of the alphabet as your text (or any other nonsense sounds), play a short scene with another actor. Define a strong action for yourself, such as one of the following:

Trying to get the other person to lend you money

Trying to get the other person to give you directions how to get somewhere

Trying to make the other person understand a piece of bad news

Trying to make the other person understand how you feel about him or her

Trying to make the other person get angry about some terrible act of injustice

Trying to make the other person feel ashamed for having done something wrong.

In each case, fill in the specific details of the situation in your own mind, enough to allow you to play the scene, but don't tell the other person in advance what your action is going to be. After the scene is over, ask the other person to tell you what your action was. If the other person didn't understand, ask for suggestions on how you might have succeeded.

3. Take a speech from a play or a passage of text from a short story or novel and perform that speech essentially as the author intended it to be performed. Then change the context of the speech or the identity of the person speaking or some other details of the performance to give the speech an entirely different meaning. For example, you might take the opening speech of the Stage Manager in Thornton Wilder's *Our Town* and perform it as Wilder intended, and then you might become a real estate salesperson trying to convince a client to buy a home in "Grovers Corners." Or you might become a Hollywood script writer trying to sell an idea for a screenplay to a producer. Or you might be an army general explaining the strategy for a battle to the troops, or you might be any number of other things as well.

Do not tell your audience in advance what your different interpretation of the speech is going to be. Change a few words if absolutely necessary, but otherwise try to do the speech as written. Perform the scene without any real props. Pantomime all the physical objects and details of the location that are required in your reinterpretation of the scene. After you have performed the speech, ask the members of the audience what they thought you were trying to do. Then ask them to suggest any other interpretive choices you might have made to communicate the same situation.

NOTES

1. André Antoine quoted in *A Source Book in Theatrical History*, ed. A. M. Nagler (New York: Dover Publications, Inc., 1952), p. 581.

2. Vladimir Nemirovich-Danchenko, *My Life in the Russian Theatre*, trans. John Cournos (Boston: Little, Brown and Company, 1936), p. 159.

3. Christine Edwards, *The Stanislavsky Heritage: Its Contribution to the Russian and American Theatre* (New York: New York University Press, 1965), p. 229.

4. John Corbin, "Realism of the Spirit," the *New York Times*, January 14, 1923, Sec. 7, p. 1, quoted in Edwards, p. 229.

Lesson Two

The "If-I-Were" Formula

On the stage, what passes for natural behavior is not really natural at all. Good acting has a distinctly unnatural quality that results from the demands made on all actors by the nature of live theatre. If actors really behaved exactly as if they were in their own living rooms or in somebody's office or wherever the play takes place, the results would be unsatisfactory. Actors couldn't be heard, they couldn't be seen, and their behavior would include seemingly random and unfocused movement. In other words, the stage is not a living room or an office; the stage is the stage, and that fact must be respected above all else.

To create an effective illusion of natural behavior, actors must understand where that unnatural quality of an actor's behavior properly comes from and what the component parts of the resulting illusion really are. This unnatural quality of an actor's behavior is explained in detail in Chapter Two; the component parts of the illusion are described in the following chapters.

However, actors must never deliberately try to be "stagey" in their acting. When an actor tries to do that, the result doesn't look natural either. It just looks stagey. To help combat the urge to be stagey, there is the "If-I-Were" formula. Actors say to themselves, "Now, if I were this character in this situation, how would I read that line? How would I make that cross? How would I do that piece of business?" As long as the actors' performances are consistent with their answers to those questions, their performances should seem natural. This kind of performing is what is meant by the phrase *playing with conviction*.

There is a danger that some actors will use this formula to turn every character into themselves. But the formula doesn't ask how you personally would behave in the situation of the play, but how you would behave *if you were* that character in that situation. Learning to use the formula in this way is the first step toward creating an effective performance.

Chapter Two

Playing with Conviction

Every stage setting—no matter how realistic or finely detailed—is still only a stage setting. It may look like something else, a living room or a restaurant or an office or whatever, but it is really only a set, an arrangement of flats and drapes and platforms. You know how to behave naturally when you are really in a living room or a restaurant or an office, but when you are really on a stage set, the natural way to behave is as if you were on a stage. In other words, when you are on a stage, it's not natural to behave as if you were in a living room or a restaurant or an office. When most people get on a stage, they start to act as if they were on a stage and not in the place that the setting is supposed to represent. Trying to forget about the stage and to behave as if you were somewhere else is a lot harder than it might at first appear to be.

Imagine being in the audience at a performance of Arthur Miller's *Death of a Salesman*. The curtain rises on the first act of the play, and the audience begins to concentrate on what the actors are saying. If the actors are competent, the audience sees a husband and a wife in the kitchen of their home in the middle of the night. Willy Loman, the husband, is exhausted, troubled, clearly too old for the life of a traveling salesman. Linda, his wife, is also troubled, concerned. "You didn't smash the car, did you?" she asks.

Now consider the same scene from the point of view of the actors: They don't see a cozy little kitchen in the middle of the night. They see a number of brightly colored lights shining in their eyes. They see an arrangement of canvas flats and other scenic elements designed to suggest a kitchen. They see the spatter painted on those flats and the dutchmen on the facings and the stage braces holding it all up. They hear the coughs and whispers in the audience, not to mention the shuffling of the four people who are late taking their seats in the fourth row. If the actor playing Linda opens the refrigerator door, she notices that the air inside isn't cold. If she opens a drawer to pull out a spoon, she knows that only one of the three drawers on the set is functional and will hold only the spoon the property assistant has placed there for her to use in that scene. She can see beyond the set and into the wings, where the stage manager, wearing a pair of headphones, is standing less than twenty feet away at a lighted desk. She may even be able to perceive other members of the crew lounging about in the shadows and other actors waiting to make their entrances. When she speaks to the actor playing Willy, she can see face powder that he accidentally spilled onto one trouser leg, makeup stains around the top of his shirt collar, and age spots stippled onto his hands with a makeup sponge. And when she says, "You didn't smash the car, did you?" she has to try to forget she knows he's going to answer, "I said nothing happened. Didn't you hear me?" She also has to try to forget that she has heard him say that line thirty or forty times in rehearsal, but at the same time she has to remember that his "Didn't you hear me?" is her cue to say, "Don't you feel well?" And in spite of all that, she has to make it believable.

Take a moment to look at the illustrations that accompany this section. In Figure 2–1, we see two actors rehearsing a scene on a stage. Notice that even as we look at that photograph, we start to wonder about the scene they might be rehearsing. From their body positions, we imagine that they might even be rehearsing the scene just described from *Death of a Salesman*. We automatically try to see them as the characters they are playing in the place where the scene might be taking place. Now look at Figure 2–2. In this view we see what the actors see. The overpowering sensation is one of being on a stage and facing the rows of seats that will be filled with people when the final performance is given. And yet, the actors have to forget about those seats and try to act as if they are in another place entirely.

A real Linda Loman would surely know how to behave naturally if she were really talking to her husband in the kitchen of their own home. But an actor playing the role of Linda Loman doesn't have it so easy. How is it possible to act naturally in the completely unnatural circumstances of a live performance on a stage? (It is one of the great ironies of the stage that everything the actors do is created, rehearsed, and executed for the sole benefit of the people in the audience, but when the actors actually step out in front of that audience, the actors are supposed to try to pretend that those people don't exist and that all the action of the play never even happened before.)

Initially, many beginners conclude that the way to make everything believable for the audience is for the actors themselves to try to believe that

FIGURE 2-1.   The Stage as the Audience Sees It.   *Even though these are only actors rehearsing a scene without costumes or scenery, we immediately start to imagine these missing elements. We tend to see them not as actors on a stage, but as characters in a play.*

everything on the stage is real. The idea seems perfectly logical: If the actors can somehow convince themselves that they are really the characters they are playing and that the scenery is really what it represents, then their behavior cannot help but be natural in those surroundings.

The idea seems logical, but it isn't very practical. Even if actors can believe that the set and the costumes and the makeup are all real, actors don't start rehearsing a role with any of these things already in existence. For an average nonmusical play, the actors may spend from two to four weeks in rehearsal with only masking tape on the floor to indicate the details of the set and only folding chairs and card tables to indicate the furniture. If the actors playing Willy and Linda have to convince themselves that three stripes of masking tape, two folding chairs, and a card table are really the Loman kitchen before they can act naturally, rehearsals aren't going to move ahead very quickly. Trying to believe that everything on the stage is real is really doing it the hard way.

And even if actors could produce authentic natural behavior by believing completely in the reality of the setting, the results would probably be

FIGURE 2-2. The Stage as the Actors See It. *In contrast to the previous photograph, the perspective from the actors' point of view is very different. The actors are more aware of the presence of the audience than of any illusion of time and place.*

undesirable. Again, try to imagine that you are watching the actors playing Willy and Linda onstage, but now try to imagine the same performance from the point of view of an observer in the wings. From this point of view, we see that they aren't really behaving the way people behave naturally in their own kitchens at all. The differences are striking: For one, the actors' body positions tend to be forced out toward the audience; in a real kitchen, people can turn their bodies in any direction they want. For another, the actors' voices are unnaturally full and loud; people usually don't bellow like that in their own kitchens at 2:00 in the morning. In other words, if actors on a stage really behaved just exactly as if they really were in the kitchens of their own homes, the results wouldn't look natural on the stage.

The secret of achieving natural behavior on the stage is for the actors not to try to believe that everything on the stage is real. The fact is that natural stage behavior is nothing like natural behavior offstage. Everything the actors do onstage has a distinctly deliberate quality. Also, everything seems a little larger than life; gestures, movements, facial expressions—all seem broader and more expansive than the way most people behave in their own kitchens. Perhaps one way to sum up this quality of natural stage behavior would be to say that stage behavior is like offstage behavior, only more exaggerated; however, that that summary would be *wrong*.

On the stage, exaggerated behavior tends to look like exaggerated behavior, not natural behavior. Exaggeration is fine for actors appearing in an "Olde Tyme Mellerdrammer," but otherwise, good stage behavior is not an exaggeration of offstage behavior. Even in the case of plays that require highly stylized acting, such as Restoration comedies or Greek tragedies, exaggeration and excess on the stage always look just like exaggeration and excess.

Then why does stage behavior look exaggerated? The answer is that good stage behavior is based on natural offstage behavior *but stripped away of everything nonessential to the performance of the role.* As a result, what remains seems slightly out of proportion. The following example should help to clarify this point: Consider the experience of watching home movies, candid films of friends and family taken at picnics or birthday parties. One easily observable quality of such films (besides their frequent lack of interest) is the jerky, random behavior of the people on the screen. Other than the "posed" shots in which the subjects are aware of being on camera, people shift their heads and swing their arms and sway from side to side and slouch and lean and turn away from the camera in the most annoying and undramatic fashion. And the key word here is indeed *undramatic*. That jumble of disconnected and unfocused behavior is what natural behavior really looks like; because natural behavior is such an unfocused jumble, home movies are usually boring to watch. But when we watch actors on a stage (again, as if from the wings), we notice how often the actors aren't moving at all. Trained actors know how to hold still when other actors are moving or saying lines. Offstage, people are free to put up their feet or scratch their heads or move about as they like—but onstage, never!

Natural stage behavior requires good body control. One reason is that movement attracts the audience's attention. A good actor knows not to move when the audience is supposed to be looking at someone else. If Biff or Happy decides to scratch his nose while Linda is saying her famous line "Attention must be paid!" there are going to be angry words in the greenroom at intermission.

An actor should prepare a role by choosing only the quintessential movements, gestures, reactions, and so on, that the part requires. The actor should reject everything that is not absolutely essential. In *An Actor Prepares,* Stanislavski exhorts his students to eliminate all "superfluities" with the words "Cut 90 per cent!"[1]—by which he means that the actor should get rid of everything except that which is absolutely necessary to the performance. Great acting is thus the result of great choices as well as great omissions.

Here we face a fact that is something of a paradox, and yet it is a fact of essential importance. The illusion of natural behavior onstage is created as much—or more—by what the actors leave out of the performance as by what they include. To understand why these omissions are of such importance, we need to understand a few key facts about the nature of illusions in general.

ACTING AND MAGIC

By definition, an illusion is not the thing it appears to be. For example, a black and white photograph is actually a piece of paper on one side of which has been attached an emulsion of gelatin and silver salts. Some of the salts, because of their sensitivity to light, have darkened to form a pattern. Therefore, a photograph is not an actual likeness of someone's Uncle Freddy—a photograph is only a piece of paper with stains on it. But someone might look at those stains and see a likeness of Uncle Freddy in his or her imagination. The likeness is strictly an illusion; the reality is the salts and the emulsion. Another example is the flashing green, red, and blue dots of a color television screen. If you look at the dots when you are very close, the dots themselves are all you can see. But if you step back a foot or more away from the dots, moving images may be easily recognized. The images are the illusion; the reality is the flashing dots of colored light. In this way, an illusion is never the thing it appears to be.

There is a certain definable pleasure created by illusions. In *The Poetics*, Aristotle puts great stress on this pleasure in his exposition of the nature of tragedy:

> Objects which in themselves we view with pain, we delight to contemplate when reproduced with minute fidelity: such as the forms of the most ignoble animals and of dead bodies.[2]

What Aristotle means is that the body of a dead man on display would be a repulsive sight; but a statue of a man, perhaps that of a famous writer or political leader, would be a work of art and, as such, a pleasurable sight. A statue made of marble is not a human being; it is only a piece of stone. But if that piece of stone has been shaped to recall the form and features of a certain person, then an illusion of that person is created in the minds of people looking at that statue. The recognition of that illusion (that is, how the stone has been shaped to resemble the person) is a pleasurable occurence. In the same way, the fascination we feel at a wax museum comes from the pleasure we derive from recognizing artfully costumed wax dummies as famous people. The pleasure does not come from thinking that the wax figures are actually the people they represent. In fact, wax models don't resemble their real-life counterparts in more ways than they do. They don't breathe, they don't move, the coloring of wax flesh is never as complex as that of real skin, and there are usually no discernible blemishes or moles or other minor skin imperfections that everyone has naturally. Like all illusions, wax dummies are really nothing at all like what they are intended to represent, but they're fun to look at anyway.

For precisely that reason, a person looking at a statue or a wax dummy does not have to be told to try to imagine the identity of the person being represented. The process of forming illusions in our imaginations is fun—we do it all the time. In fact, we do it automatically. We are always ready to "fill in the blanks" and find the image in the flashing dots or the stains in the gelatin emulsion. And audiences who come into the theatre are no different. However, it can also be said that some illusions are more effective than others.

Consider the following example: A man steps before an audience and announces that as everyone watches, he is going to saw his assistant in half. No one in the audience believes this event is actually going to take place, but everyone keeps watching in anticipation of the pleasure of being deceived. As the magician sets to work, what he actually does is very different from what he appears to do. With the help of his assistant, he skillfully manipulates his stage props to create an illusion of separation. There is no real dismemberment, but the audience perceives that the seemingly cruel act has taken place. And they are delighted.

But think for a moment about all the details that the magician tastefully omits from his performance. If he really wanted the audience to believe that his assistant was being murdered in such a horrible way, there would be screaming and struggling; he would have artificial blood covering the saw and pouring out onto the stage; he could even produce cleverly simulated human limbs and organs to dispel any remaining doubt. But such effects would be repulsive and gratuitous. Instead, the magician shows the people only enough to get them to think what he wants them to think. Once they have the idea, he leaves the rest to their imaginations. And that is exactly what every good actor should do also. Actors should not try to overwhelm the audience with too many details; the idea is to give the people only enough details to get them thinking in the right direction—and then let the people imagine the rest for themselves.

Suppose the magician decided to add the screaming and the blood and the dangling organs. Wouldn't those additional details increase the effectiveness of the illusion? No. In fact, details of that kind might destroy the illusion completely. The audience knows that it has come into the theatre to see a performance; they have faith that the separation of the hapless assistant into two parts is only going to be a trick. When the trick is performed, the audience might be willing to believe that the assistant's top and bottom halves appear to have been temporarily disconnected, but they would never accept that the blood and all were real. Indeed, the magician wouldn't even want want them to believe that. If the people watching the magician thought such details were real—even for just a second—they would be horrified. They might even try to stop him or run from the theatre to summon the police. Obviously, the magician doesn't want that to happen; therefore, there are limits to what he can do to make the illusion naturalistic. Within those limits, any phony organs, dripping blood, and screaming would have to be perceived as fake. And seeing something that is so obviously fake can only get in the way of the audience's imagining the illusion that the separation is real. In this way, the success of the illusion depends absolutely on the absence of any inappropriate details, no matter how naturalistic. Show the audience too much, and there is no illusion.

To return again to the actors playing Willy and Linda, all the ways in which the scene doesn't resemble a husband and a wife in their kitchen do not distract from the effectiveness of the scene; the missing details make it possible for the audience to see the *illusion* of a husband and wife in their kitchen. The kitchen walls are canvas and wood, not real plaster and paneling. The actors' body positions are unnaturally forced out; the actors don't turn as freely as people really do in their own homes. And they hold still when they aren't speaking; they don't scratch and wiggle at random. Since so many such naturalistic details are missing, the people in the audience must supply all of those details in their imagination. If these actors somehow were able to provide every single missing detail, they would have the same problem as the magician who tried to show the audience too much—there would be no illusion. Of course, the only way for the actors to supply everything the scene required would be to have the audience stand in the bushes outside the window of someone's actual kitchen in the middle of the night and silently watch a real husband and a wife arguing inside. Therefore, we may conclude that no matter how naturalistic the scene is supposed to be, on the stage some details are going to have to be omitted. Realism for actors is a matter of degree, not an absolute quality.

Still, even the best actors are sometimes tempted to do it the hard way. Sir Laurence Olivier has told the following story about himself and Dustin Hoffman when they were working together on a film called *The Marathon Man*. Olivier was playing a fiendish doctor, a Nazi war criminal who comes to New York to secure his finances. Hoffman was playing an innocent man whom the doctor suspects of having information about a plot against him. In a chilling sequence, Hoffman's character is tortured by the doctor. When the day came to film that sequence, Olivier arrived on the set in fine spirits after a good night's sleep. Hoffman, however, had gone without sleep for two days to help him authentically create the appearance of his character's exhaustion and bedraggled physical condition. Olivier took one look at Hoffman and said, "Why don't you try *acting*, dear boy? It's so much easier!"

In sum, the magician and the actor share much in common in the way they should prepare for their performances. First, the magician works out a clear and very specific idea of the illusion he wants the audience to see. Not only is the idea clear and specific, but it is also something that is well within y to bring off successfully (in other words, just the separation, not d and guts). He does not, as so many actors do, set himself complicated, abstract, mystical, and (therefore) unattainable goals. The magician knows that the audience will imagine a great deal more than it is shown; he only worries about one thing at a time. Second, the magician selects every detail of the illusion with great care. Since he is not really going to saw anyone in half, he is limited in what he can actually do and still be convincing. He experiments with different gestures and props and even with what he is going to say while he is doing the trick. He does not, as so many actors do, take the first line reading or the first gesture that comes to mind and never try anything else. Finally, the magician knows that it is not necessary for him to believe that he is sawing anyone in half to make the audience imagine it; it is necessary, however, that he not do anything or allow anything to be seen that might break that illusion. To that end, he carefully checks his props and stage machinery to make sure that nothing is showing which shouldn't be. Too many actors worry about believing in everything when they should be more concerned about checking their performance to make sure they are not accidentally doing something that contradicts the effect they are trying to create. (For example, an actor might be sitting in a chair and playing an angry scene; the actor might feel the emotion deeply, but the illusion could be spoiled if the actor's legs remain crossed accidentally in a casual manner that is inconsistent with the emotion.)

However, there is one important difference between the actor and the stage magician. The actor pretends to be someone else, whereas the magician is a magician. The actor and the magician must simplify the performance to provide only necessary details. Through simplification, they both create their illusions. But the actor has to take those details a step further than the magician does. The magician does not need to make the audience really believe that he is sawing anything, only that the metal blade of the saw passes through the place where the body of his assistant should be. But actors must never "go through the motions" of anything. Whatever the details are that have been chosen for the performance, they must be done with conviction, as if the actors were really doing what they seem to be doing. The audience readily accepts the unnatural conventions of stage behavior, and they are more than willing to imagine all the missing details, but the audience is not willing to accept any detail presented without conviction.

ACTING IN EVERYDAY LIFE

Acting—in the broadest sense of the word—is not found only on the stage. Acting is a fundamental, necessary social skill that all people are expected to have to some degree. In truth, our parents are our first acting teachers. If little Johnny doesn't particularly care for his Aunt Martha, then Mother teaches him early on not to say "Ick!" when Aunt Martha kisses him. Little Johnny also learns that if Grandma gives him a copy of *Winnie the Pooh* and he already has two other copies under his bed, then he had better smile and say, "Thank you! Gee, it's just what I always wanted!" And he'd better make Grandma believe it, too! When Grandpa starts telling his old, boring stories, little Johnny is taught to look interested and not to wiggle and yawn. Soon Johnny becomes his own tutor. He learns how to pretend to be asleep when Mother comes rushing into his room to find out what just crashed at eleven o'clock at night. He learns how to make Mother believe that he wasn't eating cookies and chips all afternoon and really just isn't very hungry for dinner. He even learns that Mother can be manipulated after she says no to something if he looks properly distraught.

As life goes on, the stakes get higher and the acting becomes more complex. At one time or another, nearly everyone has had to take a job that was unpleasant and demeaning; but if you needed the money, you put on the uniform and smiled and swallowed your true feelings. Nearly everyone has had to deal with people that are unfriendly or treacherous or just downright nasty; but if those people were your employers or co-workers or even your friends, you had to treat them like long-lost relatives. Nearly everyone has had to put on an act to impress someone else, either for personal favors or for advancement. And of course, at one time or another everyone has had to tell a lie and make it stick, either for your own sake or to protect someone else. Anyone who can't successfully do these things when the need arises is not going to be a very successful human being. Everyone must be able to do this kind of acting.

Costume and characterization are also involved in this kind of offstage acting. For example, most people have certain modes of dress that they feel are appropriate for them. Some people see themselves as sex symbols or rock stars and dress accordingly. Other people may wish to be less conspicuous and therefore reject clothing that seems too trendy or too eye-catching. Most people feel a need to wear casual clothing in order to feel relaxed. Everyone feels "dressed up" when they put on their best clothes. People who wear uniforms at certain jobs often notice that they don't feel quite like themselves when they are dressed for work. Sometimes people deliberately decide to change the way they dress or wear their hair just because they're tired of the character they've been playing.

There are even certain very extreme moments in life when we actually rehearse and costume ourselves just as if we were going to be in a play. Consider a man who has an interview for an important job. He carefully plans what he is going to wear and what he is going to say and how he is going to act. Knowing that everything is going to be under close scrutiny, he frets and sweats over every detail to be sure that his appearance makes exactly the right impression. The most important factor he wants to project is that he is competent for whatever the job may require—whether or not he actually believes that. He knows that people who are truly competent sometimes fail to project that image, and as a result they are passed over in favor of people who are less competent but more self-assured.

From the previous example, we can see that whenever a person wants to make a deliberate impression on someone else, a whole mental process is activated. That person intuitively begins to seek out the right appearance and right physical attitude and right way of speaking and right everything else that will get the idea across. And it is precisely this same process of seeking and planning that the actor needs to initiate in the preparation of a role for the stage. (In Laurence Olivier's autobiography, *Confessions of an Actor,* he remarks, "For what is acting but lying, and what is good acting but convincing lying?")[3]

In order for actors to achieve conviction on the stage, they must activate the same mental process they use when they have to be friendly to their relatives, get a job, or tell a lie. Fortunately, activating this process is really very simple. Once actors have conceived the idea to be communicated, they just have to think, "Suppose I were that person and I were really in that situation. If I really wanted to get across this idea, how would I go about doing it?" This mental proposition completely eliminates the step of actually pretending to be someone else and trying to imagine what that other person's feelings might be. From this point of view, actors start immediately with their own knowledge of how to get things done in the world. Starting from this approach, they seek out the right way to make the desired impression in the same way that they might prepare for an interview or plan how to tell a lie or pick out the right clothes to wear on a special occasion. Actors' own good intuition and judgment lead them to the most effective way to create the desired effect.

The actor who wants Linda Loman to be believable for the audience must put herself into Linda's place by asking, "What would I do *if I were* that person in that situation. *If I were* married to a man who had come home unexpectedly in the middle of the night, how would I respond to him? *If I were* worried that he might be falling apart, how would I speak to him?" It doesn't matter whether or not the actor is personally like Linda Loman; she doesn't have to feel like Linda in order to imagine herself in the kitchen of her own home at night and with her own husband, who is possibly having a mental breakdown. Anyone ought to be able to imagine herself being in that situation and have some idea of how to behave. She thinks to herself, "*If I were* Linda Loman, how would I say the line, 'You didn't smash the car, did you?'" And using this "If-I-Were" formula, her intuition should lead her to a way to say that line with conviction.

This approach to acting is not my invention. Most good actors of the last several hundred years have all discovered some variation on this formula for themselves, either consciously or unconsciously. Stanislavski glorified this simple idea by calling it the "Magic If." At the same time, however, he stressed the additional concept of "the given circumstances." He observed that actors should not use the "Magic If" to turn every character into themselves. To avoid that tendency, actors should consider how they would behave if they were their characters, but only in the actual given circumstances of the play. In other words, the actor playing Linda Loman must not say to herself, "If that were my husband and I were really worried about his having a nervous breakdown, I would never say, 'You didn't smash the car, did you?'" But Linda Loman does say that; it's part of the given circumstances, and the actor playing that role has got to study those circumstances until she finds how it would be possible for her to say that line with conviction.

The real value of the "If-I-Were" formula is that it helps the actor not only to find ways of playing that are convincing but also to stay away from ways of playing that are not convincing. As was noted before, the sheer immediacy of being on stage acts like a powerful narcotic on many performers; otherwise normal, sensible people start behaving in the most peculiar ways whenever they step onto a stage. They know there is something "stagey" about the way actors behave on stage, and so they assume they are supposed to try to be "stagey" too. Then they posture and pose and rant and intone and generally carry on like invaders from space. It doesn't seem to matter to these people that their behavior has no known precedent in human life; they don't want anyone to forget for a moment that they are actors! I once had the experience of directing two beginners in a scene from Jean Anouilh's *Antigone*; the actors playing Antigone and her sister, Ismene, were so preoccupied with the high seriousness of the scene and the tragic intensity of the language that their performances were becoming ludicrous. I reminded them that they should be trying to create the illusion of two sisters having a serious discussion about their brothers. That thought hadn't occurred to them. They were so busy playing tragedy, they forgot to be sisters. They started trying to imagine how two sisters might discuss the events described in this scene. Instantly, the histrionic excesses vanished and a compelling, convincing scene emerged.

To summarize, beginners need to realize that playing with conviction does not mean that actors should try to believe everything happening in the play is real. "Conviction" is something actors must try to achieve in the minds of the audience. Actors want the audience to feel that the right details have been presented and that they have presented them as if they were really doing them, and not (like the magician) only pretending to do them.

DIALOGUE AS CODED INFORMATION

At the beginning of this chapter, we considered the problem of the actor trying to create the illusion of natural behavior in the completley unnatural situation of a live performance on stage. The solution is that the actors have to supply certain absolutely essential details, and they must be supplied, unlike the magician, with conviction. The question to be answered now is how does the actor know which details are absolutely essential?

The answer, as will be explained more fully in the following chapters, is that the actor absolutely needs to supply details that define three categories of information: the *situation,* the *relationships,* and the character's *objectives.* When the actor communicates this information to the audience (with conviction), then the audience will be able to form an effective illusion of natural behavior.

And where do these details come from? They are derived from a very careful reading of the script—the entire script, not just the actor's own dialogue alone. A reading of the whole play is required because the playwright usually states explicitly very few of the details that the actor needs to know. Almost all of the essential details that actors require have to be inferred from the dialogue. As was stated before, dialogue is a kind of code; everything actors need to know that is not stated in so many words is implied by the dialogue. But to break the code and draw the correct inferences, actors must know the key, which is that they must know in advance what information to look for.

How actors break the code of the dialogue and infer the necessary details in those three categories is the subject of the next several chapters.

SUMMARY

Acting is the process of creating an illusion of natural behavior. The behavior of actors in performance is not really natural because the fact of being on stage requires actors to modify their behavior in ways that are peculiar to the stage alone. Some of these modifications include a tendency to force body positions open to the audience's view, a need to use fuller and louder voices than are common in everyday conversation, and a conscious elmination of all unnecessary movements. The audience accepts such behavior as natural because these changes encourage it to form the illusion the actors are trying to create.

As much as possible, the actor should try to simplify the performance; the best illusions leave room for the audience to become involved in the illusion-making process. The actor has a lot of information that must be supplied, and the more simply and effectively it can be conveyed, the better. The information supplied by the actor is the physical context in which the author's dialogue takes place. As was noted in the first chapter, it is the actor's behavior that gives the meaning to the words the playwright has created.

Creating this illusion is relatively easy because all audiences come to the theatre ready to see an illusion on the stage. In general, audiences are more than willing to supply the missing elements in their own imaginations.

This fact creates a special need for actors to create only behavior that is consistent with the audience's expectations. To help actors avoid line readings, movements, or business that might break that illusion, there is the "If-I-Were" formula. This is a mental device that encourages actors to use their own ability to act as needed in everyday, social situations. Using this formula, actors should be able to achieve conviction and believability in their acting.

EXERCISES FOR CHAPTER TWO

Chapter Two stresses two important principles: (1) Good acting is simple acting; all unnecessary details must be stripped away. (2) All actions must be performed with conviction, as if the actor really were the character in the situation of the play. The "If-I-Were" formula should be used to guarantee the authenticity of each action performed. The following exercises are designed to help students develop their mastery of simplicity and conviction.

1. Imagine that you are seated at a table in a fine restaurant. Imagine also that a good meal has just been placed before you by the waiter. In pantomime, act as though you were actually eating that meal.

    Try to imagine very specific foods. Give thought to the size and shape of the dishes, silver service, glasses, and any other items that might be before you on the table. Constantly ask yourself, "What would I do *if I were* in this restaurant and actually eating these foods?" Try also to eliminate all unnecessary gestures and business; be especially careful not to use your face in a "stagey" manner to indicate eating.

    When your pantomime is complete, ask your audience to try to guess what you were eating. Ask if they felt that any part of your pantomime was unrealistic or unnecessary. Ask if there were any details you performed that were not really needed in order for them to guess what you were eating.

    If necessary, you may need to imagine you can actually see or taste the foods that you are pretending to eat. However, don't forget that the goal of the exercise is to execute all the details of eating consciously, with simplicity and conviction—not to "hypnotize" yourself into thinking that you actually see and taste the foods you are pretending to eat.

2. Try performing the following pantomime: "The Letter on the Table." You pretend to walk into a room as if you were just passing through on your way to somewhere else, when suddenly your attention is drawn to a letter lying on top of a table. You stop your movement and step over to the table. You pick up the letter and read the address. Then you sit down and open the letter. You read silently, then replace the letter as you found it and leave the room.

    Make up specific details about the scene you are going to perform. Decide who you are, where you are, why you are passing through this room, to whom the letter is addressed, and what it says. Remember to figure out all these details as specifically and exactly as possible, but don't tell your audience anything before you perform your play. Act out your play as simply as possible. Use only details that you would really do if you were actually that person in that situation. Don't throw in anything just to try to get across some piece of information. Play with conviction.

After your performance is over, ask your audience to tell you who you were and what the letter was all about. Don't worry if the audience didn't understand everything you were trying to get across; they probably will not, and that goal is not the point of the exercise. Then tell them what your play was about and ask if you did anything that was not completely correct for that situation. Ask if any details did not seem truly convincing, if there were any that a person actually in that situation might not do or would do differently. Ask for any suggestions for things you might have done that would have communicated the story of your play more completely and yet would still have been authentic. If your audience thought your performance had conviction, you succeeded.

3. Take a short, emotional speech from a play or a piece of poetry and memorize the lines. Try to imagine that you are the character speaking in the situation implied by the words. Act out the speech and give yourself full license to move and gesture as much as you like. Then try performing the same speech again seated in a chair, and try to remain still as you speak; make no movements or gestures unless absolutely necessary. Continue to imagine yourself as the character actually in this situation, but try to imagine some compelling, dramatic reason why the character is speaking while moving as little as possible.

Then do the speech again, allowing yourself complete freedom of physical expression, but eliminate all the gestures, movements, and facial expressions that you have discovered you don't really need.

Try performing this revised version of your speech for an audience, and then ask them if they found your performance convincing. Ask them particularly if they thought any of your movements or gestures were unnecessary. Can they suggest other alternatives to the choices you made? Did they feel you did enough to be convincing? Try the scene again with any changes your audience suggests and decide whether or not their suggestions work for you. Be like the magician discussed in this chapter—don't be easily satisfied; keep experimenting until you find the quintessentially right physical expression, and then disregard all others. Let in nothing that is not absolutely appropriate to the illusion you are trying to create.

NOTES

1. Constantin Stanislavski, *An Actor Prepares* trans. Elizabeth Reynolds Hapgood (New York: Theatre Arts Books, 1936), p. 153.

2. *Aristotle's Poetics*, trans. S. H. Butcher (New York: Hill and Wang, 1961), p. 55.

3. Laurence Olivier, *Confessions of an Actor: An Autobiography* (New York: Simon and Schuster, 1982), p. 20.

Lesson Three

Public Space, Private Space, and Personal Space

People automatically adjust their behavior to the nature of wherever they happen to be at any given moment. In other words, there are differences in the way people might behave in their own bedrooms or in the living rooms of friends or in a restaurant. Since these adjustments are natural and spontaneous in everyday behavior, we take them for granted. But on the stage, these adjustments have to be consciously created by actors as a fundamental part of the illusion of natural behavior. If the scene of the play is a living room or a restaurant, actors must consciously make the same adjustments in their behavior that they would naturally make if they were in these locations.

There are two ways in which these adjustments affect the actor's behavior. One reflects the character's relationship to the scene of the play. The other reflects the character's specific reason for being in that place at that particular moment.

To portray the first type of adjustment, actors must understand that there are three different ways in which a character may be related to a place. The place may be a public space (just passing through), a private space (restricted access), or a personal space (strangers not allowed). Some of the ways in which people adjust their behavior to each of these types of places are described in Chapter Three.

The second type of adjustment is reflected primarily in the blocking of the play. Actors must motivate their movements to make them consistent with their characters' reasons for being wherever they may be.

Making these two types of adjustments is what is meant by the phrase *playing the situation.*

Chapter Three

Playing the Situation

One of the main principles of realistic acting is that actors create everything on the stage. Of course, actors don't literally design the costumes and build the set and write the script, but they do give all these things meaning.

The first element on the stage that actors must "create" in this way is the place where the play takes place. The place must be first for a very logical reason: In life, the behavior of every person is a function of wherever that person happens to be at any given moment. For example, a man might take off his shoes and put up his feet on the furniture at home, but he would probably not do such a thing in the home of a friend. In the same way, a woman might laugh out loud while reading an amusing book in her own living room, but she would probably stifle that response if she were sitting next to a stranger on a bus. Therefore, even if the scenic technicians provide a setting that resembles a living room, it is still up to the actors to create the illusion of a living room by using that setting as if it were a living room.

Consider the situation in Tennessee Williams' play *Cat on a Hot Tin Roof*. The story revolves around Big Daddy and his two sons, Brick and Gooper. The doctors have just discovered that Big Daddy is dying of cancer, and at the time the play begins, all the members of his family know the truth of his condition—but no one has told him. The occasion is a birthday party for Big Daddy. His older son, Gooper, has arrived with his wife and children to try to make a favorable impression on his father in hopes that he will be awarded control of Big Daddy's estate in the will. Big Daddy favors his younger son, Brick, but he and his wife, Maggie (the "cat" of the title), are having marital problems aggravated by Brick's drinking. If Maggie can't get Brick to shape up, she fears that Big Daddy will cut him out of the will.

All the scenes of the play take place in the same location. The stage directions state,

> The scene is a bed-sitting room and section of the gallery of a plantation home in the Mississippi Delta. It is early evening in summer. [1]

For the original Broadway production in 1955, designer Jo Mielziner provided a skeletal setting that used a minimum of scenic elements and only faintly suggested the setting as Williams describes it. But Mielziner was one of the finest designers ever to work in the American theatre, and he knew what he was doing. His setting for this play is as well known and highly regarded as his settings for the original productions of *The Glass Menagerie* and *Death of a Salesman,* settings that also used a minimum of representational elements. For *Cat,* Mielziner deliberately omitted a lot of unnecessary naturalistic detail to encourage the audience to use its imagination. In other words, it was up to the actors to use Mielziner's set to make the audience see the "bed-sitting room" Williams had in mind.

However, this room has a distinctly different meaning for each of the characters in the play, and these different meanings affect how each actor will "create the set." Maggie must create an unhappy bedroom where she is trying to cover up her troubles with her husband. Brick must create a hiding place, where he is trying to drink away the guilt he feels over the recent death of his closest male friend. Big Mama must create the feeling of a room where she knows something is being hidden from her. Big Daddy must create just another room in his private domain, where he may stroll about at will. Gooper and his wife must create the enemy camp. The actors playing these characters must determine the different ways their characters might behave in that particular room under those particular circumstances. Each actor must think "*If I were* that character, how would I behave in such a room if that's what that room meant to me?"

A character's behavior is thus affected by the situation in two different ways: passively and actively. The passive effects may be observed in the way people move, perform certain actions, respond to certain objects, and so on; such passive effects are usually inhibitory, but not always. The active effects may be observed in the specific activities people feel free to perform in a given place. In other words, the passive effects are reflected in *how* people do things; the active effects are reflected in *what* they do. In the latter case, these choices are particularly important because they often determine a large part of the blocking of each scene. The passive and active effects of the situation on a character's behavior are never fully stated in the text of the play; they are the first piece of coded information that must be derived from the dialogue.

READING THE SCRIPT

It may surprise some beginners to learn that actors have not always been given whole scripts to study. Before the proliferation of offset printing and photocopying, actors were frequently given only partial scripts, called *sides*. Each side would contain only one character's lines, cues, and stage directions, and the actors would never really know what was going on in the whole play until they all met for the first reading. Sides were a practical necessity when scripts had to be copied out by hand, and they also made it harder for plays to be pirated before the Copyright Act of 1919. Some play-leasing companies still occasionally send sides to amateur groups, especially in the case of certain older musicals, but their use is no longer common.

Actors might conclude that sides are rarely used today because of the ease with which whole scripts can be duplicated inexpensively. But the same technology that makes it possible to duplicate whole scripts makes it possible to duplicate sides as well. Sides became unpopular with the rise of realistic acting. In previous times, performances might be dominated by stars who would devise the staging to emphasize their own acting at the expense of everyone else. For such actors, giving sides to the supporting actors reinforced the subordination of all the other actors to the star. But giving all the actors in a play their own complete scripts reinforces the way each actor contributes to the total effect of the performance as a whole.

Beginning actors are reminded of such things here to point out the responsibility implied when an actor is given a whole script to study instead of merely a side to memorize. With a complete script in hand, each actor becomes a full and equal partner in the production, not just another cog in the machine. All the individual performances must fit together and express the sense of the whole play, and for that reason, actors must first strive to grasp the sense of that whole before beginning work on their individual parts. If that were not the case, actors would still be using sides.

Therefore, as early in the rehearsal process as possible, actors should find the time to read the whole script from start to finish. They should read slowly and carefully, trying to visualize all the characters and the actions and trying to hear all the lines as if the characters were actually speaking them aloud in the theatre of the imagination. This reading should be purely intuitive, not intellectual; there will be time later to think about what everything means. Just as the audience watching a performance fills in all the missing elements in its imagination, so should the actors allow the printed words to suggest in their own imaginations all the missing elements of production. Some scripts will come alive in the mind more easily than others.

But actors should be able to "see" and "hear" every script to some degree. During this reading, it is particularly important to read all the playwright's stage directions carefully, word for word. In later readings, these directions may be skimmed, but for the "first reading," absolutely every word in the script should be studied and thought about. Only by this kind of slow, detailed reading can actors gain a sense of the whole play at once.

Actors should do a "first reading" whether or not they have had any previous exposure to the play. If the play has been read or seen before, actors should push out of mind all previous memories to insure a fresh and spontaneous response. If at all possible, the play should be read in one sitting to get a sense of its rhythm. But regardless of how many separate occasions are required to finish the "first reading," actors should try to read leisurely and without distractions. The point is to do everything possible to allow the imagination complete freedom to work directly on the playwright's text.

From this kind of intuitive reading, actors should get a clear vision of the play as a whole and how their particular characters function within it. Often these imaginary productions will be quite detailed, including specific line readings, ideas for business, details of physical appearance and dress, and even blocking that actors may want to try out later in rehearsal. In this way, actors can gain a creative foundation on which to base their performances— a foundation derived directly from the playwright's text.

But what happens when actors don't take the time to do this kind of reading? If they read the script initially, as so many actors do, only to find and underline their own lines, their ideas are going to have to come from someplace else, someplace other than the text. Actors may have to fall back on character stereotypes or vague memories of other actors' work. But a proper "first reading" will ensure that the actors' characterizations will be truly original and creative.

Once the "first reading" of the play has been completed, the actors need to determine the playwright's controlling idea, or *theme*. Many actors balk at the idea of having to think about a play's theme; they feel that themes are the business of critics and scholars, not actors. But every well-written play demonstrates certain fundamental principles through the structure of the action. In other words, something happens, and then something else happens, and then other things happen, and these events all lead to some inevitable conclusion. By looking at the order in which these incidents occur, anyone should be able to perceive the principles the playwright is trying to demonstrate. For example, *Macbeth* is a play rich in levels of abstract meaning. Scholars and critics have written endlessly about the meaning of the color symbolism, the various occult elements, the mysterious identity of the third murderer, and so on. An actor could spend years reading all the volumes that have been written about this play. But for an actor preparing to do a role in *Macbeth*, the structure of the action demonstrates one fundamental principle in particular: the destructive effects of obsessive ambition. There are many ambitious people in this play, and their obsessions cause them all varying degrees of misfortune. Realizing that fact is an important first step in bringing any of these roles to life in production.

Theme as a controlling principle of play structure is not found only in classic tragedy. In Neil Simon's *Barefoot in the Park,* the theme has to do with excess and moderation; each of the four main characters suffers from excess of one kind or another, and as the play progresses, each must become more moderate in some way. An actor preparing to perform a role in *Barefoot* will find that theme a valuable key to the "code" of the dialogue as a whole. In Mary Chase's *Harvey,* the theme is stated explicitly in the speech made by the cab driver, who appears only briefly in the last act of the play: The gentle lunacy of Elwood P. Dowd is much more desirable than the selfish, grasping normalcy of the other characters. That speech is an important indication to the actors who portray the normal characters that they must not play their roles too broadly; everything they do must be firmly grounded in reality in order to make the audience feel that the cab driver's words are appropriate. The ideas developed by these playwrights may not have the weight or the complexity of the ideas found in *Macbeth,* but such fundamental principles are present to some degree in all well-written plays.

Next, actors need to do a *technical* reading of the script. At this time, actors should mark all their own lines and entrances and exits. Also, any character description given in the stage directions or indicated in other characters' lines should also be carefully noted. Actors should pay particular attention to any comments made by other characters about their own characters, especially when such comments are made when their own characters are not on stage to hear them. For example, if one character happens to remark, "Oh, he's always so jittery," the actor playing the character under discussion should carefully note that comment, whether or not he feels that the comment is justified. Somehow, within the context of the play, the actor's character must eventually do something to make that observation meaningful. Also, any references to props or costume pieces need to be noted and evaluated. If, for example, the script says a character is to enter carrying a concealed letter that is later revealed in the scene, the actor knows that the letter is absolutely required. However, if the stage directions state that the character wears a coat and carries a briefcase and neither of these things are ever referred to directly in the dialogue or have any bearing on the action, the actor may assume they are optional.

Once actors have completed the "first" and the "technical" readings, they are ready to get up and start acting.

CREATING THE SET

To the question "Where does the play take place?" most people will give answers like "the kitchen of Willy Loman's home" or "Castle Elsinore" or "a bed-sitting room in Big Daddy's house." Although these answers are perfectly correct, they are not the ones that really start the creative juices flowing. The reason should be obvious: no one has ever been in Willy Loman's kitchen or Hamlet's Castle Elsinore or Big Daddy's bed-sitting room. These places are totally imaginary. (Never mind that there actually *is* a Castle Elsinore; Shakespeare never went there and didn't really have that actual castle in mind when he wrote the play.) It's hard to know how one might act in a place where one has never been, let alone a place that doesn't exist. Before the actor can start to create any of these places, a way must be found to make the locations more immediate.

A better answer to the question "Where does the play take place?" would be for the actor to start by personalizing the location in terms of the actor's own character. If an actor were playing Linda Loman, she might answer, "the kitchen of my own home." If a man were playing one of the Loman boys, he might answer, "in my mother's kitchen." It doesn't matter if "the kitchen of my own home" or "my mother's kitchen" is nothing like what either Arthur Miller or the scene designer for the production had in mind. What matters is that the actors already have some idea of how people behave in their own kitchens, and that experience is immediate and personal and ready to be exploited for the stage.

If an actor were playing Hamlet, he might answer the question (in the case of the scenes on the battlements), "on the fortified walls surrounding my castle." Very few actors have been brought up in a castle, but almost everyone has been in a place that is similar in some way, such as a pioneer stockade at a tourist attraction or an actual castle in a foreign country or even at the top of the high walls surrounding a courtyard of some kind. Once the actor begins to think along these lines, the "If-I-Were" formula will bring back personal memories that can be pressed into service in the scene.

Actors playing the roles of Brick and Maggie might find it useful to conceive of the location a little differently from the way in which Williams has described it. They might be better off to answer the question, "in our hotel room." Big Daddy's house is no hotel, but the way Brick and Maggie are using the room, it might just as well be, and the actors playing the roles have undoubtedly stayed in such rooms at one time or another and undoubtedly will get some strong associations from this approach through the "If-I-Were" formula.

These three examples also illustrate the three general types of places that actors need to understand: The castle at Elsinore is an example of a *public* place, a place where anyone already inside the castle presumably could pass through at any time. The kitchen of Willy Loman's house is an example of a *private* place, a place where only people who know each other are likely to be found, although not a place where any one person might have some measure of control over who might be there. Brick and Maggie's "hotel room" is an example of a *personal* place, a place where they have some say about who may come in. A good rule of thumb for the actor to use in deciding whether a setting is private or personal is to ask whether or not the actor's character might feel free to change clothes in that place if circumstances warranted. If the answer is no, the place is probably more private than personal.

Public places may be both interiors and exteriors. Edward Albee's *The Zoo Story* is set in a park; Murray Schisgal's *Luv* is set in the middle of a bridge; Arthur Miller's *The Crucible* contains an important scene between John Proctor and Abigail Williams that takes place in the woods at night. Interiors are usually places of business. Mark Medoff's *When you Comin' Back Red Ryder?* is set in a diner; Lanford Wilson's *The Hot L Baltimore* takes place in the lobby of a decaying hotel. Other examples of public places include the settings for Jerome Lawrence and Robert E. Lee's *Inherit the Wind* (a courtroom dominated by a vista of the courthouse square) and William Inge's *Bus Stop* (a lunchroom on the bus route between Kansas City and Topeka).

There are several generally observable characteristics of people's behavior in public places: (1) They generally have very strong and very obvious reasons for being there. In *The Zoo Story*, Peter has come into the park to relax and read a book. In *Inherit the Wind*, each and every character has a direct relationship to the trial. Why a character is in a public place is frequently the most significant starting point for developing the physical performance. (2) People are usually less demonstrative and expressive of their feelings in public than elsewhere. Often they do not want to attract unnecessary attention to themselves in public. (3) Except in restaurants and bars, people tend to do more standing around than in private or personal places. When they do sit down, they seldom sit to make themselves comfortable; frequently, furniture in public places is not very comfortable. People often sit on the edges of chairs or they sit very formally, as if expecting to be moving on to some other place in a moment. (4) People who know each other often tend to stay together in groups and not spread out across a whole room, as they might do in a private place. Strangers tend to keep as much distance from each other as possible, and they try to avoid eye contact. (5) Most people generally keep their attention primarily on their own business; everyone looks around at everyone else from time to time, but no one likes to be caught staring at a stranger. The result is that individuals and groups of strangers tend to create little islands of awareness around them that do not include other people's similar islands.

One of the chief differences between the nature of public and private places is that everyone in a private place is likely to know or have business with everyone else there. Private places can be exteriors as well as interiors also. Arthur Miller's *All My Sons* takes place in the yard of the Keller home; the second act of Anton Chekhov's *The Cherry Orchard* is set on the grounds of Madame Ranevskaya's estate; the middle act of Oscar Wilde's *The Importance of Being Earnest* is set in the garden of the Manor House. However, interior settings are more common, and they are most frequently large living rooms. Clifford Odets' *Awake and Sing!* is set in the front room and the adjoining dining room of an apartment; Frances Goodrich and Albert Hackett's dramatization of *The Diary of Anne Frank* is set in three rooms that comprise the top floor of an office building in Amsterdam; Garson Kanin's *Born Yesterday* is set in the sitting room of a large suite in a hotel.

The behavior of people in private places tends to be equally distinctive: (1) There is usually much more sitting in private places than in public. People usually make for the furniture as soon as they come in the door. Also, once someone has sat in a particular chair, the chair tends to "belong" to that person as long as the person remains in the scene. After the person gets up for some reason, he or she will generally sit down again later in the same chair unless there is some specific reason to sit elsewhere. Actors must respect this idea particularly; they must not sit on three different chairs in the same set during a two-minute scene unless specific circumstances within the play compel them to do so. (2) People sit to make themselves more comfortable in private places than in public places; people also have a tendency to "abuse" the furniture—although this characteristic is not usually true of extremely wealthy or aristocratic characters. People sit on the arms of chairs, put their feet on the coffee tables, lean on the edges of cabinets and counters, and so on. (3) In a private room, people who know each other can spread out all over the set, whereas in a courtroom or a restaurant, they tend to stay together. As a result, there are no "islands of awareness." (4) Self-expression is much freer; an argument would probably be louder in a private place than in a public one.

The most observable quality that differentiates personal places from private ones is the degree of control that one or more characters have over who may enter. If an actor is playing a character with that kind of control over the location of the action, the actor should think of the setting as a personal place. The most common types of personal places are small apartments or bedrooms. Tennessee Williams' *A Streetcar Named Desire* features a lot of dialogue in Stanley and Stella's bedroom; Bill Manhoff's *The Owl and the Pussycat* is set in an intimate apartment; the first act of George Bernard Shaw's *Arms and the Man* is set in Raina's bedchamber. Certain other locations may be used as private places as well. Ronald Harwood's *The Dresser* is set in the dressing room of an aging theatrical star; Elmer Rice's *Counselor-at-Large* is set in a metropolitan law office; Henry Higgins' study in Alan Jay Lerner and Frederick Lowe's *My Fair Lady* is certainly his own personal place. These places are personal places only for the people who control them, but for other people who are invited in as visitors, they are essentially only private places.

People exhibit three common characteristics of behavior in their own personal places that are not likely to be seen elsewhere: (1) They are much freer about their personal appearance and what they wear. They take off their coats and throw them over the backs of chairs; they parade around in their bathrobes; in general, they really make themselves at home. (2) They usually have lots of personal objects around them—photographs, nick-nacks, clothing, books, and so on. Also, people are frequently (but not always) messy in their own personal places, whereas they would be more careful to clean up after themselves in a private place. (3) In their own personal places, people might be likely to sit in half-a-dozen different places in succession without claiming any one place as their own; a visitor in a personal place would probably still "stake a claim" on one chair at a time. In general, an actor who is playing a scene in what is considered to be that character's personal place should make a special effort to use the objects and furniture to create the impression that the character really does belong there.

The previous suggestions can be condensed into the following general principles:

1. The less familiar a character is supposed to be to a particular location, the less that character is likely to move around in it. Consider how restrained you are likely to be the first time you visit the home of a friend; after you've been there a few times, you feel freer to go exploring at will.

2. The more familiar people are to a particular place, the more they tend to abuse the furniture. As a general rule, no one aspect of the way an actor works on a set tells more about that character's relationship to the setting than the way in which the actor uses the furniture. People usually sit very tentatively or very correctly in public places; they tend to be more comfortable in private places, where more comfort is usually provided; and they are inclined to be fairly free with the furniture in their own personal places.

3. The more a person is directly related to a certain place, the more casually that person will tend to dress. When most people get home from a hard day at work, they often pull off their shoes, drop any objects they brought with them onto the first convenient horizontal surface, and flop down on the most comfortable article of furniture. A character who exhibits that sort of behavior is usually in that character's own personal place; that character is not concerned about someone uninvited walking in unannounced.

4. The less familiar a person is to a particular place, the more restrained that person's mode of expression is likely to be. This fact is particularly important to remember when playing emotional scenes. People generally restrain their emotions until they are ready to burst when they are in public and private places; this tendency can help actors create building tensions during very intense sequences. In their own personal places, people usually let their emotions out quickly. Upon meeting some opposition, they often try to get the offending party to leave the place or they try to pull back to their favorite corner of the room and hide. (An example of this kind of behavior is found in Tennessee Williams' *The Glass Menagerie*; Laura keeps drifting toward the old phonograph when her mother questions her about business school.)

5. In any given scene, different characters will probably not have the same general relationship to the setting, and the actors must find appropriate behavior to point out these contrasting relationships. In other words, in a two-person scene set in the bedroom belonging to only one of the characters, one person must treat the setting as a personal space and the other must treat it as a private place. An audience should be able to tell from the actors' behavior alone whose

bedroom it is. The principle of contrasting behavior is very important; actors must seek out ways to express the different relationships that their characters have to each scene. This contrast is a significant part of the illusion of natural behavior.

These guidelines only represent tendencies of behavior, not absolute rules that have to be followed slavishly. In fact, there are numerous situations in which a given character's behavior might deliberately be inconsistent with that character's actual relationship to the place in order to make a point. However, with these guidelines in mind, consider the following situations:

Suppose you are to play a scene that is set in the public lounge of a bus depot. What are some of the things you might want to do (and not do) to create the illusion of your relationship to this setting? Stop reading now and give the question some thought before reading the material that follows.

To show that your character is in a bus depot, you probably should not immediately sit on the furniture. People in such places tend to do more standing around than sitting. If you do sit, remember not to spread out and make yourself as comfortable as you would in a living room. Also, you should "keep your eyes to yourself" and not stare at other people in the same scene. If you are in the scene with another person, the two of you should stay as close together as possible. If the scene requires any kind of emotional display, you will want to act as though you are deliberately trying not to attract attention; you simply cannot carry on as loudly or as freely as you could if you were in private.

(If any of these ideas occurred to you before you read them, you may consider that you are getting the idea quite well. If other ideas occurred to you, they may be equally valid as long as they conform to the general guidelines that were given earlier for portraying a public place.)

Now consider the problem of playing a scene in someone else's living room (not your own). What are the specific ways in which you could make apparent to an audience your character's relationship to the space in which the scene is to take place? Again, please stop reading and try to come up with some ideas before reading on.

In order to communicate that you are in someone else's private place, you will probably do more sitting than standing. When you are moving around, don't handle objects or go "poking around" as you might do if this place were your own living room. When sitting, make yourself comfortable, but don't abuse the furniture. Remember also that the first chair in which you sit should be the only chair in which you sit unless circumstances compel you to sit elsewhere. You will want to pay attention to all the other actors who are supposed to be in the same room; there are no "islands of awareness." You may move away from another actor with whom you came into this living room; there is no need to stick together as in a bus terminal.

Now ask yourself how you might show that you are in your own living room and not someone else's. Again, try to answer the question before reading on.

Your own personal relationship to the room can be demonstrated in several ways. You will probably move around the room more than you would if this were not your living room. You should find reasons to handle the objects in the room with familiarity. You can sit in more than one place, and you may want to find ways to "abuse" the furniture by sitting on the arm of a chair or by putting your feet up. But the best action you can perform to establish that this is your living room is to take off or loosen an article of clothing; take off your shoes or throw your coat on the back of a chair, things you would probably not do if you were in someone else's living room and most certainly not if you were in a bus terminal. If you have an emotional scene to play, you can really give free reign to the expression of your emotions.

These guidelines are offered only as suggestions to help actors in the early phases of rehearsal. When the actors are walking around the rehearsal hall and staring at the masking tape on the floor and trying to read the lines out of the script in hand, they often find it hard to relate to the imaginary setting of the play. Classifying the type of place according to the character's general relationship to the setting can thus be extremely helpful during this phase of the work.

Before going on to the matter of blocking a scene, the purpose of this whole section needs to be emphasized one final time. The matter of creating a character's general relationship to the setting is not optional; it is a fundamental requirement of realistic acting. As an actor, you must consciously and actively seek out ways to communicate this information to your audience.

BLOCKING THE SCENE

With the previous observations on the nature of public, private, and personal spaces in mind, we are now ready to discuss the process of blocking a scene. The term *blocking* refers to the actors' pattern of movement around the stage. In most productions, the director has the initial responsibility to set this pattern, but because actors always have input into the final form, they also need to understand the factors that make good blocking.

Blocking is one of those aspects of acting that point up how the illusion of natural behavior differs from the real thing. For example, if we were to go to the home of a friend, we might settle down in chairs around our friend's kitchen table and talk for more than an hour without getting up. But on the stage, if actors entered the stage and played a scene while seated around a table for an hour, the effect would be very unsatisfactory. Why?

One reason is that movement is needed to create visual variety for the audience. Even if the stage directions state that the actors are to enter, sit, and act without moving for an hour and a half, good actors and directors know that the scene probably should not be staged in that way. Within a matter of minutes, the audience may lose interest and stop listening to what the actors are saying. Of course, there are certain playwrights, such as Samuel Beckett and Harold Pinter, in whose plays characters may be forced to remain in one place for dramatic reasons. In those plays, the lack of action can be fully as involving as the frenetic movement associated with farce. However, unless there is a significant dramatic reason for actors to stay in one place, movement—whether specified in the stage directions or not—is essential to maintain the audience's attention.

Also, actors must move in order to communicate the context of the spoken words. By the way the actors move, they communicate their characters' relationships to each other, their states of mind, their wants and desires, the intensity of their feelings, and a thousand other pieces of information that are virtually impossible to communicate effectively without moving. It is possible for actors to remain seated for long periods of time on the stage without moving and to communicate some of this information by changing their body positions, posture, gestures, and so on, but the effect is like trying to play tennis with your shoelaces tied together. It can be done (to a limited extent) but never so well as when the body's full potential for movement is utilized. Actors have got to move and move often or they become only "talking heads," and their words are empty and without color and substance.

Some scenes are structured so that the necessary movements are implicit in the lines. But more often than not, actors and directors have to invent reasons for the characters to move. In doing so, they must observe the most important principle of good blocking: all movement on the stage must be motivated. Wandering around the set to no apparent purpose is absolutely not permitted. (Motivation for blocking is not to be confused with the more complicated matter of psychological motivation, which is considered in Chapter Five; motivation for blocking refers only to the consciously determined reason why a character moves from one place to another onstage.)

A good rule of thumb to use for working out the movement in a scene is this: A motivated movement is a movement towards something or someone. Human beings seldom move from one place to another unless there is something in that other place that interests them in some way. Even when the primary need to move is a need to get away from someone or something, the movement away must also be a movement toward someone or something else. The movement need not reach its destination; this kind of interrupted movement (or "broken cross" as some people like to call it) is perfectly permissible as long as the original impetus for the movement is clearly toward a specific person or object. The only real exception to this rule has to do with pacing, which is a kind of behavior that people sometimes exhibit as the result of an unsettled state of mind. When characters are experiencing great confusion, actors may wander about without a specific focus, but they should be careful to use pacing in this way only when no other satisfactory reason to move can be found.

The reason that unmotivated movement is not allowed in realistic acting is, as stated before, that the actors' movements are an important channel of communication to the audience. Unmotivated movement sends confusing signals to the people watching the play. When an actor moves, the audience assumes there is a reason for that movement and tries to understand what that reason is. Unmotivated movement is a lot like nonsense words inserted into the middle of an otherwise meaningful sentence: You are reading along and suddenly you find words that don't make any sense; you stop and wonder what is going on, and the next thing you know, you have forgotten what the sentence was about in the first place. In other types of acting, unmotivated movement is permitted to some degree, but not in realistic acting.

The requirement that all movement be motivated forces the actor to become actively involved with the setting. The objects found on the stage become the actor's best friends: They provide the most obvious motivation toward which movements can be made. Ironically, many actors and directors alike think that working on a minimal set or a bare stage is easier than working on a full set. Actually, working on a bare stage can be extremely hard because of the difficulty in motivating movement without physical objects to move toward. On such a stage, actors must establish imaginary objects and people in order to motivate their blocking.

To find motivation for blocking, the actor should begin with another fundamental truth of human nature: No one ever enters or remains in a given place unless that person has a specific task that can only be performed there. Once actors have analyzed their characters' passive relationship to the setting of the scene, they need to find their active reason for being there, that is, the specific task that their characters came into that place to do. Hamlet goes up on the battlements to find out if there really is a ghost up there; Linda Loman goes into her kitchen to find out why Willy has returned home unexpectedly; Maggie is in the bed-sitting room to get ready for the party in honor of Big Daddy's birthday. The specific reason why each of these characters is in these places usually becomes the primary source of motivation for movements in these scenes.

Sometimes, no active task is immediately inferable from the situation, and the actor may have to supply one. In that case, the actor must remember that the specific activity any character feels free to perform in a given setting must still be consistent with that character's general relationship to the environment. In other words, in a living room scene, one standard technique used to motivate blocking in an otherwise static sequence is to have one character prepare food or drink for the others. However, that technique will work only if the first character is in that character's own living room, not if the character is in someone else's.

To find an active reason for a character to be in a given setting, the actors simply need to ask themselves, "Why am I in this place?" Finding a suitable answer to this question will usually provide appropriate ideas for blocking. To demonstrate how answers to this question may help the actor motivate blocking, we will now consider a specific scene: an excerpt from the first act of Mary Chase's play *Harvey*. This popular comedy was first produced in New York in 1944 and has become a favorite with amateur theatre groups at all levels. The author states,

> The action of the play takes place in a city in the Far West in the library of the old Dowd family mansion and the reception room of Chumley's Rest. Time is the present. [2]

The story revolves around a delightful eccentric, Elwood P. Dowd, and his invisible companion, Harvey (actually a "Pookah," a faerie spirit in the form of a large rabbit with extraordinary powers). Harvey is perceived as an embarrassing delusion by Elwood's similarly eccentric sister, Veta Louise Simmons. In the first scene, Veta (a widow) is attempting to introduce her daughter, Myrtle Mae, to society. Veta is hosting an afternoon tea to which have been invited most of the town's wealthiest matrons. The layout of the Dowd library is described in the stage directions:

> . . . a room lined with books and set with heavy, old-fashioned furniture of a faded grandeur. The most conspicuous item in the room is an oil painting over a black marble Victorian mantlepiece at the lower part of the wall at stage L. This is the portrait of a lantern-jawed older woman. There are double doors at R. These doors, now pulled apart, lead to the hallway and across to the parlor, which is not seen. Telephone is on small table L . . . [3]

Read the following scene slowly and carefully. Try to imagine it being played out in your imagination as if you were an actor doing a "first reading." Once you feel you have adequately visualized the lines, read the scene again and underline all the stage directions and motivations for movement. Then act out the scene as written. If at all possible, work with another actor. If that is not possible, imagine yourself in the role of Veta and try to work through her blocking as if there were another actor playing Myrtle with you.

For study purposes, this scene does not have to be performed by two women. In the classroom, the scene can be performed just as easily by a man and a woman or two men. When the need arises, casting can be altered in this way for all of the other scenes presented for acting in this book. If you are at all uncomfortable with that suggestion, you need to remember that the characters in any play are only illusions created by the actors. Changing the casting in this way will only help you to see this more clearly. Also, men playing women's roles and women playing men's roles are ancient and honorable traditions of the theatre. Ideally, the scenes should be performed by male and female actors as specified by the playwrights. But for learning purposes, students need not feel themselves limited strictly in this way.

Follow the stage directions very carefully and try to be aware of how well they help you to establish your character's relationship to the setting. Try to find the characters' specific reasons for being in this room at this time.

Scene Number One: *Harvey*

At the start of the play, the voice of a soprano singing offstage can be heard. Then Myrtle enters the room to answer the telephone; the caller is the society editor of the local newspaper. Myrtle Mae summons Veta to speak with her. After the phone call, the following scene takes place:

MYRTLE: Mother—Mrs. Chauvenet just came in!
VETA: (*arranging flowers on phone table*) Mrs. Eugene Chauvenet Senior! Her father was a scout with Buffalo Bill.
MYRTLE: So that's where she got that hat!
VETA: (*as she and Myrtle start to exit*) Myrtle, you must be nice to Mrs. Chauvenet. She has a grandson about your age.
MYRTLE: But what difference will it make, with Uncle Elwood?—Mae!
VETA: Myrtle—remember! We agreed not to talk about that this afternoon. The point of this whole party is to get you started. We work through those older women to the younger group.
MYRTLE: We can't have anyone here in the evening, and that's when men come to see you—in the evenings. The only reason we can even have a party this afternoon is because Uncle Elwood is playing pinochle at the Fourth Avenue Firehouse. Thank God for the fire house!
VETA: I know—but they'll just have to invite you out and it won't hurt them one bit. Oh, Myrtle—you have got so much to offer. I don't care what anyone says, there's something sweet about every girl. And a man takes that sweetness, and look what he does with it! (*Crosses to mantel with flowers.*) But you've got to meet somebody, Myrtle. That's all there is to it.
MYRTLE: If I do they say, That's Myrtle Mae Simmons! Her uncle is Elwood P. Dowd—the biggest screwball in town. Elwood P. Dowd and his pal—
VETA: (*puts hand on her mouth*) You promised.
MYRTLE: (*crossing above toble, sighs*). All right—let's get them into the dining room.
VETA: Now when the members come in here and you make your little welcome speech on behalf of your grandmother—be sure to do this. (*Gestures toward portrait on mantel.*)
MYRTLE: (*in fine disgust*) And then after that, I mention my Uncle Elwood and say a few words about his pal Harvey. Damn Harvey! (*In front of table, as she squats.*)

VETA: (*the effect on her is electric: She runs over and closes the doors. Crosses behind table to C*). Myrtle Mae—that's right! Let everybody in the Wednesday Forum hear you. You said that name. You promised you wouldn't say that name and you said it.

MYRTLE (*rising, starting to cross L*): I'm sorry, Mother. But how do you know Uncle Elwood won't come and introduce Harvey to everybody? (*To mantel. Places flowers on it.*)

VETA: This is unkind of you, Myrtle Mae. Elwood is the biggest heartache I have. Even if people do call him peculiar he's still my brother, and he won't be home this afternoon.

MYRTLE: Are you sure?

VETA: Of course I'm sure.

MYRTLE: But Mother, why can't we live like other people?

VETA: Must I remind you again? Elwood is not living with us—we are living with him.

MYRTLE: Living with him and Harvey! Did Grandmother know about Harvey?

VETA: I've wondered and wondered about that. She never wrote me if she did.

MYRTLE: Why did she have to leave all her property to Uncle Elwood?

VETA: Well, I suppose it was because she died in his arms. People are sentimental about things like that.

MYRTLE: You always say that and it doesn't make sense. She couldn't make out her will after she died, could she?

VETA: Don't be didactic, Myrtle Mae. It's not becoming in a young girl, and men loathe it. Now don't forget to wave your hand.

MYRTLE: I'll do my best. (*Opens door.*)

VETA: Oh dear—Miss Tewksbury's voice is certainly fading!

MYRTLE: But not fast enough. (*She exits.*)

If you have tried acting out this scene according to the supplied stage directions, you probably felt that it was somewhat static. You may have become aware that most of the information contained within those directions has very little direct bearing on the actions implied by the dialogue. Only one stage direction actually bears directly on any of the spoken words—"gestures toward portrait on mantel." (Readers who are familiar with *Harvey* will recall that the playwright is deliberately calling the audience's attention to the portrait, which will be the source of certain important sight gags later in the play.) Even the direction to Veta to close the doors after Myrtle says "Damn Harvey!" is not absolutely essential, although the idea seems perfectly logical under the circumstances.

Many of these stage directions may not even have come from the playwright. The source for the stage directions found in the published versions of most plays is the prompt script kept by the stage manager of the original professional production. This prompt script is supposed to be the most authoritative text of any production. Many of the director's and actors' ideas for blocking, business, effects, and so on, are left in the published version largely as a guide for amateurs in staging their own productions. But these directions need not be followed slavishly; to disregard them is not necessarily to be unfaithful to the playwright's original intentions. The stage directions descended from the original professional production represent the solutions that one director and one group of actors found to the creative problems of the script; other productions will inevitably require different solutions.

Let's look at the stage directions in this scene more carefully. Two of the directives for movement seem odd. The first is the direction to Myrtle to squat after her "Damn Harvey!" The idea that Myrtle would sit suddenly at the moment of being most upset may not be the best way for an actor playing that role to communicate how Myrtle feels. The second odd direction has Myrtle carrying flowers to the mantle. But if she is convinced that her life is doomed because of her uncle, why does she care whether the flowers are on the mantle or not? If anything, the flower business seems to suggest that Myrtle is not as upset as she claims to be. But later in the first act, Elwood will indeed come in and introduce Harvey to all of Veta's guests just as Myrtle fears—and the result of that action will be that Myrtle will be outraged and will persuade Veta to have Elwood committed. The consequences of this situation are so serious that the actor playing Myrtle may want to find a stronger action than arranging flowers on the mantle.

Another problem with the stage directions for this scene is that once the phone call that preceded the dialogue has been completed, there is no clear reason why these characters stay in this room (other than to serve the playwright's need to communicate plot exposition to the audience). Why don't Veta and Myrtle Mae just turn around and go back to their guests across the hall—especially given the arrival of the all-important Mrs. Chauvenet? Staying to rearrange the flowers doesn't seem a sufficiently compelling reason under the circumstances. The illusion of natural behavior demands better motivation.

To solve the problem, put yourself in the place of an actor preparing to play Veta. Try to *play the situation* yourself. Ask yourself, "Why is my character in this place at this time?" Because no obvious answer can be found in the text, become creative. Use the "If-I-Were" formula and say to yourself,

Now if I were Veta Louise Simmons and giving an afternoon tea under these circumstances and if I had been called away from my guests to talk on the phone, why might I choose to stay away from my guests for a few moments? If I really were that person in that situation, what might be my motivation to stay there instead of going back into the other room immediately?

Think about parties you personally have given or attended. How did you feel? What did you do? Apply your personal knowledge of similar situations to this problem and try to come up with some good reasons for being there—reasons that can be turned into ideas that will motivate blocking. Stop reading now and try to imagine some answers; then compare your thoughts with the discussion that follows.

BLOCKING THE SCENE FROM *HARVEY*

As stated earlier, a character's general relationship to a particular setting (public, private, or personal) determines how all actions within that place may be performed. For Veta and Myrtle, the Dowd library setting is actually a personal place; the fact that Veta can close the doors indicates clearly she has control over who may enter. Since one of the most characteristic actions that people perform in their own personal places is to use the furniture, one good way to start "creating" the set is to sit down in it. (Did this idea occur to you? Good! You are definitely getting the idea.) This action is nowhere indicated in the dialogue (except for Myrtle's squat); in fact, the lack of indications to sit tends to make the library seem more like a public place.

Is sitting justified under the circumstances? Yes. Considering how much this occasion means to Veta and how much effort and strain must have gone into the preparations, she might welcome a moment to get off her feet while the attention of her guests is occupied by the soprano performing in the next room. The actor playing Veta might easily use the "If-I-Were" formula to show the hostess escaping for a moment to rest her feet. Perhaps if the actor playing Veta wanted to strengthen the reason to sit, she could remove one shoe and massage her foot as if the shoe were brand new and one size too small—an action that would help to reinforce the idea that this room is her personal space. Look at Figure 3–1, which shows two student actors working on this scene. Notice how your immediate impression of this picture seems to be that the woman rubbing her foot must be in her own personal space. A person simply does not do something like that in a public place (particularly a person so obviously dressed up) or in a room where just anyone might walk in.

If Veta chooses to play the situation in this way, Myrtle's specific relationship to the setting is thereby explained indirectly. She is waiting for her mother to put her shoes back on before they can both go back in to their guests. Once Myrtle has finished watching Mrs. Chauvenet come in, she could then cross to her mother to complain about Uncle Elwood. Perhaps Veta might then notice that Myrtle's dress needs straightening; she might stand and cross to Myrtle and fuss with the costume as she says, " . . . you've got so much to offer."

This business is illustrated in Figure 3–2. Again, this action would usually not be performed in a public or private place. If Veta has not yet slipped her shoe back on, Myrtle's "All right—let's get them into the dining room," might be interpreted as a directive to Veta to put the shoe back on so they could go back to their guests. Veta might then sit as before to put on the

FIGURE 3–1.
A Scene from *Harvey.*   *Veta, seated, rubs her foot as her daughter, Myrtle Mae, looks on. Notice how the image immediately suggests a person in her own personal space.*

shoe. The gesture toward the portrait that follows might be particularly comic if done from the chair.

These movement and business ideas are examples of what actors sometimes call *independent activities.* An independent activity is a piece of business added to the scene (and therefore independent of it) to provide motivation for movement. Such activities need to be selected and used with care because they can change the meaning of a scene in ways that the actors may

FIGURE 3–2.
A Scene from *Harvey.*   *Veta fusses with Myrtle's dress. Again, this action is something that would only be done in a personal space.*

not intend. For example, there is the business of Myrtle taking the flowers to the mantel when she is obviously so upset. This flower business is, in effect, an independent activity already supplied by the script; but as we have already observed, it has the effect of making Myrtle's anger seem less important than it really is to the action of the play.

To express real anger, people sometimes get rough with objects and even throw them in order to let off a little steam. The choice for the actor playing Myrtle to throw something to express her anger would be another example of "playing the situation." Perhaps as Myrtle exclaims, "Damn Harvey!" instead of squatting as the stage directions suggest, she might make a wild gesture that would accidentally knock over the flowers already in place.

This action could then provide motivation for blocking the rest of the scene. As Veta speaks the next line, she could close the doors (a sensible idea under the circumstances) and then cross to the mess on the floor and start setting things right again. (See fig. 3–3.) Myrtle probably wouldn't help to clean up at first; she really sees no point to the tea party in the first place.

FIGURE 3–3. A Scene from *Harvey.* *Myrtle Mae has knocked over the flowers, and Veta, kneeling, picks up the mess. Myrtle's knocking over the flowers suggests her emotional state at this point in the scene, and Veta's cleaning up the mess helps to reinforce her relationship to this place.*

She really doesn't care if things get spilled or broken in the house at all. But after Myrtle has apologized, she too could move to help her mother—an action that would help to reinforce the apology.

After having stooped down to clean up the flowers, Veta might need a small mirror on one of the walls to straighten her hair as she says, "I've wondered and wondered about that." Myrtle might then cross to Veta on her next line. The next move is to exit from the room, and the scene is blocked—and the characters' general and specific relationships to the setting have been communicated to the audience through the movements.

PREPARING A SCENE FOR CLASS

As a student actor, you will be expected to be your own director whenever you have to prepare scenes for presentation in class. Then not only must you establish your character's relationship to the setting, but you must literally create that setting as well.

In those situations, your first step is to make up a groundplan—an imaginary arrangement of furniture, doors, windows, and so on—that will fit into the space where your performance is to be given. The primary function of any groundplan is to provide a framework in which the actors can motivate whatever movement is required. (The function of the scene design as a whole is to interpret the play, and the groundplan is an element of that design; but from the actor's point of view, the primary function of the groundplan is to provide motivation for movement.) As such, the groundplan must provide for appropriate entrances and exits and a sufficient number of acting areas.

An *acting area* is usually defined as anyplace on the set where an actor can go to play a scene; to go to that place, there must be some object or group of objects to motivate the movement. A group of objects together, such as a table and chairs or a sofa and a coffee table next to each other, would actually define only a single acting area, not one acting area for each object. But a door in one part of the stage, a desk and a chair in another, and another chair all separated from each other would define three acting areas. Even for a short scene in a classroom, three acting areas in any groundplan is usually the minimum needed. On a full stage for a whole play, seven or eight acting areas may be required. More is not necessarily better in scene work; actors should be careful not to put so many objects on the stage that movement around them is difficult; the purpose of the objects is to facilitate movement, not get in the way of it. Also, there should be space between areas that can be used for between-area playing.

Whenever you have to devise a groundplan for a scene, remember the following:

1. Use imagination in choosing objects for the groundplan; don't depend on the text. Use the "If-I-Were" formula to figure out what kinds of objects might be

found in a particular setting. As much as possible, try to pick typical things that will quickly communicate the intended location. Unusual or unique objects are acceptable only if they don't send conflicting signals to the audience.

2. All furniture and other objects should be set in a realistic relationship to each other. As much as possible, the arrangement of objects should immediately suggest the place being represented. This consideration is more important than setting furniture to relate to the stage or opening up furniture positions to the audience. (Jo Mielziner can do fragmentary settings on Broadway but, in a class-room, try to use arrangements that your audience can recognize easily.)

3. Plan only for objects that are actually going to be used in the scene. Don't throw in objects or set dressing for effect. (Remember the need for simplicity.) If some-thing is not being used, get rid of it. If something is put on the set, someone had better use it at some point in the scene.

4. Try to get the furniture out into the playing areas; don't set all the furniture up against imaginary walls so that there is one big open playing space in the middle of the stage. Leave room to play on the upstage side of things if at all possible. However, the exact center area of the stage should be left open; this place is the strongest area of any stage and it should be saved for an actor to use in a strong moment. Otherwise, objects at exact center tend to get a very strong emphasis that they usually don't deserve.

5. During the scene, try to use all the possible playing areas of your groundplan. Avoid playing all the scenes in the upstage areas. Place objects in the downstage right and downstage left areas whenever possible; objects in these areas help to balance the setting as a whole and make it easy for actors to get into these areas at the appropriate moments.

6. Don't obstruct entrances with pieces of furniture or other objects. In life, chairs and tables and sofas are rarely placed directly in front of doorways, and the same logic should be followed onstage.

7. In blocking the scene on the groundplan, try to keep the audience's focus mov-ing around the stage. Remember, one of the primary reasons for movement is to create visual variety. After a scene has been played for a while in one area, try to move the focus to another area, then to another, and so on. Also, try not to repeat any single configuration of actors within that setting. If people be-come aware that they have seen the actors in exactly those same places before, they will assume that there is some significance to this fact when frequently there is not.

8. The downstage areas should be used for intimate or quiet scenes; the upstage areas should be used for louder or violent scenes. This rule can be disregarded if circumstances warrant, but otherwise it should be respected.

SUMMARY

Throughout this chapter I have stressed the need for actors to create the setting for the play by devising the appropriate passive and active responses that their characters might have to that particular setting under the particular circumstances of the play. First, actors should read the whole play carefully, trying to visualize the action in their imagination. Then they should analyze the action of the play to discern the playwright's theme (the idea or principle implicit in the order of the incidents of the play.) Then they need to read the script again to discover all the essential details that pertain only to their individual characters.

After the technical reading, actors need to classify the setting as public, private, or personal space. Using the characteristic behavior that people commonly manifest in such places as a guide, actors can then determine the specific reason for their presence in that place and how to express that reason through motivated movement. Throughout this process, the actor refers to the "If-I-Were" formula to draw on life experiences as a ready reservoir of creative ideas.

In effect, the actor has to find the answers to five questions:

1. Where does the scene take place? (Generalize and personalize the answer.)
2. What is the nature of my character's relationship to this place? Is it a public space, a private space, or a personal space?
3. What are some significant ways in which my character's relationship to this place might be expressed? ("*If I were* that person in that place, how might I behave?")
4. Why is my character in this place at this time? What is my character's specific reason for staying here and not going somewhere else?
5. How can I convey this reason?("*If I were* that person, what would I do to communicate my reason for staying here?")

Answering all these questions in succession will enable the actor truly to *play the situation*.

EXERCISES FOR CHAPTER THREE

The primary focus of Chapter Three is on the ways in which the actor "creates the set" through movement. The following exercises are designed to help students increase their awareness of the ways in which the actor communicates a character's general and specific relationship to the setting of the play.

1. Create a simple arrangement of rehearsal furniture by using a few chairs and tables. The arrangement should not immediately suggest any particular place; it should only be an area where people might enter and sit down. In your own imagination, however, make it into a public, private, or personal place. Fill in the details of the story in your own imagination.

    Somewhere in this setting there is a valuable object that you have lost and that you must search for and find. Use the "If-I-Were" formula to try to imagine how you might make such a search in such a place. The scene is to end when you find the object that you are looking for.

    Perform the scene for other actors who are doing similar scenes, but without telling each other where the scenes are supposed to take place. Each actor should use the same arrangement of furniture. After each scene, discuss where the scene appeared to have taken place according to the actor's behavior. Try to help each other think of other ideas that might be attempted according to the nature of each person's location. Notice how many ways different people in the same general type of place (public, private, and personal) use the furniture in similar ways even though the specific locations may be different.

2. Devise a short pantomime based on the following information to be communicated to the audience: Choose a specific location that can be communicated with the use of a single chair, such as a living room, public library, department store, cocktail lounge, bedroom, park, garment-fitting room, examining room of a doctor's office, restaurant, and so on. Classify the place as a public, private, or personal space to your character.

   Then assume that you are in that place to wait for someone else who is supposed to meet you there. Now choose a simple action that could be performed in such a situation, such as reading a book or magazine, working a crossword puzzle, checking the contents of your purse or wallet, or writing a note or letter. Perform the action in a way that is consistent to your general (passive) relationship to this place; use the specific reason of waiting for another person as the basis of motivating the movement. Let the whole scene run no longer than a minute, and use no sounds or spoken dialogue (or pretended dialogue) to aid you.

   At the end of your scene, ask your audience to identify where it took place. Ask for suggestions for any other details that you could have added to the scene to help to communicate the nature of your general relationship to the place. Ask if they can think of other choices for blocking, consistent with your purpose of waiting. Ask if you used any details that did not seem appropriate to the given circumstances of the scene.

3. Look at the dialogue for the scene from *Harvey* again. Try to imagine how the same lines would be affected by a change in the locale. For example, how might the same scene be played in the kitchen of the house? In an upstairs bedroom? On the front porch? Try to imagine specific reasons why the characters might actually be in such places within the given circumstances of the scene. Try to imagine other specific bits of business that could be used to motivate movement.

   If you performed the scene as written with another actor, work with that actor to devise a new groundplan that moves the action to another location. Follow the guidelines for creating a groundplan for a class scene. Use the characters' specific reasons for being in those new locations to evolve a new blocking plan for the scene.

   Perform your version of the scene for other actors and ask for their responses to the ways in which the scene was changed by the new locations.

4. Find a short scene of dialogue for two people from a play that is familiar to you. The scene should run for no more than two or three minutes at most. Find another actor to work with and learn the lines so that each of you knows the parts very well. Now try performing the scene in settings different from the one originally intended by the playwright. Make one public, one personal, and one private. In each situation, be certain that you have good specific reasons for being in the places you imagine. Explore the differences that the different scenes require in terms of movement, relating to the objects you find in the place, and degree of emotional expression.

   For example, you might pick part of the quarrel between General St. Pe and his wife that occurs in the second scene of the second act of Anouilh's *The Waltz of the Toreadors*. In this scene, each character believes that the other has been unfaithful and uses the occasion to make various accusations. (This is a long scene, but only a few minutes of the beginning would do very well for this exercise.) You might try playing the scene as if it occurred at an airport terminal (a public place), an elevator stuck between floors (a private place), and a hotel room (a personal place.) Try to use a minimum of physical properties on the stage; try to let your acting alone convey where the scene takes place.

Then clearly define the characters' specific reasons for being in those places so that you can translate those reasons into ideas for blocking. At the airport terminal, they might be waiting for a flight on which only one character is leaving. Try to use your own memories of waiting for an airplane or a bus to suggest specific ideas for movement and business. In the elevator, they might be on their way to see a lawyer for a divorce. Try to imagine what people actually stuck in such a situation might really do. In the hotel room, they might be getting dressed for an important dinner party. Whatever specific reasons you choose for your characters, try to translate those objectives into the use of imaginary properties and specific motivations for movement.

Then perform your three scenes for an audience without telling it in advance where the scenes are supposed to take place. Afterward, ask the audience to tell you where the scenes occurred. Ask for any suggestions of other details you might have added to communicate the situation more effectively. Ask also if there were any moments in which certain details did not seem appropriate.

NOTES

1. Tennessee Williams, *Cat on a Hot Tin Roof* (New York: Dramatists Play Service, Inc., 1958), p. 5.

2. Mary Chase, *Harvey* in *Fifty Best Plays of the American Theatre* selected by Clive Barnes (New York: Crown Publishers, Inc., 1969), volume 3, p. 101.

3. Ibid.

Lesson Four

The *Who,* the *What,* and the *Need*

In a complete characterization, an actor communicates two fundamentally different kinds of information to the audience. One kind deals primarily with the character's identity; the other, with the character's personality. Identity is discussed in the following chapter; personality is the subject of Chapter Eight.

Information about a character's identity is communicated to the audience in different ways. Part of the information is communicated by the actor alone, through movement patterns, speech patterns, voice, makeup, and costume. This type of information includes the kind of facts that might be found on a driver's license or a passport application. The information can be communicated by an actor without reference to any other characters in the play. We can call this category of information the character's *Who.*

Other information about a character's identity includes facts about family background, occupations, personal relationships, and so on. This kind of information can only be communicated through reference to other actors. We can call this category of information the character's *What.*

Of these two categories, the *Who* is the more difficult to communicate effectively because it requires the use of technical skills in voice, speech, and movement. The *What* is easier because role relationships among characters are signaled primarily by the habitual distances at which people in different relationships keep each other.

One other category of information includes the *Need* relationships that bind together the characters in a play. These *Need* relationships are expressed through certain interpretive choices rather than any objective detail of appearance.

Actors must provide information about the *Who,* the *What,* and the *Need* to communicate the full identity of any character in a play.

Chapter Four

Playing the Relationships

As discussed in Chapter Two, the characters of the play are not really on the stage; the actors are on the stage, but the characters are illusions created in the minds of the audience members. Unlike the way things are done in the movies, the process of characterization is not one of transformation but one of sending the right signals to the audience so that they will see the characters for themselves—even when the audience sees something completely different from what it is supposed to imagine.

Two somewhat extreme examples may serve to illustrate the truth of that last statement. On Broadway, actor Philip Anglim originated the title role of *The Elephant Man* without the use of any special "monster" makeup. He used only physical contortions and slurred speech to suggest the identity of the hideously deformed John Merrick. As in the case of Mielziner's setting for *Cat on a Hot Tin Roof*, no laziness or inexperience was involved; the purpose was to invite the participation of the audience's imagination. No monster makeup was used because it would actually have been distracting to a live audience in a theatre. Just as the audience watching the magician described in Chapter Two would never believe in fake blood and dangling organs, the audience watching Philip Anglim would have accepted elaborate latex makeup as just elaborate latex makeup, not actual physical deformities—and seeing the makeup would have inhibited the audience's imagining the real deformities.

In a similar situation, the first production of *Harvey* originally included an actor in a huge bunny suit as the title character, but the producers soon realized that his presence was too distracting. What the audience saw on the stage was a man in a bunny suit, not a Pookah named Harvey; a Pookah is an imaginary creature, but a man in a bunny suit is really only a man in a bunny suit. In effect, the actor in the rabbit costume got in the way of the audience's imagination. Fortunately, the idea was scrapped before the show opened, and the play went on to be an enormous success. Once again, we see that on the stage, what is not real is better left for the audience to imagine.

However, when the film *The Elephant Man* was made, actor John Hurt was literally submerged in latex prosthetics to play the same role. Movie audiences would never have accepted the same approach to Merrick's appearance as that used on the stage. The illusion of a film requires that each frame be composed of elements that look absolutely like what they are supposed to be. A film audience willingly imagines things that are not actually shown (for example, when a movie stuntman is shown falling off a building, but the audience has to imagine the body actually hitting the pavement), but it is never willing to pretend that it sees something other than what is actually on the screen. A stage audience will accept the sight of a wire holding up Dracula's bat as it flies across the stage, but moviegoers would laugh at such an oversight in a motion picture's special effects. (For the film of *Harvey*, the producers still elected to leave the rabbit to the audience's imagination. Perhaps they decided that a seven-foot tall rabbit would be too distracting even for a film audience.)

These last two examples help to show why the stage encourages actors to change their identities from role to role and the camera does not. On the stage, an actor does not have to be transformed into the character down to the last minute physical detail. On camera, actors must look absolutely like the people they are supposed to portray. But in the live theatre, the audience supplies most of the details for itself. Again, the problem for the actor and the magician are very similar; the trick is to select the right details the audience needs to get their imaginations working. Too many details, such as ten pounds of latex or people in bunny suits, will just get in the way.

Then what are the right details that must be provided for an actor to create the illusion of a character's identity effectively? To answer that question, we need to look at the three fundamental categories of information that define the identity of any person in real life. And we will refer to those categories here as the *Who*, the *What*, and the *Need*.

The *Who* category consists of all the details of a person's appearance, biography, and general physical condition. This kind of information would often be found on a driver's license or a job application and includes things

like age, sex, race, and nationality. As a result, this information tends to stay the same throughout the play. The actor should be able to communicate such information without the presence of other actors and without reference to any other character in the play. For example, let us consider an example from the play *The Children's Hour* by Lillian Hellman. The story concerns two women, Karen Wright and Martha Dobie, who together run a small private school for girls, one of whom (Mary Tilford) conspires with the other girls to accuse Karen and Martha of immoral conduct. Karen's Wright's *Who* is described by the playwright as follows:

> Karen is an attractive woman of twenty-eight, casually pleasant in manner, without sacrifice of warmth or dignity.[1]

She is also an American citizen, apparently white, and quite intelligent. All this information constitutes her *Who*.

The *What* category refers to a character's family, friends, occupations, hobbies, and any other way in which the character might be related to the other people in the play. The *What* is a factor that changes constantly according to whomever each character is on stage with at any given moment. To continue with the example from *The Children's Hour*, an actor playing the role of Karen Wright would have several different *Whats* to play; at various times, she is Mary Tilford's teacher, Joseph Cardin's fiancee, Lilly Mortar's niece, and Martha Dobie's close friend and co-owner of the school that is the location of most of the action of the play. Accordingly, which one of these various *Whats* she is at any given moment depends on which of these other characters is on stage with her. And the actors playing these other roles all have their own *Whos* and *Whats* to play as well. However, only the actor playing Karen Wright can make certain other actors in turn into her students, her fiance, her aunt, and her friend and business partner. Thus, as the actor playing Karen "creates" other characters' identities in this way ("You are my student, you are my fiance, you are my aunt," and so on), the other actors in turn "create" her various *Whats*: "She is my teacher," "She is my fiancee," "She is my niece."

There is also another type of relationship to be considered, one that goes beyond the social, professional, and familial roles already described. This relationship has to do with *Need*. In most plays, the characters want and need things from each other. These *Need* relationships are usually not found anywhere in the author's stage directions or stated explicitly in the dialogue; only a thoughtful reading of the play as a whole will yield up this information. *Need* relationships represent more of the coded information in the play that the actor has to know to look for before it can be found. However, once found, the *Need* relationships bind characters together more strongly than the social and familial roles. In Tennessee Williams' *The Glass Menagerie*, Amanda Wingfield is Laura's mother (the *What*), but Laura and Amanda are

held together by more than the mother-daughter relationship alone. Amanda desperately needs Laura to have a social life that Amanda can share vicariously and through which she can relive the dream of her youth. Laura, on the other hand, desperately needs her mother to accept her as she is and to stop trying to make her into something she is not. Laura also needs her mother as her sole source of support, since she is not capable of making her own way in the world (at least in her own mind). For actors playing either of these roles, the mother-daughter relationship is given its unique quality by the *Need* relationship. The full identity of both characters cannot be understood without understanding the *Need*, the *What*, and the *Who* of these characters all together.

For the actor, creating and communicating the information that goes into each of these separate categories is what is meant by the phrase *playing the relationships*.

CREATING THE *WHO*

Creating a character's *Who* is done by changing one's external appearance. This change is accomplished primarily by technical means, including makeup, costume, and rhythms of speaking and moving. Since this book is not about technique, the discussion that follows will not deal with the technical problems of changing one's *Who* but with the aesthetic problems. These problems center around two main issues: how much change is necessary and what kinds of changes are necessary.

Many beginning actors tend to have a blind spot when it comes to really looking at their own appearances onstage. Their feeling seems to be that if their normal appearance is more or less suitable to the role, they don't need to make any changes. A young woman offered the role of Karen Wright might feel that all she needs to do is to look glamorous. After all, the only statement Lillian Hellman makes about Karen Wright's appearance is that she is "attractive." A young man offered the role of her fiance (Joseph Cardin) might be content to put on a suit, comb his hair, and take his first entrance without giving any other thought to the matter. The effect is to make the role fit the actor's appearance (like movie stars do), instead of the other way around.

But when an actor goes onstage, no matter what the actor's appearance may be, the audience perceives that appearance as part of the illusion of the character as a whole. Actors need to look hard at their own appearances in a mirror and ask themselves if what they see is really exactly what the playwright has in mind. If a young woman playing Karen Wright can look at herself in the mirror and honestly say, "Yes! If I were in the audience, I would be convinced that the person I see now in the mirror is Karen Wright," then she should be content with her own appearance as is. If a young man playing the role of Joseph Cardin can honestly look at his own reflection and say,

"Why, hello there, Dr. Cardin!" then he is ready for his first entrance. But the chances of such a thing happening, if actors are really going to be honest with themselves, are not very good. Whoever the young woman and the young man in this example may really be, they are not Karen Wright and Joseph Cardin. Surely, there must be some ways in which these actors don't exactly resemble the characters they are to perform. Would Joseph Cardin, a doctor, have that kind of haircut? Would Karen Wright, a teacher, wear that kind of makeup? Actors are not the people they pretend to be, and any inconsistencies in appearance will send the wrong signals to the audience. "Close" is not good enough.

There is a possibility, however, that an actor may look in the mirror and like the reflection. In that event, the actor is saying, "That look is what I would create if I had to create something." If the actor can truly say this, nothing really needs to be changed. But it isn't enough just to look in the mirror and say, "Well . . . I guess it'll do." Any details that are appropriate may be left alone, but the illusion of natural behavior demands that if some details aren't right, they must be changed. In other words, actors need not worry about changing every detail of their appearance just for the sake of change; the only details that have to be changed are the ones that simply aren't right. Your goal as an actor is to change your appearance so that it is consistent with how *you* would look if *you* were that character (the "If-I-Were" formula again). Your appearance must provide the right details to communicate the essential details of your character's *Who*—you do not have to transform yourself into something you're not.

To return again to the example from *The Children's Hour*, what does it really matter that Karen Wright is " . . . an attractive woman of twenty-eight, casually pleasant in manner" and so on? In a contemporary production, an actor playing that role could just as easily be attractive or unattractive, tall or short, thin or heavy, younger or older, and of any race or nationality. What really matters in terms of the play is that Karen Wright is Mary Tilford's teacher, Joseph Cardin's fiancee, Lilly Mortar's niece, and Martha Dobie's close friend and co-owner of the school. What cannot be changed is that Karen Wright somehow makes one of her students hate and attack her, breaks off her engagement with her fiance, is deserted by her aunt at the apex of a major crisis, and refuses to deal with her close friend's confession of affection and thereby partially causes that friend's suicide. Creating the illusion of someone who is attractive and casually pleasant is really inconsequential compared to the problem of creating the illusion of a person who could believably be the focus of these catastrophic events.

Contemporary theatre yields up many examples in which the casting of the actors and/or the way certain *Whos* have been played were not what the playwright originally specified. Such alterations are very common in Shakespearean productions; Orson Welles' production of *Julius Caesar*, which moved the story to a modern, facist state, and Joseph Papp's award-winning

Much Ado About Nothing, which moved the setting to an American small town at the turn of the century, are notable examples. Black actor Cicely Tyson appeared as the Welsh schoolmistress in a Broadway revival of *The Corn Is Green* with an otherwise all-white cast. When the British cast of *Whose Life Is It Anyway?* was nearing the end of its Equity-permitted run on Broadway, the playwright was encouraged to revise the script slightly to change the situation to an American hospital in order to keep the show running in America. But Brian Clark changed more than just the location; in the original version, the story centered around a man, but in the revised version, the central role became a woman, played by Mary Tyler Moore in her Broadway debut. Even more extreme mismatches of age and physical type occur all the time in operatic productions.

Therefore, how to begin to think about a *Who* is not to think about any predetermined notion of the character's appearance but to evaluate the character's background generally: Where does the person live? What are the person's economic circumstances? What is the person's educational level? What is this person's daily routine like? How much and what kind of physical activity is this person required to do? What kind of personal habits does this person have? Then, you apply the answers to those questions to yourself to try to imagine how you would look if all those factors applied to you. The important thing about such questions is that they are general questions, and therefore, the answers can be applied to someone other than just the character as described by the playwright.

To transform the answers to those questions into specific details of physical appearance, actors should think about people they know who correspond in some way to their character's general background. It is not necessary to find one person who fits all the characteristics that the actor has identified. In essence, what the actor should be trying to do is to borrow characteristics from several different people to use in creating the actor's own *Who.* Then the actor can use the "If-I-Were" formula to say, "If I were of that same social background or if I were in that same line of work, I would look like that or act that same way, too."

For an actor playing Karen Wright, the place to start is not with "twenty-eight years old, casually pleasant . . . " The place to start is with the answers to the kind of questions just suggested: She is obviously well educated; she would have to be in order to run the school. Obviously she is not wealthy, but she would have to adopt a manner of dress appropriate to the economic level of the wealthy girls who are the students. Since this school is also something of a "finishing" school, it may also be assumed that her manners and general deportment would be very correct at all times. It is obvious that she should be a person of great energy, whose day must be long and tiring. (She is probably very grateful for a chance to sit down whenever one appears.) It should be a relatively easy matter for any actor to project herself into these circumstances and, by thinking back to people she might know who in any way have similar *Whos*, to modify or change her own physical appearance to one that will communicate these qualities to an audience. To make the point again, *any* female actor—regardless of age, height, length of hair, or facial structure—can find ways to communicate the illusion of a high educational level, not being wealthy herself but dressing to serve a wealthy student body, possessing great energy, and so on.

To sum up, you have to look at yourself in the mirror and identify any ways in which your own appearance is inappropriate to the background— the *Who*—of the person you are to play. You don't need ten pounds of latex to transform yourself into something you're not. But you do have to fix any details that don't fit. Like the magician, it is not important to make every-thing authentic (blood and screaming), only to make sure that nothing shows that will break the illusion you are trying to create. Then the audience will do the rest in their own imaginations. Remember, Philip Anglim didn't ac-tually look anything like the real John Merrick in the Broadway play, but the way he moved, spoke, and responded to others was otherwise consistent with the character. Given that his deformities were left for the audience to imag-ine, all other details of his appearance and actions were appropriate to that character. As a result, the audience imagined the presence of the "Elephant Man" for themselves.

When you start working on changing your own *Who* is important also. You should start making changes as early in the rehearsal process as possible. The first step is to start working in appropriate rehearsal clothing. For ex-ample, if the director of a production of *The Children's Hour* has determined that Karen Wright would wear a skirt and blouse in the first act, the actor rehearsing the role is not doing herself a favor by wearing jeans and a tank top in rehearsal. She is never going to find the right physical reality for that character until she begins to dress like her. Changing one's habitual mode of dress can have a profound effect on how one feels about oneself, as was noted in Chapter Two. If a young actor playing Dr. Cardin keeps showing up for rehearsal in sweat pants and a football jersey, he is not going to find the right approach to the character, no matter what else he does. The more quickly the actor can begin to approximate the mode of dress for the char-acter, the more quickly the actor will begin to develop a feeling for that char-acter's *Who*.

In addition to changing one's personal style of dress for rehearsals, cer-tain other changes can be useful in creating a new identity as well:

1. How people wear their hair frequently says more about them than any other single quality of personal appearance. Actors, both men and women, should pay particular attention to the way their life models wear their hair and begin experimenting with such stylistic changes.
2. Another important determining characteristic of a person's identity is the way that person carries body weight. Close observation of different types and ages of people will reveal that no two people carry their weight in exactly the same

way; some people tend to carry their weight in a somewhat forward manner, and others tend to drag their weight behind them as they move. Some people carry their heads over their shoulders, and others out in front of them like a crane. Posture is another related feature that should be studied as well, particularly in relation to different ages.

3. Closely related to the placement of body weight and posture is the curious business of how different people sit down and stand up. Again, close observation of other people will reveal that no two people tend to get into or out of a sitting position in exactly the same way. When specific patterns of standing and sitting can be identified and when these patterns can be associated with a particular identity that actors want to communicate to the audience, they will find that changing their normal patterns of standing and sitting can make a dramatic difference in their *Whos.*

4. Less immediately noticeable but equally important are patterns of walking. Does the person pick up the foot all the way before setting it down again, or does the person shuffle the foot from step to step? Does the person set the weight down slowly on the foot, or does the person drop the weight and walk with a stomp? Does the person tend to keep the toes pointed ahead, or are the toes

FIGURE 4–1.   The First of Three Illustrations of How an Actor Changes Identity and Personality.   *Student actors Catherine Stork and David DeWitt perform Neil Simon's* The Last of the Red Hot Lovers. *In the first act, "Elaine" tries to seduce the somewhat reluctant "Barney." Notice how this character's sexually aggressive personality is suggested through posture and body position. Compare the actor's appearances in these scenes with their appearances in the scenes from* Macbeth *that appear in the next chapter. Notice how simple changes in manner of dress and hairstyle alone create dramatic changes in the way their identities and personalities are perceived.*

pointed in or out? When actors change the type of stride they normally use, the transformation effected by this one change alone can be quite astonishing.

5. In the same way, changing one's habitual length of stride can also create unusual effects. Although length of stride is normally a factor of height and whether or not someone is in a hurry to get somewhere, it is also true that it can be affected by different ages and weights as well. For example, if a relatively thin actor is trying to pretend to be heavier through costume padding, the actor must also remember to change the length and type of stride. Nothing looks less convincing than a fat actor who walks like a thin one.

To conclude this section, the reader is invited to examine the accompanying photographs from a student production of Neil Simon's play *The Last of the Red Hot Lovers*. The story revolves around Barney Cashman, a middle-aged owner of a fish restaurant. In each of the three acts of the play, Barney invites a different woman to his mother's apartment (when his mother is away) in a futile attempt to have an extramarital affair. In this student production, each of the three female characters was performed by the same student actor, Catherine Stork. As an acting exercise, the transformations were accomplished completely without the aid of makeup. The emphasis was on wigs, costumes, posture, and all the other elements previously listed.

FIGURE 4-2. From the Second Act of *The Last of the Red Hot Lovers*. *Catherine Stork portrays the flaky, pot-smoking "Bobbie Michele." Notice that her costume and appearance are not drawn from stereotypes (Bobbie is a fledgling actor). Notice also how her decision to kneel on the couch in this way suggests her eccentric personality.*

In Figure 4–1, we see the character of Elaine Navazio. Notice how the choice of the dress and wig is used by the actor to communicate Elaine's cold, predatory nature. In Figure 4–2, a different hairstyle, costume, and way of using the couch create the flaky identity of Bobbie Michele. In Figure 4–3, the hairstyle, glasses, scarf, purse, and coat create the appearance of the paranoid character Jeanette Fisher. On the stage, the same actor was perceived as three completely different characters. Of course, the audience knew that the same person was playing all three roles, but through the physical details noted, the illusion of three different people was created. In each case, the actor approached the roles by trying to imagine how she would dress, move, and wear her hair if she were the character. The results were original and convincing.

In conclusion, then, it may be seen that changing one's own *Who* into that of the character is not a matter of magic or alchemy but of choosing the right details of physical appearance that fit the general background of the character—and eliminating anything that doesn't.

FIGURE 4–3.   From the Last Act of *The Last of the Red Hot Lovers.   Catherine Stork plays depressed, paranoid "Jeannette." As in the previous pictures, changes in hairstyle and clothing effect a change in identity not drawn from a stereotype. Notice the contrast between the way this character relates to the sofa and the way the other characters do.*

CREATING THE *WHAT*

Although the *Who* tends to be a somewhat flexible quality of a character's identity, the *What* is not. Once the playwright has established the social, professional, and familial relationships that exist among the characters of a play, these relationships are fixed. It would be unthinkable, for example, for a director to make Lilly Mortar into Karen Wright's mother (instead of her aunt) or to make Joseph Cardin into Karen Wright's brother (instead of her fiance). Whatever else may be true about the relationships among the characters of any play, these roles (aunt, uncle, friend, enemy, doctor, patient, and so on) are fundamental qualities that may not be tampered with or adjusted.

Just as the nature of these relationships is rigid and nonmalleable, the way that they are expressed also follows certain fairly rigid patterns. The most important external characteristic is the habitual distances people generally maintain between each other. As a general rule, how closely one person will allow another person to approach comfortably indicates the nature of the relationship between them. Actors need to analyze the relationships between the characters and then to translate that information into relative distances.

This characteristic of human behavior has been observed and commented on by many people. Dr. Edward T. Hall, an anthropologist at Northwestern University, devised the term *proxemics* to identify the field of study of this phenomenon.[2] He labeled four distinct distances that define interpersonal relationships: intimate, personal, social, and public. The intimate distance is anything between physical contact and about eighteen inches; this distance is reserved only for intimate friends or family members. The personal distance extends from eighteen inches to about four feet, the farthest distance at which one person can comfortably reach out to touch someone else; this is a distance reserved for friends and acquaintances. The social distance extends between four and seven feet; at this distance, people conduct impersonal business or talk to each other at cocktail parties. Beyond about seven feet, a public distance, people tend not to be related to each other.[3] Hall also noted further distinctions, for example, between close personal and far personal, but they are not particularly important to this discussion. On the stage, the distances between people cannot be so easily quantified because actors have to make adjustments in relative distances to reflect the size of the theatre and the nature of the stage used for a particular production.

Once again, it must be stressed that these distances are *habitual* distances. People who are not related to each other are often forced within intimate distance in elevators and crowded restaurants. But given their free choice in the matter, they would be more comfortable farther apart. From an audience's point of view, the principle has to do with the relative distances at which different characters in a play usually locate themselves from each other, not the absolute farthest or closest distances they have ever approached each other.

Consider an example from the musical play *My Fair Lady*, based on Shaw's *Pygmalion*. An actor playing the role of Professor Higgins relates in the following ways to these other characters: He is Colonel Pickering's friend; he is Mrs. Pearce's employer; and he is a virtual stranger to Alfred P. Doolittle, Eliza's father. Whatever choices the actor playing Higgins may wish to make about Higgins' *Who*, he will have fewer choices in establishing Higgins' relationships to the other characters. The one character in the play whom Higgins should approach most closely is Mrs. Higgins, his mother. (One of the peculiarities of *My Fair Lady* is that it is a love story without a love scene between the principals.) Colonel Pickering should be allowed no closer than a proper personal distance. Mrs. Pearce should be kept at a social distance because his relationship with her is essentially impersonal and businesslike. And Alfred P. Doolittle should be kept at the greatest distance because he is essentially a stranger.

But at what distance does Higgins keep himself habitually from Eliza? The formula here is a little different because of Higgins' control over Eliza while she is studying to improve her speech. During this part of the play, Higgins is at various times close to Eliza (in fact, touching her at will), and at other times very far away, almost as if she had momentarily ceased to exist. In effect, he is not actually relating to her as a person at all. This is the basis of all "power" relationships. When one person is portrayed as having "power" over another, the conventional distances between them are otherwise not respected. Higgins is not concerned with Eliza's feelings until she purposefully begins to distance herself from him at the end of the play. When Higgins is denied the kind of intimate distance to her which formerly he was allowed at will, it is clear that the relationship between them has undergone a fundamental change.

Actors may choose to vary habitual distances between certain characters during a play as a way of commenting on the changing nature of their relationships. In *Who's Afraid of Virginia Woolf?*, Martha begins to put her husband, George, at some distance while she begins to move closer to Nick, a man she has only just met. Her assignation with Nick at the end of the second act needs to be prepared for by an increasing closeness between the two characters. In *Hedda Gabler*, the scene between Hedda and Judge Brack at the beginning of the second act has Hedda playing with the distance between her and the Judge, eventually prompting him to suggest that she consider having an affair with him. The scene between Nina and Trigorin in the second act of *The Seagull* involves the same kind of process; as Nina grows more and more infatuated with the famous writer, she tries to decrease the physical distance between them as well. At first Trigorin seems to resist these advances, although in the fourth act of the play it is revealed that Nina later becomes his mistress. In all these examples, controlling and changing distances is a way of commenting on the nature of the relationships being played.

To move from the specific to the general, the formulas for differentiating between various relationships (or *Whats*) by different distances kept between actors are as follows:

1. The illusion that certain characters are strangers or otherwise not related is created when they remain at the greatest possible distance from each other. If an actor is forced by the design of the set or the blocking into closer proximity, the actor can still maintain the illusion that the other actors are strangers by behaving the way strangers always behave when they are forced together: by turning their bodies away from each other, avoiding each other's gaze, avoiding any kind of physical contact, or if all else fails, just looking very uncomfortable about the whole situation.

2. The illusion that certain characters are related in some professional capacity is created by keeping them at the so-called social distance, generally just beyond touching range. This is the distance at which the illusion of doctor and patient, teacher and student, employer and employee, and other such relationships are normally maintained. Of course, a doctor or a teacher may have occasion to approach the patient or student, but the purpose of closer proximity must always be clear—the doctor examining the patient or the teacher demonstrating something to the student.

3. The illusion that certain other characters are friends or distant family members (aunts or uncles but not parents or offspring) is created by having them maintain a closer distance yet, usually within touching distance but generally not closer than twelve to eighteen inches. Actual physical contact between these actors is possible, but the idea is generally to be close without touching.

4. The illusion that certain other characters are intimate friends, lovers, spouses, or members of one's own immediate family is created by allowing them habitually to be within intimate distance and, most particularly, to touch. The single most important quality that signals intimate relationships on stage is physical contact. And this kind of contact is usually casual, not at all the kind of deliberate contact made between a doctor and a patient or strangers in an elevator. People in intimate relationships deliberately sit close to one another, stand touching one another, or otherwise establish physical contact without having to find an excuse or even a special occasion for it. In fact, the principle at work here may be stated even more strongly: If actors trying to portray these kinds of intimate relationships do not use intimate distances and casual physical contact, the illusion of these relationships is simply not created.

It is this last category that causes the most trouble for many beginning actors. A cast of actors usually starts out as a combination of strangers, casual acquaintances, and occasionally one or two close friends. In rehearsal, the people as actors will tend to respect the appropriate distances at which they would normally approach each other as colleagues, not as characters. To use a specific example, a man and a woman who may never have met before the auditions for a particular play might be cast as husband and wife. In the course of working on the play, they pass from being complete strangers to the equivalent of being business associates. Unless it occurs to them to think about it (or to the director to do something about it), they are going to keep themselves habitually at a distance from each other that is appropriate to their real-life relationship but thoroughly inappropriate to the nature of their role in the play as husband and wife. Or worse, if they should occasionally be required by the script or by the director to hug or kiss, their unaccustomed intimacy may create a feeling of awkwardness in them and in the audience as well. Nothing is more illogical (but nonetheless frequently seen in all levels of amateur theatre) than two people trying to kiss each other while at the same time maintaining the greatest distance possible from each other with their bodies.

The greatest problem does not occur in the playing of love scenes. Love scenes are awkward by their very nature. What happens in a love scene is that two characters become closer to each other than they were before. In essence, then, a love scene is a kind of transition scene in which someone who has been previously a personal friend (and kept generally at that distance) is transformed into a new, intimate friend (now allowed at an unaccustomed closer distance). The experience is supposed to be awkward. The two people involved should not appear as though they do this sort of thing every day.

The greatest problem arises in playing those kinds of relationships in which intimate distance and casual physical contact are just that: casual, habitual, and expected. Husband and wife is one obvious example, but the list also includes father and son, mother and daughter, brother and sister, and even close personal friends of the same sex. All these kinds of relationship require actors to function at personal distances that will often be at odds with the natural distances they are most comfortable with outside of rehearsals.

The only cure for this kind of problem is for actors to make peace with themselves about the issue of touching. You may be a person who doesn't like to be touched by complete strangers, or even "business associates" and friends. However, the creation of the illusion of intimate relationships requires a certain amount of touching. If you are going to be an actor, you are going to have to make that sacrifice. You don't necessarily have to like it, but you mustn't shrink from physical contact when the nature of the role requires it.

Related to the issue of touching is that of personal modesty. The whole profession of acting is basically rather immodest. After all, most people don't usually try to attract attention in a crowd the way that actors do on a stage. Anyone who is truly modest usually doesn't go into acting in the first place. But even actors find their personal modesty occasionally compromised by the language and actions of some contemporary plays. It is not really the place of this book to argue for or against contemporary standards in theatrical practice. But actors should make a point of determining exactly what is going to be expected of them in the course of any production before they accept a role. Once the nature of the play has been explained and once the actors have accepted their roles, they should not then start asking the director to make changes because they don't feel comfortable with a particular piece of business, a particular line of dialogue, or a particular costume that was clearly a part of the role from the beginning.

To be more specific, many contemporary plays contain characters who use profanity and/or vulgarity. Many actors are not bothered by this kind of language, but many others are. Those who have difficulty saying things on-stage that they wouldn't say offstage should remember that the way a given character speaks in a play is intended to be part of the illusion of that character, not a comment on the actor cast in the role. An actor who plays a murderer in a play does not have to be a potential killer offstage. The same is equally true of actors who play homosexuals, child molesters, and rapists. An actor may play a character with a dirty mouth and the morals of a socio-path, but the actor should not feel that playing that role constitutes an endorsement of that kind of behavior. Audiences sometimes have trouble understanding this fact, but actors must be clear on this point. Whenever actors are truly offended by the way certain characters speak or act, they should simply decline to play those roles. Actors should not make a habit of asking the director to change all the expletives to *darn* and *phooey* just because they don't personally believe in using that kind of language.

CREATING THE *NEED*

The final type of information an audience requires to complete the illusion of a character's identity is the character's *Need* relationship to the other characters in the play. The qualities already discussed have their roots in human psychology, but the *Need* relationships owe more to art than to life. Both the *Who* and the *What* are based upon observations of human behavior generally, but the *Need* is something that is derived from the structure of the play itself. In effect, the *Need* relationships are really the cement holding the play together. These relationships are not expressed by changes in posture or by distances between people or by any other direct physical equivalents; rather, they are reflected in the nature of various interpretive choices that actors make.

The *Need* relationship may be defined simply in terms of what any given character in a play wants or needs from any other given character. These *Need* relationships are usually strongest among the major characters, but supporting and minor characters often have strong ones as well. Frequently the *Needs* may be contradictory, or in some instances they may be the reverse of a normal need (such as a situation in which a character may absolutely detest some other character). But *Need* relationships are always there in some form, and actors must find them and bring them out.

Finding and understanding the *Need* relationships becomes most important whenever characters in a play seem to have strong conflicts with each other. To give an example from *The Children's Hour* again, the *What* relationship between Karen Wright and Mary Tilford is that of teacher and student, respectively. However, Mary Tilford hates Karen Wright, and Karen Wright has no reason to like Mary either. And yet within the structure of the play itself, it is clear that these two characters do need each other. In Karen Wright's case, she needs Mary as a student in her school, in just the same way that she needs all the other girls in the school. Without Mary and the other wealthy girls (and the esteem of their wealthy parents), the school would go out of business. If the character of Karen Wright had no *Need* relationship to Mary Tilford at all, Karen would probably have dismissed Mary from the school long before the time of the play. But she hasn't done so, and that fact indicates that Karen must need Mary for some reason. That *Need* is then expressed in the way that Karen has to be careful how she handles Mary, no matter how little she actually likes Mary or her antics.

In her own way, Mary needs Karen, too. To be specific, Mary needs her to revenge all the imaginary acts of cruelty that Karen has perpetrated on her. Mary's ego is so great that she can never allow someone like Karen to get away with treating her as if she were just any other student in the school. Also, Mary knows that her grandmother would not let her leave the school unless Mary can come up with a very good reason, and so she makes it look as if Karen and her friend Martha Dobie are guilty of immoral conduct. In other words, Mary may hate Karen, but she needs Karen—in a perverted way—as her ticket out of the school she hates so much.

In this example, we see how these two characters work to create part of each other's identity through a synthesis of the *What* and the *Need*. An actor playing Karen Wright creates the identity of Mary Tilford by treating the actor in that role as her student (the *What*). However, in reality, Mary is more than just a mere student; in the situation of the play, Mary is also something that Karen needs for the sake of her livelihood. Mary's full identity to Karen is both that of a simple student and a kind of spoiled, temperamental "meal ticket." In turn, the actor playing Mary Tilford "creates" the identity of Karen by treating that actor as her teacher. However, Karen is really more than just a teacher to Mary; she is her persecutor and a premise that will get her out of the hated school. Karen's full identity to Mary is both that of teacher and scapegoat. In both cases, the full identity is clearly a combination of the *Need* and the *What* together.

Sometimes, the *Need* relationships in a play are obvious, such as in the example from *The Glass Menagerie* at the beginning of this chapter. It was noted that Amanda needs Laura in order to relive an old dream, and Laura needs her mother to accept her as she is and to protect her. Sometimes, however, the *Need* relationships are much harder to see. Again in *The Glass Menagerie*, it is much harder to find Tom's *Need* for his mother; the problem is intensified by the fact that Tom does finally desert his mother and sister at the end of the play. But good playwrights rarely go to the trouble of inventing and writing dialogue for characters that are not needed by other characters. Whatever characters the playwright has provided are there for a reason. Try to imagine what *The Glass Menagerie* would be like without Tom. Of course, the play couldn't function without Tom because there would be no one to invite the Gentleman Caller to dinner. And if Tom's function in the play is to provide the Gentleman Caller, an actor playing Tom has to ask himself, "Why does Tom bring his friend to dinner?" The answer to that question is well prepared for in the course of the play—to please his mother. And that answer defines his *Need* relationship to his mother: He needs to please her. If he really didn't care what she thought, he would have moved out much earlier, certainly at the point at which he and Amanda have a bitter quarrel about Tom's spending too much time at the movies. But Tom doesn't move out of the house at that point; he stays in that crowded little apartment because he feels a powerful need to find some way to please Amanda. And when his attempt to do that by bringing his friend home for dinner turns into a catastrophe, he then concludes that nothing he will ever do will please her—and that's when he finally leaves for good. An actor playing Tom creates the identity of Amanda, partly by treating her as his mother and also by treating her as a person whom he needs to please. Amanda's full identity as created by the actor playing Tom is a combination of both these elements together.

Once actors have defined their *Need* relationships to the other characters in the play, they should begin to find their *Needs* coloring and giving dimension to various interpretive choices. In the case of Tom, if the actor begins to internalize the idea that Amanda is his mother and that he really wants to please her, he will begin to find a new source of energy in the playing of even the most ordinary and banal dialogue. For example, in the first scene of the play, Amanda criticizes Tom's table manners and admonishes him to chew his food more thoroughly. Tom responds:

> I haven't enjoyed one bite of this dinner because of your constant directions on how to eat it. It's you that makes me rush through meals with your hawk-like attention to every bite I take. Sickening—salivary glands—mastication![4]

If the actor playing Tom takes that speech as an all-out attack on Amanda, the play has nowhere to go; that is, if he chooses to respond to his mother's comments by showing the audience that he can't stand her, the audience is going to wonder why he doesn't just move out. (In other words, the audience will not be able to form a satisfactory illusion of Tom's character; something will seem out of place.) But if the actor playing Tom remembers that he really wants to please his mother and that this *Need* is the basis of her identity to him, he is led to another choice in interpreting that speech. The subtext of the speech becomes, "I am irritated with you because nothing I do seems to please you, even the way I eat my food!" If the actor reads that speech as a plea for acceptance, the audience will better understand the nature of Tom's relationship with Amanda. (The audience will be able to form a satisfactory illusion of Tom's character in their minds.)

This example illustrates another principle beginning actors must understand. Audiences don't care about characters who don't care about other characters. It might be possible, even perhaps justifiable, for an actor to play Tom as if he really hated his mother—she certainly gives him ample enough cause. But audiences don't like to pay ten, twenty, or fifty dollars a ticket and then sit for two or more hours to watch people who don't really need each other but keep hanging around to shout at each other anyway. Again, if the characters weren't important to each other, the playwright would have left them out of the play. Finding a *Need* that holds the characters to each other is necessary not only for creating the illusion of natural behavior, but also for getting the audience to care about the characters. Michael Shurtleff in his book *Audition* sums up the matter very strongly:

> The actor should ask the question, "Where is the love?" of every scene, or he won't find the deepest emotional content. This does not mean that every scene is about Romeo and Juliet-type love; sometimes the scene is about the absence or the deprivation of love. But by asking "Where is the love?" you come up with an answer that will involve you emotionally with more immediacy than if you fail to ask that question.[5]

In essence, then, an actor should always try to find (or if necessary, invent) a *Need* for all the other characters in the play with whom the actor's own character actually has scenes. The actor should then find ways to use those *Needs* in every scene, particularly in those scenes in which there is strongly expressed conflict between characters.

SUMMARY

To create an effective illusion of a character's identity, the audience must receive three different types of information. The first of these is the *Who*, which is communicated primarily by the actor adopting a physical appearance based on the general background of the character and the actor's own reference to life-models. The second type of information is the *What*, the specific social, professional, or familial roles in which the characters belong. This information is communicated primarily by the relative distances between the actors. The third type of information is the *Need*, which is the way of defining what each character wants or needs from most or all of the other characters in the play.

In the process of creating this information, actors are expected to change their physical appearances as much as necessary, but always remembering that changes should be made for the sake of interpretation and not for the sake of effect alone. Also, in the creation of intimate relationships, actors must be ready for close personal distances and physical contact. And finally, strong *Need* relationships are part of the quality that makes a performance interesting to an audience. Although it is possible to do a play about people who have no use for each other, no one would want to watch it.

EXERCISES FOR CHAPTER FOUR

The most important principle illustrated in this chapter is the way that actors' appearances and the distances between actors communicates important information to the audience about each character's identity. The following exercises are intended to help students demonstrate these principles at work.

1. Each person has individual movement patterns that are subtle but very distinctive. Try the following exercise with a group of people: Have one member of the group walk onto the stage, sit down in a chair, get up again, and then walk off. The person being the model in this scene should not try to "act" or assume a character but simply perform the action as naturally as possible. Then try to perform the same action *exactly* as the model did it. Try to copy exactly such details as length and type of stride, carriage, the position of the neck over the shoulders, use of the hands while sitting and standing, and so on. You should discover that it is extremely difficult to copy another person's pattern of movement exactly with any great success. However, if you do succeed in doing so, you should feel an odd sensation that you have been magically transformed into that person. If you can make yourself move like someone else, you won't feel like yourself at all.

   A variation on the same game may be played by a more experienced group. Each person assumes a number, all the numbers are written on strips of paper and placed in a hat or bowl, and everyone draws another person's number at random. Each person then demonstrates his or her own personal patterns of moving as just described; afterward, each person in turn tries to act like the person whose number he or she has drawn. At the end, the group tries to guess who was imitating whom.

2. Consider the following pantomime: A person waits alone onstage. Another person enters and hands that person an imaginary object (letter, book, apple, hammer, and so on) in such a way that makes clear what the object is. The first person uses that object in some appropriate manner and hands it back. Then the person who brought in the object leaves the stage.

   Put yourself in the place of the person bringing the object into the room. Imagine a specific relationship with the person you will find there and a specific location in which the scene is to take place. For the relationship, decide if it is best described as intimate, personal, social, impersonal, or "power." Decide also if the place is a public, private, or personal one. But do not reveal any of this information to the other person in advance. Try to convey the nature of the situation and the relationship through your acting. Do not use any gestures or imaginary business that you would not really use if you were actually in this place or in this relationship. Use the "If-I-Were" formula to inform your behavior.

When the scene is over, ask the other person to guess where the scene took place and what the relationship was. If there are observers, ask them to guess as well. Ask which details of your acting made the sense of the scene clear. Ask if there were any details that the other person found confusing. Solicit suggestions on other choices you could have taken to make the information clearer.

3. Take the scene from *Harvey* or another scene of your choice and try changing the *What* relationships between the characters. For example, Veta might be Myrtle's psychiatrist, or Myrtle might be Veta's mother. Remove any references in the text to the actual relationships between the characters, and try to avoid inserting any new references that spell out what your new ideas are. You may also have to change certain specific bits of business, but don't let the original version of the scene intimidate you. Make a radical change in the characters' *What* relationships, and then change the scene as needed to get it to work.

Perform the scene without telling your audience where the scene takes place or what the new relationship is. Then ask your audience to guess the nature of the new relationships between the characters. Pay particular attention to the different spatial relationships that different *What* relationships are going to require and how they affect the scene.

Afterward, ask your audience to guess what the new relationships were. Then ask for their suggestions as to other choices you might have made to communicate the same ideas.

NOTES

1. Lillian Hellman, *The Children's Hour* in *Lillian Hellman: The Collected Plays* (Boston: Little, Brown and Company, n.d.), p. 9.

2. Edward T. Hall, *The Hidden Dimension* (New York: Doubleday & Company, Inc., 1966), p. 1.

3. Hall, pp. 110–120.

4. Tennessee Williams, *The Glass Menagerie* in *50 Best Plays of the American Theatre* selected by Clive Barnes (New York: Crown Publishers, 1969), p. 140.

5. Michael Shurtleff, *Audition: Everything an Actor Needs to Know to Get the Part* (New York: Bantam Books, 1980), p. 36.

Lesson Five

The Six Fundamental Objectives

The most difficult part of the illusion of natural behavior for the actor to create is the illusion of purpose. The difficulty arises from several sources: A character's purpose is constantly changing from moment to moment. A playwright seldom gives the actor any direct information about purpose, and as a result, actors are usually left to figure it out on their own. But the biggest problem is that purpose can only be communicated to an audience indirectly.

There are two different ways to understand purpose in human behavior. Consider the following example: A man walks onto the stage and says to the people he finds there, "Anyone for tennis?" One way to explain the purpose of that action is to ask what is the character's motivation, that is, why did he say that? The answer is that he probably needs a tennis partner. The other way to explain the purpose is to ask what objective is he trying to achieve, that is, what is the desired result his action is intended to bring about? The answer in that case is that he probably is trying to get someone to play tennis with him.

The concepts of motivation and objectives work together to communicate purpose to an audience. Before an actor can play a specific action, the actor must first understand what the character's motivation is. But as is explained in the following chapter, motivation must then be translated into a particular desired result that each specific action is intended to achieve. The audience can then deduce from the way the actor plays that action what the character's motivation is.

There are only six possible desired effects that any action can have on another person:

1. To get information from another person
2. To communicate information to another person
3. To make another person do something
4. To stop another person from doing something
5. To make another person feel good
6. To make another person feel bad

These six possible desired effects define the six fundamental objectives.

Chapter Five

Playing The Motivation

In Chapter One, we observed two qualities that set apart realistic acting from other types of acting: the way actors relate to the setting and the way actors play actions. In the two previous chapters, we have seen how actors relate to the setting and to each other. Now we are ready to explore the nature of actions and how they communicate information to an audience.

Consider the following example: We are walking down a deserted city street at twilight, and suddenly we see a man throwing a brick through the window of a store. Instantly, we step back into the security of a doorway to watch the man's further behavior. Several minutes later, the police arrive and ask us what we have seen. We relate the facts of the incident as we observed them, and then we are asked to draw a conclusion. "Why do you think he did it?" the policeman asks us.

If you think about it, the policeman's question is somewhat remarkable. The man with the brick was a complete stranger to us. We never saw him before. We don't know anything about him. How should we know why he threw the brick? But in spite of that fact, we have probably already formed a conclusion about the man's purpose based on our observations, possibly without even realizing that we have done so. The remarkable fact is that without consciously intending to do so, the man probably told us a lot about the reason he tossed the brick through the window. The policeman just naturally assumes that we "heard" what the man "said" through his actions. Human nature dictates that we should have already formed an opinion on the matter.

What are some of the possible conclusions we might have drawn already? The man might have been trying to rob the store. Or he might have been trying to get revenge on the owner of the store for some reason. Or he might have been just trying to make trouble. If he had been trying to rob the store, he might have been a drug addict trying to get money to support his habit, or he might have been someone down on his luck who was trying to get money to support his family. If he had been trying to get back at the owner of the store, the owner might have done something to the man to make him angry, or the man may have simply imagined that the owner had tried to take advantage of him in some way. If the man had just been trying to make trouble, he might simply have been angry with society, or he might have been trying to make some sort of political statement. And there are other possible explanations as well.

How could we possibly know which one of those explanations might have been his true purpose? We can't know for sure, but by observing certain details of the event, we can make an educated guess. If the man's movements had been stealthy and if he had taken something from inside the window and run away with it, we would have assumed that robbery was indeed his motivation. If he had been bold and not taken anything but pleasure in the act of breaking the glass, we would have assumed that revenge was his motivation. If he had been just walking along the street, stumbled over the brick, and then, on the spur of the moment, tossed it through the window before running away, we would have assumed that the man was simply a troublemaker. In other words, the reason he threw the brick probably would have been reflected in his actions. And by thinking about other details of the event (such as his age, manner of dress, pattern of movement, and so on), we could draw further conclusions about his identity (drug addict, a person down on his luck, urban terrorist, or whatever) that would tend to confirm our initial conclusion as to why he tossed the brick in the first place.

Again, we would probably draw such conclusions about the man's behavior before we even realized we had done so. As we have observed in the discussion of illusions, human beings automatically tend to "fill in the blanks" of what they observe. But in this case, there is no illusion involved. We were watching a real man throwing a brick for a real reason. Therefore, the principle being demonstrated here is a little different. In drawing conclusions about the man's purpose based solely on observing his actions, we are demonstrating our belief in a fundamental principle of human behavior, namely that the man had a purpose in the first place. We assume—and the principles of modern psychology dictate—that people always have reasons for everything they do. No one can do anything for absolutely no reason whatsoever. A person might not be consciously aware of the purpose behind a certain action (as when a person with a mental disorder steals something without knowing why), but nevertheless, there is a purpose for that action somewhere deep down inside that person's psyche. We accept as an axiom that there are reasons for everything that people do, no matter how bizarre or seemingly thoughtless.

Because we assume that all human behavior is purposeful, we assume that the purpose is always reflected in human behavior. Or to turn that proposition around, not only is all human behavior purposeful, but it looks purposeful as well. Just as our behavior constantly adjusts to reflect our relationship to the environment and to other people, our behavior constantly adjusts to reflect the purpose of our actions as well. Even in situations in which we try to conceal the purpose of our behavior (such as when we tell a lie), what we are really trying to do is to disguise our actual purpose by assuming the appearance of another.

The policeman in our example knows that the purpose of people's behavior is evident (or at least partially evident) just by looking at them. The same principle holds true in the theatre as well. An audience knows that all human behavior has purpose, and therefore, by looking at the behavior of the actors on the stage, the audience should be able to guess the purpose behind the characters' behavior. (This is the reason an audience watching realistic actors shouldn't need to understand the language being spoken in order to understand the meaning of the words.)

However, actors are not the people they portray. Their behavior will not adjust automatically to reflect their characters' purposes any more than their behavior will automatically adjust to the imaginary setting of the play or to the other characters. Actors must consciously make their characters' behavior appear purposeful in the same way that they must consciously create the proper responses to the situation and to the relationships. And audiences can tell when actors are behaving purposefully and when they are not. Sometimes actors will speak with no apparent connection to what their bodies are doing; that is, sometimes their gestures and movements will contradict what they are saying. Sometimes actors will stare off into space when not speaking and shift their weight from foot to foot in the middle of a scene. Occasionally, they will race through long speeches without moving at all because they don't understand the meaning of what they are saying. In such situations, even untrained observers can tell that something is wrong. In life, people always have valid, active reasons for being wherever they are and for doing whatever they are doing, and their behavior always reflects those reasons. Whenever characters in a play don't appear to have a purpose for every moment they are onstage, their behavior does not seem natural.

Creating the illusion of purpose is the most difficult part of the actor's job. Unlike a character's relationship to the setting and to the other characters, a character's purpose changes from moment to moment. Actors must create the illusion not of one purpose, but of a continuous string of purposes, each of which must be clear by itself as well as differentiated from all the others. Furthermore, a character must continue to appear to have purpose even when the character is not speaking. In life, people don't stop having a purpose to their behavior whenever they stop talking, and on the stage, characters must retain the appearance of purpose as well.

And therein lies one of the biggest headaches for the actor. Purpose, like *Need,* is never spelled out in the script. Actors have to infer their characters' purposes from a careful reading of their lines. And, as we shall see, playwrights are even more oblique about specifying purpose than they are about about indicating *Need* relationships. But actors must also derive purpose from the spaces between the lines as well as from the lines themselves. There must never be a moment on the stage when actors are without a purpose for their characters, even when there are long sequences of action in which they have no lines at all from which to guess what those purposes might be. Therefore, this part of the actor's job involves more work than any other.

Because creating the illusion of purpose is such a large and complex problem, the subject has been spread out over three chapters. This chapter deals with the relationship between purpose and behavior and how the actor goes about expressing the one through the other. Chapter Six focuses on the process of deriving purpose from the script. Chapter Seven deals with the separate problem of differentiating between one purpose and the next within a single scene.

MOTIVATION AND BEHAVIOR

The word that is most often used to designate purpose is *motivation,* meaning simply the need or desire for something that a person does not already possess. In saying that all human behavior is motivated, we are saying that human behavior is an unending series of attempts to satisfy needs or to fulfill desires of one sort or another. For example, eating could be an attempt to satisfy the need for food. Sleeping could be an attempt to satisfy the need for rest. Calling a friend on the telephone could be an attempt to satisfy the need for companionship. Watching the television could be an attempt to satisfy the need for diversion. Or to turn the examples around, we could say that hunger could be a motivation for eating, exhaustion could be a motivation for sleeping, loneliness could be a motivation for calling a friend, and boredom could be a motivation for watching television.

As we have already observed, a person's motivation tends to be reflected in that person's behavior. In other words, when people are eating, sleeping, calling a friend on the telephone, or watching television, their behavior should reflect if their motivations are hunger, exhaustion, loneliness, or boredom. All human behavior *appears* to be motivated because it *is* motivated. There is no such thing as unmotivated behavior.

In the previous examples, we have considered only one motivation and one corresponding action at a time. However, life is rarely that simple. A single action may reflect several motivations at once, and a single motivation may incite several actions, both directly and indirectly. The same is true of characters in plays. For example, no one single motivation is sufficient to explain all the various actions of Shakespeare's Macbeth. In a major role of this kind, the actual number of motivations can seem almost infinite.

(In the discussion that follows, I assume that the reader is already familiar with *Macbeth*. If you are not, you may want to consult a plot summary before reading on.)

The most basic type of character motivation includes all the possible needs and desires that are built into the plot of a play. This category may be described as a character's situational motivation. In the case of Macbeth, these factors include his desire to be king of Scotland and his need to please his ambitious and ruthless wife. After the murder of the King, Macbeth needs to lie to cover up his guilt; his desire to know more about his future motivates him to go back to the witches for more prophecies; and so on. All these wants and desires are simply a function of the plot of the play.

In addition to situational motivation, a character's emotional needs and corresponding emotional state at any given moment may motivate certain actions as well. When Macbeth runs out of the dining hall in the middle of dinner with the King, his emotional state is partly responsible. Part of the problem is his fear that the other people in the room may be suspicious of what he is contemplating. Part of the problem is also his shame of even daring to think about murdering the King so soon after having been accorded many honors in battle. In other words, Macbeth flees the room at that moment to alleviate his fear and shame. Later in the play, when he returns to the witches, it is his need to vent his anger and frustration that makes him threaten the witches: "Deny me this, and an eternal curse fall on you!" Under such circumstances, emotions can be considered as motivations.

In addition to situational and emotional motivations, certain peculiarities of personality may also motivate a character's actions. In other words, some people do certain things just because that's the way they are. It has already been noted that Macbeth and his wife are very ambitious people. Ambition is certainly a kind of need, and therefore it motivates many of Macbeth's actions. In the same way, Macbeth is also an honorable man, at least at the beginning of the play; in other words, he has a need for honor, and that need motivates several other of his actions. It is, in fact, the tension between these two motivations in his personality that makes him the unique and fascinating character that he is. It may also be said that Othello is jealous, Oedipus is proud, and Katherine the Shrew is spiteful. As a general rule, the personality of any character in a play is actually based on certain unique and ongoing needs that motivate many of that character's actions.

Probing more deeply into a character's individual wants and needs, actors may find what may be described as psychological motivations. For example, Lady Macbeth, in the first act, says:

> Come, you spirits
> That tend on mortal thoughts, unsex me here
> And fill me, from the crown to the tow, top-full
> Of direst cruelty!

After reading that speech, some actors may conclude that she has a subconscious desire to be a man. That piece of speculation is fueled in part by the way she dominates her husband in the first two acts of the play. Any such speculations on the subconscious desires that motivate a character's behavior may be classified as psychological motivations.

Certain other types of motivation may also figure into an actor's thinking. One type has been discussed in the previous chapter, namely, the *Need* relationships existing among the various characters. Macbeth needs his wife as a counselor, an accomplice, and a spiritual comforter. Another area of motivation is all the functions expected of Macbeth as a leader, first as a victorious general and later as king. There is an additional category of purely physical motivations: The castle is drafty (need to put on a warm cloak), the night is dark (need to light a torch), Macbeth is tired (need to go to sleep), and so on. All these needs require the character to respond in some way. And the list goes on and on.

Thus, the large number of possible motivations for a character like Macbeth presents a very serious problem to any conscientious actor. It is possible to read into this script so many different motivations that an actor may be easily overwhelmed. Also, since sitting around and thinking about a character's motivation can be a lot of fun, there is a very real danger that some actors will spend so much time thinking about motivation that they forget to get on with the business of acting itself. How do you know when you have figured out everything that you need to know? How do you know when it is time to stop?

To answer that question, we have to delve more deeply into the relationship between motivation and behavior in acting. And the first fact that we have to understand about that relationship is that actors cannot play motivations directly. Try to imagine that you are an actor who has just been told to walk onto a stage and play the motivation of hunger. You step out in front of the curtain and try to remember what it's like to be hungry. You think about all the food you like to eat, or you try to remember last Thursday when you were late getting home and were absolutely starving by the time you finally ate dinner. And your mouth starts to water, and you lick your tongue around your lips, and you even start to rub your stomach with your hand. There! You are now playing the motivation of hunger directly. You are feeling hunger, and you look as if you are hungry. Anything wrong with that?

Yes. You look ridiculous. That kind of behavior has absolutely no counterpart in natural behavior whatsoever. If you're really hungry, you grab a candy bar or you call for a pizza or you find a friend and say, "You busy for lunch?" In life, people who are hungry don't stand around licking their lips and rubbing their stomachs; they get something to eat. Only on the stage would someone actually stand around and try to pretend to be hungry; anywhere else, someone who's hungry does something about it. The motivation of hunger cannot be communicated directly by playing the need; it can only be communicated indirectly through the action of food-seeking.

Now imagine that you are going to try to play the motivation of hunger again. This time, however, you start by picking an action directed toward satisfying the need for food. Perhaps you pantomime opening and devouring a brown-bag lunch. Perhaps you pretend to be a person at a buffet supper who is sampling each dish while loading up two or three plates at the same time. Actions such as these could be used to communicate the motivation of hunger convincingly as it is communicated in life.

You're on the right track, but you're not home yet. Choosing the right action to play does not automatically guarantee that you will convey the right motivation. To be specific, the action of eating does not by itself communicate the motivation of hunger. People often eat for other reasons besides the need for food. Sometimes people eat because they're terribly unhappy and want to cheer themselves up. Sometimes they eat because they've got nothing else to do and need something to pass the time. Sometimes people eat because they've just tried out a new recipe and need to decide whether or not to make that dish for a party. Sometimes they eat because they're trying to convince Mom that she's still a great cook (when she isn't). Thus, the action of eating may be used to convey many different motivations.

However, when people are unhappy, their eating reflects the need to cheer themselves up, not the need for food. In the same way, when people are really hungry, they don't eat the same way as when they are just trying to pass the time, judge the results of a new recipe, or convince someone of something. As noted at the beginning of this chapter, our behavior adjusts spontaneously according to the nature of our purpose. To play the motivation of hunger, you must not only choose the right action to play, but you must play that action as if you are trying to satisfy the need for food. (Obviously, the "If-I-Were" formula applies here as well.)

To communicate any character motivation properly, actors must first choose appropriate actions to play and then play those actions in such a way that the purpose of those actions is clear. It is the audience's perception of the desired result that the action is intended to bring about which makes it possible to determine the actor's motivation.

But again, we are still talking about only one motivation and one action at a time. In the case of Macbeth, we have observed many different, even conflicting, motivations affecting his behavior at any given moment in the play. For example, at one point in the play, he says to his wife, "I dare do all that may become a man; Who dares do more is none." On the one hand, he is an ambitious man; with the King soon to be asleep under his very roof, he sees the opportunity for unlawful advancement. But on the other hand, he is a man of honor, a valiant soldier, and one of the King's most trusted associates. He has a need for honor that is almost as great as his need for advancement. And his banquet hall is full of guests; something has got to be done before they all get suspicious. But his wife is questioning his valor; he has a need to make her content. All these factors come to bear on this one moment. Given that Macbeth's action at that moment is to say those words to his wife, how can an actor perform that action to communicate all those various needs at once?

To find the answer to that question, let's leave the theatre and consider a similar situation in life. Consider a college freshman taking notes in an English class as the instructor lectures on *Beowulf*. What are some of the possible motivations for this behavior? Does the note-taking result simply from a basic human need to know about *Beowulf*? Not likely. Very few college freshmen suffer from that need. Perhaps the student is taking notes as a result from the need to pass the final examination for the course. That need is more likely, but where does that motivation come from? Possibly it comes from a need to get an education, a need to get ahead in the world, a need to keep Mom and Dad happy since they are paying the tuition; or perhaps the motivation is simply a need to stay busy in class to keep from falling asleep. It is even possible that the student really does want to learn about *Beowulf*. But more likely than not, the student's behavior can only be fully explained by a combination of all these motivations together, as any one of these motivations alone does not provide sufficient explanation.

If it is true that our behavior spontaneously adjusts to reflect our motivation and if it is true that our student's note-taking is motivated by all these various needs, then how is it possible that all these motivations are reflected in this one simple action?

The answer is that every motivation does not produce an automatic response. For example, a person may feel hungry and not do anything about it. The person may be too busy to eat or on a diet or fasting as an act of religious devotion—or there could be any number of other reasons. Except in the case of extremely urgent needs (a person is drowning and needs air; someone is on fire and needs to roll on the ground), any one state of need does not automatically incite a corresponding action. There is an intervening step that must take place first—an act of deliberate choice by the conscious mind.

Before any action is initiated, there is always a definite moment when the conscious mind says, "*Now*, let's get something to eat. *Now*, let's go to bed. *Now*, let's telephone so-and-so. *Now*, let's watch television." The whole cause-and-effect relationship between motivation and behavior is consciously controlled by the mind in this way. And the conscious mind can only choose to attend to one need at a time. If you're talking on the phone and you suddenly get hungry, your conscious mind delays the food-seeking activity until you are off the phone. If you start to feel tired while you are driving your car, your conscious mind tries to delay the action of lying down to go to sleep until you can get home to your bed.

In the case of the freshman taking notes on *Beowulf*, many different motivations may be required to explain that student's presence in the class. But the student's conscious mind can only deal with one of those motivations at a time. Therefore, we ought to be able to observe that student's behavior at any given moment and make a fairly shrewd guess about what one need is motivating his behavior *at that one particular moment*. In other words, we can imagine that if the student were merely taking notes to stay awake, the behavior *at that moment* would be noticeably different from taking notes to pass the final exam or taking notes in the excitement of just having grasped some significant insight into the nature of the poem or trying to impress the instructor. The point is this: no matter how many different motivations the student might have for being in that class and taking those notes, we ought to be able to tell *at any one moment* what specific need the student's conscious mind was giving its top priority: keeping awake, passing the test, understanding the poem, or trying to impress the instructor.

The same principle applies to the actor playing Macbeth. No matter how many different motivations may be inferred from the text, the actor must do just what people in life do—consciously determine Macbeth's most pressing need *at that particular moment* and perform that speech as if he were really trying to satisfy that one need.

But isn't that approach going to make the performance rather one-dimensional? Does the actor simply ignore all those different levels of motivation that we catalogued earlier? Shouldn't the actor do something to get all those various nuances across to the audience?

No. But the audience will probably grasp all of those different motivations, anyway. If the actor plays one motivation at a time, the result is going to be a convincing illusion of natural behavior. If the illusion is convincing, the audience members are going to figure out all that other information for themselves. And they are going to do it in just the same way that the actor figured it all out originally: the audience will take what information it is given and imagine the rest. Remember the man and the brick? When he threw the brick through the window, he wasn't trying to communicate anything to us at all; he was just trying to break the window. We took what information we could observe, and we inferred the rest. And when we drew our conclusions, we were doing just what an audience does when they create the illusion of a character's purpose for themselves in their imagination.

At the risk of repetition, I want to stress again that the actor's task is not the same as Dr. Frankenstein's—actors don't have to assemble enough pieces of flesh to build a living human being, only the *illusion* of one. The audience will do most of the work for the actors if they just give the audience enough information to get started.

Finally, we see the answer to the question we left unanswered earlier in this section: How do you know when you have figured out everything that you need to know? The answer is that you need one and only one motivation for each moment that you are on stage. To avoid being swamped by a tidal wave of possible motivations, actors should follow this procedure: First, they should read the script to determine their characters' most pressing motivations from moment to moment. Then for each moment they are onstage (whether speaking or not), actors should pick the one and only motivation that seems to be the most immediate in that character's conscious mind. Next, actors must determine an appropriate action that can be used to express that motivation. Finally, they should perform that action in a way that seeks to achieve that desired result. In following this order, actors are only duplicating the order in which all human behavior comes about naturally: The conscious mind selects the most important motivation and then initiates action directed at achieving a desired result that will satisfy that need.

To end this section, it will be helpful to review the major principles we have covered thus far:

1. A motivation is a state of need or desire for something that a person does not already possess.
2. All human behavior is motivated. There is no such thing as unmotivated behavior.
3. A person's actions always adjust spontaneously to reflect the person's motivation.
4. An actor cannot play a motivation directly. Motivation can only be expressed as a quality of an action.
5. The quality of action that communicates purpose is the desired result the action is intended to create.
6. Even though a person may be acting from many different and contradictory motivations, the conscious mind can only work to achieve one desired effect at a time.
7. By determining the desired result of any action and observing the details of the situation and the character's identity, an audience can guess most or all the motivations that incited that action.

No matter how numerous or complex a character's motivations may be, the actor simply has to play each individual action—one at a time—to achieve only a single desired result. The trick is to play the *right* action to achieve the *right* desired result. The problem of finding the right action will be discussed in the next section, and the problem of communicating the right desired result will be discussed in the section after that.

OBJECTIVES AND ACTIVITIES

The word most often used to designate the desired result that an action is intended to bring about is the *objective*. (As we shall see in the next chapter, the concept of an actor's objective includes more factors than just the desired result, but the desired result is always the most important part of every objective.) By definition, an objective is something that doesn't exist. If the desired result were already in existence, there wouldn't be any need to try to bring it about. Once an objective is achieved, it ceases to exist. Therefore, an audience never actually sees a character's objective in anything that the actor says or does. An objective is something that the audience always infers from the way a character performs a given action.

Furthermore, it is part of the definition of an objective that it is reflected by action that is consciously directed. However, not all actions require conscious control. Therefore, before we can fully understand how objectives may be inferred from consciously-directed behavior, we need to distinguish between behavior that is consciously-directed and behavior that is not.

There are certain procedures that all people learn to perform as a matter of habit or routine. For example, most people can tie their shoes or make their beds without having to think about what they are doing while they are doing it. In fact, it is possible to do either of these things and sing a song at the same time (an action that does require conscious control.) Most procedures of this type are better done without thinking about them. Without thinking about it, a man may be able to tie his own tie in the morning when he is getting ready for work, but if he has to explain to someone else how to tie a tie (an act that requires thought), he may experience considerable difficulty. Walking is another procedure that we all do without thinking. And yet, if a person is in a catastrophic accident and temporarily loses the ability to walk and has to learn to walk again, that person soon realizes just how complicated a procedure walking can be if we have to think about it and control it deliberately.

Any procedure that can be performed without conscious control will hereafter be designated as an *activity*. The brain has to turn some procedures into activities as a direct consequence of being able to direct only one action at a time. The following example will illustrate how this process of transformation happens and why. If you have ever had to learn how to drive a car, you may recall the sensation of sitting behind the steering wheel and being overwhelmed with things to worry about all at once. Simultaneously, a novice driver must consciously steer the car, watch what other cars are doing, work the accelerator, shift the gears, control the speed, and follow the driving instructor's orders. The novice driver must give conscious attention to every single aspect of controlling the vehicle at once because none of the individual procedures that constitute driving a car have yet become routine (that is, activities). In order to survive this ordeal, drivers must learn to perform these procedures without having to concentrate on them one at a time: Shifting gears must become a matter of habit; regulating speed must become a function of foot pressure on the accelerator pedal; watching the other drivers in front and behind must become an automatic rhythm. When all of these separate skills are mastered, driving the car itself stops being the objective and becomes an activity. For most experienced drivers, the mechanical process of driving a car requires very little conscious control.

In exactly the same way, all activities are procedures that were once objectives (including walking, talking, eating, writing, reading, and so on). Every person must turn some objectives into activities or a person would never be able to get through the day.

This distinction between objectives and activities gives us some important insights into the working of the conscious mind, insight that is of significant consequence to the actor. To return to driving, once control of the car is no longer an obstacle to be overcome, the conscious mind moves on to a new objective: learning which streets to drive to get from one place to another, such as from one's home to one's job. Once a satisfactory route has been learned, driving that route becomes an activity. Then the conscious mind finds a new objective to occupy its attention: finding some way to pass the time between leaving home and arriving at work. One way to satisfy that need is to listen to the radio; another is to make conversation with a passenger; if neither of these distractions is available, the driver may simply daydream. (And if we watch other people driving their cars, we can usually tell if their objective is to control the car, to find a way to get somewhere, or to pass the time while they drive by habit.) In other words, the conscious mind immediately moves on to new objectives as soon as old ones are achieved.

Now imagine that you have become an experienced driver. You are driving to work on a route that you have been driving everyday for years. You have a passenger in the car with you, and you are trying to explain to that person how to make an omelet. Suddenly, a small child runs out in front of the car. You see the child and instantly your conscious mind assumes full control of the operation of the vehicle; all conversation is suspended until the objective of avoiding a collision has been achieved. Anyone who has had such sudden emergencies while driving (including a blowout or another driver pulling out of a parking space without warning) will undoubtedly recall the feeling: an instant heightening of all the senses accompanied by an intense awareness of the total operation of the vehicle—a sensation very similar to that of learning to drive. Because of the danger, the activity of driving the car suddenly became the objective of driving the car again. Then when the emergency is over and you have had a chance to calm down, you remember that you were trying to explain the mysteries of the omelet to your friend. There being no more pressing problem that requires your attention, you go back to your conversation about cooking to pass the time.

This example demonstrates several important principles. First, when one need (to pass the time) was superceded by a higher priority need (to avoid running over the child), the conscious mind instantly "switched gears" from the lower-order problem to the higher-order one. The conscious mind could not pursue two objectives (explaining the omelet and avoiding the collision) at the same time. Before the child ran out in front of the car, you could talk about omelets and drive the car at the same time because driving was only an activity. You were technically doing two things at once, but only one of them (explaining the omelet) required the attention of your conscious mind. There are many situations in which a person may *appear* to be playing more than one objective at a time, such as in the case of a person who is cooking an omelet while talking on the phone. But what is really going on in that situation is that the conscious mind is rapidly shifting its attention back and forth between objectives. If the cook gets too involved with conversation, the omelet may burn. If the omelet starts to burn, the cook will have to put down the phone. The mind may shift focus among several different objectives at once, but the mind still may only deal with one of these at a time. A juggler may get several plates twirling in the air on bamboo sticks at the same time, but the juggler can only focus on one plate at a time. How many plates are kept twirling at once depends on how good the juggler is at dashing about from pole to pole.

Another principle demonstrated by the example of driving the car is that the conscious mind is never without an objective to pursue. When the operation of the vehicle no longer requires conscious control, the driver's mind automatically turns back to the need to pass the time. At no time is the conscious mind without a problem of some sort to occupy its attention. This principle is a direct counterpart to the principle that all human behavior is motivated; in effect, human beings are never without objectives of one sort or another to occupy their time, and therefore, everything they do is done for a reason. When a person has absolutely no other problems to solve, there is always the need to find something to do to pass the time. In effect, the need to pass time is the objective of last resort.

But the most important principle which the driving example illustrates is the way that the brain assigns priorities to different objectives. The phenomenon of higher order and lower order motivations has long been the object of study and speculation by psychologists. Among them, Abraham Maslow suggests the concept of a "hierarchy of relative prepotency" based on the relative importance of various human needs (or motivations.) Maslow describes what he calls the process of homeostasis, "the body's automatic

efforts to maintain a constant, normal state of the blood stream," as the basis
of this hierarchy. From this need evolve certain physiological needs, of which
the most prominent is hunger. Once the physiological needs of the organism
have been satisfied, certain lower order needs emerge, of which the next
highest on the ladder is what Maslow calls the "safety" needs, meaning any
needs that pertain to a person's well-being. Maslow states,

> Practically everything looks less important than safety and protection (even
> sometimes the physiological needs, which, being satisfied, are now underesti-
> mated). A man in this state, if it is extreme enough and chronic enough, may
> be characterized as living almost for safety alone.[1]

Somewhat lower in priority are the needs for affection and a sense of belonging. When those needs are satisfied, Maslow maintains the next needs
which emerge are the needs for a person to feel valued.

> All people in our society (with a few pathological exceptions) have a need or
> desire for a stable, firmly based, usually high evaluation of themselves, for self-
> respect, or self-esteem, and for the esteem of others.[2]

Finally, Maslow recognizes the need for self-actualization.

> A musician must make music, an artist must paint, a poet must write, if he is
> to be ultimately at peace with himself.[3]

Maslow's hierarchy confirms the fact that human beings are never without specific objects to pursue. At last, we can see why seemingly unmotivated
behavior onstage is so disastrous. When actors shuffle about from foot to
foot or stare off into space or move about at random during their scenes,
such behavior looks unnatural because the character suddenly seems without
a need (or motivation) for the conscious mind to satisfy—a situation that
could never occur in real life. For this reason, actors must have objectives to
play for every moment their characters are onstage. When an actor focuses
on a specific problem (such as finding out why Willy Loman is back from his
sales trip much earlier than expected or why Laura Wingfield quit typing
school months ago and never told anyone), the possibility for random or pur-
poseless behavior is virtually eliminated. If we are trying to find out why
somebody smashed up our car or why somebody has been lying to us, we
don't shuffle about and stare off into space. We direct all our behavior toward
achieving an answer to our questions. Only in this way does our acting appear
truly realistic.

The remaining problem for the actor is how to determine the appropriate desired results that define the objectives. Fortunately, finding a character's desired result at any given moment in a play is relatively easy to do:

To find the objective, you simply have to find the obstacle. And for most scenes, finding the obstacle is obvious.

THE SIX FUNDAMENTAL OBJECTIVES

Obstacles can be of two types. One is located in the environment (trying to get the door open, trying to find the hidden letter, and so on). Environmental obstacles are obvious; they are always found in the stage directions, and therefore, they do not present a problem of interpretation for the actor.

The other type of obstacles, those located in other characters, are always found in the dialogue. If there are two characters onstage together and they are talking to each other, they have to be each other's obstacles. Common sense dictates that a playwright would have difficulty writing a scene in which two people talked to each other without making each other the focus of their mutual objectives. If there were no need for them to speak to each other, there would be no dialogue. But if they are speaking, there must be some need to speak, and that need must define an objective—a need to have an effect of some sort on the other person.

This fact greatly simplifies the actor's search for the desired result of a character's actions; although there may be an infinite number of motivations for the behavior of a character, there are only six possible desired effects that one person may seek to have on another:

To get information. An enormous amount of time in any play is usually devoted to characters who are trying to get information from each other. Who are you? What do you want? What are you doing? What did you just do? What happened? What does it mean? What are you going to do? Linda Loman tries to find out what happened to the car. Veta wants to know what's bothering Myrtle. No matter what the particular details of the situation may be, the objective is always played fundamentally in the same way. The obstacle is that someone else has information that is needed. As an actor, you must use the "If-I-Were" formula and ask the questions in the dialogue as if you were really trying to make the other person tell you what you want to know. You must then focus on what the other actor is saying in response, and that focus on listening is the most characteristic sign of this objective. You must try to block out of your mind that you know what the other character is going to say. When the desired information is revealed, you must respond as if you were hearing the facts for the very first time. Until you get the information that your character needs to know, then the character who has that information is the obstacle.

To communicate information. This objective is the mirror image of the first one; just as characters have to find out things about each other, other characters have to inform them. But this category also includes more ag-

gressive objectives, such as trying to convince, to persuade, or to make someone understand something. The obstacle in this case is always the other character's lack of understanding. The desired result that the actor seeks in playing
this objective is the look of recognition from another character that indicates
he or she now really understands. When Myrtle says to her mother, "Thank
God for the Fourth Avenue Firehouse," she is trying to make her mother
understand how she feels. When Macbeth says, "I dare to all that may become a man," he is trying to convince Lady Macbeth that he is not a coward.
To play this objective, an actor saying any of these lines must focus on the
lack of understanding within the character to whom the line is directed. As
an actor, you have to use the "If-I-Were" formula to imagine how you would
try to persuade or convince that other character of whatever facts you have
been given to communicate. You must seek to create that look of recognition
from the other actor that says, "Ah, yes—I see now what you're getting at."
You must forget that you know how the other actor is going to respond and
really focus on the obstacle of the other character's not knowing.

To make someone do something.   The focus in this case is on actually
forcing another character to perform a physical action, not merely to understand or to perceive something. To get you to loan me five dollars, to get
you to do me a favor, to get you to make a phone call, to get you to leave
the room, to get you to get rid of Uncle Elwood—these are all examples of
various attempts to precipitate a specific action. To play this objective, the
actor must focus on the person that is the obstacle and do whatever is necessary until that person performs the desired action. As an actor, you must
use the "If-I-Were" formula to imagine how you might really try to persuade
the other character to do what your character needs to have done. You must
forget you know whether or not your objective is going to be achieved. Not
knowing whether or not the person is actually going to do whatever is desired
can make this a powerful objective to play. You must direct all your energy
at the obstacle of the other person's inaction.

To stop someone from doing something.   This is the mirror image of
the previous objective, although they are usually not connected in the same
way as are the first two objectives. The obstacle in this case is always that
the other person is doing something that you, as a character, want to stop.
This particular objective often involves your taking a definite physical action.
To stop people from leaving the room, you may have to grab them and hold
them back; to get people to stop talking, you may have to threaten them or
shout to get their attention. Usually, this particular objective is played to
completion. As an actor, you have to use the "If-I-Were" formula to figure
out how you would stop the other character from acting if you were really
in that situation. At the risk of being repetitive, the action must be performed
without being aware of whether or not the person can be stopped. Only in

that way can the obstacle of the other person's activity be overcome with conviction.

To make someone feel good.   This objective is similar to that of communicating information, but the desired result is more than a look of understanding from the person who is the obstacle; the objective is a fundamental change in his or her mental state. In the scene with Myrtle and Veta, Veta takes on the objective of making Myrtle feel better about herself. To play that objective, an actor playing Veta has to focus on the obstacle: the way in which the actor playing Myrtle projects a lack of self-confidence. Myrtle is bitter about how her uncle is limiting her social life; the actor playing Veta has to focus on that bitterness and do everything possible to make it go away. As an actor, you have to use the "If-I-Were" formula to recall how you might try to make other people feel better about themselves. You have to focus on all the things the other person is doing that project a bad self-image and then attack that bad self-image just as you would in a real-life situation. The result you are looking for is a certain brightening of the other person's spirits. You have to forget the fact that you know whether or not that objective is going to be successful and direct your efforts toward the obstacle of that other person's attitude.

To make someone feel bad.   Again, this objective is the mirror image of the previous one. To play this objective, you have to focus on the obstacle, the other person's sense of well-being or pride or whatever. You have to look hard at the other actor and observe all the signs that indicate good feelings, and then you must do everything in your power to make those signs change. You have to use the "If-I-Were" formula to put yourself in the position of someone who really wants to hurt someone else. You have to do everything you would do in real life to overcome the obstacle of the other person's sense of well-being.

Using these six fundamental objectives as a frame of reference, the actor can usually discern exactly what desired effect a character is trying to create at each moment in a play. Let us now examine this process at work in a specific scene. The following excerpt is from *Macbeth*, Act One, Scene Seven (a scene to which several references have already been made in this chapter). Read the scene over carefully as if you were an actor doing a "first" reading.

Scene Number Two: *Macbeth*

Act One, Scene Seven, begins with a stage direction calling for a parade of servants bringing dishes to the banquet. After they have passed, Macbeth enters as if fleeing from the hall. He then delivers a famous soliloquy, which begins, "If it were done when 'tis done, then 'twere well/It were done quickly." In this familiar speech, he voices several objections to the planned murder of Duncan, and he ends with the words,

> I have no spur
> To prick the sides of my intent, but only
> Vaulting ambition, which o'erleaps itself
> And falls on the other side.

Since this speech is delivered while Macbeth is alone onstage, we must assume that his objective is to sort out his own feelings. But a moment later, Lady Macbeth enters as if she had just followed him from the banqueting hall. From that moment, her objectives and his objectives are concerned with each other.

LADY MACBETH: He has almost supped. Why have you left the chamber?
MACBETH: Hath he asked for me?
LADY MACBETH: Know you not he has?
MACBETH: We will proceed no further in this business.
He hath honored me of late, and I have bought
Golden opinions from all sorts of people,
Which would be worn now in their newest gloss,
Not cast aside so soon.
LADY MACBETH: Was the hope drunk
Wherein you dressed yourself? Hath it slept since?
And wakes it now to look so green and pale
At what it did so freely? From this time
Such I account thy love. Art thou afeard
To be the same in thine own act and valor
As thou art in desire? Wouldst thou have that
Which thou esteem'st the ornament of life
And live a coward in thine own esteem,
Letting "I dare not" wait upon "I would,"
Like the poor cat i' the adage?
MACBETH: Prithee peace.
I dare do all that may become a man;
Who dares do more is none.
LADY MACBETH: What beast was't then
That made you break this enterprise to me?
When you durst do it, then you were a man,
And to be more than what you were, you would
Be so much more the man. Nor time nor place
Did then adhere, and yet you would make both.
They have made themselves, and that their fitness now
Does unmake you. I have given suck, and know
How tender 'tis to love the babe that milks me.
I would, while it was smiling in my face,
Have plucked my nipple from his boneless gums

	And dashed the brains out, had I so sworn As you have done to this.
MACBETH:	If we should fail?
LADY MACBETH:	We fail?
	But screw your courage to the sticking place And we'll not fail. When Duncan is asleep (Whereto the rather shall his day's hard journey Soundly invite him), his two chamberlains Will I with wine and wassail so convince That memory, the warder of the brain, Shall be a fume, and the receipt of reason A limbeck only. When in swinish sleep Their drenched natures lie as in a death, What cannot you or I perform upon The unguarded Duncan? what not put upon His spongy officers, who shall bear the guilt Of our great quell?
MACBETH:	Bring forth men-children only, For thy undaunted mettle should compose Nothing but males. Will it not be received When we have marked with blood those sleepy two Of his own chamber and used their very daggers, That they have don't?
LADY MACBETH:	Who dares receive it other, As we shall make our griefs and clamor roar Upon his death?
MACBETH:	I am settled and bend up Each corporal agent to this terrible feat. Away and mock the time with fairest show; False face must hide what the false heart doth know.

The general motivations of these two characters have already been discussed at length in this chapter. Their most urgent motivations are situational: Lady Macbeth wants to get her husband back into the hall before everyone becomes suspicious. Macbeth wants to talk his wife out of the little scheme they have cooked up to cut the red tape of promotion. However, as clear as these motivations may be, they are still just that, motivations. Before actors can play this scene, they need to determine the specific desired results that individual lines are intended to achieve. For example, at the beginning of the scene, Lady Macbeth says, "He has almost supped. Why have you left the chamber?" What is the specific desired result implied by that line? Stop reading now and try to answer that question. When you have an answer in terms of one of the six fundamental objectives, compare your answer with the text that follows. Remember always to consider the objective in terms of the other person as the obstacle, in this case Macbeth himself.

One of the first principles of finding the right action to play is always to look for the most pressing, most immediate need first. (Recall the example of driving the car: The most important need always takes precedence.) The most immediate objective for Lady Macbeth at that moment is *to get information*. The obstacle is clearly her husband: He has the information she seeks. In order to play that objective, the actor playing Lady Macbeth must think to herself, "What would I do if my husband had suddenly run out on our guests and I wanted an answer in a hurry? How would I stand? How would I gesture? How would I use my voice?" Everyone at one time or another has been in the position of needing an answer in a hurry from someone else. Anyone should be able to find answers to those questions that would communicate that desired result to an audience.

But consider all the many conflicting emotions that Lady Macbeth must be feeling at such a moment: irritation at having her husband desert her at such a crucial moment in their schemes, fear at the possibility that his rash act may arouse suspicions, dread of the planned murder to follow, revulsion at having to make small talk with the intended victim over the roast boar and fried turnips. Aren't these more important than simply finding out why he has left the dining room?

No. The line is a direct question. The principles of human psychology dictate that getting information is her top priority at this moment. If something else were more important, she would have said something else. When she says "Why have you left the chamber?" she simply wants to know why he has left the chamber. (Note fig. 5–1; observe how the student actor playing Lady Macbeth is communicating this primary objective through her posture and gesture.)

Figure 5-1.
From Act One, Scene Seven of *Macbeth*.   Lady Macbeth asks, *"Why have you left the chamber?" Fundamental Objective: To get information. Notice how the actor's body position communicates this objective.*

The actor must also remember that Lady Macbeth may suspect why her husband has left the hall, but she doesn't really know why until she hears his answer. For all she knows, he could have run out of the hall because he heard someone else arriving in the courtyard or because he wanted to check out the King's accommodations or because he had just come up with a new idea that could make the murder go even more smoothly later on. Once she finds out that he left the chamber because he's having an attack of conscience and wants to withdraw, she has reason to become angry. In other words, she must not ask the question as if she already knew the answer. Of course, the actor does know the answer before she asks the question, but she has got to block that fact out of her mind in order to play the action with conviction.

As to all the various conflicting emotions that Lady Macbeth must be feeling at this moment—the evil, neurotic obsession, irritation, fear, anxiety, dread, and revulsion—the actor has to trust the playwright. If the actor has previously made good choices in playing the character's identity and the situation, all Lady Macbeth's conflicting inner states will be clearly implied by her behavior in the context of the play as a whole. Lady Macbeth herself is not worrying about communicating obsession, irritation, fear, anxiety, dread, and revulsion to her husband. All she is trying to communicate is that she wants an answer from him.

Two lines later, Macbeth says,

> We will proceed no further in this business.
> He hath honored me of late, and I have bought
> Golden opinions from all sorts of people,
> Which would be worn now in their newest gloss,
> Not cast aside so soon.

What is Macbeth's fundamental objective as he says this?

Again, looking at the most immediate level of the scene, Macbeth's fundamental objective seems to be to communicate information. But is that all that's going on at this moment?

In the soliloquy that precedes this scene, Macbeth expresses several reasons for not killing the King, but nowhere in any of it does he mention "golden opinions" or anything similar. In essence, what he tells the audience before Lady Macbeth enters is that the whole idea makes him sick because it is so unnatural. But as soon as she comes out, he starts rattling on about his public image. Isn't his real action here to try to cover up his actual feelings at this moment so that Lady Macbeth won't see how scared he is? Maybe, but looking at the action that way makes Macbeth his own obstacle, and we have already established that when he is speaking to her, she must be the obstacle. If Macbeth really wanted to cover up his feelings, why would he stand there and say anything to her at all? Why not just go somewhere else where she couldn't find him until he had a chance to get his feelings under control? If the objective does not imply some connection with her, then there is no reason for him to stay in the scene. As we noted before, the fact that one person in a scene speaks to another person always implies that each person is the other's person's obstacle to achieving a particular desired result.

Another problem with playing the action as if Macbeth were trying to cover up his own feelings is that it is essentially a negative action; it says what Macbeth is trying not to do. Macbeth might be trying not to do any number of things at this moment—not to let the servants hear what he is saying, not to let his cloak blow off in the wind, and so on. But the audience isn't interested in what he isn't trying to do; they want to know what he *is* trying to do. Therefore, objectives should always be expressed in a positive way. Common sense dictates that if people aren't trying to do one thing, they must be trying to do something else.

Our first guess seems to have been right after all. Macbeth's motivation is to call off the plot to murder Duncan. Lady Macbeth is the obstacle. Therefore, no matter how badly he wants to cover up his own true feelings at this moment, the desired result he wants to have on Lady Macbeth is to change her mind (*to communicate information.*) With this fact in mind, we could say that Macbeth's action is to tell her that he wants to call off the plan. This action is superior to the action of trying to cover up his own feelings (because it makes Lady Macbeth the obstacle), but the main verb choice, *to tell* is not completely accurate. She is not actually preventing him from telling her anything; in fact, she asked him a direct question and is waiting for the answer. The action *to tell* points to her as the obstacle but does not make clear the nature of the resistance. If she were physically restraining him from speaking at this moment, telling would require overcoming an obstacle.

More accurate verb choices to express this action include *to persuade,* *to convince,* and *to make understand.* Such verbs clearly imply an obstacle: the other person's lack of agreement or lack of understanding. Therefore, let's say that Macbeth's objective is *to convince* Lady Macbeth that they should call off the murder. An actor playing Macbeth could then say to himself, "Now, if I were really trying to convince somebody in this way, how might I stand? How might I speak? How might I move?" Surely, this is a situation that everyone has shared at one time or another. It may be hard to imagine oneself as a Scottish warlord in the Middle Ages who is plotting to murder a king, but it is very easy to imagine trying to convince someone not to do something. Anyone should be able to play such an objective with conviction. (See fig. 5–2.)

But what about the fact that Macbeth may not be expressing his real feelings? Doesn't the actor have to get that across somehow? No. Again, the actor has to trust the playwright and the sense of the scene. It is quite clear

FIGURE 5-2.
From Act One, Scene Seven of
*Macbeth. Macbeth states, "We will
proceed no further in this business."
Fundamental Objective: To
communicate information. Notice
how the actor is clearly focused on
his partner's face, looking for some
sign of recognition from her. Notice
also how her physical attitude
suggests that she is resisting what
he is saying.*

from the context that Macbeth may not be expressing his true feelings at
this particular moment—a fact that becomes only too clear as the scene goes
on. But when the actor says, "We will proceed no further in this business,"
his objective must be to convince the actor playing his wife to call off that
murder, and the actor must play just that action as if he really wanted to
achieve that result. Never mind whether or not the character is being honest.
At that moment, Macbeth is trying to make Lady Macbeth believe that what
he is saying is how he really feels. Let audiences figure out the truth for
themselves.

To continue with the scene, Lady Macbeth responds strongly to her
husband's words:

> Was the hope drunk
> Wherein you dressed yourself? Hath it slept since?
> And wakes it now to look so green and pale
> At what it did so freely? From this time
> Such I account thy love.

What is the nature of Lady's Macbeth's action implied by this speech?

Before the actor can define the objective for a speech such as this, she
must be certain she understands exactly what the words mean. The idea of
drunken hope waking up sober and having second thoughts suggests the kind
of false courage that liquor creates in a drunk. In other words, she is accusing

Macbeth of being all talk and no action. But then she goes on to say, "From this time/Such I account thy love," implying that his professions of love to her are nothing but drunkard's boasts. To paraphrase, she seems to be saying, "You don't really love me; all that talk about making me Queen of Scotland was just so much hot air!" Her motivation is her need to shore up his faltering resolve, but her objective is *to hurt him*. (See fig. 5–3) The specific action is to make him feel ashamed of himself by comparing him to a courageous drunk who is a coward when he's sober. (And if you stop to think about it, that's a pretty clever stratagem to play on him because it has the effect of changing the subject and putting him on the defensive. Lady Macbeth is not stupid.)

Then she goes on to say,

> Art thou afeard
> To be the same in thine own act and valor
> As thou art in desire? Wouldst thou have that
> Which thou esteemst the ornament of life
> And live a coward in thine own esteem . . .

After she finishes this speech, Macbeth finally cuts her off:

FIGURE 5-3. From Act One, Scene Seven of *Macbeth*. Lady Macbeth says, *"Was the hope drunk . . .?"* Fundamental Objective: To tear down someone else's self-esteem. Notice how her whole physical attitude makes this intention clear.

Prithee peace.
I dare do all that may become a man:
Who dares do more is none.

What are the fundamental objectives implied in his lines?

These lines have already been discussed in the preceding text, but it should be pointed out that they express two different objectives. As noted in the first section of this chapter, a person's purpose changes from moment to moment; in a play, a character's purpose can change several times, even in the middle of a single speech.

The first fundamental objective is fairly direct: to stop her from speaking. His action is to silence her by a direct order. (See fig. 5–4.) It is significant that she lets him get away with that action—she stops speaking. That fact demonstrates how he is really the dominant one in this relationship, and she recognizes his authority and defers to it, no matter how much she may badger him or influence his judgment. This moment in the scene is a good example of a situation in which the very structure of the dialogue reveals an important fact about the relationship between two characters; the actor doesn't have

FIGURE 5-4. From Act One, Scene Seven of *Macbeth*. *Macbeth says, "Prithee peace!" Fundamental Objective: To stop someone from doing something. Notice, as in Figure 5–2, how the actor is focused on his partner's face to be certain that the desired result is achieved.*

to worry about getting this information across to the audience; it will be communicated just by playing the action.

The second fundamental objective is again *to communicate information,* but not the same information as before. It seems that her attack on his valor has drawn a little blood; at least, he felt the need to respond to the accusation of cowardice more than to the accusation that he doesn't really love her. (Again, the structure of the dialogue reveals that he is so certain of her feelings for him that he doesn't even take that accusation seriously.) She seems to have touched a nerve; he is having second thoughts about murdering the King, and perhaps he is wondering if those second thoughts really do indicate a lack of courage on his part. Once again, the structure of the dialogue itself communicates information to the audience, and the actor doesn't have to try to get that information across; it is communicated automatically if the actor will only play the right action.

Lady Macbeth now responds to the vulnerability Macbeth has just shown:

> What beast was't then
> That made you break this enterprise to me?
> When you durst do it, then you were a man,
> And to be more than what you were, you would
> Be so much more the man?

Now what is she up to?

As before, we must first clarify the exact meaning of the words. When she says "What beast," she is referring directly to his previous statement, "Who dares do more is none," meaning not a man and therefore a beast. In effect, he implies that ethics and morality ("all that may become a man") are the qualities that differentiate men from beasts. In other words, he is defining manliness in terms of ethics and morality. What she does in her response is to turn that definition around; she defines manliness in terms of aggression. In other words, a *real* man is someone who has the guts to go after whatever he wants. Then having changed his definition of manliness in this way, she begins to use that definition to flatter him ("then you were a *man*"). Instead of continuing to attack him, her strategy has changed radically. Her fundamental objective now is *to make him feel good.* Her objective is to shore up his faltering courage by flattering him.

Then she takes her definition of manliness one step further:

> I have given suck, and know
> How tender 'tis to love the babe that milks me.
> I would, while it was smiling in my face,
> Have plucked my nipple from his boneless gums

And dashed the brains out, had I so sworn
As you have done to this.

Her fundamental objective changes again abruptly. Now she is trying *to communicate information* to him—that she has the guts to go through with this plot even if he doesn't.

Macbeth's response is short and simple: "If we should fail?" What is his fundamental objective here?

Don't be misled by the question mark. His fundamental objective is *to communicate information,* not to get it. At last he says what is really on his mind. He is terrified by the cost of failure. The simplicity and directness of the words that Shakespeare has given Macbeth to say here suggests the enormity of his fear. If, instead, Macbeth had launched into an eighteen-line speech about what happens to regicides, we would have to assume that he had his emotions under control. But instead, he simply cries out, "*If we should FAIL?*" This man is scared. The actor doesn't need to huff and puff and work up a full load of emotional steam to convey this motivation; Shakespeare's choice of words does it all for him. All he has to do is play the action. His fundamental objective is to make Lady Macbeth understand just how awful the price of failure is going to be.

But is Lady Macbeth frightened? Not really:

> We fail?
> But screw your courage to the sticking place
> And we'll not fail. When Duncan is asleep . . ,
> . . . What cannot you and I perform upon
> The unguarded Duncan?

What are the fundamental objectives implied in this speech?

Now Lady Macbeth can see that all his talk about honor and "golden opinions" was merely a cover-up for the real issue: his terror. First, her desired result is to silence him. Her "We fail?" is almost a slap in his face. Then, having got back the floor, she proceeds to deal with the fear he has expressed. There are two ways to look at the desired effect she wants to achieve, and they are both perfectly proper. One way is to assume that his attack of cowardice is a reflection of his self-esteem at this moment; in other words, the speech that follows represents an attempt on her part to build his self-esteem back up by reminding him how perfectly foolproof their clever little plan is. The other way is to assume that she is trying to get him to do something (to calm down) by showing him how easy the plan is. Either way, for an actor playing Lady Macbeth the desired result is to see a change in Macbeth's physical attitude. From that perspective, we can see that she is actually using a little humor to help her along: "swinish sleep" and "spongy officers." She is so confident that she can actually make jokes at this moment.

Obviously she achieves her desired result because he responds:

> Bring forth men-children only,
> For thy undaunted mettle should compose
> Nothing but males.

Why does he say this?

The most obvious way to explain what Macbeth is doing at this moment is to say that he is trying to show his wife that he now has his fear under control. But as has been already pointed out, the objective of "showing" does not imply an obstacle. Lady Macbeth is assumed to be the obstacle, and from that point of view, we realize that he has a need to *convince* his wife that he has his emotions under control. But still, what he is saying to her sounds more like a compliment than an argument. In point of fact, what he says is a compliment. Therefore, the most obvious desired result would be the fundamental objective of trying *to make her feel good.* Of course, Lady Macbeth seems to be feeling pretty confident of herself already, but perhaps Shakespeare is trying to point out that she may perhaps have more doubts about what they are planning to do than she is willing to let on to her husband. After all, they do support each other in this crisis, and in the latter part of the play, Lady Macbeth does seem to go virtually insane—two facts that suggest she is human after all. Also, we need to remember that these two people are husband and wife. It is extremely desirable that actors playing these roles should find places in the script that allow them to express their feelings for each other. Therefore, the idea that Macbeth might actually be trying to build up her self-esteem at this moment is perfectly possible. Also, by implication, his having the presence of mind to pay her that compliment at this moment must clearly show her that he has his fear under control. (See fig. 5-5.)

In the next line he says,

> I am settled and bend up
> Each corporal agent to this terrible feat.
> Away, and mock the time with fairest show;
> False face must hide what the false heart doth know.

What is Macbeth's final objective in this scene?

At first glance, an actor might be tempted to say that Macbeth's fundamental objective here is again to convince his wife that he has his feelings

FIGURE 5–5.
From Act One, Scene Seven of
Macbeth. *Macbeth says, "Bring
forth men-children only . . ."
Fundamental Objective: To build up
another person's self-esteem.* Notice
that he is now touching her in a way
that reaffirms their relationship as
man and wife. This touching,
although nowhere called for in the
script, is an actor's choice that helps
to convey their Need relationship and
to make them more interesting as
characters as well.

under control. However, the most striking thing about this speech is that
Macbeth seems to be giving orders again for the first time in the scene since
he ordered his wife to be silent. Clearly, he is taking charge again, and the
actor's phrasing of this objective should reflect that change. Then the fundamental objective must be to get Lady Macbeth to do something: to go back
into the hall with him. (See fig. 5–6.)

As the previous discussion demonstrates, the way that the actor phrases
a character's objectives provides an important psychological bridge to the
imaginary world of the play in which that character exists. Objectives are
universal human goals that enable an actor in a high school in New Jersey
or a community theatre in Kansas to portray a medieval Scottish king. An
actor who portrays Macbeth does not have to have committed murder or
been a king or even have ever been to Scotland. An actor doesn't need to
have anything in common with the personality of any character in a play in
order to act that character successfully. But the actor does have to find the
universal human objectives that the character of Macbeth tries to achieve
from moment to moment in the play itself. Every actor, no matter how like
or unlike Macbeth, has had to communicate information to someone, to get
information from someone, to make someone do something, and so on. These
fundamental objectives are what actors have in common with the characters
they play. Through the medium of these objectives, actors find the way to
play any character with conviction and naturalness. In other words, Macbeth

FIGURE 5-6. From Act One, Scene Seven of *Macbeth.* *Macbeth says, "Away, and mock the time with fairest show." Fundamental Objective: To get someone else to do something. Notice how the actor really seems to be waiting for her to move. Also, go back now and look at Figures 5–1 through 5–6 again; notice how they tell the story of the scene in visual images alone. A person who did not understand the language being spoken by the actors should be able to follow the action of the scene from the actors' behavior alone.*

doesn't try to persuade, to convince, or to reassure his wife any differently from the way in which you or I might try to persuade, to convince, or to reassure someone close to us if we were in similarly desperate circumstances. The best, most dependable approach to playing any role is, thus, a careful study of the objectives derived from a close reading of the script.

To summarize this section, the following are principles for phrasing objectives illustrated in the scene from *Macbeth:*

1. Always look for the most immediate, highest priority needs first.
2. Unless you are totally alone onstage (as in the case of a soliloquy), try to locate the obstacles to be overcome in other characters onstage, not in yourself.
3. Avoid negative objectives. Common sense dictates that you can only play what a character is doing, not what a character is *not* doing.
4. Avoid all self-serving objectives such as "to show" or "to tell." The main verb choice for an objective should always clearly imply the nature of the resistance that must be overcome to achieve the desired effect.
5. Finally, when the nature of the objective is not immediately apparent, look for the obstacle, and the desired effect will usually become clear.

SUMMARY

A lot of material has been covered in this chapter, but there are only a few key principles to remember:

First, all human behavior has purpose and appears purposeful. By the way in which we perceive the desired result that another person's behavior is designed to bring about, we can usually infer the person's motivation. The same exact principle holds true for the way in which an audience observes the behavior of the characters in a play and determines their motivations.

Second, a person in a given situation may be acting as a result of many different motivations, but the conscious mind of that person can only seek to create one desired result at a time. In fact, human behavior results from a continuous and unbroken series of desired results that the conscious mind seeks to create.

Third, not all behavior is consciously controlled. Certain procedures (which once required conscious attention to learn) can be carried out without direct conscious control. Such procedures are called *activities*. In creating the illusion of purposeful behavior, an actor must be careful to differentiate between a character's activities and objectives. Objectives always result from the presence of an obstacle that has to be overcome to achieve the desired result. At any given moment in a play, a character may or may not have an activity to perform, but a character (like a person in real life) is never without an obstacle that requires the attention of the conscious mind.

Fourth, whenever two or more characters are onstage together, the actors playing those roles should assume that the obstacles are always located in the other characters. As a result, the specific desired results that their characters seek to attain are almost always variations on the six fundamental (general) objectives. By using those fundamental objectives as guidelines, actors can quickly perceive the specific results that their characters want to achieve.

EXERCISES FOR CHAPTER FIVE

The major principle demonstrated in Chapter Five is that a character's motivations are communicated to the audience as a quality of the character's actions. The following exercises are intended to help students better understand this process.

1. Try an improvisation like the one in which the actor plays the motivation of hunger. Decide on a motivation for yourself or pick one from the following list:

    cold
    despair

anger
exhaustion
fear
curiosity
loneliness
depression
happiness

Before you start, think about all the obvious, stereotypical ways in which such motivations might be played—all the clichéd sign language that should be avoided.

Then choose an appropriate action based on a need to achieve a particular desired result over a specific obstacle. Perform your scene in pantomime, and do not tell your audience in advance what your motivation is going to be. After you have performed, ask the audience to guess what motivation you were playing. If they guess something other than what you intended, try to determine exactly what you did that led them to that conclusion.

2. In a similar exercise, pick an action that does not necessarily in and of itself suggest a motivation. Choose one of your own or pick one from this list:

cooking a meal
reading a book
getting dressed
walking a pet
shopping
cleaning your living room
doing your laundry

Then pick a motivation that is not directly related to that action, such as any on the list of motivations for the previous exercise. Decide how you might perform one of these actions in a way designed to bring about a desired result evolved from that motivation. For example, in what ways could "walking a pet" serve to relieve loneliness, despair, and so on.

To succeed at this exercise, you must define the obstacle very carefully so that performing the action becomes a true objective, not merely an activity. If at all possible, work with other actors who choose the same action but different motivations. Perform your improvisations separately and then try to guess what each other's motivations might have been. If your audience does not guess the motivation you had in mind, try to determine what you did that led to the wrong conclusion.

3. Take a short speech from a play or a piece of poetry (such as Macbeth's "If it were done when 'tis done" soliloquy). Then pick one of the six fundamental objectives, ideally one that was not the original intention of the author of the speech. Choose an acting partner and have that person join you onstage, but without telling that person your objective.

To make this exercise work, you will have to imagine a particular place where this scene takes place. Be sure to decide whether it is a public, private, or personal one to you. You will also have to imagine a full identity for your character (a *Who*, a *What*, and a *Need*). Make appropriate choices for blocking, business, gesture, and so on, that will communicate the situation and the relationship just as if you were in a play. Then perform the speech. When you are done, ask your partner to guess what you wanted him or her to do (in terms of the six fundamental objectives). Then ask what details of the situation and your identity your partner was able to figure out from your performance. If you have an audience, ask them how much information they obtained from your acting. If they inferred something you did not intend, be sure they get to tell you what you did that led them to that conclusion.

4. Take a scene from a play of your choice and analyze the character's objectives in the same way as we analyzed the scene from *Macbeth*. Ask yourself for each moment that your character is onstage—not just for each moment your character is speaking—which one of the six fundamental objectives best describes your character's motivation.

    When you have completed your analysis, get a friend (or friends) to help you perform the scene in pantomime. Try to avoid any "story-telling" pantomime whose primary purpose is to communicate information to the audience in sign language (as in the game of charades). Use only those movements, gestures, and so on, that you would actually use if you were saying the words.

    Then perform the scene for an audience. Reveal the situation and the characters but not what is going on in the scene itself. Perform the scene just as if you were speaking the words but without moving your mouth or lips. After the performance, ask the audience to tell you everything they understood of the scene from your pantomime. Ask what they thought your motivations were. If there is something you wanted them to understand that they did not pick up from your performance, ask them to suggest anything you should have done to communicate the missing details of the scene. There will be certain specific details of the dialogue that the audience will not follow from your pantomime, but those details are not important for this exercise. What you want to know is if the audience understood your primary objectives, your motivations, the situation, and your relationship to the other character. If you communicated all this information without using the words, then you are well on your way to becoming a skilled realistic actor.

NOTES

1. Abraham H. Maslow, *Motivation and Personality*, 2nd ed. (New York: Harper & Row, Publishers, 1970), p. 39.

2. Maslow, p. 46.

3. Ibid.

Lesson Six

"I am trying to . . . by . . ."

Using the six fundamental objectives as a guide, actors can go through the script and chart out all the specific objectives their characters try to achieve. This process is known as doing a *beat breakdown*. In performance, a "beat" is a unit of behavior that defines a specific objective; every time a character's objective changes, the actor's behavior must also change in some perceivable way. The *beat breakdown*, therefore, becomes a kind of blueprint for the playing of the role.

As noted in the previous chapter, the desired result is the most important element of any objective. However, the desired result is not actually an element of an actor's behavior; by definition, the desired result is something that doesn't exist. What the audience actually sees are the three other elements of an objective, each of which is reflected in the actor's behavior. They are as follows:

1. The obstacle to be overcome (the person from whom the desired result is to be obtained)
2. The strategy (how the character is trying to bring about that result)
3. The cost (what the character is going to lose if the desired effect is not obtained)

How each of these three elements is reflected in the actor's beat is explained in the following chapter.

Chapter Six

Playing the Objective

What are you doing right now? Go on, answer the question. That's right—you are reading this book. But that is only an activity. You already know how to read; reading is not something that you have to think about in order to do. So, let me ask the question again, and this time I want you to answer in terms of your objective: What are you doing?

The answer is you are trying to understand the meaning of this strange exercise. You are trying to figure out what point I am trying to make by the strange opening of this chapter. (Or, you answered the question in some similar way.)

You have just demonstrated another important principle of the way that objectives work. In life, people usually know and can state what their objectives are at any given moment. Ask people what they are doing, and they will give you answers, such as "I am trying to find out what's going on here," "I am trying to get you to understand my problem," "I am trying to finish my laundry," and so on. Of course, they probably didn't think through their objectives in so many words before attempting to pursue them (any more than you thought to yourself, "Now I will try to understand this chapter," before you started to read). But when asked, people usually can express their objectives more or less in terms of a specific desired result they are trying to achieve at any given moment.

Just as people can usually say what their objectives are, actors should be able to say what their characters' objectives are. A director ought to be able to stop actors at any moment in rehearsal and ask, "Why did you say that? Why did you do that?" and they ought to be able to answer according to the specific desired result that their characters want to achieve.

There are, of course, certain circumstances in which people can't or won't say what their real objectives are. Such circumstances usually involve situations of extreme emotion, such as when two people are having a scream-ing match. People do sometimes lose control over themselves and do things (that is, try to achieve certain results) that they may not have consciously desired. For example, a man might become very angry with his wife and start saying things to hurt her. If a referee to this shouting match were to stop the man and ask, "Why did you say that?" he might very well deny that hurting anybody's feelings had been his actual intention. He might not even understand that causing hurt had been his real purpose at that moment, even though two hours later he might be willing to admit the truth to himself. However, as a general rule, people can usually say in so many words what effect they are trying to achieve through their behavior. If actors are really playing their objectives, they ought to be able to do the same.

Some actors, though, object to being asked to verbalize all their char-acter's objectives. They feel this procedure forces them to intellectualize the role and deny the possibility of spontaneity. Actually, the reverse is true. If actors say the words and execute the movements without understanding their specific purposes, their performances have to be mechanical, not sponta-neous. And worse, if actors then try to change the blocking or otherwise throw in a few new ideas just for the sake of variety, the results are liable to be disastrous. When actors clearly understand (and can verbalize) the desired result implied by their lines, spontaneity is insured. As long as actors have a clear idea of what the desired result is supposed to be, they are free to do almost anything consistent with the situation and the character relationships to achieve the objective. In other words, not knowing your objectives makes it difficult, if not impossible, to know what to do with your role; knowing your objectives liberates your creativity. Good acting demands that actors be really focused on each other and really trying to achieve their desired results in each rehearsal and each performance; and therefore, the results have to be different every time.

Some other actors object to verbalizing all the objectives because of the occasional difficulty of finding the right words to express a particularly ob-scure desired result. In such circumstances, actors sometimes cry out, "I know what it is—I just can't say it!" But again, the reverse is true. Objectives are consciously determined; if the actor can't say what the objective is, then the actor does not know it. An objective is not an impulse or a subconscious urge. Until actors can say what the desired effect is supposed to be, they can't possibly know how to communicate it. Of course, they may not know what one or more specific objectives are just from reading the script alone. Certain specific objectives may not be clear until the scene is worked in rehearsal. But the fundamental objectives should be clear, and by working with one of those six fundamental objectives in mind, actors should be able to figure out their specific objectives eventually.

There is yet another reason why actors need to know precisely what their objectives are: If they don't know, then they are probably playing what are sometimes called "nonobjectives."

PLAYING NONOBJECTIVES

If an actor is not consciously playing a legitimate character objective derived from one of the six fundamental objectives, then there is some other aspect of the character or the situation or the language that is occupying the actor's conscious mind. One such example was given in the last chapter: the actor trying to play the motivation of hunger directly, instead of indirectly through an action directed at a desired result. *Playing the motivation* in this way is a type of nonobjective. A catalog of some of the more common nonobjectives follows:

Playing the result.   This nonobjective occurs when an actor anticipates the effect of an action or a plot development that has not yet occurred. A good example, as noted in the previous chapter, would be if Lady Macbeth were to say the line "Why have you left the chamber?" as if she were already accusing Macbeth of being a coward. Result playing is the most common nonobjective. The best way to guard against it is for actors always to force themselves to forget that they know what is about to happen. Sometimes, though, in the case of extremely familiar plays such as *Macbeth*, actors may know certain scenes so well that it becomes almost impossible to block out the knowledge of what is going to happen. The solution is to define the objectives very precisely and to play them exactly, always using the "If-I-Were" formula to guarantee conviction.

Playing the stereotype.   This is an error that most often occurs in supporting or minor roles, but it can be a problem for leads as well. It occurs when an actor has a preconceived notion of how a character should behave and then reads every line in a way that is consistent with that stereotype alone instead of exploring the full range of possibilities within that character's identity. Such stereotypical characters are common in comedy and in farce: the dumb blonde, the foolish old man, the blustering boss, the nagging wife, and so on and so forth.

Consider the problems that playing Lady Macbeth in this way might create. Many actors have a preconceived image of her as an old crone and a monstrous villain. In the scene analyzed in the previous chapter, she appears to be quite bloodthirsty. However, playing Lady Macbeth as an old crone and a bloodthirsty ghoul and nothing else for four acts of the play would alienate an audience. No villain—no matter how villainous—sees himself or herself as a monster twenty-four hours a day. In the analysis of Lady Macbeth's speeches in the last chapter, a broad range of possibilities was suggested, including the use of flattery and even intentional humor. Any actor who wants to be successful with this role should try to realize all these possibilities, not just play a one-dimensional villain. (I once saw an excellent production of *Macbeth* at the Old Vic in London, in which Diana Rigg played Lady Macbeth as a young, vibrant, and frequently rather pleasant woman. The result was striking—a welcome relief from the stereotypical interpretation of the role. When she did the speech about bashing out the baby's brains, the effect was particularly horrifying because she didn't look like the type of person who would do something like that. But murderers rarely look or act like murderers all the time. The secret is that Rigg played Lady Macbeth's objectives, not some simple, preconceived notion of her character.)

Playing the subtext.   Subtext is the level of meaning that lies beneath the literal meaning of the words a character is saying. To recall an example from an earlier chapter, someone may say the words "I love you," but what the person actually means may be very different from the literal meaning of the words themselves. Of course, someone's subtext may be the same as a person's "text"—they do not necessarily have to be contradictory—but usually when actors talk about a character's subtext, the assumption is that the meaning of the subtext is different in some way from the literal meaning of the lines.

Naturalistic plays, in particular, often call for an extensive use of subtext in this latter sense. A good example is found in William Inge's *Come Back Little Sheba*. Lola, the central character, is a frustrated and emotionally immature, middle-aged housewife. In a significant scene in the first act, she engages in a seemingly innocent piece of dialogue with the milkman, who talks to Lola about body-building. In the context of the play as a whole, however, the scene is far from innocent; from an analysis of the situation, an actor playing Lola will realize that she is really flirting with this man. Perhaps it would be going too far to suggest that she is actually trying to seduce him, but clearly she is enjoying a kind of sexual fantasy while she talks to him about cottage cheese and coffee cream. An actor playing Lola in this scene must be aware of this subtextual level and find objectives to bring it out.

The abuse of subtext occurs when the actor chooses to substitute the subtextual level of the dialogue for the objectives. A problem of this sort was described in the scene from *Macbeth* described in the previous chapter. When Macbeth says, "He hath honored me of late, and I have bought/Golden opinions from all sorts of people," his objective is to try to talk his wife out of murder. But in the latter part of the scene, it becomes clear that Macbeth is really covering up his true feelings. His fear is the subtext of this speech. However, if an actor playing Macbeth chooses to play the fear instead of the objective, the result will be decidedly peculiar. Reading the speech in a whiny, frightened voice would defy logic—Macbeth is trying to talk his wife out of murder (the line says so), not show her how frightened he is. Playing the subtext on that line would be a mistake.

Playing the mood or the emotion.   This nonobjective can be a problem in any scene dominated by a strong sense of atmosphere or single emotion. Melodramatic plays are particularly vulnerable; if something mysterious is happening in an old house during a thunderstorm at midnight, sometimes the actors inadvertently make their objective to try to communicate to the audience how spooky and weird it all is. Or in a tragedy, during a scene in which some awful act of fate is being revealed, everyone on stage may try to bring out the ponderous seriousness of the events. This kind of mood-playing is often the source of some of the most dreadful evenings audiences are asked to spend in the theatre. Mood and atmosphere are essentially functions of the situation; the actors must continue to play their objectives truthfully and naturally and let the mood take care of itself.

Playing the audience.   Actors who engage in this particular nonobjective usually do so in every role they play. They think that their purpose in being onstage is to get the audience to like them. They seek ways of reading lines, doing business, crossing from place to place, and wearing their costumes to serve the primary objective of making themselves as attractive as possible to the people watching. These actors frequently refuse to change their customary hairstyle, to wear ugly or unflattering costumes, and to use coarse language or perform seemingly vulgar actions, and they insist on being the center of attention whenever they are onstage. Sometimes even otherwise talented actors become tempted to flirt with the audience in certain scenes in which they feel they are giving a particularly brilliant line reading or when they are appearing in a particularly attractive costume. If actors will consistently think through their objectives, this error (like all the others of this type) can be avoided.

Playing the style.   This is an error that is particularly common in Shakespearean productions, but it can also occur in Restoration or Victorian plays as well as in certain types of farces and musical comedies. What happens is that actors become carried away with the stylized way of speaking and moving; they start to focus on communicating the style itself and forget to play the objectives. In Lady Macbeth's famous speech that begins "I have given suck and know how tender 'tis . . ." there is a temptation for the actor to use dramatic vocal inflections that such sentiments seem to require. But an actor must not allow being Shakespearean to become the objective, instead of the real objective of shocking or shaming Macbeth.

A variation of this fault occurs in plays that require heavy dialects and foreign accents, such as British or French or American southern. An actor can become so involved in the highly stylized manner of speaking that the objectives become unimportant. This is a trap particularly in comedy. Many actors can get laughs just by talking in a dialect. The temptation then is to play the dialect for the laughs and to forget about the objectives.

There are other possible nonobjectives as well, but the point here is only to demonstrate that when actors are not playing legitimate objectives, they are inevitably playing something they shouldn't. To ensure that actors have good legitimate objectives in mind, they need more than just the six fundamental objectives; they need specific objectives that express the particular and unique problems their characters are trying to solve.

OBJECTIVE-SEEKING BEHAVIOR

As mentioned in the previous chapter, the desired result is only one part of a character's behavioral objective. In fact, three additional items of information are necessary to define a complete objective. And it is these other three parts that an actor actually realizes onstage. Those details are the factors that actually make the audience understand the desired result. Together, these three qualities define what we will now call *objective-seeking behavior*.

The first of these has already been identified: the *obstacle*. The quality of an actor's behavior that identifies the obstacle is the actor's point of focus, that is, *where the actor is looking*. In the case of the six fundamental objectives, the obstacle is always another person onstage. The only way to know if the desired result has been achieved is by looking at the person who is the obstacle. Therefore, the actor's point of focus is the element of behavior that reveals the obstacle. From reading the script, the actor has to figure out who is the obstacle at each moment in the scene so that he or she can focus on that person.

Objective-seeking behavior is always clearly focused in this way; activities are not. However, activities are intimately related to a character's objectives. Going back again to the scene from *Macbeth*, we note that when Macbeth says, "Bring forth men children only," his objective is to build up his wife's self-esteem; his motivation for that action is a need to convince her that he has his emotions under control. How he goes about achieving that result is by flattering her. But the act of paying her the compliment is technically only an activity. There is no obstacle; she is not opposing his flattery in any way. Building up his wife's self-esteem is the desired result, and therefore she is the obstacle (his point of focus) to achieving that effect, but the actual act of flattery is merely an activity in the service of that objective.

Activities used to bring about a specific desired result are the second component of objective-seeking behavior. In order to differentiate between an independent activity and an objective-related activity, we will hereafter refer to the latter type as the character's *strategy*. A strategy is an activity that is directed toward overcoming an obstacle but that does not in itself present an obstacle to be overcome. In other words, Macbeth's activity (flattery) is directed at a specific obstacle (Lady Macbeth) to bring about a specific desired result (building up her self-esteem). Perhaps at the same moment, however, Macbeth is whispering so as not to be overheard by the people in the hall, and he is also clutching his cloak around his shoulders to keep it from being blown off in the high wind. Whispering and clutching the cloak are also activities, but they are technically independent activities because they are not directed at the one obstacle who is his point of focus at that moment.

If that last point seems confusing, recall the example of learning to drive the car. When getting from place to place was the obstacle, driving the car was the strategy; when the route was learned, passsing the time became the desired result, talking to the passenger became the strategy, and the driving itself was only an independent activity, not a strategy.

Choosing strategies is a matter of interpretation for the actor, and as such, it is the area in which actors have the greatest degree of creative freedom. When Macbeth says, "I dare do all that may become a man," his desired result is to communicate information to his wife (specifically that the deal is off). But what is his strategy? Perhaps the line could be said in a very cool, deliberate way; in that event, his strategy would be to reason with her. Perhaps the line could be played with a sudden outburst of anger: in that event, his strategy would be to threaten her. Perhaps the line could be played as a cry of wounded pride; then his strategy would be to plead with her. And there are other possibilities as well. Reasoning with her, threatening her, and pleading with her are all valid strategies, and there is nothing in the script that says which one should be used. It's entirely up to the actor (or the actor and the director together) to decide. Ideally, an actor should take the time to try more than one strategy and see which one works best. For any role in any play, there are always many different strategies that can be played successfully to achieve any single desired result.

The last factor of behavior to be considered, and the final component part of a specific objective, is the intensity with which the character tries to achieve the desired result. To give this factor a name, some actors use the term *cost*. In other words, if the character fails to achieve the desired effect, how much is he or she going to lose by that failure? How much is that failure going to "cost"? If, for example, Macbeth is trying to convince his wife that he wants boar instead of pheasant for dinner, the cost is very low. If she wants pheasant and he decides to capitulate just to bring an end to the debate, he loses very little in the process. But if Macbeth fails to convince his wife that he is not a coward, the cost is very high—his whole sense of personal esteem is at stake. Since the cost is so high, the actor must play that objective with great intensity. He must say, "I dare do all that may become a man" with great intensity, as anyone might argue for something important.

All four component parts of an objective may now be listed: (1) the *desired result* that the character wants to achieve, (2) the *obstacle* that must be overcome, (3) the *strategy* that the character uses to overcome the obstacle, and (4) the *cost* of failure. In terms of the actor's actual performance onstage, the physical equivalent of the obstacle is the actor's point of focus, the physical equivalent of the strategy is the activity directed at that obstacle, and the physical equivalent of the cost is the intensity with which the actor directs the strategy at the obstacle. If the audience can clearly see what the obstacle is, how the character's actions are being directed toward it, and how badly the character wants to overcome it, the audience should be able to guess the desired result easily. In this way, the audience creates the illusion of the desired result by observing the actor's point of focus, the activity, and the cost.

Deducing all a character's objectives from a script can sometimes be a tedious and time-consuming process. But if actors know what information they need, their job will be speeded up considerably. To that end, there is a little magic phrase that will help the actor speed up the process of analysis:

"I am trying to . . . by . . ."

By reading the script carefully and filling in the blanks correctly for each moment the character is onstage, the actor may be reasonably assured of having enough information to create the proper objective-seeking behavior.

This formula is carefully constructed to account for the first three elements of any objective and to get the actor personally involved in that objective. The formula is stated in the first person. "*I* am trying to . . ." not "Macbeth is trying to . . ." The whole concept of actors playing objectives depends on actors using their own personal experiences filtered through the "If-I-Were" formula. Therefore, right from the beginning, they need to think of their characters' objectives as their own. The second part of the formula, ". . . am trying to . . ." suggests the all-important difference between objectives and activities. Whatever words the actor chooses to fill in the formula must make sense in that context. In other words, "I am trying to show my feelings" doesn't make sense as a statement. Who's stopping you? But "I am trying to convince my wife that I am not a coward" does make sense; the choice of words defines the resistance being provided by the obstacle ("my wife" is the obstacle, and the fact that she doubts my valor is the nature of the resistance). The last part of the formula, ("by . . .") requires the actor to identify the strategy to be used, for example ". . . by reasoning with her," " . . . by putting her in her place," ". . . by threatening her," and so on. (The formula does not contain an element directly related to the cost factor, except by implication. How cost is revealed through the playing of objectives will be demonstrated in the next chapter.)

For the moment when Macbeth says, "I dare do all that may become a man," the formula might be filled in to read

I am trying to convince my wife that I am not a coward by reasoning with her.

With these words, the actor identifies the desired result (communicating information), the obstacle (Lady Macbeth), and the strategy (reasoning with her). The nature of the resistance is also clear: She seems to think I am a coward; I cannot simply *tell* her I am not a coward, I must *convince* her of that fact. Although the formula does not state the cost explicitly, common sense dictates that it must be high. Failure to achieve that objective would be tantamount to admitting cowardice. The actor then says to himself, "If I were that person in that situation, how would I go about performing that action?" The answer should result in a convincing illusion of natural behavior.

Taken together, each of the four components of a specific objective— the desired result, the obstacle, the strategy, and the cost—are all qualities of behavior that should be apparent to an audience. And if the actors playing Lord and Lady Macbeth have also established their characters' relationship to the situation and to each other, the illusion of natural behavior will occur. By observing the actors' behavior alone, the audience should be able to determine that the two actors on the stage are husband and wife and that they are clearly in a public place. The audience should also be able to tell that the man is opposing his wife in a matter of some great importance to them both. When the actor playing Macbeth says, "I dare do all that may become a man," the audience should see that he is defending his valor. And this is the important thing—the audience should be able to understand all these things whether or not they can understand the language the actors are speaking. The behavior of the actors alone should be sufficient to communicate virtually the entire meaning of the words. This is how the Moscow Art Theatre could tour America to widespread acclaim while performing exclusively in Russian. This is the ideal toward which all realistic acting should strive.

THE BEAT BREAKDOWN

Another advantage of the "I am trying to . . . by . . ." formula is that it helps to clarify certain subtle changes in a character's motivation that need to be reflected in the character's behavior. In the scene from *Macbeth*, we observed that Macbeth's general objective is to try to talk Lady Macbeth out of murdering the King. But in the actual playing of the scene, Macbeth seeks to achieve that same result more than once with different strategies. Depending on the actor's choice, Macbeth at different times might use reason, threats, pleas, and fear. In turn, Lady Macbeth uses attacks on Macbeth's personal valor, flattery, boasts, and even humor to achieve her goal of getting him to stick to the plan. Since each of these different strategic ploys is indicated to the audience by different activities, there have to be significant changes in the actor's behavior each time the strategy changes. Common sense dictates that every time the character's objective changes in any way, there has to be a corresponding and observable change in the actor's behavior as well. If the actor's behavior doesn't change, how does the audience know that the objective has changed?

Onstage, the behavior that corresponds to a specific objective is called a *beat*. Everything an actor does to communicate a single desired result, obstacle, strategy, and cost constitutes one "beat" of behavior. Whenever there is a change in any element of the objective (a new desired result, a different obstacle, a shift in strategy, or an increase or decrease in cost), the actor has to create a new beat to show that the change has occurred. Using the "I am trying to . . . by . . ." formula, an actor can go through the script and chart out each objective to be played in turn, noting where the beat changes have to occur. Charting out a character's objectives in this way is sometimes called a *beat breakdown*.

Beginning actors need to practice doing beat breakdowns to gain expertise at putting objectives into words. To that end, read the following scene from Oscar Wilde's *The Importance of Being Earnest*. This play dates from 1895, and it is one of the most popular plays with high school, college, and community theatres. Since this play is so familiar, the plot (which is extremely complicated) will not be recalled here. All the reader needs to know is that the two characters in the scene, Gwendolen and Cecily, are meeting each other for the first time and they both discover as the scene progresses that they both seem to be engaged to the same man (Ernest Worthing). In fact, they are engaged to different men, but—unknown to them—neither of their fiances is actually named "Ernest".

Armed with that information, read the following scene carefully as if you were an actor preparing to play the role of Gwendolen. Try to visualize the scene in your imagination. Then use the six fundamental objectives to help you identify the specific desired results Gwendolen tries to bring about. Starting with Gwendolen's first line, ask yourself (as if you were Gwendolen), "What am I trying to do?" Then answer yourself using the "I am trying to . . . by . . ." formula. Once you have an answer in that form, read on until you feel that it no longer applies because she has changed her desired result, strategy, or cost. Wherever you feel that change has occurred, draw a line across the page to indicate that your behavior as an actor should change also. Then use the "I am trying to . . . by . . ." formula to phrase Gwendolen's next objective. Go through the whole scene, figuring her objectives in this way. Number each section of dialogue between the lines, and then write down

each of Gwendolen's corresponding objectives on a separate piece of paper. Be sure that you are trying to imagine how the scene might be played and not just reading the words on the page. Your objectives must account for all the spaces between the lines and all the times Gwendolen is simply listening to Cecily as well. (In other words, there are certain "hidden" objectives in these lines that you cannot find if you are not trying to imagine how the scene will play.)

Scene Number Three: *The Importance of Being Earnest*

The scene takes place in the garden of a substantial country estate. Cecily and Gwendolen have just introduced themselves to each other, and according to Oscar Wilde's stage direction, they both sit, presumably on some sort of garden bench.

GWENDOLEN: Perhaps this might be a favorable opportunity for my mentioning who I am. My father is Lord Bracknell. You have never heard of papa, I suppose?

CECILY: I don't think so.

GWENDOLEN: Outside the family circle, papa, I am glad to say, is entirely unknown. I think that is quite as it should be. The home seems to me to be the proper sphere for the man. And certainly once a man begins to neglect his domestic duties he becomes painfully effeminate, does he not? And I don't like that. It makes men so very attractive. Cecily, mamma, whose views on education are remarkably strict, has brought me up to be extremely shortsighted; it is part of her system; so do you mind my looking at you through my glasses?

CECILY: Oh, not at all, Gwendolen. I am very fond of being looked at.
(Gwendolen takes out a lorgnette from her purse and carefully examines Cecily. Then she puts away the lorgnette before going on.)

GWENDOLEN: You are here on a short visit, I suppose.

CECILY: Oh no! I live here.

GWENDOLEN: Really? Your mother, no doubt, or some female relative of advanced years, resides here also?

CECILY: Oh no! I have no mother, nor, in fact, any relations.

GWENDOLEN: Indeed?

CECILY: My dear guardian, with the assistance of Miss Prism, has the arduous task of looking after me.

GWENDOLEN: Your guardian?

CECILY: Yes, I am Mr. Worthing's ward.

GWENDOLEN: Oh! It is strange he never mentioned to me that he had a ward. How secretive of him! He grows more interesting hourly. I am not sure, however, that the news inspires me with feelings of unmixed delight. I am very fond of you, Cecily; I have liked you ever since I met you! But I am bound to state that now that I know you are Mr. Worthing's ward, I cannot help expressing a wish you were—

	well, just a little older than you seem to be—and not quite so very alluring in appearance. In fact, if I may speak candidly—
CECILY:	Pray do! I think that whenever one has anything unpleasant to say, one should always be quite candid.
GWENDOLEN:	Well, to speak with perfect candor, Cecily, I wish that you were fully forty-two, and more than usually plain for your age. Ernest has a strong upright nature. He is the very soul of truth and honor. Disloyalty would be as impossible to him as deception. But even men of the noblest possible moral character are extremely susceptible to the influence of the physical charms of others. Modern, no less than Ancient History, supplies us with many most painful examples of what I refer to. If it were not so, indeed, History would be quite unreadable.
CECILY:	I beg your pardon, Gwendolen, did you say Ernest?
GWENDOLEN:	Yes.
CECILY:	Oh, but it is not Mr. Ernest Worthing who is my guardian. It is his brother—his elder brother.
GWENDOLEN:	Ernest never mentioned to me that he had a brother.
CECILY:	I am sorry to say that they have not been on good terms for a long time.
GWENDOLEN:	Ah! That accounts for it. And now that I think of it I have never heard any man mention his brother. The subject seems distasteful to most men. Cecily, you have lifted a load from my mind. I was growing almost anxious. It would have been terrible if any cloud had come across a friendship like ours, would it not? Of course, you are quite, quite sure that it is not Mr. Ernest Worthing who is your guardian?
CECILY:	Quite sure. (a pause) In fact, I am going to be his.
GWENDOLEN:	I beg your pardon?
CECILY:	Dearest Gwendolen, there is no reason why I should make a secret of it to you. Our little country newspaper is sure to chronicle the fact next week. Mr. Ernest Worthing and I are to be married.
GWENDOLEN:	My darling Cecily, I think there must be some slight error. Mr. Ernest Worthing is engaged to me. The announcement will appear in the *Morning Post* on Saturday at the latest.
CECILY:	I am afraid you must be under some misconception. Ernest proposed to me exactly ten minutes ago. (Cecily shows her diary to Gwendolen.)
GWENDOLEN:	(after looking at the diary through her lorgnette again) It is very curious for he asked me to be his wife yesterday afternoon at 5:30. If you would care to verify the incident, pray do so. (She produces a diary from her purse and shows it to Cecily.) I never travel without my diary. One should always have something sensational to read in the train. I am so sorry, dear Cecily, if it is any disappointment to you, but I am afraid I have the prior claim.
CECILY:	It would distress me more than I can tell you, dear Gwendolen, if it caused you any mental or physical anguish, but I feel bound to point out that since Ernest proposed to you he clearly has changed his mind.

GWENDOLEN: If the poor fellow has been entrapped into any foolish promise I shall consider it my duty to rescue him at once, and with a firm hand.

CECILY: Whatever unfortunate entanglement my dear boy may have got into, I will never reproach him with it after we are married.

GWENDOLEN: Do you allude to me, Miss Cardew, as an entanglement? You are presumptuous. On an occasion of this kind it becomes more than a moral duty to speak one's mind. It becomes a pleasure.

CECILY: Do you suggest, Miss Fairfax, that I entrapped Ernest into an engagement? How dare you! This is no time for wearing the shallow mask of manners. When I see a spade I call it a spade.

GWENDOLEN: I am glad to say that I have never seen a spade. It is obvious that our social spheres have been widely different.

At this point in the dialogue, the women are interrupted by the entrance of servants who have come into the garden to serve afternoon tea.

When you have finished your beat breakdown for Gwendolen, read the analysis that follows. Compare your breakdown of the beats with the version in the following section.

In looking over how the beat changes occur in relation to the lines, you will notice that the changes do not necessarily occur each time a character begins a speech. For example, there seems to be a beat change right in the middle of Gwendolen's second speech. Then there seems to be a long beat that continues through several exchanges of dialogue. In Gwendolen's speech beginning "Ah! That accounts for it," there seem to be two or more changes occurring within the same passage. There is even at least one beat change where there is no dialogue at all—where Gwendolen is to inspect Cecily through her lorgnette. As we are about to see in doing a beat breakdown, actors cannot be guided by how the words appear on the page.

1	GWENDOLEN:	Perhaps this might be a favorable opportunity for my mentioning who I am. My father is Lord Bracknell. You have never heard of papa, I suppose?
	CECILY:	I don't think so.
	GWENDOLEN:	Outside the family circle, papa, I am glad to say, is entirely unknown. I think that is quite as it should be. The home seems to me to be the proper sphere for the man. And certainly once a man begins to neglect his domestic duties he becomes painfully effeminate, does he not? And I don't like that. It makes men so very attractive.
2		Cecily, mamma, whose views on education are remarkably strict, has brought me up to be extremely shortsighted; it is part of her system; so do you mind my looking at you through my glasses?
	CECILY:	Oh, not at all, Gwendolen. I am very fond of being looked at. (Gwendolen takes out a lorgnette from her purse and carefully examines Cecily. Then she puts away the lorgnette before going on.)
3	GWENDOLEN:	You are here on a short visit, I suppose.
	CECILY:	Oh no! I live here.
	GWENDOLEN:	Really? Your mother, no doubt, or some female relative of advanced years, resides here also?

	CECILY:	Oh no! I have no mother, nor, in fact, any relations.
	GWENDOLEN:	Indeed?
3	CECILY:	My dear guardian, with the assistance of Miss Prism, has the arduous task of looking after me.
	GWENDOLEN:	Your guardian?
	CECILY:	Yes, I am Mr. Worthing's ward.

4	GWENDOLEN:	Oh! It is strange he never mentioned to me that he had a ward. How secretive of him! He grows more interesting hourly. I am not sure, however, that the news inspires me with feelings of unmixed delight.

5		I am very fond of you, Cecily; I have liked you ever since I met you! But I am bound to state that now that I know you are Mr. Worthing's ward, I cannot help expressing a wish you were—well, just a little older than you seem to be—and not quite so very alluring in appearance. In fact, if I may speak candidly—
	CECILY:	Pray do! I think that whenever one has anything unpleasant to say, one should always be quite candid.
	GWENDOLEN:	Well, to speak with perfect candor, Cecily, I wish that you were fully forty-two, and more than usually plain for your age.

6		Ernest has a strong upright nature. He is the very soul of truth and honor. Disloyalty would be as impossible to him as deception. But even men of the noblest possible moral character are extremely susceptible to the influence of the physical charms of others. Modern, no less than Ancient History, supplies us with many most painful examples of what I refer to. If it were not so, indeed, History would be quite unreadable.

7	CECILY:	I beg your pardon, Gwendolen, did you say Ernest?
	GWENDOLEN:	Yes.
	CECILY:	Oh, but it is not Mr. Ernest Worthing who is my guardian. It is his brother—his elder brother.

8	GWENDOLEN:	Ernest never mentioned to me that he had a brother.
	CECILY:	I am sorry to say that they have not been on good terms for a long time.
	GWENDOLEN:	Ah! That accounts for it. And now that I think of it I have never heard any man mention his brother. The subject seems distasteful to most men.

9		Cecily, you have lifted a load from my mind. I was growing almost anxious. It would have been terrible if any cloud had come across a friendship like ours, would it not?

10		Of course, you are quite, quite sure that it is not Mr. Ernest Worthing who is your guardian?
	CECILY:	Quite sure. (a pause) In fact, I am going to be his.

11	GWENDOLEN:	I beg your pardon?
	CECILY:	Dearest Gwendolen, there is no reason why I should make a secret of it to you. Our little country newspaper is sure to chronicle the fact next week. Mr. Ernest Worthing and I are to be married.

12	GWENDOLEN:	My darling Cecily, I think there must be some slight error. Mr. Ernest Worthing is engaged to me. The announcement will appear in the *Morning Post* on Saturday at the latest.
	CECILY:	I am afraid you must be under some misconception. Ernest proposed to me exactly ten minutes ago.

13	(Cecily shows her diary to Gwendolen.)

14	GWENDOLEN:	(after looking at the diary through her lorgnette again) It is very curious for he asked me to be his wife yesterday afternoon at 5:30. If you would care to verify the incident, pray do so. (She produces a diary from her purse and shows it to Cecily.) I never travel without my diary. One should always have something sensational to read in the train. I am so sorry, dear Cecily, if it is any disappointment to you, but I am afraid I have the prior claim.
	CECILY:	It would distress me more than I can tell you, dear Gwendolen, if it caused you any mental or physical anguish, but I feel bound to point out that since Ernest proposed to you he clearly has changed his mind.
15	GWENDOLEN:	If the poor fellow has been entrapped into any foolish promise I shall consider it my duty to rescue him at once, and with a firm hand.
	CECILY:	Whatever unfortunate entanglement my dear boy may have got into, I will never reproach him with it after we are married.
16	GWENDOLEN:	Do you allude to me, Miss Cardew, as an entanglement? You are presumptuous. On an occasion of this kind it becomes more than a moral duty to speak one's mind. It becomes a pleasure.
	CECILY:	Do you suggest, Miss Fairfax, that I entrapped Ernest into an engagement? How dare you! This is no time for wearing the shallow mask of manners. When I see a spade I call it a spade.
17	GWENDOLEN:	I am glad to say that I have never seen a spade. It is obvious that our social spheres have been widely different.

FIGURE 6-1. Gwendolen's Beat Breakdown.

Compare your beat breakdown with fig. 6-1, and then check your list of beats against the following list:

The Importance of Being Earnest: Gwendolen's Beats

1. I am trying to make friends with her by making small talk.
2. I am trying to get permission to look at her by asking.
3. I am trying to find out more about her by asking.
4. I am trying to make Cecily understand that I don't approve of her by expressing my disapproval.
5. I am trying to make her understand my disapproval by explaining it.
6. I am trying to warn her away from my fiance by appealing to her sense of morality.
7. I am trying to find out what she wants by asking.
8. I am trying to verify the truth of what she has just said by asking.
9. I am trying to make friends with her by explaining my conduct.
10. I am trying to verify the truth of what she has just said by asking.
11. I am trying to find out what she means by asking.
12. I am trying to straighten her out by announcing my engagement to Ernest.
13. I am trying to verify the truth of her claim by looking in her diary.
14. I am trying to straighten her out by showing her my diary.
15. I am trying to straighten her out by threatening her.
16. I am trying to straighten her out by attacking her.
17. I am trying to straighten her out by ridiculing her.

You will observe that there are three specific desired effects that are played more than once. The first is Gwendolen's efforts to make friends with Cecily. The second is Gwendolen's efforts to get information out of Cecily. The third is the major effort at the end of the scene to try to straighten out Cecily on the subject of who is actually engaged to "Ernest." In playing these objectives, particular stress has to be placed on the strategy to be sure that the desired effect appears to remain the same.

The beat breakdown provides an approach to the physical level of the scene, which is not easy to realize because (like the scene from *Harvey*) the action is static and talky. The dialogue only specifies two distinct actions, both of which occur only in a tangential way to the dialogue itself; the first is Gwendolen's use of her lorgnette to stare at Cecily, and the second is the exchange of the diaries. The danger in playing this scene is that the acting will thus become as static and talky as the dialogue. Of course, some people feel that if Wilde wrote the scene that way, it should be played that way, and indeed, I have watched this scene played several times by actors who sit and talk and do nothing with their bodies beyond the business with the lorgnette and the diaries. The result usually is not very interesting nor very funny. The lines are only funny by themselves when they are read on the page; when actors perform them, they don't become funny unless the actors make them funny. The lines have absolutely no meaning until the actors give them meaning by how they move, gesture, change position, look at each other, and so on. Fortunately, the beat breakdown of the scene clearly indicates where the characters' behavior must change in perceivable ways according to the progression of the objectives. If reading the lines alone does not suggest to the actor playing Gwendolen how to use her body in this scene, the beat breakdown does:

Beat One

GWENDOLEN: Perhaps this might be a favorable opportunity for my mentioning who I am. My father is Lord Bracknell. You have never heard of papa, I suppose?

CECILY: I don't think so.

GWENDOLEN: Outside of the family circle, papa, I am glad to say, is entirely unknown. I think that is quite as it should be. The home seems to be the proper sphere for the man. And certainly once a man begins to neglect his domestic duties he becomes painfully effeminate, does he not? And I don't like that. It makes men so very attractive.

I am trying to make friends with her by making small talk.

Making small talk is a familiar social ritual. Gwendolen should sit at a polite distance from Cecily, smile, gesture pleasantly, and speak with animation.

There is another way to play this beat, however. Instead of playing the objective, a close look at the situation provides a rare example of a moment when it might be more effective to play a subtext. The next beat provides an important clue. From a polite distance, Gwendolen is not able to see Cecily's features clearly, and the longer she talks with Cecily, the more concerned she becomes about the need to have a good look at her. After the first few lines of the speech, Gwendolen might play a beat change—that is, play a different objective—even though the words of the speech continue to suggest the formalities of polite conversation.

> I am trying to find out what she looks like by getting close enough to see without my glasses.

Gwendolen might then begin to stare and squint at Cecily rather pointedly, perhaps even moving in to an intimate distance in order to get a good look. If she became completely involved in this activity while continuing to speak the innocuous lines, the effect would be quite comic and would help to set up the next beat.

Beat Two

GWENDOLEN: Cecily, mamma, whose views on education are remarkably strict, has brought me up to be extremely shortsighted; it is part of her system; so do you mind my looking at you through my glasses?
CECILY: Oh, not at all, Gwendolen. I am very fond of being looked at.

> I am trying to get permission to look at her by asking.

All the animation of the previous beat should cease. What has happened here is that this beat represents a higher order need than the previous beat. Gwendolen should become very still and stare at Cecily intensely. She must really look at Cecily to get the answer she wants, and then she should respond with some kind of acknowledgement, perhaps a nod to mean "Thank you, Cecily."

There follows the unnumbered beat of Gwendolen's peering at Cecily through her lorgnette. In order to generate some movement into this otherwise static scene, the actor playing Gwendolen might choose to leave the purse with the lorgnette in another part of the stage. Thus, she would have a reason to stand up, walk to her purse, take out the lorgnette, peer at Cecily, show her disapproval, and put the glasses away. This beat is unnumbered because it is not part of the text, which serves as the basis for the beat break-down. However, in performance this beat is played in the same way as any other beat. (See fig. 6–2. Note that the actor playing Cecily has chosen to pose for Gwendolen to admire, an idea derived directly from her previous line.)

Beat Three

GWENDOLEN: You are here on a short visit, I suppose.
      CECILY: Oh no! I live here.
GWENDOLEN: Really? Your mother, no doubt, or some female relative of advanced years, resides here also?
      CECILY: Oh no! I have no mother, nor, in fact, any relations.
GWENDOLEN: Indeed?
      CECILY: My dear guardian, with the assistance of Miss Prism, has the arduous task of looking after me.
GWENDOLEN: Your guardian?
      CECILY: Yes, I am Mr. Worthing's ward.

I am trying to find out more about her by asking.

FIGURE 6–2. A Scene from *The Importance of Being Earnest.   Cecily poses so that Gwendolen may inspect her through her glasses. Notice that Gwendolen's fundamental objective is to get information, while Cecily's fundamental objective is to communicate information.*

Notice that the previous objective of making friends with Cecily is not resumed at this point; therefore, it would probably be a mistake for Gwendolen to sit down next to Cecily as before. What is going on here is that Gwendolen at first glance has taken a liking to Cecily and has wanted to make her a friend. But now Gwendolen doesn't know what Cecily is; consequently, withdrawing to a more impersonal distance seems justified. Since this is a beat of asking questions and many people like to pace when they are conducting an investigation, perhaps Gwendolen might now pace. Pacing indicates an unsettled state of mind, and that state is certainly appropriate to Gwendolen at this time.

Beat Four

GWENDOLEN: Oh! It is strange he never mentioned to me that he had a ward. How secretive of him! He grows more interesting hourly. I am not sure, however, that the news inspires me with feelings of unmixed delight.

I am trying to make Cecily understand I don't approve of her by expressing my disapproval.

Suddenly Gwendolen stops pacing. Her posture changes. Possibly she moves even further away from Cecily, or possibly she adopts a physical attitude not unlike someone lecturing a naughty puppy or a child. The idea of moving away from Cecily again indicates how their former friendly relationship is now deteriorating. However, an actor playing this part should be careful to motivate the movement away as a movement toward something else, perhaps another table or bench in the same garden scene.

Beat Five

GWENDOLEN: I am very fond of you, Cecily; I have liked you ever since I met you! But I am bound to state that now that I know that you are Mr. Worthing's ward, I cannot help expressing a wish you were— well, just a little older than you seem to be—and not quite so very alluring in appearance. In fact, if I may speak candidly—
CECILY: Pray do! I think that whenever one has anything unpleasant to say, one should always be quite candid.
GWENDOLEN: Well, to speak with perfect candor, Cecily, I wish that you were fully forty-two, and more than usually plain for your age.

I am trying to make her understand my disapproval by explaining it.

There is an element in this beat that is distinctly conciliatory. Perhaps Gwendolen feels that she has been a little too strong in the previous beat;

perhaps she senses a certain amount of hurt and confusion in Cecily's behavior and suddenly feels a need to explain herself. Whatever the reason, the conciliatory tone suggests that Gwendolen needs at least to step toward Cecily again, as if to say that there is nothing personal in her disapproval of Cecily. There's nothing wrong with you, Gwendolen seems to be saying, it's just that you claim to be the ward of my fiance! Perhaps to reinforce that point, she might even touch Cecily on her shoulder while remaining as far away as possible.

Beat Six

GWENDOLEN: Ernest has a strong upright nature. He is the very soul of truth and honor. Disloyalty would be as impossible to him as deception. But even men of the noblest possible moral character are extremely susceptible to the influence of the physical charms of others. Modern, no less than Ancient History, supplies us with many most painful examples of what I refer to. If it were not so, indeed, History would be quite unreadable.

I am trying to warn her away from my fiance by appealing to her sense of morality.

In essence, she is warning Cecily not to get any ideas about abusing her relationship with Mr. Worthing as his ward by trying to snag him for her own husband. There is nothing conciliatory about this beat. Gwendolen needs to move away from Cecily again.

But look ahead: Gwendolen gets so caught up in giving warnings that Cecily has to interrupt her. This fact suggests that perhaps Gwendolen does not look at Cecily during this speech; frequently, when people are giving warnings to other people, they do not look at them directly in order to seem even more superior. And since Gwendolen began this moral sermon with the name "Ernest," Cecily must have responded much earlier than her next line. If Gwendolen looks at Cecily throughout this speech, she will see that Cecily wants to say something. Therefore, Gwendolen should perhaps walk away from Cecily, who then might even have to follow her around the garden to get her attention.

Beat Seven

CECILY: I beg your pardon, Gwendolen, did you say Ernest?
GWENDOLEN: Yes.
CECILY: Oh, but it is not Mr. Ernest Worthing who is my guardian. It is his brother—his elder brother.

I am trying to find out what she wants by asking.

Gwendolen's previous objective having been interrupted, she would want to stand still until she finds out what Cecily wants. Apparently, Gwendolen's reaction is to be skeptical at first. If Cecily stepped over to her to interrupt her, perhaps Gwendolen might step away from her slightly for the next beat.

Beat Eight

GWENDOLEN: Ernest never mentioned to me that he has a brother.
CECILY: I am sorry to say they have not been on good terms for a long time.
GWENDOLEN: Ah! That accounts for it. And now that I think of it I have never heard any man mention his brother. The subject seems distasteful to most men.

I am trying to verify the truth of what she has just said by asking.

This is another beat of interrogation, but the cost factor has been going up. Therefore, instead of pacing as in the previous interrogation, Gwendolen should stand still and focus on Cecily strongly.

Beat Nine

GWENDOLEN: Cecily, you have lifted a load from my mind. I was growing almost anxious. It would have been terrible if any cloud had come across a friendship like ours, would it not?

I am trying to make friends with her by explaining my conduct.

This beat represents a return to the first objective that Gwendolen played in this scene and it is important to bring that fact out. The actor playing Gwendolen should probably sit next to Cecily as in the first beat. However, since Gwendolen nearly made Cecily an enemy by accusing her of having designs on Gwendolen's fiance, the cost factor has just gone up again. Gwendolen should have to work a little harder at making friends with Cecily than in the first beat, perhaps sitting even closer than before.

Beat Ten

GWENDOLEN: Of course, you are quite, quite sure that it is not Mr. Ernest Worthing who is your guardian?
CECILY: Quite sure. (a pause) In fact, I am going to be his.

I am trying to verify the truth of what she has just said by asking.

This is also the resumption of an earlier beat. Probably she would lean back away from Cecily slightly or change her behavior in some other way to differentiate this objective from that of the previous beat. If at all possible, her tone of voice or expression or something should recall the way she played beat eight. Again, though, this objective should be played more emphatically. Common sense dictates that if this objective were not very important to her, she would not have interrupted her previous objective to return to this one.

Beat Eleven

GWENDOLEN: I beg your pardon?
      CECILY: Dearest Gwendolen, there is no reason why I should make a secret of it to you. Our little country newspaper is sure to chronicle the fact next week. Mr. Ernest Worthing and I are to be married.

I am trying to find out what she means by asking.

This is really a long beat of reaction. The news that Gwendolen receives is a catastrophic surprise. The best way to play this whole beat would probably be just to freeze. (See fig. 6–3.)

Beat Twelve

GWENDOLEN: My darling Cecily, I think there must be come slight error. Ernest Worthing is engaged to me. The announcement will appear in the *Morning Post* on Saturday at the latest.
      CECILY: I am afraid you must be under some misconception. Ernest proposed to me exactly ten minutes ago.

I am trying to straighten her out by announcing my engagement to Ernest.

This is the beginning of a long series of recurring beats. As the beats go forward, Gwendolen becomes progressively more distant from Cecily. But since this is the beginning of a series of similar beats, the first move should not be too extreme. Perhaps Gwendolen might simply try to get as far away from Cecily as possible while remaining seated on the same bench.

Beat Thirteen

I am trying to verify the truth of her claim by looking in her diary.

FIGURE 6-3. A Scene from *The Importance of Being Earnest.* *Cecily announces her engagement. Gwendolen freezes at Cecily's news. Notice that Cecily's decision to embrace Gwendolen reinforces the fact that Cecily believes Gwendolen to be her friend. The choice also helps to intensify Gwendolen's panic at what she has just heard and to motivate her to put some distance between them immediately.*

The action is self-explanatory. (See fig. 6–4.)

Beat Fourteen

GWENDOLEN: It is very curious for he asked me to be his wife yesterday after-noon at 5:30. If you would care to verify the incident, pray do so. (She produces a diary from her purse and shows it to Cecily.) I never travel without my diary. One should always have something sensational to read in the train. I am so sorry, dear Cecily, if it is any disappointment to you, but I am afraid I have the prior claim.

CECILY: It would distress me more than I can tell you, dear Gwendolen, if it caused you any mental or physical anguish, but I feel bound to point out that since Ernest proposed to you he clearly has changed his mind.

I am trying to straighten her out by showing her my diary.

Note that this beat does not begin where the stage direction states that Gwendolen "produces" the diary from her purse. The intention to use the

FIGURE 6-4. A Scene from *The Importance of Being Earnest.* *Cecily shows Gwendolen her diary. Notice how Gwendolen has now increased the distance between her and Cecily. Notice also how Cecily is focused on Gwendolen, watching for a look of understanding on Gwendolen's face.*

diary to straighten out Cecily begins earlier, as she begins the movement to get her purse. She might then simply stand by her purse and hold the book out at arms's length for Cecily to cross to. After Cecily finished reading Gwendolen's diary, she might walk contemptuously back toward the bench where she had been sitting to indicate her lack of concern. Gwendolen's attempt to straighten out Cecily thus meets with failure, but she does not give up. Clearly, the cost continues to go up.

Beat Fifteen

GWENDOLEN:　If the poor fellow has been entrapped into any foolish promises I shall consider it my duty to rescue him at once, and with a firm hand.

CECILY:　Whatever unfortunate entanglement my dear boy may have got into, I will never reproach him with it after we are married.

I am trying to straighten her out by threatening her.

From the way that Gwendolen moves toward Cecily as she says this line, the implication of the physical threat ("a firm hand") can easily be communicated. Again, though, the objective is not achieved. Therefore, Gwendolen would probably move forward again into the next beat to indicate the ever-increasing strength of her resolve.

Beat Sixteen

GWENDOLEN: Do you allude to me, Miss Cardew, as an entanglement? You are presumptuous. On an occasion of this kind it becomes more than a moral duty to speak one's mind. It becomes a pleasure.

CECILY: Do you suggest, Miss Fairfax, that I entrapped Ernest into an engagement? How dare you! This is no time for wearing the shallow mask of manners. When I see a spade I call it a spade.

I am trying to straighten her out by attacking her.

Gwendolen's forward movement, now more determined than in the previous beat, probably carries her virtually nose to nose with Cecily. The actor must forget that she knows what Cecily is going to say and do next. She must keep her focus on Cecily with great concentration as if she were preparing herself to meet whatever challenge Cecily might offer. Again, this beat ends in failure. Where can Gwendolen go next?

Beat Seventeen

GWENDOLEN: I am glad to say that I have never seen a spade. It is obvious that our social spheres have been widely different.

I am trying to straighten her out by ridiculing her.

The very nature of this beat suggests an idea for Gwendolen's next movement. If her apparent desire is to ridicule her opponent, perhaps she might want to turn away suddenly and pretend to sit as before in her former place on the garden bench. That move would have the effect of leaving Cecily poised for combat but with no one to fight. (See fig. 6–5.) The effect would be to undercut Cecily, as if to say that Gwendolen wasn't even taking her seriously as an opponent. Cecily's response to that strategy might be to move as if to strike Gwendolen or knock off her hat or something of the sort, but that action would be thwarted by the appearance of the servants to lay afternoon tea. In effect, Gwendolen would then be the winner of that point by default.

FIGURE 6-5.
A Scene from The Importance of Being Earnest. *At the finale of the scene, Gwendolen sits to communicate her contempt for Cecily. Notice how Gwendolen's body is turned slightly away from Cecily, which has the effect of increasing the impression of contempt.*

The choices of how to play these beats are all rather obvious, perhaps too much so for an actual performance. Also, Cecily's role in this exercise was severely limited in order to focus only on Gwendolen; in actual performance, Gwendolen would have to make several adjustments according to the way Cecily played her beats. Also, another actor might choose to interpret the same beats and objectives very differently. The point has not been to show how the scene must be played, only how the scene might be played. The key lesson to be learned from this analysis is that every time the objective changes, there has to be a corresponding change in the actor's behavior.

SUMMARY

Merely understanding a character's motivation and objectives is not enough for the actor. Once the motivation has been studied, the actor needs to translate it into specific objectives. If the actor does not know what the objectives are, then they cannot be communicated to the audience; worse, the actor runs the risk of playing nonobjectives instead, which are not part of the illusion of natural behavior.

A character's specific objectives have four component parts: the obstacle (indicated by the actor's point of focus), the strategy (the specific activity aimed at overcoming the obstacle), the cost (the intensity with which the activity is directed at the obstacle), and the desired result (which is something that the audience infers from observing the other three qualities of the performance).

Every time the character's objective changes, there must be a corresponding and apparent change in the actor's behavior. These changes in behavior create units of behavior called *beats*. By going through a script and charting out the character's objectives, the actor creates a blueprint for the physical performance called a *beat breakdown*. The beat breakdown will then give the actor important clues about how to express all the bodily changes inherent in the changing objectives.

EXERCISES FOR CHAPTER SIX

If the beat breakdown is done according to the "I am trying to . . . by . . ." formula, the resulting list of objectives describes what the scene is going to look like. Each objective specifies three qualities of the actor's behavior: the obstacle (where the actor is looking), the strategy (what the actor is doing), and the cost (how important that action is). The following exercises are designed to help students increase their awareness of how the obstacle, the strategy, and the cost are reflected in behavior.

1. Prepare a short improvised scene with another actor. Each of you should determine very specific conflicting objectives at a relatively high level of cost. Presume a personal or an intimate relationship (not social, business, or "power"): husband and wife, two brothers, two sisters, father and daughter, mother and son, and so on. Set the scene in a private or personal place. Or use one of the following suggestions:

    You are a husband and wife who own only one car. At breakfast in your own kitchen, you each try to get the other's permission to take the car for the day. The husband says he needs the car for a meeting with a client, and the wife says she needs the car for a variety of errands. However, in reality, he is trading in the car on a new one for her birthday, and she is driving a neighbor woman in secret to a battered wives' clinic.

    You are two brothers who meet in one of your living rooms. One brother wants to have the annual family reunion in one place, and the other brother favors another. In reality, however, the first brother is close to bankruptcy and can't afford to go anywhere else (and doesn't want anyone to know), and the other brother has already agreed to a clandestine meeting at the other place with business associates to close a big real estate deal (which cannot be even hinted at in fear of its being called off.)

    You are a mother and daughter. The daughter has invited the mother over to her small apartment for dinner. The mother (a widow) wants to persuade the daughter to move back home, but the daughter wants to persuade her mother to go on a trip with her. In reality, the mother needs her daughter's financial support and is too proud to ask for it. The daughter, however, has been receiving threatening phone calls; she does not want to go away alone but is reluctant to tell her mother for fear of alarming her.

    Work out the details of the situation thoroughly in advance, but do not plan what is to happen in the scene. On your own, plan at least three different strategies you might use to bring the other person around to what you want. Use the "If-I-Were" formula to put yourself in the place of your character and to stimulate your imagination.

Perform your improvisation for an audience without previous rehearsal, and then ask them if they understood what your strategies were and the real cost you were playing.

In playing this exercise, be careful not to keep using a given strategy after its effectiveness has been exhausted. If a new strategy occurs to you while playing, use it. One of your goals should be to use as many different strategies as possible. Be careful also not to allow the scene to become static and talky. Each time you change your strategy, change your behavior in some way. Don't forget to play the situation—use the objects in your setting to help you motivate your movements.

2. Look again at the list of beats for the scene from *Earnest*. Examine Gwendolen's strategy for the beats in which her desired results were to make friends, get information, and straighten out Cecily. As an exercise, determine different strategies for those moments. Let your imagination take over. Use the "If-I-Were" formula to try to put yourself into Gwendolen's position and ask yourself what strategies you as a person might use in such a situation to accomplish such goals.

Create a new beat breakdown for Gwendolen that reflects your own strategy. Deliberately strive for effects that are different from the ideas already discussed but are possible under the circumstances. Then act out the scene with the person who played Cecily before but without telling her how you intend to change the strategies. Observe how new choices of strategy demand different choices for blocking and business.

Afterward, discuss the results with your partner and with the audience who observes the scene. Ask the audience to tell what your new ideas were. If they cannot, ask for suggestions on how you could have made your new ideas more apparent.

3. Try doing a beat breakdown for Cecily, but (for the sake of an exercise) change important details of her identity or the situation. For example, consider any of the following changes:

Cecily *is* very plain and nearly forty years old.
Cecily has been warned in advance that her fiance is having an affair with another woman, but she doesn't know whom.
Cecily is really in love with someone else entirely and wishes she could get out of her engagement to Ernest Worthing.
Cecily has murdered the person she believed to be Ernest Worthing about five minutes ago, and the body is lying on the ground just behind the hedge.
Cecily is suffering from an incurable, terminal disease and has less than four months to live.

Plan Cecily's beats carefully to reveal any new movement, business, or gestures that these changes will require. Then perform the scene with a Gwendolen who keeps the same beats as before—but who is not forewarned what changes Cecily is going to make. Afterward, discuss the results with your partner and with the audience.

4. Practice in doing beat breakdowns and phrasing out specific objectives is essential to develop the ability to play objectives well. Go back to the scenes from *Harvey* and *Macbeth* and try to do a complete beat breakdown for the characters you played before. Follow the guidelines for phrasing out objectives that were given in this and the previous chapters. Try not to develop too many objectives actually to play. If possible, act out the scenes again with these objectives in mind. Make whatever changes in the blocking are now suggested by your changes in strategy or desired results.

Lesson Seven

Completed and Interrupted Objectives

In performance, an actor must communicate not only the nature of each objective in turn but also the moments at which one objective changes to another. If the audience cannot tell when one objective ends and another one begins, the actor's performance will seem muddied and unclear. Therefore, actors have to create the beat changes as well as the beats themselves.

Beat changes follow a peculiar logic all their own, depending on whether or not the character intends to try to achieve the same desired effect again. The attempt may be repeated because the first attempt was interrupted or because the first attempt met with failure, but there still remains a possibility that another strategy will succeed. The attempt may not be repeated either because the desired effect was acheived or because there is no further possibility of success. In each case, the way the actor plays the beat change must communicate to the audience whether or not there is an intention to continue.

Effective beat changes are one of the most important single indicators of convincing acting. Beat changes cannot be rehearsed and planned like all the other elements of performance. They are a function of the actor's ability to concentrate properly in performance.

Chapter Seven

Playing the Beat Changes

Communicating the nature of each individual objective one at a time is not all that the actor has to do; the transition from one objective to the next must also be carefully created. As this chapter will demonstrate, the way in which actors create the transitions between objectives may be fully as important as how they choose to play the objectives themselves. Just as a person's behavior adjusts to reflect the nature of each objective being pursued by the conscious mind, the behavior also adjusts to reflect the transitions between objectives as well.

To show how these transitions are perceived, read through the following example carefully and try to visualize exactly the action being described:

A man walks into the kitchen of his own home after working in the yard on a hot day. He is very thirsty. As he enters the kitchen, his intention is to get a bottle of beer out of the refrigerator. He opens the door and reaches toward the rack on the door where the bottles of beer are usually kept, but there is no beer. He moves around the various objects on the refrigerator shelves in the hope that the beer may be hiding somewhere among the plastic cartons, jars, and miscellaneous items wrapped in aluminum foil. But no bottle of beer can be seen. Then he begins to move around the various objects on the refrigerator shelves again, now looking for anything cold to drink. After a moment, his gaze falls on a single six-ounce can of tomato juice in the back corner of the lowest shelf. He pauses for a moment and then pulls out the can. Apparently in the absence of beer, tomato juice will have to do.

After closing the refrigerator door, he begins to stroll toward the kitchen table with the cold can of juice still in his hand, his intention apparently to set the can on the table. But suddenly the phone on the wall begins ringing. He changes direction for the phone and lifts up the receiver. After a few moments of conversation, he suddenly realizes that his hand is still wrapped around the cold can, and he quickly sets it down on the nearby counter.

Once the phone call is completed, he picks up the can again and carries it over to the table, where he seats himself in a kitchen chair. He pulls off the mylar strip at the top of the can and raises the juice to his lips. He drinks about half the juice and then stops. The back of his throat feels cold, and so he puts down the can for a moment. While waiting, his eyes glance around the kitchen absently to pass the time until he is ready to drink again. A moment later, his eyes return to the can, he drinks, and the can is empty. There is a brief pause while he considers whether to try to find something else to drink or to go take a shower. A second later, he stands, tosses the empty can into the trash container, and leaves the room.

As you visualize the scene in your imagination, you see that the man's behavior adjusts as he goes from objective to objective, even when the action itself remains basically the same. For example, the action of rummaging around in the refrigerator adjusts to reflect two different objectives. His sifting through the contents of the refrigerator to find a hidden bottle of beer has a different quality from his searching through the contents of the refrigerator to try to find something else cold to drink. Both actions are very similar, but there is be a noticeable difference between them because two different objectives are involved.

What makes the difference noticeable is the moment at which the first action stops and the next one begins. In our imagination, we see a distinct moment when the man realizes that there is no beer to be found; he then starts rummaging around again for something else. However, if we did not observe that moment of transition, we would probably see only one continuous action (and therefore, only one objective, not two separate objectives as the nature of the situation demands). The adjustment in behavior between the two actions is so slight that without the moment of transition, we might not notice the change.

This example is trivial, but understanding this last point is vital to understanding the material that follows. When the man realizes that there is absolutely no beer to be found, there is a definite moment when his behavior registers that failure. If an actor were to act out this little scene for an audience, he would have to play that moment; he would have to show the audience when the search for the beer stopped and the search for something else began. If he did not play that moment of transition, the audience would not see two, clearly differentiated objectives. They would only see an action that starts out as one thing and ends up as something else. The effect would be unnatural. The way the conscious mind works, the failure must be grasped and accepted before the second objective, searching for something else to drink, can be formulated. Therefore, the lack of an appropriate moment of transition would be confusing. The illusion of natural behavior would be broken.

These moments of transition occur throughout the imaginary scene, and they break up the man's behavior into the little units called *beats*. (Remember that a beat was defined in the last chapter as a unit of behavior that defines a single objective.) A beat breakdown for this scene would include moving toward the refrigerator, looking for a beer, looking for something else, taking the juice to the table, answering the phone, setting down the can, talking on the phone, walking to the table again, drinking, and leaving. Each beat is marked by a distinct moment of transition that separates it from the next. Human behavior, thus, constantly alternates between beats and beat changes. Onstage, the performance of an actor must be the same. When an actor reaches the end of each objective, there must be a proper moment of transition in behavior to signal that the conscious mind of the character is moving on to another objective. And as we shall see, the reverse formula is true as well: whenever there is a noticeable change in the actor's behavior (intentional or otherwise), the audience perceives that there has been some change in the character's objective.

BEATS AND MUSIC

The word *beat* annoys some actors because it does not immediately suggest anything concerned with behavior. The word is most commonly used in discussions of rhythm and music. How did it come to be used as a theatrical term to designate units of behavior?

The term was probably popularized by Stanislavski, who used it in *An Actor Prepares* to designate the small segments into which an actor divides a role for the purpose of learning it. He draws an analogy between the task of an actor working on a role and that of a man carving a turkey. The turkey cannot be consumed whole; it must be cut up into bite-sized portions, each of which must then be chewed thoroughly before swallowing.

Stanislavski may or may not have been thinking of music when he used that word in *An Actor Prepares*, but the comparison of music and acting is appropriate. There are many qualities that are shared by beats of music and acting. One is the way in which the rhythmic beats of a melody progress in a definite, unvarying order. The second beat of a given melody cannot occur until the first has been completed. In other words, in acting as well as in music, beats can only happen one at a time, one right after the other. If two beats are allowed to overlap, the results are very unpleasant. Two musical examples may help to bring this point out more emphatically: First, if you have ever taken dancing lessons or learned choreography for a musical, you will recall how important it is to do everything on the right beat of music. Each step must be completed on the proper beat before the next step can be initiated. Second, have you ever been to a concert given by an amateur orchestra in which some of the musicians are a beat ahead or behind everyone else? If the beats of music start to overlap, the effect is chaotic and discordant. In acting as well as in music, the beats must follow in the correct order.

Another point of comparison is the way in which the beat changes give a sense of tempo and rhythm to the performance. In a musical composition, the beats may alternate very slowly or very quickly, and the speed may even change, as in the various movements of a symphony or sonata (medium fast, very slow, very quick, medium slow, and so on). In addition, the pattern of stressed and unstressed beats creates the rhythms, such as the march, the waltz, the polka, and so on. In an actor's performance, the patterns of beat changes may create a sense of tempo and rhythm as well. Some characters change beats very quickly, some change only infrequently, and some alternate between tempos. Also, the way in which some beat changes are very pronounced and some very subtle creates a pattern; some characters may be regular and marchlike in the way they work on their objectives, others more lyrical and waltzlike; and some may have erratic rhythms that seem comic or grotesque.

In acting, just as in music, variations in tempo and rhythm help to sustain the audience's interest and give the acting a sense of texture. And the reverse is true also: The lack of significant variations in tempo and rhythmic patterns can make an audience lose interest in the performance. Some actors never play any noticeable beats at all; they simply recite their lines and wander through their blocking. Some actors play objectives but do not separate them properly, and the lack of perceivable beat changes produces an effect not unlike hearing a musician play a single note on a violin for several minutes without letup. Even professional actors are sometimes guilty of giving "one-note" performances such as these.

Still another point of comparison between acting and music is the way in which there may be recurring melodies, or leitmotives, in music and the way in which there are usually recurring beats in an actor's performance. Recurring beats are units of behavior aimed at creating the same desired results but with different strategies, costs, or obstacles. In the scene from *The Importance of Being Earnest,* we observed three recurring beats in Gwendolen's role (note the second exercise at the end of Chapter Six). As a composer repeats a single theme in a musical composition, the listener begins to recognize that melody as a major theme; as an actor tries to achieve the same desired result more than once, the audience begins to perceive those attempts as a major action of the play.

However, composers do not usually repeat a single melody over and over again without using some variations. Sometimes composers will change the key in which the melody is played or the part of the orchestra in which the melody is heard; or they may change parts of the melody, add ornamentations, slow it down, speed it up, or add a counter melody. The way in which composers develop the major musical themes of a composition often defines its entire form, and the listener becomes involved in perceiving each new variation as it is played. In exactly the same way, actors must play recurring beats with appropriate variations. You may have seen plays in which there are interrogation scenes (such as a lawyer questioning a witness or a wife grilling a faithless husband) in which one actor may have asked all the questions in the same way, with basically the same tempo, vocal inflections, and gestures. The result was, undoubtedly, tedious. Repetition without variation is monotonous both in music and in acting. This lack of variation is one of the most common faults of beginning actors.

Recurring beats in acting are extremely common, and they are extremely important. Their importance can be illustrated in part by another reference to the man with the tomato juice in the refrigerator. The storyline of this little pantomime is not particularly interesting: A man enters his kitchen, gets something to drink, and leaves. Who cares? No one, perhaps because none of the man's objectives is very interesting. Trying to find beer in the refrigerator is not as interesting an objective as trying to talk one's spouse out of murdering the King of Scotland. But if Macbeth had mentioned those "golden opinions" to Lady Macbeth and she had responded, "I guess you're right—let's just call the whole thing off," Macbeth's objective wouldn't have been very interesting either. The problem with the man and the tomato juice is not that what he tries to do is boring but that he succeeds at everything he tries to do. Had he met with a little opposition at some point, the scene would have been more interesting.

In the scene from *Macbeth*, the quality that holds our attention is how much difficulty the two characters have in trying to achieve their conflicting objectives. They have to keep working away at each other, first trying one approach and then another. It is this sense of a mighty struggle to overcome seemingly immovable obstacles that gives a performance interest, not the specific nature of the obstacles themselves. Remember that Beethoven took two notes, repeated one of them twice, and created the basic theme of one of the most popular symphonies ever written—Dee-dee-dee-DAAA—the main theme of the first movement of the Fifth Symphony. In the kitchen scene, the action threatens to become interesting, if only for a moment, when the man can't find the beer and starts looking for something else. Suppose that the scene had taken an entirely different turn at that moment. Suppose that instead of allowing himself to be satisfied with tomato juice, the man had renewed his search with greater intensity—first throwing out everything in the refrigerator onto the floor, then throwing out everything in the cupboards, and finally ransacking the whole house to find his precious bottle of beer. His repeated failure to find what he wanted, coupled with renewed and increasingly ferocious attempts to achieve his goal, would hold our interest very well indeed. In music, recurring themes give a sense of structure and form to a complete work; in acting, recurring beats serve something of the same purpose. In each case, what holds our interest is not the fact of the recurrence alone; it is the nature of the variations that the composer and the actor create on their basic themes.

To bring the musical analogy to a conclusion, it will be useful to summarize the points that have been made in this section:

1. The separation between the beats must be clear and distinct in music as well as in acting.
2. Beats must never be allowed to overlap.
3. Variation in the tempo and rhythm of the beat changes is a desirable quality.
4. Recurring beats create interest in a role and help to suggest a sense of structure within the play as a whole, just as recurring themes suggest structure in longer musical compositions.

Having observed the importance of beat changes to the work of the actor, we need now to observe the different types of changes and what they tell an audience about the actor's objectives.

TYPES OF BEAT CHANGES

There are two fundamentally different types of beat changes, and the example of the man in the kitchen contains illustrations of both: First, the trip to the table with the cold can of juice was interrupted by the ringing of the telephone; in other words, the objective of getting to the table was abandoned in favor of the objective of answering the phone. But when the phone call was completed, the conscious mind shifted back to the problem of getting something to drink, and the man's trip to the kitchen table was resumed. This example reveals an objective that is momentarily suspended. Second, the man's attempt to find beer in the refrigerator was a complete failure, and therefore he had to change to the new objective of finding something else to drink. This example reveals an objective that is played to completion. In this way, some objectives are *suspended* and some are *completed*. The distinctive qualities of each type of beat change will now be discussed in detail.

Completed objectives. An objective is completed whenever there is no intention to bring about the same desired result again—no matter whether the attempt met with success or failure. For purposes of playing the beat changes, success and failure are not the determining qualities; what counts is the lack of intention to try again. When the man searched for beer in the refrigerator, the attempt met with failure; there was no possibility of playing that same objective again because there was no beer to be found. When he tried to quench his thirst by consuming all the juice in the can, the attempt met with success; the juice having been consumed, there was no intention to play that same objective again either. Usually when an objective has been completed in this way, the conscious mind then "shifts gears" to a lower level of need. (Presumably, whatever objective the conscious mind is playing at any given moment represents the highest level of need that the mind has to work on at that moment.) When the can of juice in the refrigerator was located, the mind shifted to the less pressing need to sit down. When the juice had been consumed, the mind shifted to the lower-level need to clean up. Thus, the lack of intention to try again is usually indicated by the conscious mind's shift to a lower level of need.

As a general rule, there are two qualities of behavior that make a completed objective look like one: The first is that the actor pauses to recognize and register the success or failure of the attempt. (This kind of pause is often called, appropriately, a *beat pause*—meaning simply a moment when the conscious mind is pausing between beats in order to figure out what to do next.) The second is the resulting change of body focus, position, or posture, usually accompanied by a release of tension. When the man in the kitchen finally sits down after talking on the phone, we can imagine his registering his relief: He's been out in the yard and he's tired; at last he gets to sit down. When Lady Macbeth finally hears her husband tell her to "Bring forth men children only," she would probably show a considerable release of tension also: The fight is over; she can relax and get back to dinner with the King. Regardless of whether an actor has succeeded or failed at reaching a specific goal, the energy that went into that effort has been spent; what energy remains is then usually redirected at a lower-order need.

Suspended objectives.   An objective is suspended whenever the attempt to achieve it is met by failure or by interruption but the character still wants to try again (regardless of whether or not such an attempt is ever made). When the man started to walk toward the kitchen table, that attempt was momentarily interrupted by the higher-order need to answer the phone. In a similar way, when the man tried to deal with the person on the phone, that attempt was interrupted by the intrusion of the higher order need to set down the cold can. In both cases, however, the man still intended to drink the juice eventually; the objectives were suspended by interruption, not abandoned. In the scene from *Macbeth*, Lady Macbeth's first attempt to stop her husband from backing out of their plan meets with a momentary failure when Macbeth shouts, "Prithee peace!" (He is the dominant one in that relationship, and therefore, she has a higher-order need to defer to his authority.) We know her beat is suspended because a moment later she tries to achieve the same desired result again with another strategy. Thus, a beat change at the point of an interruption usually involves the conscious mind shifting to a higher-order problem; the beat change at the point of a momentary failure usually involves the conscious mind shifting to another strategy. In neither case is tension released; if anything, tension is increased and carried over into the next beat.

The primary quality that makes a suspended objective look like one is this "carryover" into the next beat. It may involve retaining body focus, position, or posture. When the man stops moving toward the table in order to answer the phone, he does not heave a great sigh of relief and pull up a comfortable chair next to the phone; he's waiting until he can get rid of whoever is on the phone so he can sit down at the table. In a like manner, when Lady Macbeth is interrupted while trying to talk her husband into completing their plan, she would certainly keep her focus on Macbeth while he talks. (Look at fig. 5-4 again; note how the actor playing Lady Macbeth retains her focus on her husband even after he has silenced her—she clearly seems to have more to say.) A suspended beat may also be followed by a beat of recognition or surprise at having been interrupted or thwarted, but such beats are usually played much more briefly than the beats of recognition that follow a completed beat.

Retaining tension at the beat change of a suspended objective is an important factor in playing recurring beats. As a character makes repeated attempts to achieve a single desired result, the cost factor always increases. In other words, when a playwright has dictated that a character goes after the same desired result more than once, the actor has got to show the audience that it is worth it to that character to make another attempt; a second effort must always take a little more energy than a first try. For example, the third time that Gwendolen tries to straighten out Cecily, she must be trying harder than her second and first attempts because neither of them were successful; the more energy Gwendolen puts into each of those repeated attempts, the more she shows the audience how much she wants to marry Ernest. This factor of increasing intensity as beats recur is another way in which actors can increase the audience's interest in a scene. If the character appears to care enough about achieving a particular goal not merely to try again but also to try again harder and harder each time, then achieving that goal becomes important for the audience as well.

(In the days of the silent movies, comedians Laurel and Hardy specialized in two-reel films that created audience involvement through recurring beats. In *The Music Box*, which won an Academy Award, their repeated attempts to push a piano up an impossibly steep flight of concrete steps become more and more hilarious as their failures are met each time with renewed and more determined effort.)

To summarize, there are four major types of beat changes as determined by the character's intention or lack of intention to try again to achieve the same desired result:

1. Completion as a result of success
2. Completion as a result of absolute failure
3. Suspension as a result of interruption
4. Suspension as a result of momentary failure

Completed beats are usually followed by the shift of the conscious mind to a lower order of need, regardless of success or failure. As a result, there are a change of focus and a release of tension. Suspended beats are usually followed by the mind shifting to a higher-order need (interruption) or remaining at the same level of need with greater intensity (momentary failure). The intention to try again is revealed in some sort of physical carryover into the next beat.

This summary of the different types of beat changes points out an important fact about beats themselves. No two objectives can ever be completely alike. An objective is made up of a desired result, an obstacle, a strategy, and a cost. Whenever an objective is terminated, either by completion or suspension, those same four factors cannot possibly exist again in the same way. If the objective is completed, the desired result has to change; logic dictates that it cannot be played again. If the objective is suspended, either the cost or the strategy has to change. In the case of an interruption, logic dictates that if the cost were high enough originally, the character would never have allowed the interruption to occur in the first place. Therefore, the cost has to go up or the desired result isn't worth going after again. Or in the case of momentary failure, logic dictates that because the previous strategy didn't work, a new strategy must be played or there is no point to the repetition at all. And since logic dictates that no two objectives can ever be the same, logic also dictates that no two beats of an actor's performance should ever be completely alike either. If an actor does play two or more beats in the same way, the effect is not natural. Once again, the illusion of natural behavior is broken.

Also, the way a beat change is perceived determines how the audience understands the nature of the objective, regardless of what the actor intends. If the beat ends with the actor changing focus and losing tension, the audience assumes that the objective has been completed. If the beat ends with the actor carrying over energy into the next beat, the implication is that the objective is suspended and the character is not through trying to achieve that particular desired effect. And if the audience can't tell where one objective ends and the next begins, it won't know what is going on and, very quickly, won't care. As a result, actors must give conscious attention to their beat changes or risk confusing and losing the audience. Like the process by which the audience seeks to fill in the missing elements of the illusion of the performance as a whole, this process goes on all the time regardless of whether the actors wish it to or not. If the actors don't control their beat changes to send the right signals to the audience, the audience will draw their own conclusions—right or wrong—anyway.

THE ACTOR'S DOUBLE CONSCIOUSNESS

Beat changes are another aspect of natural human behavior that has to be consciously simulated in order to create a convincing illusion. However, unlike the character's relationship to the setting and to the other actors, actors cannot plan and rehearse their beat changes in advance; and the explanation for that fact goes right to the heart of what good realistic acting is all about.

There are two reasons why beat changes cannot be planned and rehearsed. First, each performance of every play is a unique event. There are thousands of details that are never the same two performances in a row. Consequently, if the beat changes are meticulously rehearsed and performed the same way in every performance, they are going to seem unnatural. For example, recurring beats require increasing cost, which is reflected in the increasing intensity with which a character tries to bring about a particular desired result. But the increasing intensity must be proportional to the intensity of the resistance provided by the character who represents the obstacle. Since no two performances are ever going to be exactly the same, the amount of increase for each beat change will only be known as each change occurs. For some performances, the increases will be rapid and meteoric; for other performances, the rhythm will be slower and the changes will build more gradually. Actors who play their beat changes the same way in each and every performance are not really paying attention to what is going on around them. Their acting is, therefore, not convincing.

Second, in performance good actors actually play many more beat changes than they plan to play. In life, we constantly make subtle adjustments in our facial expressions, vocal inflections, gestures, and so on, that are spontaneous responses to all the changes going on around us all the time. On the stage, actors usually make the same spontaneous responses as they play their objectives, and these responses are all perceived by the audience as beat changes (however subtle) as well. Actors who play a lot of beat changes in this way seem more natural than those who play very few. It is simply not possible to plan in advance every conceivable nuance and subtlety in the way a character goes about trying to play a given objective. In every performance, things are going to happen that have never happened before and things that have happened before are not going to happen again in the same way; actors must respond to all these unplanned and unanticipated details as well. The absence of these little, spontaneous beat changes looks decidedly unnatural. In other words, actors must respond to what is actually going on around them, not what they wish were going on or what they thought was going to go on or what went on at rehearsal. The beat changes must be a response to the reality of each moment as it happens. And if they are not there, the reason must be that the actor is not paying attention to the performance, and therefore, the actor is not really playing the objectives.

Then, should the beat changes be left entirely to chance and accident in performance? No. The actor must go through the script and note each place in the dialogue where a beat change is indicated and what kind of a change it should be. But as was stated in the first chapter, the script itself is only the starting point from which the performance is evolved. The actor uses the beat changes indicated by the dialogue as a starting point from which to create all the beat changes that each individual performance requires. And the actor creates all those changes as a natural result of playing the objectives with conviction.

But actors are not the characters they pretend to be, they are not in the place they pretend to be, and they are not really doing what they pretend to be doing. How is it possible for the beat changes to come about *naturally* from playing objectives that aren't real in the first place?

Again, the answer takes us deeper into the heart of what good realistic acting is all about. In the discussion of conviction in Chapter Two, the "If-I-Were" formula was introduced to point out how actors perform the actions of the play as if they really were the characters in those situations. As was further discussed in Chapter Five, those actions are based on the fundamental objectives that each and every person has played at one time or another in that person's own life. What happens on the stage, then, is that the objectives themselves aren't real (I'm not really trying to straighten you out by threatening you; I'm not really trying to convince you to murder the King of Scotland), but the *way* actors play those objectives is just as real as if the objectives themselves *were* real.

Consider the mental state of a woman driving a car in a cross-country race. Before the race begins, she studies the course slowly and carefully, noting where to turn, where to brake, where to accelerate, and so on. But when the time comes to run the race itself, she doesn't think about the course. She directs all her attention toward what is happening in the race. The driver must know and remember the course, but her focus must be on making all the spontaneous adjustments required by the maneuverings of the other drivers. Always the objective foremost in the driver's mind is to get ahead and to win the race, but that objective is predicated on an awareness of the race course itself within which that objective has to be achieved. In other words, there are rules dictating how the race is to be driven. The race is an artificial situation in that the driver is not at liberty to take a shortcut across town or to throw hand grenades at the other drivers to disable their vehicles. The goal has to be achieved within the rules of the game. And within those restrictions, the driver adjusts her driving to the maneuverings of the other drivers as she seeks to achieve her objective.

In the same way, the actor notes where the important beat changes have to take place and plans how they should be handled. But in the performance itself, the actor's focus has got to be on what is happening in the scene. If the actor's concentration is good, the beat changes will then come about naturally as the actor responds to how the other performers are playing their objectives. Just as winning the race is real to the driver, the objectives are real to the actor. The fact that the actor must achieve those objectives within the artificial restrictions of the performance in no way makes them any less real than the objective of winning the race is to the driver.

But even so, there is an important difference. The actor knows what is going to happen next; the driver does not. In fact, the intensity with which the driver concentrates on the objective of winning the race is a function of the fact that losing the race (not achieving the objective) is a very real possibility. The driver may know the race course intimately, but on that course are drivers whose movements cannot be known in advance. To win the race, she must not let her mind wander; she must pay attention to every detail of what the other drivers are doing. In effect, she plays the objective of trying to win the race just by paying attention to what the other drivers are doing.

Just like the driver, actors should focus on every single detail of the performance in progress. No two performances are ever completely alike; there are surprises constantly. Good concentration requires that actors not allow their thoughts to wander. During a performance, actors should not be thinking about who may be sitting in the audience, where they are going to eat dinner after the show, whether or not they can make another actor laugh by making funny faces from the wings, or anything else of that sort. Any thoughts that don't specifically have to do with the performance must be pushed out of mind. (Also, actors should not be thinking about the words of the phrased-out objectives from their beat breakdowns; if they do, they are likely to forget their lines. The objectives must be internalized, like the layout of the race course, not verbalized while being played.) Each actor must be looking at and thinking about the other actors in the play and constantly trying to determine if the desired results are being achieved.

In describing the six fundamental objectives, the point was made in each case that the actor must try to block out of mind any advance knowledge of the outcome. When Macbeth says, "Prithee peace!" the effect he wants to achieve is to get his wife to stop talking. What must be going on in his mind at that moment is that he's looking at the actor playing Lady Macbeth and he's trying to say something to her and she won't stop talking and he has got to get her to shut up so that he can say what's on his mind and get her off his back! When he hears his cue to say his line, he's got to make it his first priority at that moment to get her to stop talking. And that is only possible if he blocks out of his mind at that moment that she is going to be quiet after he yells out his next line. However, he cannot get so carried away with the need to make her be quiet that he pushes her off the stage or takes out a gun and shoots her or any other such ludicrous action. Like the driver, the object is to achieve the desired result within the rules of the game.

Much has been written about the phenomenon of the actor's double consciousness in performance. The idea is that the actors are aware of themselves as the characters in the play and as actors on the stage at the same time. Heaven forbid that the actors playing the final duel between Macbeth and Macduff should get so carried away with the playing of their mutual objectives that they actually try to kill each other! There is nothing quite so disturbing, either for actors on a stage or for an audience, as the feeling that an actor has become carried away in feigning grief or anger and is out of control. Thus, the actor is supposed to be consciously aware of the reality of the objective and the fiction of the performance all at the same time.

But how is it possible simultaneously to do something that is real and not real? We have already established that the conscious mind can only pursue one objective at a time—and that principle applies to actors as well as to characters in a play. If the reader will forgive one more sporting analogy, consider the following example from the game of football: A defensive lineman squares off opposite an offensive lineman on the line of scrimmage. When the ball is snapped, they must do everything they can to frustrate each other's objectives: The offensive lineman must get past the defensive lineman and break up the play. The defensive lineman must not allow him to do it. Of course, both players know that they are only playing a game, that their efforts are strictly proscribed by the rules; they cannot get so carried away that they use knives and guns in the service of their objectives. But even so, the game itself is real. And within that particular reality, they have to stop each other from doing what each wants to do—and for them at that moment, those objectives are as real as any objectives off the football field. In effect, there is no double consciousness; there is only the reality of working to achieve a specific effect at that particular moment within a certain set of rules.

The actor must concentrate on the objectives in the same way that professional athletes concentrate on playing football or baseball or any other game. When I am playing Macbeth, I am not consciously aware of myself as Macbeth at that particular moment—that is the illusion I am trying to create; that is for the audience to see. What I am aware of is that there is another actor opposite me on the stage and that I have a particular effect I want to achieve on that actor (derived from one of the six fundamental objectives.) I know we are both actors—those are the rules of the game—but within those rules, my relationship with that actor at this particular moment is just as real as the relationship between an offensive and a defensive lineman, and I must do whatever I can to achieve the effect that I want to have on that other actor. The play may be a fiction, but my objective is real.

If you have ever played any game of any kind, you know what it means to become completely involved in the reality of the play without losing touch with the reality that you are only playing a game. That is the state of con-centration the actor seeks when playing the objectives. Those objectives be-come as real as the goals in any game—scoring a touchdown, hitting a home run, making a free throw, finessing your opponent's ace, buying Boardwalk and Park Place, or getting tic-tac-toe. Your opponent in the game is real, and in your mind you want to do everything possible to win the game within the rules. When actors play their objectives in that way, they are really playing those objectives with conviction.

And how exactly do the actors make their objectives that real? By block-ing out of their minds any advance knowledge of how the attempt to achieve each objective is going to come out. The possibility that an objective may not be achieved can be a powerful mental device to liberate the actor's en-ergy.

But trying to forget that you know what is going to happen next in a play is a negative objective, and actors aren't supposed to play negative ob-jectives. But actors don't concentrate on trying not to remember what is going to happen next. In order to block that information out of their minds, they concentrate on what the other actors are doing to the exclusion of all other thoughts. A football player may have rehearsed a particular play a hundred or more times in practice; but each moment in every game is a unique experience, and the player must concentrate exactly on what is hap-pening at each second or run the risk of failure. An actor may have played a given scene a hundred times in rehearsal and other performances, but the actor can never be certain just how any given performance is going to turn out. Actively looking for and concentrating on those details that are unique in every moment onstage is not only a way of forgetting what is going to happen next; it is also what is really meant by the phrase *playing the objective.* (In *The Stanislavski System,* Sonia Moore makes this point very eloquently.

> The only thing an actor can fulfill truthfully on stage as a character is a simple physical action. He can bang his fist on a table; he can slam the door; he can *ask* a question; he can *explain* something to his fellow actor; he can *threaten* or *encourage* him—and he can do all this truthfully.[1]

And notice that the actions she describes involving a "fellow actor" are clearly variations on the fundamental objectives described in the previous chapter. From each one of these single actions, built up truthfully one at a time, the actor constructs even the most complicated and contradictory roles.)

When objectives are played truthfully with the intensity of a sport, the beat changes will occur just as naturally as they do when you play any ob-jective in real life or in any game. If you are playing Lady Macbeth and your objective is to get your opponent (the other actor) to agree to go back into the dining hall with you, it doesn't matter that there is no dining hall and no one is really plotting to kill the King. Your fundamental objective (to make the other actor do something) *is* real. If you play that objective with conviction and if you don't achieve your desired result, then you shouldn't have to worry about playing the beat change by keeping your focus on the other actor and playing the next objective with increased intensity—all those factors will be there automatically. If you are playing Macbeth, you aren't going to have to worry about playing the beat change when you successfully convince the actor playing your wife that you have your courage back; if you are really looking at her and paying attention to what she is doing, you will respond automatically with a release of tension when she shows you that she is content.

In this way, we see that effective beat changes are one of the most important single indicators of good realistic acting. If the beat changes are clear and correct and appropriately abundant, it is a sure sign that the actor is concentrating properly and playing the objectives with conviction. If the beat changes are muddled, mechanical, or just not there at all, the acting is bad.

Before going on to the next section, we need to observe one other point. If the actor is concentrating properly, the beat changes should be in place properly. If, however, the actor's concentration starts to wander, he or she should not try to start creating the beat changes consciously and deliberately. That approach will only make the problem worse. The only thing for the actor to do is to try to get back in the right frame of mind by forcing out all extraneous thoughts. Good beat changes are virtually impossible to fake; they are the result of the proper mental attitude, and if that attitude is not present, they will not be right.

Scene Number Four: *The Circle*

You are now asked to imagine being a student who has just been assigned to prepare a scene for performance in your acting class. The scene selected for this exercise is from a classic drawing-room comedy by the English novelist and playwright W. Somerset Maugham. *The Circle* was first performed in 1921 and has since reappeared frequently in professional revivals, community theatres, and colleges. Objectives will have to be played with great conviction to avoid playing the accents and the style. But this is a realistic play and, therefore, a fair one to use to demonstrate all the principles of realistic acting that we have been discussing.

The Circle is in three acts, and all three take place in the drawing room of a magnificent English country house called Aston-Adey. The setting is of considerable significance to the scene because the whole feeling of the room mirrors the character of the owner, Arnold Champion-Cheney, who is a Member of Parliament. On Arnold's first entrance, Maugham describes him as follows:

He is a man of about thirty-five, tall and good-looking, fair, with a clean-cut face. He has a look that is intellectual, but somewhat bloodless. He is very well dressed.[2]

Readers who have been paying attention will realize that little of the information in that description is of practical assistance to actors preparing to do this scene. However, in describing the drawing room of Aston-Adey, Maugham makes a more significant observation:

It is not a house, but a place. Its owner takes a great pride in it, and there is nothing in the room which is not of the [Georgian] period. Through the French windows at the back can be seen the beautiful gardens which are one of the features.[3]

The situation in the play is that Arnold has a wife who is very much younger than he is (she is twenty-five) and who is thinking of leaving him. She finds being married to Arnold a lot like living in a museum, which is virtually what Arnold's home is like.

Arnold's mother deserted his father when Arnold was only five years old. She ran off with Lord Porteous, who at the time was destined for a fine career in politics, possibly even as a future prime minister. Now in much the same way, Arnold's wife (Elizabeth) is thinking of deserting him for a man much closer to her own age. His name is Edward (Teddy) Luton, and he is currently residing as a guest at Aston-Adey. Teddy is a planter in the Federated Malay States, and Elizabeth has begun to admire Teddy and the harsh, vigorous life he leads in Malaysia, a lifestyle that currently seems much more attractive to her than the "bloodless" one she is leading with Arnold.

In the first act, Elizabeth has taken a bold step and invited Arnold's mother and Lord Porteous to return to Aston-Adey so that she may meet them. Since thoughts of leaving Arnold have been on Elizabeth's mind, she has become fascinated with the story of Arnold's mother, who sacrificed everything for the sake of her love for Lord Porteous. Matters become further complicated when Arnold's father decides on the spur of the moment to visit Aston-Adey also, not realizing that his former wife and her husband are going to be there. When Arnold's father and mother (known in the play as Lady Kitty) are reunited, the father begins acting like a cad, and Elizabeth's sympathy for Lady Kitty begins to grow.

In the second act, from which the following scene is taken, Elizabeth decides to tell Arnold that she is leaving him (like his mother before her). Just before this scene, Lord Porteous challenges Arnold's authority as an expert on antiques by claiming that one of the chairs Arnold has purchased for Aston-Adey is a fake. Arnold leaves the room to find a book with proof that the chair is genuine. Eventually Elizabeth is left alone in the room, and when Arnold reenters, she decides to break the news.

Read the following scene very carefully. Try to visualize the action as you would for a first reading. Read it again for the technical details. Pick the character you would like to perform and read the scene a third time, making notes on the character's motivation. Then go through the scene a fourth time and do a beat breakdown for your character. (By the time you have read the scene four times, you will probably already have most of your character's lines memorized.)

ARNOLD: Hulloa! Oh, Elizabeth, I've found an illustration here of a chair which is almost identical with mine. It's dated 1750. Look!

ELIZABETH: That's very interesting.

ARNOLD: I want to show it to Porteous. (moving a chair which has been misplaced) You know, it does exasperate me the way people will not leave things alone. I no sooner put a thing in its place than somebody moves it.

ELIZABETH: It must be maddening for you.

ARNOLD: It is. You are the worst offender. I can't think why you don't take the pride that I do in the house. After all, it's one of the showplaces in the country.

ELIZABETH: I'm afraid you find me very unsatisfactory.

ARNOLD: (goodhumoredly) I don't know about that. But my two subjects are politics and decoration. I should be a perfect fool if I didn't see that you don't care two straws about either.

ELIZABETH: We haven't very much in common, Arnold, have we?

ARNOLD: I don't think you can blame me for that.

ELIZABETH: I don't. I blame you for nothing. I have no fault to find with you.

ARNOLD: (surprised at her significant tone) Good gracious me! What's the meaning of all this?

ELIZABETH: Well, I don't think there's any object in beating about the bush. I want you to let me go.

ARNOLD: Go where?

ELIZABETH: Away for always.

ARNOLD: My dear child, what *are* you talking about?

ELIZABETH: I want to be free.

ARNOLD: (amused rather than disconcerted) Don't be ridiculous, darling. I daresay you're run down and want a change. I'll take you over to Paris for a fortnight if you like.

ELIZABETH: I shouldn't have spoken to you if I hadn't quite made up my mind. We've been married for three years and I don't think it's been a great success. I'm frankly bored by the life you want me to lead.

ARNOLD: Well, if you'll allow me to say so, the fault is yours. We lead a very distinguished, useful life. We know a lot of extremely nice people.

ELIZABETH: I'm quite willing to allow that the fault is mine. But how does that make it any better? I'm only twenty-five. If I've made a mistake I have time to correct it.

ARNOLD: I can't bring myself to take you very seriously.

ELIZABETH: You see, I don't love you.

ARNOLD: Well, I'm awfully sorry. But you weren't obliged to marry me. You've made your bed and I'm afraid you must lie on it.

ELIZABETH: That's one of the falsest proverbs in the English language. Why should you lie on the bed you've made if you don't want to? There's always the floor.

ARNOLD: For goodness sake, don't be funny, Elizabeth.

ELIZABETH: I've quite made up my mind to leave you, Arnold.

ARNOLD: Come, come, Elizabeth, you must be sensible. You haven't any reason to leave me.

ELIZABETH: Why should you wish to keep a woman tied to you who wants to be free?

ARNOLD: I happen to be in love with you.

ELIZABETH: You might have said that before.

ARNOLD: I thought you'd take it for granted. You can't expect a man to go on making love to his wife after three years. I'm very busy. I'm awfully keen on politics and I've worked like a dog to make this house a thing of beauty. After all, a man marries to have a home, but also because he doesn't want to be bothered with sex and all that sort of thing. I fell in love with you the first time I saw you and I've been in love ever since.

ELIZABETH: I'm sorry, but if you're not in love with a man his love doesn't mean very much to you.

ARNOLD: It's so ungrateful. I've done everything in the world for you.

ELIZABETH: You've been very kind to me. But you've asked me to lead a life I don't like and that I'm not suited for. I'm awfully sorry to cause you pain, but now you must let me go.

ARNOLD: Nonsense! I'm a good deal older than you are and I think I have a little sense. In your interests as well as in mine I'm not going to do anything of the sort.

ELIZABETH: (with a smile) How can you prevent me? You can't keep me under lock and key.

ARNOLD: Please don't talk to me as if I were a foolish child. You're my wife and you're going to remain my wife.

ELIZABETH: What sort of a life do you think we should lead? Do you think there'd be any more happiness for you than for me?

ARNOLD: But what is it precisely that you suggest?

ELIZABETH: I want you to let me divorce you.

ARNOLD: (astounded) Me? Thank you very much. Are you under the impression I'm going to sacrifice my career for a whim of yours?

ELIZABETH: How will it do that?

ARNOLD: My seat's wobbly enough as it is. [meaning "my seat in Parliament"] Do you think I'd be able to hold it if I were in a divorce case? Even if it were a put-up job, as most divorces are nowadays, it would damn me.

ELIZABETH: It's rather hard on a woman to be divorced.

ARNOLD: (with sudden suspicion) What do you mean by that? Are you in love with someone?

ELIZABETH: Yes.

ARNOLD: Who?

ELIZABETH: Teddie Luton.

             (He is astonished for a moment, then bursts into a laugh.)

ARNOLD: My poor child, how can you be so ridiculous? Why, he hasn't a bob. He's a perfectly commonplace young man. It's so absurd I can't even be angry with you.

ELIZABETH: I've fallen desperately in love with him, Arnold.

ARNOLD: Well, you'd better fall desperately out.

ELIZABETH: He wants to marry me.

ARNOLD: I daresay he does. He can go to hell.

ELIZABETH: It's no good talking like that.

ARNOLD: Is he your lover?

ELIZABETH: No, certainly not.

ARNOLD: It shows that he's a mean skunk to take advantage of my hospitality to make love to you.

ELIZABETH: He's never even kissed me.

ARNOLD: I'd try telling that to the horse marines if I were you.

ELIZABETH: It's because I wanted to do nothing shabby that I told you straight out how things were.

ARNOLD: How long have you been thinking of this?

ELIZABETH: I've been in love with Teddie ever since I knew him.

ARNOLD: And you never thought of me at all, I suppose?

ELIZABETH: Oh, yes, I did. I was miserable. But I can't help myself. I wish I loved you, but I don't.

ARNOLD: I recommend you to think very very carefully before you do anything foolish.

ELIZABETH: I have thought very carefully.

ARNOLD: By God! I don't know why I don't give you a sound hiding. I'm not sure if that wouldn't be the best thing to bring you to your senses.

ELIZABETH: Oh, Arnold, don't take it like that.

ARNOLD: How do you expect me to take it? You come to me quite calmly and say: "I've had enough of you. We've been married three years and I think I'd like to marry somebody else now. Shall I break up your home? What a bore for you! Do you mind my divorcing you? It'll smash up your career, will it? What a pity!" Oh, no, my girl, I may be a fool, but I'm not a damned fool.

Directly following this dialogue, Arnold summons Teddie into his presence and demands that he leave Aston-Adey at once. Arnold will not allow Elizabeth to divorce him, and he makes it clear that he has ways of stopping her from obtaining a divorce even if she and Teddie decide to run off together. The second act ends here. In the third act, Elizabeth eventually does leave with Teddie, but it takes her another whole act of the play to make up her mind to go. This fact suggests an important insight into Elizabeth's character. She wants to go, but she hasn't yet really made up her mind to do it. If she were ready to take off, she would merely pack her bag, thumb her nose at Arnold, and walk out the door with Teddie. But Elizabeth isn't ready for so drastic a step at the time of this scene. In fact, the scene reads as if she were really asking Arnold's permission to run off with Teddie.

Arnold, on the other hand, is determined. As soon as he sees the cost of her leaving in terms of his seat in Parliament, he is prepared to stop her. Arnold's whole purpose in life seems to be to keep things in order, from his furniture to his marriage. Therefore, we can sum up the characters' motivations for the scene in this way: Elizabeth wants Arnold to give her a divorce and Arnold wants to hold his life together. The cost for Elizabeth is her love for Teddie, but that love is apparently not yet worth the guilt she would have to endure if Arnold did not give his consent; the cost for Arnold is more specific—his entire political career would be in jeopardy if there were to be a humiliating personal scandal.

The first problem that a student actor faces in trying to prepare a scene such as this one for a class is that of creating a setting. In most acting classes, this means moving around a few chairs and a prop table or two. (Of course, even actors preparing for a fully staged production would probably not have more rehearsal furniture to use.) What is required are three or four chairs put together to make a sofa, another chair (the one Arnold refers to in the scene), and maybe a coffee table and another table in some other part of the room to indicate a fireplace or a window. For purposes of the analysis here, let us assume that there will be a "sofa" at stage right (on the left as the audience looks at the stage) and a chair at stage left (on the right as the audience sees it).

The actors now need to focus on the relationship their characters have to the environment. Fortunately, the script supplies two important clues. The first is in the way that Arnold complains about people changing the positions of things in his house; obviously, this is a man who goes around the house once a day to straighten all the pictures on the walls. The second clue is Arnold's accusation that Elizabeth doesn't care about the place the way he does. (As was stated in Chapter Three, actors should always pay particular attention to the comments characters make about each other; in this case, an actor playing Elizabeth would have to take Arnold's comment as a mandate to her to find things to do in the performance that would appear to motivate that comment.) In sum, Arnold's relationship to the environment is defined by the way he keeps trying to set things in order; Elizabeth's relationship is probably more like that of a person who uses a room to live in. She wouldn't put her feet up on the coffee table, but she's not afraid to make herself comfortable. Since this is a realistic play and since the characters' various relationships to the environment are important, some hand props will be useful also. Perhaps there are magazines on the coffee table, a vase of flowers on the table by the window, and a pillow or two on the sofa; such articles would give Arnold things to straighten up during the earlier part of the scene. (The articles could all be pantomimed if desired.)

The second problem the actors have to deal with is playing the relationships. Since the nature of the *Need* relationships have already been clarified, we must now focus on the *Who* and the *What*. In the case of a classroom scene, there isn't going to be much that students can do in the area of dressing the *Who*, but they probably can costume themselves to some degree. The illusion of this scene can be strengthened if they will make some attempt at costumes that express some aspect of their characters' identities. It is not necessary in a classroom to find clothing that is correct for the period, but it is desirable, at least in a case like this, for Elizabeth to wear a dress and Arnold to wear a jacket of some kind. Furthermore, the actors would be well advised to costume themselves in ways that suggest their ages and, if possible, economic status. Arnold should be dressed very conservatively, if at all possible, and Elizabeth might consider wearing something that suggests her desire for a more exciting life.

The text supplies some important clues about the nature of the *What* relationship as well. They are, of course, husband and wife, but that is not the only significant fact. Arnold admits that he takes Elizabeth for granted; he's involved with politics and interior decoration, and demonstrating his affection for his wife hardly seems necessary to him; nor does he feel he really has time for it. Elizabeth says that she is bored with the life he expects her to lead. These clues translate into physical ideas very easily. Because they are husband and wife, there has got to be a certain close physical proximity established between them and some casual physical contact. Arnold's comments about taking her for granted can be put into physical terms by very casual pats and little hugs and other mechanical gestures of affection that appear to be obligatory and not deeply felt. Elizabeth, for her part, should be unresponsive to such overtures, even disdainful. Eventually she must work to put some distance between herself and Arnold, but whenever he starts looking hurt and angry, she has to respond by moving close to him to show the kind of feeling that she still does have for him.

The third problem the student actors have is breaking down the scene into its component beats. Knowing where the important beat changes are is an important prerequisite for planning the movements for the scene. Therefore, the actors should do beat breakdowns before blocking the scene, but they ought to get together to discuss the scene and how they want to play it before they start to work individually on their own parts. Both this scene and the one from *The Importance of Being Earnest* have few clues for action in them. The actors will have to rely heavily on the beats to suggest appropriate actions to play.

If you have not already done so, do a beat breakdown for the character of Elizabeth or Arnold before reading on. After you have done a list of beats for your character and noted the places where the objectives change in the script, look at the sample beat breakdown and the list of beats that follows.

1

ARNOLD:	Hulloa! Oh, Elizabeth, I've found an illustration here of a chair which is almost identical with mine. It's dated 1750. Look!
ELIZABETH:	That's very interesting.
ARNOLD:	I want to show it to Porteous.

2

ELIZABETH:	(moving a chair which has been misplaced) You know, it does exasperate me the way people will not leave things alone. I no sooner put a thing in its place than somebody moves it.
ELIZABETH:	It must be maddening for you.
ARNOLD:	It is. You are the worst offender. I can't think why you don't take the pride that I do in the house. After all, it's one of the showplaces in the country.
ELIZABETH:	I'm afraid you find me very unsatisfactory.
ARNOLD:	(goodhumoredly) I don't know about that. But my two subjects are politics and decoration. I should be a perfect fool if I didn't see that you don't care two straws about either.
ELIZABETH:	We haven't very much in common, Arnold, have we?
ARNOLD:	I don't think you can blame me for that.
ELIZABETH:	I don't. I blame you for nothing. I have no fault to find with you.

3

ARNOLD:	(surprised at her significant tone) Good gracious me! What's the meaning of all this?
ELIZABETH:	Well, I don't think there's any object in beating about the bush. I want you to let me go.
ARNOLD:	Go where?
ELIZABETH:	Away for always.
ARNOLD:	My dear child, what *are* you talking about?
ELIZABETH:	I want to be free.

4

ARNOLD:	(amused rather than disconcerted) Don't be ridiculous, darling. I daresay you're run down and want a change. I'll take you over to Paris for a fortnight if you like.
ELIZABETH:	I shouldn't have spoken to you if I hadn't quite made up my mind. We've been married for three years and I don't think it's been a great success. I'm frankly bored by the life you want me to lead.
ARNOLD:	Well, if you'll allow me to say so, the fault is yours. We lead a very distinguished, useful life. We know a lot of extremely nice people.
ELIZABETH:	I'm quite willing to allow that the fault is mine. But how does that make it any better? I'm only twenty-five. If I've made a mistake I have time to correct it.
ARNOLD:	I can't bring myself to take you very seriously.
ELIZABETH:	You see, I don't love you.

5

ARNOLD:	Well, I'm awfully sorry. But you weren't obliged to marry me. You've made your bed and I'm afraid you must lie on it.
ELIZABETH:	That's one of the falsest proverbs in the English language. Why should you lie on the bed you've made if you don't want to? There's always the floor.
ARNOLD:	For goodness sake, don't be funny, Elizabeth.
ELIZABETH:	I've quite made up my mind to leave you, Arnold.
ARNOLD:	Come, come, Elizabeth, you must be sensible. You haven't any reason to leave me.
ELIZABETH:	Why should you wish to keep a woman tied to you who wants to be free?

	ARNOLD:	I happen to be in love with you.
	ELIZABETH:	You might have said that before.
	ARNOLD:	I thought you'd take it for granted. You can't expect a man to go on making love to his wife after three years. I'm very busy. I'm awfully keen on politics and I've worked like a dog to make this house a thing of beauty. After all, a man marries to have a home, but also because he doesn't want to be bothered with sex and all that sort of thing. I fell in love with you the first time I saw you and I've been in love ever since.
	ELIZABETH:	I'm sorry, but if you're not in love with a man his love doesn't mean very much to you.
	ARNOLD:	It's so ungrateful. I've done everything in the world for you.
6	ELIZABETH:	You've been very kind to me. But you've asked me to lead a life I don't like and that I'm not suited for. I'm awfully sorry to cause you pain, but now you must let me go.
	ARNOLD:	Nonsense! I'm a good deal older than you are and I think I have a little sense. In your interests as well as in mine I'm not going to do anything of the sort.
	ELIZABETH:	(with a smile) How can you prevent me? You can't keep me under lock and key.
	ARNOLD:	Please don't talk to me as if I were a foolish child. You're my wife and you're going to remain my wife.
	ELIZABETH:	What sort of a life do you think we should lead? Do you think there'd be any more happiness for you than for me?
7	ARNOLD:	But what is it precisely that you suggest?
	ELIZABETH:	I want you to let me divorce you.
	ARNOLD:	(astounded) Me? Thank you very much. Are you under the impression I'm going to sacrifice my career for a whim of yours?
8	ELIZABETH:	How will it do that?
	ARNOLD:	My seat's wobbly enough as it is. [meaning "my seat in Parliament"] Do you think I'd be able to hold it if I were in a divorce case? Even if it were a put-up job, as most divorces are nowadays, it would damn me.
	ELIZABETH:	It's rather hard on a woman to be divorced.
	ARNOLD:	(with sudden suspicion) What do you mean by that? Are you in love with someone?
9	ELIZABETH:	Yes.
	ARNOLD:	Who?
	ELIZABETH:	Teddie Luton.
		(He is astonished for a moment, then bursts into a laugh.)
10	ARNOLD:	My poor child, how can you be so ridiculous? Why, he hasn't a bob. He's a perfectly commonplace young man. It's so absurd I can't even be angry with you.
	ELIZABETH:	I've fallen desperately in love with him, Arnold.
11	ARNOLD:	Well, you'd better fall desperately out.
	ELIZABETH:	He wants to marry me.
	ARNOLD:	I daresay he does. He can go to hell.
	ELIZABETH:	It's no good talking like that.
12	ARNOLD:	Is he your lover?
	ELIZABETH:	No, certainly not.
	ARNOLD:	It shows that he's a mean skunk to take advantage of my hospitality to make love to you.
	ELIZABETH:	He's never even kissed me.
	ARNOLD:	I'd try telling that to the horse marines if I were you.

	ELIZABETH:	It's because I wanted to do nothing shabby that I told you straight out how things were.
	ARNOLD:	How long have you been thinking of this?
12	ELIZABETH:	I've been in love with Teddie ever since I knew him.
	ARNOLD:	And you never thought of me at all, I suppose?
	ELIZABETH:	Oh, yes, I did. I was miserable. But I can't help myself. I wish I loved you, but I don't.
	ARNOLD:	I recommend you to think very very carefully before you do anything foolish.
	ELIZABETH:	I have thought very carefully.
	ARNOLD:	By God! I don't know why I don't give you a sound hiding. I'm not sure if that wouldn't be the best thing to bring you to your senses.
13	ELIZABETH:	Oh, Arnold, don't take it like that.
	ARNOLD:	How do you expect me to take it? You come to me quite calmly and say: "I've had enough of you. We've been married three years and I think I'd like to marry somebody else now. Shall I break up your home? What a bore for you! Do you mind my divorcing you? It'll smash up your career, will it? What a pity!" Oh, no, my girl, I may be a fool, but I'm not a damned fool.

FIGURE 7-1. Arnold's Beats.

THE CIRCLE: Arnold's Beats

The numbers correspond to the division of the scene that appears as Figure 7–1.

1. I am trying to get Elizabeth excited about my chair by showing her the picture in the magazine. (Actually, Arnold's first beat is his coming into the room to compare the chair with the picture; in performance, that would be the first beat the actor would play, but trying to get Elizabeth excited about the chair is the first beat directly derived from the script.)
2. I am trying to make Elizabeth feel guilty by chastising her.
3. I am trying to find out what's bothering her by asking.
4. I am trying to make her stop bothering me by humoring her. (Although it doesn't say so in the script, his condescending tone suggests he might go back to comparing his chair with the picture in the magazine.)
5. I am trying to put her in her place by lecturing her (rather like a father disciplining a naughty child).
6. I am trying to make her feel guilty by reasoning with her. (As late as this beat in the scene Arnold still has not grasped what Elizabeth is trying to tell him).
7. I am trying to find out what she wants by asking. (This is the first point in the scene at which Arnold seems to be fully aware that something out of the ordinary is going on.)
8. I am trying to put her in her place by impressing her with the seriousness of what she's suggesting.
9. I am trying to find out if there's another man by asking.
10. I am trying to hurt her feelings by ridiculing her.
11. I am trying to straighten her out by threatening her.

12. I am trying to make her feel guilty by talking tough.
13. I am trying to change her mind by threatening her.

A quick survey of these beats suggests that Arnold isn't a very nice guy. Three times the beat has to do with trying to make Elizabeth feel guilty about her conduct; twice he tries to put her in her place, and he makes several veiled threats as well. This all sounds pretty serious, but the actor must remember that this is a comedy. A husband who has to work this hard to create such negative effects on his wife is not a very strong character. His fury is impotent. When he resorts to clichés like "mean skunk" and "tell it to the marines" to express the full measure of his anger, he makes himself look quite ridiculous. The most telling indicator of his feelings for his wife is the length of time it takes to grasp fully what she is trying to tell him.

	ARNOLD:	Hulloa! Oh, Elizabeth, I've found an illustration here of a chair which is almost identical with mine. It's dated 1750. Look!
	ELIZABETH:	That's very interesting.
	ARNOLD:	I want to show it to Porteous. (moving a chair which has been misplaced) You know, it does exasperate me the way people will not leave things alone. I no sooner put a thing in its place than somebody moves it.
	ELIZABETH:	It must be maddening for you.
1	ARNOLD:	It is. You are the worst offender. I can't think why you don't take the pride that I do in the house. After all, it's one of the showplaces in the country.
	ELIZABETH:	I'm afraid you find me very unsatisfactory.
	ARNOLD:	(goodhumoredly) I don't know about that. But my two subjects are politics and decoration. I should be a perfect fool if I didn't see that you don't care two straws about either.
	ELIZABETH:	We haven't very much in common, Arnold, have we?
	ARNOLD:	I don't think you can blame me for that.
	ELIZABETH:	I don't. I blame you for nothing. I have no fault to find with you.
	ARNOLD:	(surprised at her significant tone) Good gracious me! What's the meaning of all this?
	ELIZABETH:	Well, I don't think there's any object in beating about the bush. I want you to let me go.
	ARNOLD:	Go where?
	ELIZABETH:	Away for always.
2	ARNOLD:	My dear child, what *are* you talking about?
	ELIZABETH:	I want to be free.
	ARNOLD:	(amused rather than disconcerted) Don't be ridiculous, darling. I daresay you're run down and want a change. I'll take you over to Paris for a fortnight if you like.
	ELIZABETH:	I shouldn't have spoken to you if I hadn't quite made up my mind. We've been married for three years and I don't think it's been a great success. I'm frankly bored by the life you want me to lead.
3	ARNOLD:	Well, if you'll allow me to say so, the fault is yours. We lead a very distinguished, useful life. We know a lot of extremely nice people.
	ELIZABETH:	I'm quite willing to allow that the fault is mine. But how does that make

3

it any better? I'm only twenty-five. If I've made a mistake I have time to correct it.

ARNOLD: I can't bring myself to take you very seriously.

4

ELIZABETH: You see, I don't love you.

ARNOLD: Well, I'm awfully sorry. But you weren't obliged to marry me. You've made your bed and I'm afraid you must lie on it.

5

ELIZABETH: That's one of the falsest proverbs in the English language. Why should you lie on the bed you've made if you don't want to? There's always the floor.

ARNOLD: For goodness sake, don't be funny, Elizabeth.

ELIZABETH: I've quite made up my mind to leave you, Arnold.

ARNOLD: Come, come, Elizabeth, you must be sensible. You haven't any reason to leave me.

ELIZABETH: Why should you wish to keep a woman tied to you who wants to be free?

ARNOLD: I happen to be in love with you.

6

ELIZABETH: You might have said that before.

ARNOLD: I thought you'd take it for granted. You can't expect a man to go on making love to his wife after three years. I'm very busy. I'm awfully keen on politics and I've worked like a dog to make this house a thing of beauty. After all, a man marries to have a home, but also because he doesn't want to be bothered with sex and all that sort of thing. I fell in love with you the first time I saw you and I've been in love ever since.

ELIZABETH: I'm sorry, but if you're not in love with a man his love doesn't mean very much to you.

ARNOLD: It's so ungrateful. I've done everything in the world for you.

7

ELIZABETH: You've been very kind to me. But you've asked me to lead a life I don't like and that I'm not suited for. I'm awfully sorry to cause you pain, but now you must let me go.

ARNOLD: Nonsense! I'm a good deal older than you are and I think I have a little sense. In your interests as well as in mine I'm not going to do anything of the sort.

8

ELIZABETH: (with a smile) How can you prevent me? You can't keep me under lock and key.

ARNOLD: Please don't talk to me as if I were a foolish child. You're my wife and you're going to remain my wife.

9

ELIZABETH: What sort of a life do you think we should lead? Do you think there'd be any more happiness for you than for me?

ARNOLD: But what is it precisely that you suggest?

ELIZABETH: I want you to let me divorce you.

ARNOLD: (astounded) Me? Thank you very much. Are you under the impression I'm going to sacrifice my career for a whim of yours?

ELIZABETH: How will it do that?

ARNOLD: My seat's wobbly enough as it is. [meaning "my seat in Parliament"] Do you think I'd be able to hold it if I were in a divorce case? Even if it were a put-up job, as most divorces are nowadays, it would damn me.

ELIZABETH: It's rather hard on a woman to be divorced.

ARNOLD: (with sudden suspicion) What do you mean by that? Are you in love with someone?

10

ELIZABETH: Yes.

ARNOLD: Who?

	ELIZABETH:	Teddie Luton.
		(He is astonished for a moment, then bursts into a laugh.)
10	ARNOLD:	My poor child, how can you be so ridiculous? Why, he hasn't a bob. He's a perfectly commonplace young man. It's so absurd I can't even be angry with you.
	ELIZABETH:	I've fallen desperately in love with him, Arnold.
	ARNOLD:	Well, you'd better fall desperately out.
11	ELIZABETH:	He wants to marry me.
	ARNOLD:	I daresay he does. He can go to hell.
	ELIZABETH:	It's no good talking like that.
	ARNOLD:	Is he your lover?
	ELIZABETH:	No, certainly not.
	ARNOLD:	It shows that he's a mean skunk to take advantage of my hospitality to make love to you.
	ELIZABETH:	He's never even kissed me.
	ARNOLD:	I'd try telling that to the horse marines if I were you.
	ELIZABETH:	It's because I wanted to do nothing shabby that I told you straight out how things were.
	ARNOLD:	How long have you been thinking of this?
12	ELIZABETH:	I've been in love with Teddie ever since I knew him.
	ARNOLD:	And you never thought of me at all, I suppose?
	ELIZABETH:	Oh, yes, I did. I was miserable. But I can't help myself. I wish I loved you, but I don't.
	ARNOLD:	I recommend you to think very very carefully before you do anything foolish.
	ELIZABETH:	I have thought very carefully.
	ARNOLD:	By God! I don't know why I don't give you a sound hiding. I'm not sure if that wouldn't be the best thing to bring you to your senses.
	ELIZABETH:	Oh, Arnold, don't take it like that.
13	ARNOLD:	How do you expect me to take it? You come to me quite calmly and say: "I've had enough of you. We've been married three years and I think I'd like to marry somebody else now. Shall I break up your home? What a bore for you! Do you mind my divorcing you? It'll smash up your career, will it? What a pity!" Oh, no, my girl, I may be a fool, but I'm not a damned fool.

FIGURE 7-2.   Elizabeth's Beats.

THE CIRCLE: Elizabeth's Beats

The numbers correspond to the division of the scene that appears as Figure 7–2.

1. I am trying to get Arnold's attention by blaming myself. (In effect, Elizabeth is really putting on an act of being contrite; that is, the actor must play a character who is playing a character.)
2. I am trying to make Arnold understand what I want by announcing it.
3. I am trying to make Arnold understand what I want by reasoning with him.
4. I am trying to make Arnold understand what I want by spelling it out for him.
5. I am trying to make Arnold understand what I want by arguing with him.

6. I am trying to make Arnold understand what I want by demonstrating my feelings for him.
7. I am trying to make Arnold feel better by taking the blame on myself.
8. I am trying to get him to let me go by threatening him. (The threat is subtextual, and the line could be interpreted differently except for Maugham's stage direction.)
9. I am trying to get him to let me go by reasoning with him.
10. I am trying to get him to let me go by shocking him.
11. I am trying to get him to take me seriously by standing up to him.
12. I am trying to convince Arnold that Teddie is not my lover by denying the accusation.
13. I am trying to make Arnold feel better by showing my sympathy.

Elizabeth's beats reflect the difficulty she has in getting Arnold's attention. Notice how the strategy escalates each time she tries to make Arnold understand what she wants. Notice also that things seem to get a lot rougher when her objective changes to the more forceful attempt to get him to let her go. Her lack of resolve is reflected in her two attempts, however brief, to cheer up Arnold; also, her penultimate beat in the scene has her in effect denying the intensity of her feelings for Teddie.

THE CIRCLE: Staging the Scene for Class

From the analysis of the beat changes, the actors should be able to evolve ideas for staging the scene easily. The scene opens with Elizabeth onstage; since she is waiting for her husband to enter the room so that she can drop a bomb on his domestic life, she will probably not want to be seated. Perhaps she might want to pace or otherwise move about nervously for a moment or two before the actor playing Arnold enters. Perhaps also there is a small table in the performing area to designate one of the windows that Maugham has mentioned in the description of the setting. Perhaps she might end up by that table as if looking out of the window. Arnold's first beat clearly requires him to cross to her to show her the picture (see fig. 7–3); he would undoubtedly want to stand very close to her to reinforce the relationship as husband and wife. On his second beat, he would have to move to the chair to put it back in place. Elizabeth's first five lines in the play are very terse; she reponds to Arnold very abruptly as she tries to get his attention. Perhaps, then, she would choose not to move from her position by the window as she plays her first beat. During Arnold's second beat, he might move about the room to straighten various objects. At the beginning of his third beat, he would stop what he was doing and turn his full focus on Elizabeth to find out what she wants.

At the beginning of Elizabeth's second beat, she should move toward Arnold as she makes her announcement. But he misses the meaning of her

FIGURE 7-3.   A Scene from *The Circle*.   *At the beginning of the scene, Arnold tries to get Elizabeth interested in the picture in the book. Notice how she is focused on his face, watching for some recognition of the information that she is trying to communicate to him through her physical attitude.*

words entirely; perhaps, as suggested, he turns back to his chair to compare it with the picture. As Elizabeth begins her third beat, a continuation of the second, she might move closer to Arnold, approaching the spot where he is kneeling by his precious antique. Perhaps he continues to be too busy to notice. (See fig. 7–4.)

At the beginning of Elizabeth's fourth beat, she might move herself into Arnold's sightline or grab his arm or take his magazine away from him—anything to get him to look at her. With Arnold's next beat, he turns into a father lecturing his naughty child; at the very least he has to stand up in order to condescend to her from a proper height. But Elizabeth appears to respond to his strategy in a hostile manner. She probably moves away from him, moving more quickly and with more intensity as she tries to argue. Before Arnold's sixth beat, he has to cross to wherever she happens to be standing, perhaps touching her arm or shoulders in order to be emphatic as he declares his love for her. Elizabeth responds to this beat by moving away to show that she no longer cares for him. But Arnold is beginning to act hurt now. Perhaps he even moves to sit on the sofa as he berates her for her

FIGURE 7-4. A Scene from *The Circle.* *Arnold compares his chair to the picture of the book. Elizabeth continues to try to get Arnold's attention.*

ingratitude. (Sitting and pouting might help to make her feel guilty.) This movement would motivate Elizabeth to sit next to him at the beginning of her seventh beat as she tries to make him feel better. (See fig. 7-5.)

Elizabeth's attempt to cheer up Arnold does not meet with success, nor does Arnold's attempt to make Elizabeth feel more guilty. Perhaps growing irritated with his methods, she plays her eighth beat. If she had been leaning forward to show concern for Arnold previously, she will definitely want to back away now, both to put some distance between them and to appear more villainous as she reminds him that he can't lock her up. But that strategy doesn't work on Arnold either as he continues to try to make her feel more guilty. On her ninth beat, Elizabeth's body position probably changes again; perhaps she moves toward him once more, her hands extended toward him as she tries to reason with him.

Finally, worn down by the attempt to induce guilt in Elizabeth, Arnold turns to face her and asks simply on his seventh beat what it is that she wants. She remains calmly rational, but he undoubtedly jumps up in astonishment at the news, making wild gestures to emphasize the seriousness of the situation. Perhaps he even paces a bit to express his inner turmoil. If his move-

FIGURE 7-5.   A Scene from *The Circle.*   *As Arnold pouts, Elizabeth tries to comfort him. Note how the intimate distance and the touching suggest how she still has a Need for him, even while she is asking him for a divorce.*

ments were to take him to the opposite end of the couch from where she is sitting, he would be in a good position to lean over its back edge at the beginning of his ninth beat as he tries to find out if there is another man in her life. In response, she undoubtedly would sit up again, stiffening herself against the howl of outrage that she thinks is coming. There is a tense face-off.

But the howl of outrage turns into a burst of laughter, according to Maugham. Suddenly cheerful and smiling again, Arnold pushes off from the back of the couch, perhaps sitting on the edge as he says his lines to show his contempt for what Elizabeth has said. It is her turn to be outraged, and at the beginning of her eleventh beat, she undoubtedly stands up and steps around to confront Arnold where he is sitting. But in a surprise move, he suddenly stops laughing and stands up virtually in her face to start his eleventh beat to straighten her out by threatening her.

Almost as quickly as the face-off begins, it is over. Arnold's threatening posture softens—he is the wronged man again as he demands to know if Teddie is her lover. In response, her posture changes also; no longer on the offensive, she is now trying to convince her husband of the truth of the situation. Perhaps Arnold again begins to move around, maybe even crossing to his precious chair, now identified as his special pride and joy. (The chair is, at this point, the only friend in the room that he has.) Elizabeth's movements must follow Arnold's as she tries to keep his attention. Perhaps Arnold's spirits seem to collapse when he says, "And you never thought of me at all, I suppose," and he actually sits on the precious chair.

After a moment, Arnold's mood appears to darken again as he faces Elizabeth, leaning toward her to threaten her on his thirteenth beat. Seeing the suffering in his eyes, Elizabeth's resolve cracks again and, on her thirteenth beat, she moves toward him to touch him; but he pushes her away as he finishes his tirade: ". . . I may be a fool, but I'm not a damned fool." Curtain.

Having blocked the scene in this manner, you are now ready to rehearse it for performance. The next step is to memorize the lines and then to run through the scene a few more times to set the blocking and the business. Finally, the game plan established, the actors are free to focus on the actual objectives themselves. Try now to imagine yourself as the actor playing the role of Elizabeth, following the mental process involved in actually playing the objectives in a performance.

THE CIRCLE: Elizabeth Performs the Scene

The first moment of the scene includes a period of being onstage alone in which you must pass the time while waiting for the actor playing Arnold to make his entrance. Here again is a beat that must be played but that is not directly indicated in the script. This beat is tricky to handle well because there is no one else onstage to use as an obstacle for an objective, and yet human beings are never without objectives for the conscious mind to play. The solution is not to perform some elaborate pantomime to suggest nervous waiting—thumbing through magazines or pretending to rearrange the throw pillows or the like. The audience is going to know that such efforts are all for effect. The solution is for us to find an activity that an Elizabeth in such a situation might actually be performing at such a moment, and then to perform that activity deliberately and consciously with conviction. Perhaps Elizabeth might be rehearsing what she was going to say to Arnold, or perhaps she might be thinking about Teddie and what kind of a life they might be going to have together. You will choose to rehearse different speeches in your head, and as you are planning what to say, you move over toward the table slightly upstage and to the stage right of the couch (that is, to the audience's left). If you do this correctly, you should be so involved in the reality of your thoughts that you will not be aware of Arnold's entrance. Ideally, you might even be startled by his first line.

When Arnold finally speaks, you begin to focus on trying to get his attention. (It is probably a measure of Elizabeth's immaturity that Maugham has her go about this business in such an awkward way, but you must not be concerned with trying to play awkwardness; an objective is an objective, and every objective must be played with conviction.) You look at Arnold as he crosses to you with his magazine; you listen to what he says; you are unpleasantly surprised when he puts his hand on your arm in his enthusiasm about the picture. When you speak, you do so as coldly as possible—a tone so cold that only a insensitive moron could miss the point that something is wrong.

But Arnold goes right on babbling about his chair. You study his face, searching for some indication that he has noticed how you just spoke to him. Suddenly, he heads for the chair, making more of his snide remarks about how nobody ever puts things back where he left them. Overbearing snob! You speak again, using your coldest tone, even more emphatically trying to get him to notice you. Still he keeps babbling on about how you don't take pride in this dusty old museum, how he loves his politics and interior decoration. Good grief! When is he going to notice you? Finally, you say, "I blame you for nothing. I have no fault to find with you." Suddenly, his focus turns away from his chair—he looks at you. Now he's paying attention. "What's the meaning of all this?" he asks.

You feel a certain fleeting moment of satisfaction; all the tension that had been building up in your effort to get his attention is now relaxed. But you have a specific piece of information you want Arnold to understand. You step forward to make your announcement. You watch his face, searching his eyes for a glint of recognition that is not immediately forthcoming. You have to announce it all again: "I want to be free." Nowhere does his face betray the slightest suggestion of understanding. He turns back toward his chair. You have failed. He has misunderstood you completely.

Now you continue to move forward. The fact that he is not looking at you is very irritating. How can you make someone understand something when he isn't even giving you the courtesy of looking at you? You reason with him, but he responds, "I can't bring myself to take you very seriously."

Suddenly, an inspiration born out of desperation occurs to you. If he won't take you seriously, at least he takes that damn chair seriously. Desperate measures are called for. You sit on his chair. He looks at you, shocked. You stare right into his eyes, and slowly and deliberately, you say, "You see, I don't love you."

But the plan backfires. He was apparently so upset at having his precious chair violated in this way that he now becomes even more pompous than before. He stands and pushes you out of his chair—and you don't particularly like being pushed around. He is now lecturing you—and you don't particularly like being lectured to. You are becoming angry now—he's much denser than you might ever have imagined. You pace around—you hear him quote that old cliché about making the bed and lying in it, and you try to turn his words back on him. He senses your irritation and tells you to be sensible. Again, you argue. How can anyone be so infuriatingly stupid!

Now something happens that takes you totally by surprise. Arnold reaches out and touches you, tenderly. "I happen to be in love with you." This is particularly irritating because it is precisely what he never says to you; why does he choose this particular moment to make that little declaration? You are momentarily thrown off guard, but you recover your poise. He has to understand that the time for that sort of thing is all over now. You must show him that you have no feelings for him anymore, and therefore, you pull away. He goes on professing love, but then he sits on the couch, pouting. You can see that you are beginning to hurt him. Why does he have to make this so difficult? You listen to his words, his tone of voice. You must not allow yourself to be affected by it. You answer him coldly again; he must not be allowed to think that this tactic is going to work. He has to understand your feelings toward him. But he continues to act hurt, and his act is beginning to affect you. You don't want to hurt him, just divorce him.

After a moment you sit down next to him on the couch. You try to be consoling, but suddenly he begins to get rigid again. Obviously he is feeling hurt, but he has not been threatened by anything you have said or done so far. The time has come to escalate. You lean back in a kittenish manner; you must remind him that he must give in to your will or face the consequences. But again he lectures you like a child. His tone of voice and that superior look on his face are positively infuriating. You decide to drop the pose and lean in. He's got to listen to reason. After a moment, Arnold looks at you in a way that he has not looked at you before in the scene—really looking, really focused on you. He says, "But what is it precisely that you suggest?" Indeed, the reasonable approach seems to be getting results. You answer his question.

He jumps up, astounded. He has certainly grasped the idea now! His voice is loud, strident. He is playing this for all it's worth. You will not be drawn into this display of temper; your response continues to be cool, rational. He paces around, sputtering with rage. Suddenly, he stops as if a new thought has struck him. He leans over the back of the couch toward you. "Are you in love with someone?"

You look away. This is the question you had been hoping he would not ask. But since he has asked it, he shall have the answer. You sit up; you make yourself ready for the explosion to come. If he didn't like hearing about the divorce, he's really not going to like being thrown over for Teddie Luton. Grimly prepared now, you answer him. You watch his eyes, waiting for the fuse to burn down to the powder.

But he surprises you again. No explosion! Instead the miserable little weasel is laughing at you! This really hurts. Nothing you say or do seems to make him take you seriously. Well, you'll just straighten him out! You stand and move around the edge of the couch to confront him. He will take you seriously or else.

He surprises you again by standing up suddenly. You are virtually nose to nose. You stay firm. You look into his face searching for some sign that he has grasped the need to give you the divorce. But what you perceive in his expression is something else again; suddenly his whole posture softens. "Is he your lover?" he demands to know. The word *lover* splashes over your anger like cold water. The very idea! Who does he think you are? What is he attempting to accuse you of? He sputters some more and eventually collapses into his precious chair with more of that hurt look on his face. You are shocked; it's as if he had accused you of being unfaithful! You must convince him of the truth of the situation: You have not deceived him; you have been very honorable. He must believe you! This is agony! You didn't really want to hurt him like this.

Finally, his whole demeanor changes again. You sense his posture stiffening. He starts threatening you. You can't stand to see him suffer like this. You move toward him to touch him—he's taking this all wrong! But he pushes you away. You listen to him wallowing in self-pity. "Shall I break up your home? What a bore for you!" he mocks. You would give anything to take this all back again. What a disaster!

. . . And suddenly the scene is finished. The acting stops, the illusion vanishes, and the game is over.

Some people might conclude that the process as described here is close to that of self-hypnosis. Actually, nothing could be further from the truth, any more than football players become hypnotized while playing a football game. The opposite effect is more the case: The actor's senses become heightened in order to take in as much as possible of what the other actor is really saying and doing at each moment in the scene. It is that sense of really looking at and really listening to the other person that this description has attempted to capture. And because the actor's conscious attention is preoccupied with the moment-to-moment reality of the scene, he or she cannot be thinking about what is going to happen next. Several times in this fictional attempt to be in Elizabeth's mind, we have seen how Arnold's behavior was surprising and unexpected, and those surprises fuel the actor's energy and sense of involvement.

SUMMARY

In performance, how the actor links together the various objectives becomes an important indicator of the quality of the performance. The moments of transition between the objectives are called *beat changes*.

One type of beat change indicates that the objective has either met with failure or success and there will be no further attempt to seek the desired result. The other type of beat change indicates that the objective was interrupted or suspended and that the person plans to attempt to achieve the same desired result again. Of the two, the second type is particularly important. When repeated attempts are made to achieve the same desired result, the effect is that of recurring beats with increasing cost, which help to build the audience's interest and the actor's intensity.

In rehearsal, the actor roughs out all the major beat changes that are indicated by the dialogue. In performance, the actor guarantees the spontaneity and integrity of the beat changes by focusing on the specific details of what the other actors are doing. As a result, the actor is able to forget how the attempt to achieve each objective in turn is going to turn out. By focusing on the reality of the other actors in this way, each actor becomes involved with the reality of the objectives—just as football players become involved with the reality of their opponents' movements during each play of the game.

EXERCISES FOR CHAPTER SEVEN

The two most important principles covered in this chapter are the way the beat changes determine the nature of the beats and how the actor must concentrate on what is happening in the performance to block out any knowledge of what is going to happen next. The following exercises are designed to help actors improve their abilities in these areas.

1. Develop a pantomime based on the idea of repeated attempts to achieve the same objective (that is, recurring objectives). Choose an objective that allows the possibility of repeated attempts that can end in failure, such as the following:

   Trying to make the toaster (or any other kitchen appliance) work
   Trying to stop the faucet in the sink from leaking
   Trying to fit too many suitcases into the trunk of the car
   Trying to open a jar or a drawer that is stuck
   Trying to carry too many items from one place to another

   Build up the circumstances (the situation and your character identity) and set the cost for these objectives at a moderately high level in order to motivate your repeated attempts. Use the "If-I-Were" formula to put yourself into the situation so that you can play it with conviction. The story may end with either success or failure, but in either case be sure to play a completed beat at the end.

   Perform your pantomime for an audience, and afterward ask them to comment on your beat changes. Could they tell absolutely the moments at which you changed strategy? Could they see the cost rising as repeated attempts were made? Were there any moments that they didn't believe? Any suggestions for improvement?

2. Try the following improvised scene, similar to the story of the man looking for beer in the refrigerator: Imagine yourself in a situation in which you are searching for something, an exercise that will require you to repeat the same or similar actions but with different objectives:

You are a scholar in a library who is looking for a particular piece of information.

You are a secretary in an office who is looking for a missing file.

You are a man in his own garage who is looking for a particular tool to accomplish a particular job.

You are a customer in a shoe store who is looking for a particular type of shoe.

In each case, your initial objective (like that of the man and the refrigerator) meets with failure, and therefore you have to keep changing objectives while your essential actions remain the same (looking at books, going through drawers, examining shoes, and so on.)

Plan to work with another actor in this scene to provide two or more interruptions. The scholar might be interrupted by another scholar also looking for a book; the secretary might be interrupted by a boss or another secretary; the man might be interrupted by his wife; the customer might be interrupted by a salesperson or another customer. These interruptions should not be rehearsed; the actor causing the interruptions should enter the scene at random. After each interruption, you must remember to return to the objective you were playing previously but with renewed intensity. The scene should end with success in whatever your final objective turns out to be.

Ask your audience if your beat changes were clear or if you seemed to be performing one long, muddy action. Ask if they understood the different objectives you were playing. Ask if the audience perceived your cost increasing as the scene continued. Ask also if they can suggest any improvements in the way you differentiated the beats from each other.

3. The following sequence of dialogue is essentially nonsense:

    A: Seventeen is my lucky number.
    B: People make their own luck.
    A: People have trouble with unexpected events.
    B: The unexpected can be good or bad.
    A: Bad news is never lucky.
    B: Good news can be bad for some people.
    A: Some people make their own good news.
    B: Seventeen is my number for good news.

    Learn these lines in sequence so that you can play the role of either A or B. Using these lines, perform the following exercise: Assume the role of A and build up the details of a scene in your mind—a situation, an identity, and an objective. For example, you could be a spy trying to make the other person say a password. You could be trying to pick up someone in a bar. You could be trying to sell a customer a book about luck. You could be a psychiatrist interviewing a patient. Whatever details you choose, try to set the cost moderately high.

    For performance, the person playing B will remain seated throughout the scene. You will begin the scene with an entrance. (Remember to motivate your blocking by playing the situation.) B will not know the details of your scene, and therefore B's responses to your line readings will be unpredictable. Your task is to pay attention to every detail of how B speaks and responds to you. You must then try to infer the meaning of B's line readings and play your objectives accordingly.

Since the dialogue begins and ends with similar statements, you can continue the conversation by repeating your first line. Try to play the scene until your initial objective is completed, either by failure or success.

Reverse roles and play the same scene with someone else but with yourself playing the role of B. Do several such improvisations, and discuss them later with your partners. Try to isolate the moments when you really were paying attention to what your partner was doing and the moments when you really were not.

4. Have your instructor or a friend take a short scene that you have not seen before and prepare sides for you. The sides should contain your own lines and the last three or four words of each of the other person's lines. Have your instructor or friend tell you the details of the situation and the identities of the characters but not what the other person is going to do or say. When you get your side, you will probably be able to figure out much of that information for yourself in general, but you will not know exactly what is going to happen.

Work with your lines until you feel you know them, and then prepare to perform the scene with another actor. The two of you need to agree in advance on the details of the setting and any technical blocking that is demanded by the action, but otherwise do not block out the action in any specific detail. Then perform the scene.

The purpose of this exercise is not to give a brilliant performance—impossible under the circumstances. It is to make you aware of the process of listening and paying attention to your partner. After your performance, discuss the results with your partner. Note the moments when you really were paying attention and how you may have adjusted your line readings to accommodate the sense of something your partner did.

Repeat the exercise two or three more times. As the blocking and the other person's lines become increasingly familiar to you, try to maintain the same degree of heightened observation that you had in the first run-through.

NOTES

1. Sonia Moore, *The Stanislavski System: The Professional Training of an Actor* (New York, Penguin Books, 1965), p. 22.

2. W. Somerset Maugham, *The Circle* in *Three Comedies of W. Somerset Maugham* (New York: Washington Square Press, 1969), p. 5.

3. Ibid.

Lesson Eight

Personality

In a complete characterization, the actor communicates information to the audience about the character's identity and personality. Identity was discussed in Chapter Four; personality is the subject of the following chapter.

By observing the way an actor plays a character's objectives, the audience develops expectations about how that character may respond in future situations. Those expectations for future behavior are, in effect, the audience's perception of that character's personality.

An audience forms these expectations either when a character goes about achieving a particular objective in an unusual way or when a character is placed in a situation in which there are several possible alternative actions. The former possibilities are created primarily by the actor; the latter are created primarily by the playwright.

In creating the illusion of personality, actors must be wary of stereotypes. Stereotypes are communicated primarily through a character's appearance; personality is communicated primarily through a character's actions. Stereotypes can be useful to actors in small or in one-dimensional roles. But stereotypes are based on fixed patterns of action and response, and in the case of longer or more complex roles, these fixed patterns can often interfere with portraying the multiple levels of motivation inherent in the characters. Lady Macbeth is not just a maniacal murderer; Othello is not just a jealous fool.

Actors must realize that personality is a function of the way the objectives are played, not the character's physical appearance alone. Establishing the character's identity and establishing the character's personality are two fundamentally different processes.

Chapter Eight

Characteristic Behavior

The process by which an actor communicates a character's identity was discussed at length in Chapter Four. Briefly, identity was described as a combination of three different types of information: the *Who*, the *What*, and the *Need*. Different strategies for communicating the information in each of these three categories were also discussed. There is yet another type of character information that was not discussed, nor could it be effectively until the concepts of beats and objectives had been introduced and examined. This category includes all the subjective attributes of a character that aren't part of the *Who* or the *What*. This category includes all the information that most people refer to when they use the word *character* in everyday life.

The word *character* is commonly used outside of the theatre in many different ways. One common usage is to designate peculiar or idiosyncratic behavior. In this sense, someone who behaves in an amusing or unconventional way is known as a "real character." Actors who specialize in certain types of roles such as gangsters or spinsters or servants are often referred to as "character" actors because their personal appearance or conventional mannerisms make them ideally suited to play such stereotypical roles. Another common usage of the word is to designate a positive personal attribute; for example, someone who displays strength of will in the face of adversity is often said to possess a lot of "character." Conversely, a person who gives in to base temptation easily may be said to have a "low character." The word is also used to designate certain tendencies to action. For example, there is Ebenezer Scrooge in *A Christmas Carol*. When he is approached to donate money for the poor, he declines to be generous. Generosity is not part of Scrooge's "character"; that is, he tends to be a miser. After Scrooge has been visited by the three spirits, his "character" changes; he becomes a very generous and outgoing man. In this last sense, *character* designates an independent psychological entity alongside *ego, temper,* and *sexuality.* All such uses of the word *character* convey information about people over and above their simple identities.

As different as these various usages of the word may be, there is one common idea that unites them. Consider the adjectives that people commonly use to describe "character": *kind, mean, happy, cooperative, selfish, intelligent, sloppy, neat, stingy, generous, thoughtful, careless, spiteful, quick, slow, bright, dim,* and (everybody's favorite all-purpose word) *nice.* Each of these terms when applied to a particular person predicts a certain way in which that person is likely to behave in the future. If a man is perceived as generous, we expect him to give in easily to requests for favors. If a woman is perceived as intelligent, we expect her to understand complex problems quickly.

To designate all such tendencies, dispositions, and eccentricities, the word *personality* will be used in the following discussion. Although *character* in its fullest sense includes what most people mean when they use the word *personality,* the former can imply other things as well. Most people use the word *personality* primarily to predict a given person's future behavior. Therefore, it will be used hereafter to refer to all character expectations that are not part of the *Who,* the *What,* and the *Need.*

In everyday life, other people's personalities may remain mysterious to us even after we have known them for a long time. In other words, just when we think we know certain people, they can surprise us. Our neighbors or our doctors or our teachers or the people from whom we buy things in stores—all of these people may have personalities (that is, may be prone to certain types of behavior) that we would never suspect on the basis of our usual dealings with them. Our neighbor may be friendly and affable beside his backyard barbecue, but then one day we learn he has been embezzling funds from his company. Our doctor may seem reserved and cold in her office, but then one day we see her at a restaurant with friends and she is laughing and outgoing. In life, most people's personalities generally remain their own business, and we tend to respect each other's privacy (although most people enjoy a juicy bit of gossip occasionally). Personality is thus a mysterious and fascinating business because we rarely get to know people well enough to be able to predict all the many ways in which they are likely to behave.

Audiences watching a play want to know as much as possible about the personality of each character, and they expect to be given that information by the actors. Part of the pleasure of going to a play (or for that matter, watching a film or reading a novel) is gained from being given insights into the mystery of other people's personalities that we would never be permitted in everyday life. In other words, communicating personality to the audience is an important goal of the art of realistic acting in general.

HOW PERSONALITY IS PERCEIVED

When actors start thinking about how to communicate a character's personality, they usually do so in terms of appearance (the *Who*). They are doing no more than we all tend to do when we think of the personalities of people in general.

When actors change their identities (their *Who* and *What*) to resemble those of their characters, they often feel their personalities changing as well. Again as discussed in Chapter Four, a change in hairstyle, wardrobe, dialect, speech, rhythm, posture, or length of stride can often produce startling and unexpected new feelings within ourselves as well as a new effect on others. When actors put on wigs or false mustaches or wear their hair differently or dress in a different style or mode, they tend to feel such changes even more acutely. When actors change their appearances to look like different people, they tend to *feel* like different people as well.

In making these changes, actors need to be aware that a change in identity alone, no matter how differently they feel as a result, is not enough to communicate a new personality. In fact, the one sensation can often get in the way of producing the effect of the other. Actors can sometimes change their identities with wigs, mustaches, canes, eyebrow pencils, funny shoes, clunky costume jewelry, pipes, eyeglasses, and endless black lines on their faces—all without necessarily creating new personalities. Consider a seventeen-year old boy in the class play who wants to portray a mature, middle-aged man: He glues on a mustache, grays his temples, and smokes a pipe onstage. But no matter how differently such gewgaws make him feel about himself, he will not project the personality of a mature man if he still *acts* like a seventeen-year-old boy. Of course, it is perfectly possible for a seventeen-year-old boy to create the illusion of a mature personality; the fault is not with age but with technique.

The problem with the young man in this example is that he has confused identity and personality. To be specific, he has allowed himself to be taken over by a certain stereotype of appearance that is conventionally associated with the type of personality he is trying to create. That's what a stereotype is—a physical appearance that immediately suggests a particular personality: the dumb blonde, the gangster, the librarian, the used car salesman, and so on. A customary physical appearance, mode of dress, manner of speech, and so forth, go with each of them, and anyone who looks like, dresses like, or talks like one of these stereotypes is assumed to possess that personality. The problem with the young actor is that he has a stereotypical image of "Dad," and he has adopted the look, dress, and speech of that stereotype. But in doing so, he has not created a sense of genuine personality. The truth is that a person may communicate maturity without wearing a mustache, graying the temples, or smoking a pipe; there is absolutely no connection between the one and the other (in the same way that there is no necessary connection between the action of eating and the motivation of hunger).

A character's actions are much more important in creating the illusion of personality than a character's appearance. In the scene from *The Circle*, it was observed that Arnold isn't a very lovable sort. From his actions, we may conclude that he has the personality of a mean coward. But to communicate that personality, an actor playing Arnold must not make a conscious effort to look like or act like a mean coward (an error previously identified as *result playing*). If the actor really wants to communicate Arnold's personality to the audience, he has to play Arnold's objectives: to straighten out his wife, to hurt her feelings, and to make her feel guilty. For strategy, he uses threats, derision, and condescension. Anyone who would do all that to his wife is a mean coward—who cares what he looks like! Furthermore, an actor playing Arnold's objectives truthfully would have to realize that Arnold doesn't see himself as a mean coward; Arnold isn't deliberately trying to act like a mean coward—so why should the actor? It is for the audience to conclude that Arnold is a mean coward based on his actions (in the same way we saw that in order to play the motivation of hunger, an actor must play an appropriate action to achieve an appropriate desired result).

We have looked at other examples of the same process at work. In the same scene, Elizabeth's actions suggest her immaturity, and an actor playing that role should play those actions, not the appearance of a silly little twit. Bear in mind that if she acted like a silly little twit, the audience would never accept the fact that she has two men (Teddie and her husband) both willing to fight for her. In the scene from *Macbeth*, Lady Macbeth's actions suggest that she is a bloodthirsty villain, and an actor playing that scene has to play those actions, not the appearance of an old witch. Remember, the King is willing to spend the night as the guest of the Macbeths, something he surely would never do if she always acted like the Wicked Witch of the West. If anything, actors playing Arnold, Elizabeth, and Lady Macbeth should try to create an identity that doesn't immediately suggest their personalities at all. Then the audience will judge personality solely on the basis of the actions, and the stereotype will never get in the way.

A stereotype is fine to use when the role is written as one and all the character's behavior is consistent with it. But otherwise, stereotypes can lead actors away from a character's true personality: They tell the actor how to behave in only one way. Going back to the seventeen-year old boy with the pipe, this stereotypical image may work when the part requires "Dad" to talk philosophically with his "Son" about playing nicely with the other kids on the block. But it is not going to be of much use in the scene in which "Mom" asks "Dad" for a divorce, or the one in which the Hispanic neighbors next door accuse "Dad" of being a bigot, or the scene in which "Dad" tears up the living room to find the hidden bottle of gin. Adopting the stereotypical appearance of "Dad" may help the young actor to feel more mature, but the resulting inner feelings are not going to be much help if the role itself makes more complex demands than the stereotype allows.

Another reason that stereotypes are troublesome is that they are frequently not authentic. For example, ask a young woman to play the role of a librarian. How is she going to dress? She might tie up her hair in a bun, put horn-rimmed glasses on a chain around her neck, and wear a white blouse with a high collar. But have you ever seen a real librarian who deliberately dressed that way? I have not. Ask a young man to play the role of a used car salesman. How is he going to dress? A loud tie and an equally loud sport coat and patent leather shoes and a smelly cigar? Again, all those accoutrements are just playing the stereotype. But ask yourself honestly, if you were really trying to sell used cars, would you dress like that? Probably not. These stereotypical patterns are not based on reality. They can be valuable if you have to convey the impression of a character in a small role in a hurry. But these images are going to confuse the audience if you are trying to play a realistic character. What if the librarian in the play has to crusade against book-burners, play a romantic love scene, and rescue children from a burning building? Suppose the used car salesman is a widower with children, foils a robbery attempt at gunpoint in the showroom, and is elected as a resentative to Congress from his home district? In such situations, the stereotypes just get in the way.

But the influence of some stereotypes can often be very profound, and as a result, simply focusing on a character's objectives may not be sufficient to shake free of it. In that situation, actors can usually break its hold by focusing on the *Need* relationships among the characters. In the case of Arnold in *The Circle*, the effects of the stereotype of the mean coward can be dispelled if an actor concentrates on Arnold's very real *Need* for Elizabeth, as he makes clear in his own lines. If he is neglectful and condescending toward her in his actual behavior, he doesn't see his behavior that way at all. In his mind, he and Elizabeth lead a stimulating and useful life and know a lot of important people; and he really does love her within his definition of the proper type of married love. From his point of view, he loves her and needs her and is determined to keep her. If an actor focuses on that motivation, the stereotype of the mean coward will fall apart, and he can play the role with conviction. What he mustn't do is to put on a smoking jacket, an ascot tie, and a mustache and play the stereotype of an effeminate, aristocratic prig. The actor does want to dress to communicate the character's identity (age, economic status, political career, and aristocratic background), but he doesn't want to make Arnold so obnoxious that we could never imagine Elizabeth ever marrying him or anyone ever voting for him. If the actor only plays the objectives and not the stereotype, the audience will form the correct impression of Arnold's personality perfectly.

In essence, then, the audience perceives personality (like motivation) as a function of a character's actions. But not all the actions played by actors communicate personality, any more than all of a character's actions communicate motivation.

CHARACTERISTIC BEHAVIOR

In 1933, the animators at the Walt Disney Studio were grappling with this same problem. They realized that the characters they had created in previous cartoons lacked personality. In other words, the bunnies and mice and birdies were not creating audience expectations for future behavior. After working on the problem consciously, the studio achieved its first real success in this area with a cartoon called *The Three Little Pigs*. To create a sense of personality in a cartoon character, they realized that they first had to abandon character stereotypes. Next they had to invest their characters with specific details that set them apart as individuals. Then the characters had to be given movements and gestures that reminded the audience of how people with similar personalities really behave in life.

The reader has surely seen this film and will recall that two of the pigs are porcine delinquents, whereas the third (called Practical Pig) is an accomplished architect and stonemason. The individuation of the two delinquents from their brother Practical is achieved in part through significant differences in their respective identities: They are all dressed very differently (the *Who*). Their role relationships (the *What*) are differentiated by having the two delinquents play together while Practical is splashing mortar around the eaves. Also, the way they treat each other (the *Need*) is underscored by the fact that the delinquents ridicule Practical at one point, but he is still willing to protect his brothers when the wolf attacks them.

Details in the settings are used to reinforce their separate identities even further. All the pigs have pictures on the walls of their respective houses. The two delinquent pigs have pictures of pig athletes and pig hula girls, but Practical Pig has family pictures on his walls, including a sow feeding several suckling pigs (entitled "Mother") and a string of sausages (entitled "Father"). Practical even takes his bricklaying so seriously that he has built himself a brick piano and a brick bedframe. In this way, the identities of the pigs are communicated and differentiated from each other—even though all three are identical as cartoon pigs.

In addition, the animators have given the pigs certain pieces of behavior that seem familiar and strike us as extremely appropriate. After being warned to watch out for the wolf, the two delinquents dance and sing about how they will massacre the wolf if he dares to come around. At the height of their revel, they hold their musical instruments (a violin and a flute) as if they were submachine guns and make appropriate sound effects. (Surely, every little boy taking violin lessons has at one time or another pretended that his violin case contained a machine gun.) The behavior seems typical of little boys who talk big but who are really just little boys. Meanwhile, Practical is working on the roof of his house and taps a brick, breaking it to make it just the right size—exactly as a bricklayer in real life would do. Practical not only is dressed as we would expect a mason to dress but has the gestures and mannerisms of a mason as well. All these details of behavior are authentic and observed from life, not developed from stereotypes.

And when the wolf does appear, the two delinquents do just what we'd expect them to do—flee in terror. When the wolf shows up at Practical Pig's house, he does just what we'd expect him to do—lets in his brothers to protect them. (Blood, after all, is thicker than mortar.) And when the two delinquents realize that their brother's brick house is going to stand against the wolf's windy assaults, they come out from hiding to dance and sing with the same bravado as before—just exactly what we'd expect them to do under the circumstances. At the end of the film, after the wolf has been sent away for the last time, Practical Pig decides to test his brothers' mettle by knocking on the piano with his fist. In spite of their musical courage, the sound of the knocking alone is enough to strike terror in their cowardly hearts again and send them flying under the bed—just as we'd expect them to do. Not only have the animators differentiated these characters visually, but also they have created expectations in the minds of the people watching, and then reinforced these expectations by fulfilling them as the film progresses.

All these details are examples of the phenomenon of *characteristic behavior* (meaning simply behavior that is appropriate to character). This is considerably different from the kind of behavior that we associate with stereotypes. The behavior of the two delinquent pigs may suggest the aggressive play of little boys, but they are not "Our Gang" kids in any sense: They build their own houses (albeit of straw and sticks), they play musical instruments, and they dance and sing. This kind of behavior is not what most people generally associate with any one stereotype alone. Their brother Practical is no stereotype of anything either: He is a clever mason, an accomplished pianist, and when the wolf begins to assault his brick garrison, a wily tactician as well. He values his brothers enough to protect them from the wolf, but he is not above playing a little trick to teach them a lesson in humility. Even the wolf in this cartoon has an unusual approach to things: Instead of growling and skulking around (as all previous cartoon wolves had done), this wolf at one point dresses up as an orphaned sheep in a basket and at another point as a door-to-door salesman. No stereotype here either. Each of these characters behaves in unique ways to fulfill their objectives—ways that are fully consistent with their inner natures but not with any stereotypes.

Theoretically, any details of a character's behavior can be considered characteristic, but there are at least three requirements that behavior must meet before an audience will take notice. The first requirement is such behavior must be *significant* behavior. It must clearly result as a matter of choice, not inevitability. For example, when Practical warns his brothers that they had better be aware of the danger caused by a wolf in the neighborhood, they respond with derision. That is their choice. They might have responded by promising to be careful, or they could have reacted with terror at the mention of the wolf. The fact that they choose to make fun of their brother's caution when they obviously have no reason to feel secure tells us a great deal about their characters. This response is not the only one possible under the circumstances, and therefore it is extremely significant. In the scene from *The Circle*, Arnold finally takes the hint and tells Elizabeth that he loves her. But instead of trying to convince her of that fact, he then wanders off into a costly digression, explaining how romantic love is less important to him than politics and interior decoration. The impression created by that piece of behavior is that Arnold is insensitive and selfish. Another man in the same circumstances would probably have not tried to argue as Arnold did. Therefore, his behavior is significant. However, if Arnold were nothing but the stereotype of the selfish husband, he would never have said that he loved her in the first place. Therefore, his behavior is characteristic and not stereotypical.

The second requirement for characteristic behavior is that it must be based on authentic sources. The way that the pigs use their instruments as guns and the way that Practical Pig works with bricks all seem well observed. When they use their instruments like automatic weapons, the business is authentic. We say to ourselves, "Yes, that's right. That's just the way little boys might act." Finding and using authentic detail of this kind often requires actors to do research into the behavior and details that are appropriate to the background of the characters. For example, Marlon Brando trained with boxers and observed their behavior as the basis of his characterization in the film *On the Waterfront*. Not every role requires an actor to do this kind of work, but a successful characterization does require truthful, familiar, and well-observed characteristic details of behavior.

A third requirement of characteristic behavior is that there has to be some kind of repetition or reinforcement. A stereotype creates expectations of behavior instantly upon recognition of the type. A true personality takes a little longer to form in the mind of the audience. In the case of the pigs, their natures are suggested by the way they use their instruments as toy guns. But their personalities only become clear later when those initial impressions are confirmed by the pictures on the walls of their houses and by the way they respond to their brother's warnings. Then when they become cocky again in the security of the brick house, their behavior is not only predictable, but it also strikes us as familiar and truthful. We begin to feel we know these pigs; we can imagine how they might act in other circumstances. And at the risk of being repetitious, we form those expectations on the basis of their actions, not on the basis of their appearance.

To recapitulate, characteristic behavior is

1. *Significant*—the result of conscious choice, not inevitability
2. *Authentic*—based on observation of people with similar personalities and recognizable as such by the audience
3. *Reinforced*—echoed in details of identity (the *Who*, the *What*, and the *Need*) or in subsequent action

Ideally, characters should create their own stereotypes through a synthesis of their identity and characteristic behavior. Certain familiar stereotypes can even be traced directly back to the invention of certain actors, such as the stereotype of the bigot derived from Carroll O'Connor's characterization of Archie Bunker in the television series "All in the Family," or the stereotype of the vampire created by Bela Lugosi's characterization of Count Dracula in the stage play and film versions of *Dracula*.

But O'Connor's Archie Bunker had a number of redeeming qualities, not the least of which was that whenever his daughter's well-being was jeopardized, he always rose to her defense. Also, Lugosi's Dracula represented the first time a monster such as a vampire had been portrayed with such sophistication and charm. These examples in particular illustrate another way in which characteristic behavior communicates personality—through contradictory tendencies.

SIMPLE AND COMPLEX PERSONALITIES

Most people have personalities that seem to embody contradictory tendencies. As stated before, people are forever surprising us by their behavior. Of course, when we get to know surprising people better, we usually come to realize that we would not have been surprised by their behavior if we had just known them a little better. In other words, what we previously thought were contradictions in their personalities are only elements that we hadn't recognized before. Not surprisingly, we find people who surprise us to be more interesting than people who don't. In fact, people who never do anything unexpected are usually rather dull.

Audiences are the same. They prefer characters who surprise them—but only as long as any unanticipated behavior seems probable (in other words, if the actors have given the audience clues that properly prepare for such surprises).

There are fundamentally two different types of surprising characters. Some have natures that seem to be made up of many different elements, comprising wants and needs that don't immediately seem consistent in every respect; they are frequently called *complex* characters. Their behavior is difficult to predict because they are capable of actions that cannot be predicted on the basis of their previous behavior. On the other hand, some characters behave in ways that are always consistent and predictable; they are sometimes called *simple* characters. However, they sometimes surprise us by the way their behavior is predictable even in situations in which we would expect them to do something different. The terms *simple* and *complex* are not intended to imply any value judgments on the skill with which the playwright has fashioned the roles, only to indicate whether or not the characters embody contradictory tendencies.

Complex characters can be created by the playwright in two ways. The first is the way in which a complex character's behavior does not fulfill the audience's expectations. In *Death of a Salesman,* the audience's impressions of Willy Loman as a good father and husband are inevitably shattered by the revelation of him as a philanderer on the road. In the last act of *Harvey,* Veta creates a pleasant surprise by suddenly moving to stop Dr. Chumley from giving Elwood a shot that will make him stop seeing Harvey the Pookah forever. In Chekhov's *The Three Sisters,* the audience is inevitably surprised at the strength of will exhibited by the character of Natasha: In the first act, she runs from the dining room in which she has been mocked by the three sisters of Andrey, her fiance; but by the end of the play, she has managed to take over the whole house from the sisters and virtually expel them from their own home. In *The Children's Hour,* the failure of Karen Wright to deal with Martha Dobie's declaration of affection is an unpleasant surprise; Karen's previous actions in the play have led us to expect more strength of character from her. In each of these examples, the playwright gives the character an action that does not seem consistent with previous behavior.

The other way in which a playwright creates a complex character is by the way in which a given character's potential for behavior is not immediately suggested by the character's apparent stereotype. Many roles of this type should already be familiar to the reader. Shakespeare's Caliban has always fascinated audiences because of the unlikely combination of a horrible exterior with a sensitive nature. Shaw built several plays around the idea of external appearance being at odds with internal nature, including *Pygmalion, Arms and the Man,* and *St. Joan.*

Playwrights often create simple characters who can be just as fascinating as complex ones, particularly when they remain completely consistent to their natures even in the face of conflicts that might force other people to change. For example, the fact that Oedipus continues to stay the course and try to uncover the identify of Laius' murderer becomes very remarkable when he begins to suspect that he himself is the murderer he seeks. Any other man in the same circumstances would have called off the investigation as soon as the evidence began to turn sour, but not King Oedipus. A character who behaves that way in that situation must have complex reasons for remaining steadfast, and Oedipus is no exception. He is extremely proud and stubborn, characteristics that he demonstrates several times before the evidence begins to point to him as the killer. His pride is enormous, so much so that he cannot abandon the search for the murderer after he has announced that he will carry out that search to the end. His pride, stubbornness, and guilt are all at war with each other, and yet the result is a simple character who does just what he says he is going to do. Therefore, even though his actions are predictable, there is an inner complexity that is in itself surprising and fascinating to observe.

From the way in which the playwright fashions complex characters, the actor can derive the final clue to creating the illusion of personality, and it is simply this: A personality is a collection of contradictory elements that are really unified. A stereotype, by contrast, is a collection of unified elements without any contradictions. In playing a complex character, the actor needs to find and bring out the unifying qualities. In playing a simple character, the actor needs to find and bring out the complex qualities. In both cases, the illusion of a personality is created when complex elements are finally unified. Again, the actor achieves this effect by how the objectives are played.

A complex character that offers such problems is Nora in Henrik Ibsen's *A Doll's House*. In the last act, audiences who are not previously familiar with the story are frequently taken by surprise when Nora announces that she is leaving her husband and family. Throughout the play, Nora has depended on other people to take direct action for her. The actor performing the role of Nora must somehow prepare the audience to accept the sudden emergence of "backbone" in her character, but without making it actually predict what is about to happen. Nora has plenty of provocation to leave her husband, but the audience has to be surprised when she reveals that she has the courage. Even so, the audience has to be willing to accept that courage when it is finally manifested in her actions.

A close analysis of Nora's actions throughout the play reveals that Ibsen has carefully prepared Nora's character for this moment. Nora demonstrates that she loves her husband (Torvald) very deeply, but that love is based on her expectation that he would do anything at all, undergo any sacrifice, to protect her. He has a particular image of her as a kind of beautiful porcelain doll, and she doesn't want to do anything to spoil that image. Furthermore, Nora feels that she is worthy of Torvald's love because she herself arranged for a personal loan during a period when Torvald was so sick he almost died. The loan enabled them to spend enough time in a warmer climate for Torvald to recover. Torvald thinks the money was an inheritance from her father; she has never told him the truth because the loan was obtained under slightly fraudulent conditions, which if they ever came to light, could possibly hurt

Torvald's career. Therefore, Nora's position is certainly complex enough for any actor.

But how has Ibsen prepared for Nora's final action? In the first act, there is a peculiar scene that seems to be almost unnecessary, but on closer inspection, the actions are revealed to convey important information about Nora's personality. The play takes place at Christmas, and Torvald reprimands Nora for being a spendthrift. Nora sheepishly accepts his reprimands and sulks a bit; a moment later, Torvald hands her more money. (This incident precedes any of the exposition about the loan or Torvald's illness.) The first impression an audience is likely to receive from this scene is that Nora is a little nit and Torvald is a saint for putting up with her nonsense. The way that Nora manipulates her husband in this scene does not seem to suggest that she is capable of taking any responsible action on her own at all. But an actor playing this scene has to realize two important facts that only become clear later in the play. The first is that Nora needs to get money out of Torvald in order to make another payment on the loan; the same piece of dialogue also has a puzzling reference to how in the previous Christmas Nora had disappeared for almost three weeks while she supposedly made presents for the family that nobody ever saw. As we learn from later dialogue, she had been working hard to keep household expenses at a minimum by sewing things to sell for money. The second fact is that Nora desperately needs to feed Torvald's image of her as a little spendthrift so that he will not get suspicious about all the money he gives her. The hidden cost of this peculiar exchange between her and Torvald is surprisingly high; she is, in fact, playing a rather dangerous game with Torvald. The way the actor plays Nora's objectives in this scene is absolutely vital to preparing the audience to accept her departure at the end of the play.

There is a world of difference between trying to squeeze more money out of Torvald to waste on her own personal indulgences and Nora's trying to convince him she is a spendthrift in order to keep him from guessing the truth about their financial situation. Also, there's a great deal of difference between Nora's working Torvald for a little more spending money that she doesn't really need and scraping up the last few coins necessary to make the payment, run the household, and buy everybody presents. If she plays the scene like Scarlett O'Hara trying to decide which of her beaus will be allowed to bring her ice cream, Nora's exit with the suitcase in the last scene is going to seem totally implausible. But if she plays the right objectives and sets the cost at the appropriately high level, the audience is going to be intrigued by this scene because there will be a level of meaning not immediately understandable, in spite of the first impression that wheedling the money out of Torvald is going to create.

The factors of identity can also be manipulated to affect what the audience thinks of this scene. If Torvald appears to be emaciated, careworn, and dressed in a suit that looks as though he has worn it to work every day for the last three years, the impression is going to be that Nora is an unreasonable shrew about money. If, however, Torvald is played as an aging, pot-bellied man with a taste for expensive clothes, the audience may conclude that he's a noisy buffoon. If Nora comes across as a young, pretty, flighty woman, the audience may choose to regard her as the stereotype of the manipulating wife. But if she appears more matronly, plainly dressed, poorly rested, and obviously too old to be playing this kind of game with her husband, the audience may choose to suspend judgment until they have observed more of her in action.

Playing even a simple character can create the same kind of difficulties of interpretation. Several years ago, I directed a production of Federico García Lorca's *The House of Bernarda Alba.* The story is complex, and the language is poetic and frequently obscure. The production was not going at all well in the early phases, and one of the main problems that the actors were having was with the relationship between the mother, Bernarda, and her daughters. Following the death of her husband, Bernarda determines to keep her daughters locked up in her house and away from men. The result is that Bernarda causes the daughters to become extremely resentful toward her and each other. Finally, one of them takes her own life when she mistakenly believes that Bernarda has shot and killed the daughter's would-be lover. Throughout the play, Bernarda is nasty to everybody, and the whole mood of the production was being affected by this character's seemingly hateful personality.

But through a careful examination of Bernarda's motivations and the *Need* relationships to the other characters, we slowly began to realize that we were misinterpreting the situation. We had assumed that Bernarda was just a shrew; what we had missed was the fact that she was not deliberately seeking to torture her daughters by locking them up. She was sternly guarding them because she *loved* them and wanted to protect them from the kind of cruel heartbreak and disappointment she had known in her own life. Her strictness and her uncompromising morality were all grounded in her own intense desire to spare her daughters—even if against their wills—from the pain of life. The daughters, of course, don't understand or appreciate the mother's motivations (a fact that helped to explain why the actors playing the daughters didn't exactly understand what was going on in the play either). However, we began to work in rehearsals to find as many moments as possible in which the mother could consciously try to show her affection for her daughters. The result turned the entire production around, and the actors finally succeeded in creating the deep sense of tragic loss upon the daughter's suicide. The moral of the story is that the simplicity of Bernarda's character masked a depth of motivation that affected how she chose to express her love for her daughters. Once the stereotype of the nasty, hateful widow had been dispelled, it became possible to make the character fascinating as she stuck to her nature in the face of all opposition.

The infamous tea scene from *The Importance of Being Earnest* on the surface seems superficial, as do the characters of Gwendolen and Cecily. But a thoughtful analysis of the whole play reveals that their characters are predictable, but not superficial. Gwendolen and Cecily really want and need advantageous marriages that will promote their stations in society and enable them to continue the kind of existences they have been enjoying. If the scene is handled properly, the actors reveal the seriousness with which both characters approach the dilemma of who is engaged to whom. The joke of the scene is that although the social formalities create the impression of civility, the ferocity with which they each pursue their objectives indicates an almost primitive level to their desires. The scene, as anyone who has ever seen the play performed well will agree, is most effective when the seriousness of the two participants is made the most apparent. Thus, the characters become complex when actors understand (as the title of the play suggests) the importance of being earnest in playing even such seemingly trivial objectives.

In all the previous examples, the emphasis has been on creating personality by investing the characters with complex motivations. There is another way, which seems simpler initially but can create other problems if it is not handled thoughtfully. The technique is to create complexity by changing the character's identity in some striking way from what the playwright probably had in mind. One example of this technique at work was cited previously—Diana Rigg's interpretation of the young and sexy Lady Macbeth. Her identity in this production seemed, on the surface, to be more appropriate to one of Noel Coward's leading ladies than to what Shakespeare may have had in mind. But she played Lady Macbeth's objectives with great conviction. One result was that the audience could easily see why someone with her looks would want to be queen; also they could easly understand why Macbeth would be willing to kill for her. Sometimes the same effect can be achieved simply by unconventional casting, several examples of which were cited in Chapter Four. Again, as long as the objectives are still played with conviction, the effect can be very arresting.

Another version of the same idea is sometimes called *playing opposites.* Stanislavski recommended that if one is to play a villain successfully and believably, one should look for some aspect of that character's personality that is actually good. The reverse is also true; every virtuous character must have or should be invested with some petty vice. The idea is to introduce into the character—by brute force, if necessary—some element that seems contradictory or at least is at odds with the character's stereotype. The effect can be successful if the contradictory element is grounded in the character's nature. The problem with this approach is the temptation for an actor to add something into a characterization strictly for effect, something that would do nothing to illuminate the character's identity, personality, or motivation. A more dependable approach (as already discussed in the examples of Arnold and Bernarda Alba) is for the actor to focus on the *Need* relationships that are already in the script.

However the actor chooses to accomplish the effect, the presence of characteristic behavior and contradictory elements in the character's motivation are the twin factors that create the illusion of personality.

CHARACTERIZING SMALL PARTS AND WALK-ONS

The process of investing supporting roles with personality is essentially the same, but there is a shift of emphasis caused by the length of such roles.

The basic problem that every actor has to face with a small part is that there is often not very much information in the script to build on. For example, the King of France and the Duke of Burgundy are important characters in the plot of *King Lear,* but they are only in one scene in the first act. Their lines are limited to discussing who is willing to marry Cordelia if she has no dowry; they are never seen again in the entire play. The roles of Merriman and Lane, the two manservants in *The Importance of Being Earnest,* consist primarily of moving props on and off the stage. The musical *South Pacific* includes several roles for sailors and nurses, some of whom only have a line or two, almost exclusively to justify getting a large chorus onstage for the songs. All such roles have been created by the playwrights, either to serve some mechanical point in the plot or to solve some technical problem concerning people or props. Playwrights don't spend a lot of time thinking about the motivations of such characters. They depend on the actors to do their thinking for them.

Beginning actors frequently make one of three mistakes in performing such roles. One is to try to invent an elaborate offstage biography for such characters. Since there is really no way that this information can be expressed to the audience and since the playwright didn't bother thinking about these things, this kind of exercise seems totally self-serving. The second mistake is to treat the role like the playwright treated it—that is, to walk on, say the lines, and then walk off again, not thinking any more about it. That approach isn't entirely satisfactory either because the effect is not natural. In life, every person has a unique identity and a unique personality of some sort, which are reflected in his or her behavior. To see someone on a stage who does not appear to have a unique identity violates the illusion of natural behavior. The third possible mistake is to jump to the other extreme and try to turn a walk-on into a lead through the addition of some distracting behavior designed solely to attract the audience's attention. The reader may have seen the film version of the stage play *Auntie Mame.* In one sequence of the film, Mame (played by Rosalind Russell) performs a walk-on part in a stage play, but she chooses to ornament the character with loud, tinkly jewelry that distracts the actors onstage as well as the audience. Clearly this approach is not the answer either.

In order to characterize small roles effectively and to avoid these mistakes, the following two guidelines should be followed: The first is to remember that the size of the part is really determined by the time that the actor is onstage, not by the number of lines the actor is given to say. In most small roles, the amount of time the actor spends onstage is much greater than the number of lines might initially indicate. An actor can still find objectives, strategies, beat changes, and a clearly defined relationship to the situation and to the other actors onstage. Whether or not actors have been given lines, they should determine a reason for being onstage in terms of the formula for phrasing objectives and then pursue that purpose with good concentration and a sense of the reality of the situation. Even when actors are only dressing the stage in a large crowd scene, they should invent good reasons for being in that particular place at that particular moment and find something to do. (After all, people never think of themselves as an observer on the sidelines of life; everyone always has a good reason for being somewhere.) If the actor is a passive observer in someone else's scene and waiting to say two lines of dialogue after ten minutes of stage action, the same logic applies. The actor must stay alert, involved, and interested in everything that is going on—the same kind of intense looking and paying attention that an actor should use to play any objective. If actors actually have a character of some importance to play, such as the King of France or the Duke of Burgundy, they must pursue all aspects of that role just as if it were the lead. In other words, beats and objectives must be played all the time the actor is onstage—even if the actor has to make most of them up and even if they only amount to dusting the furniture or moving a broom or watching what everyone else is doing.

The other guideline is that every character requires a unique identity. If you are playing one of three butlers or one of fifteen nurses, then you should try to find some way, no matter how small to make your butler or your nurse different from all the others. Remember what Disney's animators learned about pigs: Each one must be treated as an individual. On the stage, identity and personality are illusions created by the actor, not by the playwright. In the case of insignificant roles, there may be no clues in the script to follow at all, but the actor can still invent characteristic detail and characteristic behavior to communicate to the audience the sense of being an individual. It is not necessary to develop a whole character biography or a psychological profile in order to find such touches; it is possible to be arbitrary, as long as such touches do not seem inconsistent with the play as a whole. The purpose of characteristic detail is only to make the character seem convincing as an illusion, not to call attention to the actor.

I once played the small role of an old man who had a very few lines during a long dinner scene. After thinking the matter through, I decided (based on my own observation of some elderly people) that my character was a very picky eater, and during the eating scene, I became intensely involved with the problem of carving away anything from my food that did not seem immediately appetizing. At the same time, this old man was a veteran at eavesdropping on other people's conversations (somewhat of a practical necessity because of the need to listen for the few line cues that the part involved). Having chosen good, strong objectives and having decided on ways to make this one old man an individual, and by really paying attention to everything that was happening (and thus blocking out all foreknowledge of the scene and creating corresponding beat changes), I was able to do a lot with a small part in a way that satisfied me as an actor, did not distract from the performances of other people—and even earned me a few compliments as well. Who says no one ever notices actors in the supporting roles?

Remember: No one in life feels like a supporting player. Each person is the leading actor in the play of that person's own life, and actors in small parts should play them that way as well.

SUMMARY

Creating a new identity is not equivalent to creating the illusion of personality. In this respect, actors must be particularly cautious about avoiding stereotypes, one-dimensional patterns of behavior based on certain highly generalized (and frequently not authentic) physical appearances. Stereotypes are misleading because they do not tell an actor how to deal with all the various situations in a play. The influence of stereotypes can be counteracted by a serious study of the character's objectives and especially the *Need* relationships among the characters.

Personality is the word most people use to describe a person's potential for future action based on observation of the person's past actions. From an actor's point of view, characteristic behavior creates these expectations. For any behavior to be perceived as characteristic, it must be significant, authentic, and reinforced. A true personality is also the result of seemingly contradictory actions or motivations. Playwrights create two types of characters that surprise us: complex characters (whose behavior defies our expectations) and simple characters (who remain surprisingly true to their natures in the face of conflict). In both cases, actors must analyze the objectives to find the unifying motivations that make these characters plausible even when unpredictable. Sometimes complexity can be created by the simple expedients of unconventional identities, unconventional casting, or "playing opposites." Such ideas work well as long as the objectives are played throughout with conviction. In playing supporting roles and walk-ons, the same general principles also apply.

EXERCISES FOR CHAPTER EIGHT

The main theme of this chapter is how the actor avoids stereotypes through the creation of characteristic behavior and contradictory elements. The following exercises are intended to help actors sharpen their skills at achieving those goals.

1. One of the most important goals of any characterization is to encourage the audience to predict how that character might behave in the future or in other circumstances. In the last five chapters, scenes have been presented from four different plays: *Harvey, Macbeth, The Importance of Being Earnest,* and *The Circle.* The characters in these plays have already been discussed in considerable detail, and the reader (it is hoped) has even tried playing many of them already. Pick one or two of your favorite characters from any of these plays and perform improvised scenes (by yourself or with other actors) in which your character is in a situation totally different from anything encountered in the play. For example, try to imagine Macbeth taking out a book from the public library; try to imagine Myrtle as a cocktail waitress; try to imagine Gwendolen as a police officer; and so on.

   As much as possible, try to keep your character's personality fundamentally the same. Do not try to turn your character into a stereotype, a problem that can easily occur in this exercise. Instead, use the "If-I-Were" formula to try to place the character realistically (however whimsically) into the new situation. Try to become aware of what features of your character's identity are really essential to playing that character and which ones are purely a product of that person's stereotype.

2. Recall Diana Rigg's interpretation of Lady Macbeth. Try the same idea of changing the identities of the characters in any of the scenes to observe what new complexities of personality emerge. Imagine Myrtle as a beauty queen; imagine Cecily and Gwendolen as extremely unattractive; imagine Arnold as a senior citizen; imagine Elizabeth as a doctoral candidate in philosophy; and so on.

   Try to imagine how your character's new identity would be reflected in all aspects of his or her behavior. Look for as many ways as possible to provide behavior that is significant, authentic, and reinforced. Again, the effect is not merely to be comic but to explore how different identities for these characters create new levels of complexity. Perform the scenes with the greatest degree of conviction you can manage. Do not settle for stereotypes; try to investigate all the ramifications of the new identities as you prepare the scenes for performance.

3. Develop a completely fictitious character for yourself. Invent a new identity (the *Who* and the *What*), and then choose an action that involves playing an objective on the telephone. Imagine this person calling up a creditor to complain about a bill, the IRS to get information about taxes, the police to get someone arrested, a television station to complain about the content of a program, a repair service to find out why the washing machine still doesn't work, and so on. Establish the circumstances under which the call is made and the character's motivations for making it. Then choose at random or have someone else choose for you any one of the following attributes to communicate in your scene:

stingy	generous
gullible	intelligent
crafty	innocent
bossy	cowardly
shy	extroverted
overbearing	meek

   Try playing the same scene again with a different attribute. Afterward, ask your audience to identify which attribute you were trying to play and what specific details of your performance led them to that conclusion. Ask them to suggest any other things you might have done to communicate your desired personality.

In this exercise try not to communicate the personality directly. Play your objectives and choose your strategies as a person with that particular personality might accomplish those same goals.

Lesson Nine

Empathy and Context

Emotion is a quality of acting greatly valued by actors and audiences alike. But the importance of this one quality must not be allowed to overshadow all the other qualities that make up an effective illusion of natural behavior.

The importance of emotion to the work of the actor has been debated for almost three hundred years. Although there is much disagreement in this area, there are at least two points about emotion that can be demonstrated fairly consistently. The first is the principle of *empathy*, which dictates that what audiences see and hear must strike them as authentic before an emotional response can be guaranteed. The second principle is that there is a connection between the emotions the actor feels and the expression of those emotions. Although it is difficult, if not impossible, to demonstrate an absolute cause and effect relationship between these two things, it can be demonstrated that feelings seem to be felt most strongly when they are expressed.

Chapter Nine

Emotion

As realistic acting evolved in the late nineteenth and early twentieth centuries, there evolved along with it a new emphasis on authentic emotions onstage—or, to be more precise, the authentic expression of emotions onstage. Today, realistic acting and authentic emotion have become synonymous in many people's minds, so much so that authentic emotion is often regarded as the *sine qua non* of good acting. Most audiences feel that when they are in the presence of genuine emotion, they are also in the presence of great acting. The more apparent the trauma, the more exalted the performance. Indeed, the quantity and quality of emotion are the only criteria many people use to evaluate an actor's performance.

This attitude has created an excessive emphasis on emotion in the work of some actors. For example, the ability to cry onstage is generally admired by actors and audiences alike. Tears, after all, are almost impossible to fake; one is either crying or one isn't. As a result, people who can produce tears on cue are usually considered to be good actors—even if they can't remember their lines, can't move without tripping over the furniture, and can't be heard or understood. More important, the reverse of this equation is thought to be even more true (especially by performers): Actors who cannot cry on stage are not considered to be as competent as actors who can. To cite just one example of how pervasive this attitude is, Melina Mercouri—an actor who became minister of culture in the government of Greece—was once interviewed by Harry Reasoner on the television program "60 Minutes," and to prove that she could still act, she proceeded to generate a face full of tears on command as the camera watched.

This attitude about emotion seems to be especially common among actors who have established themselves primarily as comedians. Actors with the kind of reputations enjoyed by Dick Van Dyke, Carol Burnett, Mickey Rooney, Art Carney, Jerry Lewis, Lily Tomlin, and countless others of considerable skill have all felt the need to "prove" themselves as actors by taking on highly emotional roles. The implication is that a comedian cannot be considered as a real actor until he or she has successfully played a heart-breaking or tear-jerking part. Of course, most actors also recognize that considerably more technical ability is required to play comedy successfully than drama. Rare indeed are actors such as Laurence Olivier or Glenda Jackson or Jack Lemmon who can enjoy great acclaim in both tragic and comic roles. As a general rule, most actors who can handle comedy have an easier time making the transition to serious drama than the other way around.

The identification of realistic acting and authentic emotion is so complete that many students believe that learning to act means primarily learning to emote. To that end, actors have even been known to "practice" their emotions. It is possible, as Ms. Mercouri demonstrated on "60 Minutes," to learn to cry on cue—to press a button, as it were, to turn on the tears. But the cultivation of this kind of emotion on demand involves a substantial paradox: If the presence of real emotion in an actor's playing is the ultimate indicator of authenticity, what could be phonier than real tears that have been rehearsed outside of the performance in which they are then used? Emotion onstage must be a legitimate part of the role itself, or it is not authentic in any sense.

Emotion—like motivation and personality—is something that cannot be played directly. When actors deliberately pander to the audience's desire for emotion, the results can be disastrous. We have all seen performances in which actors have deliberately given free reign to their feelings just to show how much emotion they could generate. Performances such as these are embarrassing to watch because they are self-serving and—most important of all—not natural.

Emotion is a difficult problem for all actors, but the practice of realistic acting demands solving it. Audiences expect emotion; other actors admire it; and therefore, actors work at it. But if it's practiced and nourished outside of a specific role, it can be phony and unnatural. And if it's not there in sufficient quantities, the audience is not going to be satisfied.

From all that has been said in the preceding chapters, you should already understand that realistic acting involves much more than just the authentic expression of emotions. Feeling is surely an important element of great acting, but there are many other factors that an actor has to consider as well. Learning to act means much more than just learning to emote. But how and why did all this emphasis on emotion in realistic acting come about? Before considering the proper function of emotion in the work of the actor, we need to know a little more about how this attitude developed and how it has affected the direction of actor training. Also, we need to understand more about what emotion really is and how it is generated naturally.

THE HISTORY OF THE THEORY OF EMOTION

As was mentioned in the first chapter, Stanislavski's production of the *The Seagull* was something of a landmark in the evolution of realistic acting. It was this production that clearly demonstrated the key differences between the evolving realistic acting and the presentational (or "Romantic") acting that had preceded it. Many years later, Stanislavski published a book of memoirs entitled *My Life in Art* in which he told the story of the Moscow Art Theatre's first tour to Petrograd in 1900. The engagement was a great success, and the company was treated to a banquet at which speeches were given. One of the orators supposedly said,

> A theatre has come to visit us, but to our complete amazement, there is not a single actor or actress in it . . . I hear no artfully sonorous voices; I see no actorlike manner of walking, no theatrical gestures, no false pathos, no waving of hands, no animal temperaments . . . In this theatre there are no actors and no actresses, but men and women who deeply believe. . . [1]

The rhetoric may be a little high-flown and self-congratulatory, but the statement points out an important fact. When realistic acting began to be seen, audiences were struck by the way in which the actors didn't look like actors, at least not like the presentational actors that had been seen before. The speaker notes how Stanislavski's actors expressed their emotions without "theatrical gestures" and "false pathos." When *The Seagull* had been produced originally, the production had failed because the presentational actors had not known how to portray the delicate emotions the play requires. Stanislavski directed his actors to play without "sonorous voices" and "waving of hands." Since the play was then successful, this kind of emotional expression became an important early goal of this type of acting. But what made this more natural method of emotional expression seem so revolutionary? Today, it all seems to us like just so much common sense. To understand the answer to that question, we have to understand the theory behind emotional expression in presentational acting.

Probably the first attempt at anything like a scientific theory of the emotions was based on the teachings of Aristotle (384–322 B.C.), who postulated the existence of the four so-called elemental states of being: hot, cold, wet, and dry. Aristotle and others perceived a correspondence between these basic essences and the four primary fluids, or *biles*, contained in the body: red (blood), clear (phlegm), yellow (choler), and black (melancholy). Any imbalance of these biles within the body or any impediment to their natural flow was thought to produce an emotional counterpart, or *humour*—hence our modern expression for someone who is irritable as *being in a bad humor.* A choleric personality is exhibited by someone who is easily angered. It is a melancholy day indeed for someone whose black bile isn't flowing properly. (Today, some people still deliberately take a laxative as a means of cheering up.) A person with a head cold or other excess of phlegm is often slow-moving or unresponsive; today we refer to the phlegmatic personality of someone who is sluggish and stolid. A ruddy, flushed complexion is taken as a sign of cheerfulness. In fact, the word *complexion* comes from a medieval term for the aggregate hot, cold, moist, and dry qualities of the whole body.

This theory of the emotions, as amusing as it may seem to us today, stood unchallenged through the time of the Elizabethans and beyond. Playwright Ben Jonson even inaugurated a type of comedy called *comedy of humours,* based on this theory. His plays *Every Man in His Humour* (1598) and *Every Man Out of His Humour* (1600) are examples. A more scientific theory of the emotions would not be suggested until the latter part of the nineteenth century. Charles Darwin was the first person to argue that the emotions were the result of organic processes and not by-products of bodily fluids, a theory expressed in his book *The Expression of the Emotions in Man and Animals* (1872).

In the meantime, Aristotle's theories reduced emotions to the level of clinical symptoms of bodily disorders, and since symptoms tend to be fairly uniform from one sick person to another, this approach invited the idea of standardizing the expression of the emotions onstage. As a result, actors were cast according to certain categories known as "lines of business." For example, at the Comédie Française in the seventeenth and eighteenth centuries,

> The major lines in tragedy were kings, tyrants, lovers, princesses, mothers, and female lovers, while the major lines in comedy were old men, lovers, valets, peasants, old women, coquettes, and soubrettes. In addition, there were a number of secondary lines, and the bottom rank was made up of general utility players. Certain tragic and comic lines were usually filled by the same actors. For example, the *jeune premier* (or leading male performer) played the lover in both comedy and tragedy, while the actress who played the princesses in tragedy normally assumed the roles of coquettes in comedy. As a rule, an actor remained in the same lines of business throughout his career. [2]

Part of the rationale for this system was found in the principles of neoclassicism; and in the theatre, these principles were based largely on the teachings of Aristotle. One principle of neoclassical theatre was the idea of *decorum* (or "fitness"), that is, that every age, profession, and character had certain external characteristics of movement, gesture, and speech that were common to all persons in each category. Therefore, each type would have a conventionalized manner of emotional expression as well.

Well into the nineteenth century, actors were still being cast according to their lines of business. Each actor in a given line was expected to be familiar with the standard ways to express the emotional states of each character type in that line. Some actors were even considered more adept at expressing certain emotions within a given line than others. In talking about Rachel (Elisa Felix, 1820–1858), one of the stars of the Comédie Française in the mid-nineteenth century, Oscar Brockett comments,

> She was unsuited to comedy and could not portray tenderness, womanly softness, gaiety, or heartiness; her strength lay in scorn, triumph, rage, malignity, and lust.[3]

Since emotions were treated like symptoms, they could be studied and learned by rote. The following excerpt is from *The History of the English Stage*, published in 1741. This book was supposedly written by Thomas Betterton, one of the leading actors of the English Restoration theatre, but scholars now feel Betterton was not the author. In this excerpt, student actors are advised on how certain emotions should be portrayed.

> . . . [the head] ought not to be lifted up too high, and stretched out extravagantly, which is the mark of arrogance and haughtiness . . . nor on the other side should it be hung down upon the breast . . . in rendering the mien clumsy and dull . . . Nor should the head always lean towards the shoulders, which is equally rustic and affected, or a mark of indifference, languidness, and a faint inclination.[4]

And there are many similar examples that can be found in other books on acting from the eighteenth and nineteenth centuries.

In order to play the emotions in this way, the actor has to give a lot of conscious attention to the details of movement and gesture while performing. The resulting performance may be very beautiful, but it is going to seem very artificial. However, presentational acting puts much more emphasis on beauty than on authenticity. Through the latter part of the nineteenth century, audiences were less concerned with acting that was individualized and spontaneous than they were with acting that beautifully expressed the universal qualities of man. Therefore, this approach to acting was accepted as the correct one.

Since presentational acting emphasizes conscious technique, many people argued that the actor's personal feelings only got in the way. Denis Diderot (1713–1784), the editor of the first encyclopedia, was also a playwright. In the 1770s, Diderot wrote down his views on acting in a book called

The Paradox of Acting, which was not published until 1830. In this work Diderot argues that the actor should strive to feel no emotions while performing in order that full concentration may be given to the rendering of the appearance of the emotions for the audience. At one point Diderot sharply criticizes actors who allow their emotions to rule their minds:

> What confirms me in this view is the unequal acting of players who play from the heart. From them you must expect no unity. Their playing is alternately strong and feeble, fiery and cold, dull and sublime. To-morrow they will miss the point they have excelled in to-day; and to make up for it will excel in some passage where last time they failed. On the other hand, the actor who plays from thought, from study of human nature, from constant imitation of some ideal type, from imagination, from memory, will be one and the same at all performances, will be always at his best mark . . . [5]

To Diderot, spontaneity was obviously less important than consistency. To further emphasize that point, he cites an example involving the famous English actor David Garrick:

> Garrick will put his head between two folding-doors, and in the course of five or six seconds his expression will change successively from wild delight to temperate pleasure, from this to tranquility, from tranquility to surprise, from surprise to blank astonishment, from that to sorrow, from sorrow to the air of one overwhelmed, from that to fright, from fright to horror, from horror to despair, and thence he will go up again to the point from which he started. Can his soul have experienced all these feelings, and played this kind of scale in concert with his face? I don't believe it; nor do you.[6]

However, it would be a mistake to assume that all the acting of the eighteenth and nineteenth centuries was cold and deliberate. In fact, Diderot's opinions on this subject were not universally shared, which may in part account for the fact that his *Paradox* was not published during his own lifetime. Many of the prominent actors of the eighteenth and nineteenth centuries were notoriously emotional onstage. Sarah Kemble Siddons (1755–1831) was idolized during her career for the excesses of emotion to which she permitted herself. Also known for highly emotional acting was Edmund Kean (1787–1833). Again according to Brockett,

> . . . Kean did not value grace and dignity; he was willing to cringe or crawl on the floor if he thought it necessary to convey the proper effect. Thus he tended to emphasize realism of emotion . . . Kean's style pleased the new audience, but his erratic behavior had lowered his popularity considerably before his death in 1833.[7]

"Realism of emotion" in this statement means not that Kean's emotional expression was any more authentic than his contemporaries but that it was less graceful and refined. The gestures were not always beautiful; in fact, Kean gloried in effects that were frankly grotesque by contemporary standards (such as cringing and crawling). His acting was considered to belong to a school called "Romantic."

In the United States, the professional theatre did not develop until the early nineteenth century and, as a result, the neoclassical tradition never became as firmly established here as in Europe. Highly emotional acting was much admired in the American theatre almost from the beginning. Garff Wilson, in *A History of American Acting* notes the rise of what he calls the "school of emotionalism."

> During the second half of the nineteenth century, while the actresses of the classic school were demonstrating their art in the great roles of the standard drama, another group of actresses was winning popular acclaim as purveyors of emotionalism . . . This kind of acting was developed almost exclusively by female performers for the simple reason that emotionalistic roles were not often written for men. It would have been unthinkable for a male in the American theatre with its Puritan, Anglo-Saxon background, to exhibit the kind of emotionalistic behavior which seemed probable and acceptable when coming from a lady in distress.[8]

Wilson cites as the leading actresses of this school Anna Cora Mowatt, Laura Keene, and Fanny Davenport.

The male counterpart to the school of emotionalism in America became the "heroic" style of acting, best embodied by the career and acting of Edwin Forrest (1806–1872), America's first real "star." Forrest particularly disliked the mannered, restrained classical school, and he developed a style based on strength and physical vigor. An incident from his life is relevant here because it underscores the developing American taste for emotion rather than technique. A major star of the English stage of the same period was William Charles Macready (1793–1873). Macready, an exponent of the classical school, toured in America, as did many other important English actors of his day. Macready's acting was admired by Americans with cultivated (and, therefore, European) tastes, but he was not admired by the friends and admirers of Edwin Forrest (who had "American" tastes). A feud developed between Forrest and Macready and between their partisans. In 1849, Macready was attempting to perform at the Astor Place Theatre in New York. A riot broke out between the factions, and twenty-two people were killed in the melee. This incident demonstrates an important fact about the American theatre: The preference of the popular audience for "heroic" and "emotional" acting was clear as early as 1849.

Before going on, remember that all these various approaches to emotion in acting were based on a scientific understanding of the emotions that had not progressed much further than Aristotle's four biles. In essence, emotions were still treated like symptoms: They were observed and studied and then copied. Once a particular way of expressing a particular emotion had become established for a given line of business, all actors in that line tended to copy it. Thus, in both the classical and Romantic schools of acting, actors learned how to portray emotions primarily from watching other actors. Garrick and Forrest and other prominent actors did occasionally try to improve their ability to express certain emotional states—particularly madness—through direct observation from life. But the principle was the same: observe and copy.

Eventually, the acting in both schools became very conventionalized and artificial. This is not to say that it became *bad* acting. The goal of presentational acting is not to create an illusion of natural behavior; realistic acting is the only kind of acting that makes that demand on its actors. But a new desire for realism in stagecraft and in drama began to make some people aware of how the conventions of theatrical emotion had become far removed from the natural expression of emotion in life.

One of the earliest people to challenge the established conventions in an influential way was François Delsarte (1811–1871), who studied acting at the Royal Dramatic School in Paris. Delsarte soon became disenchanted with the artificial gestures and methods of expression he was being taught there. E. T. Kirby relates Delsarte's frustration with a particular line in a particular role. The coaches at the school had been training him in the conventional way to appear pleasantly surprised at an unexpected reunion with an old acquaintance. Apparently, Delsarte could not execute the conventional gestures convincingly. Then, one day he had an accidental reunion with an old friend, and he instantly realized the difference between the postures he had been given by the coaches and the natural way his pleasant surprise had actually been expressed spontaneously. Starting from that experience, he began seriously to evaluate the whole system of conventionalized expression that he was being taught. [9]

Delsarte began by studying how people expressed their feelings in real life. He studied physiology and even visited morgues to learn about the body's full potential for expression at moments of catastrophe. From his observations, he evolved a theory of the emotions that anticipated Darwin. Rejecting the idea of emotion as a symptom of fluid imbalances, Delsarte postulated the existence of a mystical triune relationship among body, mind, and soul. Although this concept owed more to philosophy than to science, Delsarte was in effect proposing the revolutionary idea that emotions were organic processes, a function of body and mind together (not mere symptoms of fluid imbalances). What chiefly remains of his work, however, are various charts that he developed to catalogue and codify the range of human expression. These charts were recommended for study by platform speakers, and as a result, Delsarte became associated with the worst excesses of platform oratory. Worse yet were the so-called Delsarte exercises, in which women and children were dressed in Greek chitons, lined up in rows (or "choirs") and made to recite lines of poetry while gesturing in unison mechanically according to the dictates of the charts. (See fig. 9–1.) In the musical comedy *The Music Man,* the scene with the ladies' "classic dance" group performing "Three Grecian Urns" is a deliberate parody of this kind of Delsarte exercise.

Delsarte's work was very influential in two ways: In a positive sense, he opened the door to a different point of view on the nature of emotions from

FIGURE 9–1.   Remorse, Submission, and Denial—Three "Delsarte Exercises" Illustrated in *The Peerless Speaker: A Practical Manual of Elocution and Oratory* (1897). *These poses were intended to be studied and then recalled while speaking poetry. Note that the figure is pictured in a Greek costume.*

that of Aristotle. In a negative sense, his charts and exercises came to be an object of ridicule. To many people, Delsarte represented the worst, most mechanical and artificial acting. The idea that emotions could be studied and catalogued in this way became widely rejected. This is particularly ironic in light of the fact that Delsarte's initial motivation was to reform the artificiality he found in the acting of his time. But the result was to substitute one set of conventions for another. (Of course, Delsarte attempted to catalogue the expression of human emotion before the popularization of photography; had he had access to modern research tools such as motion picture film and videotape, history might have turned out very differently, as we shall see later in this chapter.)

Another early agent of change was the English critic and naturalist George Henry Lewes (pronounced like "Lewis") (1817–1878.) His career as a scientist is distinguished by a five-volume pioneering study of human psychology, *Problems of Life and Mind* (1874–1879.) His career in the theatre is distinguished by the publication in 1875 of *On Actors and the Art of Acting,* a collection of critiques and reminiscences of some of the preeminent actors of his time. Lewes' interest in psychology and theatre put him in the unique position of being influential in both fields.

Lewes' position on acting and emotion was the opposite of Diderot's. Lewes felt that emotion was the central problem of acting. He argued that great actors do indeed experience the emotions of their characters; at moments of great emotional excitement onstage, the personality of the actor becomes the personality of the character, and the actor's emotions become the character's emotions. In this fusion of outer show and inner feeling, Lewes was reaffirming the relationship among body, mind, and emotion that Delsarte had advocated. However, Lewes felt that sympathetic imagination was the key to the process, not imitation (the Delsarte approach). He agreed with Diderot that actors had to remain in control of their feelings, but he argued that these feelings gave the spark of greatness to their external expression in the role. Lewes felt that actors' feelings were derived from their memories of emotions felt in their own lives. Joseph R. Roach, Jr., writing about Lewes in *Theatre Journal,* stresses that Lewes' ideas about emotion anticipated and were indirectly influential on the work of Stanislavski. Roach summarizes Lewes in this way:

> In artists with a highly active histrionic sensibility, the intensity of memory and imagination may approach the level of "hallucination," not in the sense of madness, but in the sense of vividness, for the actions of reviving and imagining operate under conditions of artistic choice. The artist must have enough control "to select . . . only those elements which suit his purpose."[10]

Whether or not the idea of actors' using their own "memory of emotion" originated with Lewes, his writings on the subject resemble Stanislavski's concept of "affective memory," which became central to his work. The resemblance may be far from accidental. Roach points out that Lewes contributed articles to a journal called *La Revue philosophique,* edited by the French psychologist Théodule Armand Ribot (1839–1916). Ribot's treatise *The Psychology of the Emotions* was published in a Russian translation in 1898, and Stanislavski is known to have been familiar with this work. His own ideas about affective memory are thought to have been derived in large measure from Ribot's. In the chapter on emotional memory in *An Actor Prepares,* Stanislavski seems to be in perfect agreement with Lewes:

> You can understand a part, sympathize with the person portrayed, and put yourself in his place, so that you will act as he would. That will arouse feelings in the actor that are analogous to those required for the part. But those feelings will belong, not to the person created by the author of the play, but to the actor himself.[11]

Immediately after that statement, Stanislavski goes on to plead with the actor.

> *Never lose yourself on the stage. Always act in your own person, as an artist. You can never get away from yourself. The moment you lose yourself on the stage marks the departure from truly living your part and the beginning of exaggerated false acting.* [Stanislavski's emphasis.][12]

In that excerpt, we see how Stanislavski advised actors to use authentic emotions as a way to overcome the "exaggerated false acting" that was characteristic of the presentational actors of his day. By rejecting Diderot's advice and trying to stimulate their own emotions, actors could find the authentic way to express the delicate emotions required by a play such as *The Seagull.* Therefore, we see that in the early development of realistic acting, emotion was emphasized not as a goal in itself but as *a means to an end.* Through the use emotion memory, the actor could overcome the stale and artificial clichés of emotional expression that were characteristic of lines of business. Ironically, this was the same goal that Delsarte had sought; but Delsarte had tried to solve the problem through observation, whereas Stanislavski chose the device of affective memory.

In the meantime, Lewes' ideas on psychology and acting became known to another important psychologist, William James, who reviewed the second volume of Lewes' *Problems of Life and Mind* favorably in *The Atlantic Monthly* in 1875. William James (1842–1910) was an influential American scientist and philosopher. As a psychologist, he took the idea of emotions as organic processes in a startlingly different direction. His ideas on the nature of emotions are also associated with the work of the Danish psychologist Carl Georg Lange, who published a similar theory of the emotions at about the same time. As a result, even though their work was evolved separately, their joint theory is today known as the James-Lange theory of the emotions. James published its earliest expression in a journal called *Mind* in 1884. The following excerpt from this article, entitled "What Is an Emotion?" expresses the germ of the theory itself:

> Our natural way of thinking about emotions is that the mental perception of some fact excites the mental affection called the emotion, and that this latter state of mind gives rise to the bodily expression. My thesis on the contrary is that *the bodily changes follow directly the PERCEPTION of the exciting fact, and that our feeling of the same changes as they occur IS the emotion.* Common sense says, we lose our fortune, are sorry and weep; we meet a bear, are frightened and run; we are insulted by a rival, are angry and strike. The hypothesis here to be defended says that this order of sequence is incorrect, that the one mental state is not immediately induced by the other, that the bodily manifestations must first be interposed between, and that the more rational statement is that we feel sorry because we cry, angry because we strike, afraid because we tremble, and not that we cry, strike, or tremble, because we are sorry, angry or fearful as the case may be. [James' emphasis.][13]

This theory was greeted with tremendous interest, but other researchers found difficulty in establishing its validity in clinical situations. Other theories of the emotions were subsequently offered. In 1894, John Dewey proposed one based on conflict. In 1915, W. B. Cannon proposed another based on what he called "biological emergency." Sigmund Freud related emotions to the interplay of the life and death instincts. And other explanations have been offered, and continue to be offered, to the present day.

To summarize this section, we now understand why authentic emotion became an important factor in the early development of realistic acting. Stanislavski discovered that by treating emotion as part of the organic process of acting, actors could avoid the "false pathos" of presentational acting and create an effective illusion of natural behavior. This emphasis on the actor's own emotion as the basis of emotional expression onstage was a radical innovation.

EMOTIONAL MEMORY IN AMERICA

Richard Boleslavsky (1889–1937) and Maria Ouspenskaya (1881–1949) were among the first actors who left the Moscow Art Theatre (MAT) to spread the gospel of Stanislavski elsewhere. Boleslavsky left Russia in 1922 and made his way to America, where he greeted Stanislavski and the other MAT actors when they arrived in New York in 1923 for their first American tour (as discussed in Chapter One). Ouspenskaya arrived with the MAT company, but she decided not to go back with the other actors when they returned to Russia in 1924. Together, Boleslavsky and Ouspenskaya began teaching at the American Laboratory Theatre in New York. Boleslavsky also published articles about Stanislavski's theories, eventually collected into a volume entitled

Acting: The First Six Lessons (1933). In 1924, Stanislavski published a book of memoirs, *My Life in Art,* in which he describes his theories as they had evolved at that time (and as Boleslavsky and Ouspenskaya were teaching them in America). He begins by affirming that the actor must believe in the reality of the stage illusion.

> It will be said, "But what kind of truth can this be, when all on the stage is a lie, an imitation, scenery, cardboard, paint, make-up, properties, wooden goblets, swords and speares. Is all this truth?" But it is not of this truth I speak. I speak of the truth of emotions, of the truth of inner creative urges which strain forward to find expression of the truth of the memories of bodily and physical perceptions.[14]

In the mid-1920s, Stanislavski was still emphasizing that actors needed to stimulate their own emotions first and then give those emotions expression in the physical performance onstage.

Lee Strasberg (1901–1982), undoubtedly America's most influential teacher of acting, was a student for a time at the American Laboratory Theatre in 1923, and he also saw the Moscow Art Theatre in performance during its New York engagement. The son of immigrants, who brought him from Budzanow, Russia, to America at the age of seven and a half, Strasberg had previously participated only in amateur theatricals, but Boleslavsky's course, "Art of the Theatre," excited him sufficiently that he decided to become a professional actor. David Garfield, in *A Player's Place,* states that Strasberg retained the notes taken during Boleslavsky's first lecture.

> On that introductory occasion, the topic was not the System, but the two forms of acting: the kind that Stanislavski calls "the art of representation," which demands a highly skillful imitation or indication of preconceived forms of behavior, and the other kind, "the art of living the part," which requires the actor to really experience onstage. Years later [Strasberg] would recall how he sat there listening and jotting down his notes, experiencing the sensation that "this is it." Here were the means to create the kind of acting and the kind of theater he wanted to be involved with.[15]

The way to accomplish this goal was to use emotional (or "affective") memory, which was to become the key element in the approach to acting that would eventually become known in America as "The Method." Once again, it needs to be stated that Strasberg apparently perceived its use as Stanislavski had perceived it—that is, as a means of overcoming the stilted, artificial expression of emotion that realistic acting had inherited from presentational and Romantic acting. In 1941, John Gassner published a lengthy article by Lee Strasberg, "Acting and Actor Training," which is one of the few substantial pieces of writing that he created on the subject of acting. In this article, he comes down particularly hard on the James-Lange theory,

... which not only laid stress upon the outer manifestation [of emotion] but claimed that the consciousness of these outer manifestations was the emotion ... "You are afraid because you run—not you run because you are afraid." This proved such a wonderful cushion for the teachers of acting that it has distilled itself like poison as a basic premise, despite the fact that research in modern psychology has gone far beyond it. The theory has not withstood the test of the experimental evidence; and in the cognate field of the expression of emotions, experimental work tends to show that there is no expression typical of any situation ... [16]

Strasberg attacked the James-Lange theory largely because he saw it as leading backward to the abuses that had accompanied the Delsarte charts.

While it might seem that from the actor's point of view the possession of purely external media for the expression of emotions, neatly catalogued into illustrations, should be a great boon, the exact opposite is true. An actor's impulses and resources are completely choked by a predetermined physical pattern.[17]

In 1931, Strasberg joined with Harold Clurman, Cheryl Crawford, and others to form a company called the Group Theatre. Organized as an offshoot of the powerful Theatre Guild, the Group was a self-conscious attempt to organize a Moscow Art Theatre in America. The Group's organizers had read Stanislavski's account of the founding of the MAT in *My Life in Art* and proceeded along very similar lines. Strasberg became the Group's chief director and instructor of acting. During the summer of 1931, rehearsals were begun for a play called *The House of Connelly* by Paul Green, and Strasberg wasted no time in introducing Boleslavsky's techniques to the members of the new company. Clurman recalls these first sessions with Strasberg in his book *The Fervent Years*.

... the actor was asked to recall the details of an event from his own past. The recollection of these details would stir the actors with some of the feeling involved in the original experience, thus producing "mood". .... The first effect on the actors was that of a miracle. The system (incorrectly identified by some actors as the use of the exercises) represented for most of them the open-sesame of the actor's art. Here at last was a key to that elusive ingredient of the stage, true emotion. And Strasberg was a fanatic on the subject of true emotion. Everything was secondary to it.[18]

In this passage, Clurman seems to suggest that Strasberg had moved somewhat further in his thinking about the role of emotion than Stanislavski, who saw remembered emotion primarily as a means to an end. Strasberg seems to have insisted on the actor's experience of "true emotion" as a prerequisite for performance. In other words, emotion was no longer the means to an end, but the end in and of itself. (And in this attitude, we find the origin of the idea that learning to act means primarily learning to emote.)

Strasberg left the Group Theatre in 1937 to pursue a career as a director. Ten years later, Elia Kazan brought about the formation of the Actors Studio in New York as a response, in part, to the helter-skelter system of actor training in America up to that time. The concept of the Studio was to provide working professional actors with a place to practice their craft and to sharpen their skills as performers. But by 1951, Kazan's interest had taken him elsewhere, and Strasberg had become the most influential leader of the Studio's activities. Using the Studio as a forum, Strasberg taught his system of Method acting until his death in 1982, and in the process, he trained and influenced the careers of many fine stage and screen actors.

Through the influence of Stanislavski and Strasberg, emotion has become accepted as an essential part of realistic acting in America. As noted before, American audiences early on declared their preference for emotional acting. But as Wilson pointed out, American males are not normally expected to be emotionally demonstrative; at least, that expectation is not part of the American stereotype of the John Wayne/Gary Cooper strong and silent American male. When Clurman refers to the technique of emotion memory as a kind of "open-sesame," we can easily imagine that American male actors especially would have welcomed it as a way of increasing their ability to give audiences the kind of emotional acting they want. At the 1984 convention of the American Theatre Association, Lorrie Hull (senior faculty member of the Los Angeles Lee Strasberg Theatre Institute) presided over the following demonstration: Two actors with whom she had worked previously presented a scene from Edward Albee's *The Zoo Story*. One of them closed his eyes and began to visualize his memories of his father's funeral. A moment later, he began describing those details aloud—his memory of his father's body lying in an open coffin and the thoughts that had been going through his mind at that time—with the result that he began weeping openly. Then, at the height of his remembered grief, he was told to begin the scene from *The Zoo Story*, literally fusing the emotion he was remembering into his acting of the scene. (It should be noted that once actors gain practice at recalling their emotions in this manner, they can learn to speed up the recall process, even to a point at which extremely intense emotions can be recalled almost instantaneously.) No one who watched this demonstration could have doubted for a moment that the actor's grief was real.

FROM THE OUTSIDE IN

As noted in Chapter One, once the ideals of realistic acting evolved, there were dissenters almost immediately, among them Vsevolod Meyerhold and Bertolt Brecht. In the same way, not everyone approved of Stanislavski's emphasis on the actor's use of emotional memory as the primary route to authentic emotional expression.

In America, there were dissenters also. In 1934, Stella Adler, an actor in the Group Theatre, began to take exception to Strasberg's techniques. As a result, she journeyed to Paris to meet with Stanislavski in person; she complained to him that his theories were not working for her and were causing her great distress as an actor. When she explained what Strasberg had been doing with the Group actors, Stanislavski reacted strongly, and his remarks were recorded by a stenographer that Adler had brought with her to the session. At one point Stanislavski apparently said,

> For emotion, I search in the given circumstances, never in the feelings. If I try and do the psychological, I force the action. We must attack the psychological from the point of view of the physical life so as not to disturb the feeling. In each psychological action, there is some physical element. Search for the line in terms of the action, not in feeling.[19]

The Stanislavski we hear in this quotation is very different from the Stanislavski we have heard in the other quotations. Apparently his ideas on affective memory had changed somewhat since the publication of *My Life in Art*. Most Stanislavski scholars seem to feel that at some time between 1924 and 1934, he may have concluded that remembering emotion was not the most effective route to authentic emotional expression. He apparently concluded that the emotions could be stimulated more effectively by purely physical means. Unfortunately, Stanislavski's later conclusions were not to be so well known in America as his earlier ones. How did that happen?

In 1928, Stanislavski suffered a heart attack that effectively ended his career as an actor. But as a result, he turned his attention even more seriously to the development of his system and to writing. Elizabeth Reynolds Hapgood met with Stanislavski when he was taking a rest cure in Paris in 1930. According to her, Stanislavski felt that his ideas would require more than one book to develop fully. Eventually, he would write two complete books and most of a third. The first book, *An Actor Prepares,* was published in America (in Hapgood's translation) in 1936. It focuses on the inner life of the actor and seems to reflect the same emphasis on remembered emotion that Strasberg learned from Boleslavsky. When the book was published, most people assumed that it embodied the entire Stanislavski system.

Then because of the advent of World War II and other problems, the second book did not appear in America until 1949. This book, *Building a Character,* seems to be almost a radical reversal of the ideas in the first one. In this book, Stanislavski shows how many of the results described in *An Actor Prepares* can also be achieved primarily through physical means. At the end of *Building a Character,* he summarizes the contents of both books and suggests that both approaches are useful to the actor. In the first chapter of *Building a Character,* Stanislavski describes an exercise that strongly recalls the James-Lange theory (which Strasberg, you recall, rejected vehemently). A fictional student (really Stanislavski himself) creates the internal sensations of a character entirely through the adoption of various costume and makeup elements gathered at random.

A third book, *Creating a Role,* appeared finally in America in 1961, and some people argue that it represents the final form of Stanislavski's system. This form of his theories is today known as the *method of physical actions* and does not use emotion memory in the form that Strasberg taught at the Actors Studio. Sonia Moore, founder of the American Center for Stanislavski Theater Art and an expert on this latter evolution of Stanislavski's system, gave a demonstration of it at the same American Theatre Association convention in San Francisco in 1984. (And you can try this demonstration for yourself as you read along.)

First, she demonstrated an action without a motivation, in this case, a person waving a hand overhead for no apparent reason. Then she showed how an actor might choose to accomplish a specific desired result through that action—as when, for example, a person might wave to catch the attention of someone at the other end of a crowded room. Using this example of a motivated action, she asked all the people in attendance to raise one arm and hold it out in front of them. She then told everyone to motivate this pose, to build up specific reasons why someone might hold up an arm in that position. She suggested that everyone say a few sentences to themselves to build up the details of the circumstances (not unlike the verbalizing done by the actor in the Method Acting demonstration) and then to let the whole body become involved—to become, as it were, an actor really playing the action of holding out an arm in this manner. Then she told everyone to drop their arms.

After everyone had relaxed, she asked the audience if they could remember the feelings they had experienced while playing that simple action. Most people in the room said they could not. After a few moments of discussion on other points, she asked everyone to raise their arms as before with the same total bodily involvement in the action. Then she asked if everyone could remember their thoughts and feelings as before. Most people in the room could. Repeating the physical action alone brought back the feelings without having to build the mental circumstances first; in other words, the physical action stimulated the memory of the feeling without having to recall the circumstances used to induce the feeling originally. She commented that everyone should be able to recall the former sensations to some degree, but that to remember everything through re-creating the physical action alone requires practice.

This demonstration is described here because it illustrates how Stanislavski's understanding of emotional memory had expanded and evolved. Apparently, he had begun to accept the idea that Delsarte had suggested in the first half of the nineteenth century, that emotions and their physical expression are indeed related. In her book *The Stanislavski System,* Moore sums up this version of emotion memory:

> Emotional memory stores our past experiences; to relive them, actors must execute indispensable, logical physical actions in the given circumstances. There are as many different nuances of emotions as there are different physical actions.[20]

However, the difference between this point of view and Delsarte's is critical. The Delsarte approach required a deliberate recreation of the outer expression of emotion. Moore emphasizes that the actor's focus must be on performing a motivated action truthfully to stimulate the memory of the desired emotion. Just as James theorized, re-creating certain physical poses or postures can induce certain emotions associated with them.

Using modern research tools and techniques, Paul Ekman, a professor of psychology at the University of California, San Francisco, has attained some clinical results that tend to support James' theory. Ekman has done extensive research on the ways in which emotions are expressed by the face. He has concluded that there are at least six fundamental emotions that all people express on their faces in the same way. In his book *Unmasking the Face*, he describes how the face expresses happiness, sadness, surprise, fear, anger, and disgust—regardless of cultural differences.

> In one experiment, stress-inducing films were shown to college students in the United States and to college students in Japan. Part of the time, each person watched the film alone and part of the time the person watched while talking about the experience with a research assistant from the person's own culture. Measurements of the actual facial muscle movements, captured on videotapes, showed that when they were alone, the Japanese and Americans had virtually identical expressions.[21]

Ekman provides extensive photographic documentation of the expression of these six emotions. The results are startlingly like Delsarte's charts.

In the September 16, 1983 issue of *Science*, Ekman and his associates reported on a fascinating experiment in which they attempted to establish a connection between facial expressions and felt emotions. Twelve professional actors were asked to produce facial expressions appropriate to the six fundamental emotions already listed. In part of the experiment they were not told which emotion to express, only which facial muscles to contract; in another part of the experiment, they were told to use the technique of emotion memory to generate specific emotions. At the same time, researchers documented heart rate, left and right-hand temperatures, skin resistance, and forearm muscle tension. The results proved that

> Emotion-specific activity in the autonomic nervous system was generated by constructing facial prototypes of emotion muscle by muscle and by reliving past emotional experiences.[22]

One other conclusion that Ekman states in the same article has far-reaching implications for actors:

> Particularly intriguing is our discovery that producing the emotion-prototypic patterns of facial muscle action resulted in autonomic changes of large magnitude that were more clear-cut than those produced by reliving emotions (a more naturalistic process). With this experiment we cannot rule out the possibility that knowledge of the emotion labels derived from the facial movement instructions or seeing one's own or the coach's face was directly or indirectly responsible for the effect. We find this unlikely . . . We propose instead that it was contracting the facial muscles into the universal emotion signals which brought forth the emotion-specific activity.[23]

The implication seems to be that a greater intensity of feeling can be achieved by posing the expression of the emotion mechanically than by using emotion memory to generate the physical expression. Thus, Ekman's conclusions seem to cast doubt on the long-held assumption in American realistic acting that emotion has to be felt before it can be expressed authentically.

Then what is the proper function of emotion in the work of the actor? To answer that question, we must look at yet another theory of the emotions—but one that has to do more with how emotions are communicated than with how they are generated or expressed. This is the theory of *empathy*.

EMPATHY

When we look at a painting or a sculpture that stirs our emotions, we are having an *empathic* response to that object. In other words, some element in what we see reminds us of our own experience of a particular emotion, and the memory of that emotion is felt within ourselves as the emotion itself. For example, one of the most famous sculptures in the world is Michelangelo's *Pietà* in St. Peter's, Rome. This sculpture shows the Virgin Mary cradling the body of Christ in her lap. Most people who view this sculpture in person have a strong emotional response; even photographs of it are capable of stirring the emotions, although not to the same degree. To be specific, when we are moved by this block of stone, we are moved because we seem to feel the emotion that is being felt by the figure of Mary. That fact is somewhat remarkable when you consider that the statue is made of marble and, therefore, has no feeling within itself. Certainly, we have to assume that Michelangelo must have felt deep emotion in executing the sculpture. But Michelangelo died in 1564, and therefore it is unlikely that his feelings are somehow stored up within the marble to be communicated to us today.

What is actually happening when we view this sculpture is that we are affected by the expression on the face of Mary and the position of the limbs.

We recognize the expression of profound sorrow and love. In other words, those details seem familiar to us; they seem authentic. We look and we think to ourselves, "Yes, when someone mourns, that is how such a person looks." Even more, we are likely to think to ourselves, "When I grieve, that is how I look. I know how that feels." In essence, the recognition of the emotion stirs the feeling within us.

Empathy is this tendency to identify with the feelings of others. It is the assumption that someone else's feelings are just like our own. This tendency is different from *sympathy*, which is an actual sharing of feelings (such as when more than one person feels the same grief for the loss of someone else). However, in the case of Michelangelo's *Pietà*, we ourselves do not literally grieve for a piece of cold marble.

In effect, the result is similar to that of Ekman's experiments. We can look at the expression on someone else's face, and if we recognize a look of fear or happiness or sadness or whatever, we will feel that same emotion ourselves—almost as if the face and the facial expression were our own. We ourselves do not have to pose our own face into a similar expression in order to feel the emotion. The look we recognize on someone else's face is sufficient to trigger the feeling within ourselves.

Empathy is a principle similar to the audience's tendency to fill in the missing pieces of the illusion of natural behavior—it works whether or not anyone tries to make it work. When someone has a particularly good reason to feel happy, that person can "brighten up" a whole room full of people just by being there. Conversely, one person may be nervous and tense and walk into an office full of people and make them all nervous and tense in a matter of minutes—without their realizing how or why they got that way. Probably the most common example of this phenomenon is the response most people have to someone who yawns. Within seconds, everyone around that person feels like yawning, too.

The principle of empathy explains how emotion is communicated by an actor to an audience. The actor communicates feeling through some use of the body that causes the people in the audience to recognize that behavior as being similar to their own experiences of a particular feeling. Their recognition triggers their own memories of that feeling, and that memory is experienced as the feeling itself. For example, when Lady Macbeth walks around the battlements at Dunsinane and tries to rub imaginary blood off her hands in her sleep, her sense of despair and terror is not shared by the audience in any real sense—no one in the audience has helped her kill the King. Besides, the actor who plays the King is backstage in the greenroom to wait for his curtain call at the end of the performance. But from the way that she moves and gestures and breathes and uses her voice, the people in the audience recognize the emotions of despair and terror, and therefore, they feel those emotions vicariously because they have felt them in their own lives—perhaps not in the same way or to the same extent, but all people have known those feelings to some degree. All the audience must do is recognize those feelings in the actor playing Lady Macbeth, and they will feel them at that moment as well.

This point is so important and so basic to this chapter that it needs to be stated once again. The marble that constitutes Michelangelo's *Pietà* feels nothing. The emotion that we feel when we contemplate this masterpiece is our own; it does not come from the marble, the sculptor, the subject matter, or from anywhere else outside ourselves. It is our own emotion, entirely of our own creation. When we look at Lady Macbeth onstage, we are also feeling our own emotion; the actor playing this role may be feeling the passion of the moment very deeply, but we are not literally sharing her emotion. Through her emotion, she achieves physical postures and attitudes that we recognize; the act of recognizing her postures and attitudes triggers the emotional response within ourselves. Whether or not the actor playing Lady Macbeth actually feels these emotions has no direct bearing on the case; the emotions are communicated to us in the same way as the *Pietà* communicates emotion to us.

Some readers may find that last statement hard to accept. After all, a statue does not move, whereas an actor does. However, movement does not affect the process. Puppets (which are a kind of moving sculpture) can inspire deep and intense emotional responses in audiences. Steven Spielberg's film *E.T.* caused audiences to sob and blubber shamelessly when the puppet that portrayed the central character appeared to be dying. Even highly unsophisticated puppets can have similar effects. In 1933, Willis O'Brien created a gorilla puppet for *King Kong*. At the climax of the film (in a sequence which seems extremely clumsy by contemporary special-effects' standards), the big ape is riddled with bullets (fired by model biplanes.) The suffering of the ape-puppet as he finally releases his female human captive is still curiously affecting. What is particularly remarkable in this example is the fact that the sequence used stop-motion animation. In other words, O'Brien and his fellow "puppeteers" had to pose their puppets one frame at a time and then wait until the film came back from the lab before they could judge the effectiveness of their work. The same principle works in animated cartoons as well: The death of Bambi's mother or Gepetto's grief at the drowning of Pinocchio are powerfully affective moments in the animated film versions of these stories.

The fact that the principle of empathy works at all points to an inevitable conclusion about emotion and the actor: *Actors do not have to feel the emotions they portray in order to make an audience feel those emotions.* Diderot's example regarding David Garrick provides significant support for this conclusion. Garrick was clearly the most admired English actor of his day; the demonstration of technique which Diderot claims to have witnessed shows that Garrick's acting did not depend on feeling all the emotions he portrayed. In fact, Diderot claimed that Garrick had such a command of his lines of business that feeling would simply get in his way.

An effective piece of acting requires maintaining control over physical technique; indeed, I have occasionally seen actors who have become so involved in their own emotions that they forgot their technique entirely—and their acting stopped being effective. (Perhaps you have seen similar occurrences yourself.) When actors feel their emotions deeply but forget to make them an authentic part of the overall illusion of the performance as a whole, the audience's empathic response is stifled. (When Melina Mercouri demonstrated that she could cry, Harry Reasoner didn't cry also. He simply smiled and complimented her on her technique; since the tears were so obviously out of any context, they were merely interesting as a stunt.) In a like way, when we respond to the face and figure of Mary in Michelangelo's *Pietà*, we are responding not merely because we are looking at a statue of a woman who looks sad; we are responding to the expression of grief in the full context of who those figures are and what that scene is supposed to represent. The expression of grief in the figure of Mary in that grouping strikes us as authentic *in that context*.

Therefore, we can draw our second conclusion about emotion and the actor: *Whether or not the actor feels the emotion, its expression must seem authentic within the context of the dramatic situation.* In other words, the emotion must be perceived as a part of the overall illusion of natural behavior before an audience is going to respond. Without the context within which the audience can evaluate the authenticity of the emotional expression, the emotion is not going to be effectively communicated no matter how deeply felt or how beautifully expressed. To return again to Diderot's story about Garrick, Diderot does not claim that he himself responded empathically with the moods Garrick portrayed on his face. Indeed, such a response would be highly unlikely in the way that Diderot describes the incident.

Then what is the proper role of emotion in the work of the modern realistic actor?

FEELING THE PART

Emotion, as was stated at the beginning of this chapter, remains an area of great concern and great controversy in American acting. Opinion is divided whether actors should feel first and then express themselves (as in the Method demonstration described earlier) or perform the action and build the circumstances to generate the feeling (as in the demonstration of the "method of physical actions"). There seems to be ample scientific precedent for both approaches. Neither side can claim to have dominance over the other in that department. But between the warring factions, there is a middle ground where some facts cannot be disputed by either side.

First, the whole basis of modern research into the mystery of the emotions is that emotions are organic processes, not symptoms. Aristotle's biles have at last been drained away! Both approaches to acting agree that there is a definite connection between the inner sensation of feeling and its outer expression. Since these things are connected, it is possible for the dog to wag the tail or the tail to wag the dog. As was shown in the Method demonstration, the man's memories generated the physical expression; as Ekman's researches have demonstrated, posing the expression of an emotion on the face can generate the feeling itself.

But we don't really need scientific proof of this fact; many examples can be drawn from familiar situations in everyday life. For example, often our external indicators can be manipulated to produce a corresponding change in our feelings. Many people have felt the despondency that results from long periods of inactivity; that despondency can be relieved simply by physical exercise. If we act happy, we feel happy. In the musical play *The King and I*, Anna sings to her son Louis, "When I fool the people I fear, I fool myself as well." Being brave is as much a function of acting bravely as being a coward is a function of acting like one. At one time or another, almost everyone has experienced the odd transition from "horsing around" with a friend (pretending to quarrel and fight), to *really* fighting and arguing. This is a dangerous game to play because so often a "pretend" argument can turn into a real one.

Most people have felt the opposite process at work also. If you simply start to think about having a tooth drilled by a dentist, you may find that your palms start to sweat (a phenomenon you couldn't order up voluntarily no matter how hard you tried). If you start to think about a mysterious stranger who is lurking behind you and is about to put his hands around your throat, you may find that the skin on the back of your neck starts to tingle. If you start to think about getting the car you've always wanted or going out on a date with a glamorous star, you may actually find your pulse rate increasing slightly—just by suggestion alone. Thought alone can produce the feeling, and the feeling can stimulate involuntary indicators of emotion that could never be initiated by conscious, deliberate command alone.

However, our everyday experiences also tell us that the connection between the sensation of feeling and its expression is not one of simple cause and effect. In our everyday life we encounter many exceptions to the principles just discussed. In effect, we seem to have the ability to override the connection between emotion and its expression when it is to our advantage to do so. We can, when we want to, hide our feelings. For example, many people have gone to funerals and felt great sorrow (as did the man in the Method example), but they may also have felt a need to keep their feelings under control. If you have ever been in a similar situation, you know that we can keep ourselves from crying simply by not letting ourselves cry. We still feel our sorrow, but we can keep it from showing if we have to.

Again, the opposite process works also. When you get the promotion that I wanted for myself, I can make you believe that I am happy for you (because you are my friend), even though I am really very jealous of your good fortune. When I have heard a piece of extremely bad news that I know would hurt your feelings if you were to hear it, I can convince you that nothing is wrong, even though inside I am extremely upset. If you are a salesperson in a shoe store and you are on duty on the sales floor, you are expected to be charming to the customers. But suppose that your feet are killing you and your best friend is in the hospital and your automobile insurance has just been canceled and you're being evicted from your apartment tomorrow; these are all circumstances that are likely to cause you to feel less than charming. But if you want to keep your job, you are going to have to be charming anyhow. Most people can bring off that effect even under those circumstances if they have to. (As noted in Chapter Two, acting is an absolutely essential social skill.)

If the connection between the sensation of feeling and its expression is not one of simple cause and effect, exactly how are they connected? You can discover the answer yourself by trying the following experiment.

First, allowing yourself complete freedom of expression, act out Ekman's six emotions: surprise, disgust, sadness, anger, fear, and happiness. Notice how hard it is to feel happy without the external indicator of a smile, how difficult it is to feel anger without the corresponding tensing of the muscles. Notice that it is almost impossible to create any of these sensations without using some kind of suggestion or specific memory, as in the Method demonstration described earlier; you almost have to think of something that makes you feel happy or sad in order to create those feelings. Next, adopt a physical attitude that suggests complete neutrality, the absence of any strong feelings or muscle tension. Without changing any of the external indicators (no frowns, no hunched shoulders, and so on) try again to feel the same six emotions. Use the same suggestions and memories you used before. Perhaps some emotional response can be generated, but certainly not with the apparent ease and intensity that accompanied fully unrestricted physical expression. Therefore, you can see for yourself that the emotions that are felt most intensely are those that are expressed.

In essence, therefore, the relationship between the inner sensation of emotion and its external expression seems to be a lot like the relationship between motivation and behavior. The two things are related, but the conscious mind seems to control the relationship. Except in the most extreme circumstances, we control our feelings and their expression in the same way that we select which objectives to play at any given moment. From an actor's point of view, therefore, thinking sad thoughts in the hope of automatically generating the external appearance of sadness is not enough; the process has got to be helped along by the choice of appropriate behavior, that is, *consciously creating the external indicators appropriate to sorrow*—which is exactly what happens in life. To return to the example of the funeral, we can consciously control our experience of grief; we have to let ourselves go through the motions of grief, as it were, before we can feel that emotion fully. If we do not allow ourselves to go through those motions, our experience of grief is going to be severely diminished—a fact that you have just demonstrated for yourself in the previous exercise. Feeling alone does not automatically produce its external expression; in order for feeling to be fully experienced, the external expression of feeling (which is under our conscious control) must be initiated.

However, there are involuntary components to the experience of feeling as well as those external indicators that can be consciously manipulated. The sweat in our palms, the tingling on the back of our neck, and the accelerated pulse rate cannot be initiated just by conscious command. These elements are controlled—as described in previous examples—by suggestion. Sometimes, as in the Ekman findings, the suggestion provided by conscious and deliberate manipulation of the voluntary indicators is sufficient to stimulate the involuntary ones. But onstage, the problem cannot always be solved so easily. For example, many actors have been greatly frustrated because they cannot cry onstage. Try as they may, no matter how they go through the motions of crying (the voluntary indicators), they cannot generate the necessary tears (the involuntary indicators.) The reason is not that James and Ekman are wrong but that some kind of interference (or *block*) is being imposed by the actor's conscious mind. The natural connection between the sensations of sorrow and the appropriate external indicators is being interrupted. For some reason, the conscious mind is not allowing the involuntary indicators to be affected by the physical suggestion.

There can be any number of explanations for this kind of interference, but three are especially common:

1. Actors sometimes have their feelings blocked because their conscious mind thinks they are not feeling the emotions they should be feeling. They get an idea in their heads that there is a "right" feeling for a particular scene; if they don't feel that particular emotion in exactly the way they think they should, their own authentic emotions become blocked. The solution is for them to forget what they think they should be feeling and to concentrate on what they really are feeling. In the playing of any role, there should be some response brought on by the physical actions alone; the Ekman experiments make this fact very clear. Once actors stop judging their real feelings by what they think they should be feeling, they generally find the block is removed.

2. Sometimes, the actions that an actor has chosen to play lack conviction. The conscious mind is not satisfied, and an emotional block is the result. Perhaps the emotions they are trying to play are really too extreme for the motivation, or perhaps the character's behavior is not really appropriate to the situation or the relationships. As we observed in discussing the *Pietà*, the context is an important factor in generating the response; tears without the right context are not by themselves affecting for the audience or for the actor. The solution in this case is to check the details of the situation, the character relationships, the character's identity and personality, and the objectives to be sure that all the choices are convincing and appropriate. If there are bad choices being made, their removal will generally remove the block as well.

3. Actors sometimes become so preoccupied with the need to feel a particular emotion in a particular scene that they forget to play the scene. Some actors, such as Melina Mercouri, can generate certain emotions instantly; with others, the feelings are less immediate. When results are not immediately forthcoming, some actors stop trying to play their objectives and try instead to force their emotions to their will. If the emotion doesn't want to be forced in that way, the result is often a block. The solution is to stop trying to play the emotion (an error that was previously identified as a nonobjective) and put the focus back on the character's objectives, really looking at and paying attention to what is happening onstage at each moment in the performance. As in the previous case, forcing one's emotions is not natural behavior; it is, in effect, asking the body to do something that is not appropriate to the context in which emotion is felt naturally.

But ultimately, when an actor does not feel a desired emotion in spite of the correct context and the correct external expression, we have to ask whether or not actually feeling that emotion is really important. In life, we can be convincing when we pretend to be happy (when we are really jealous), calm (when we are dreading bad news), or charming (when our feet ache, our friend is in the hospital, and we are about to be evicted); therefore, we *can portray emotions onstage effectively without feeling them.* Remember, the marble statue of Mary and the stop-motion puppet of King Kong didn't feel anything either, and according to Diderot, neither did David Garrick while he played that emotional "scale" with his face alone.

Remember also that Stanislavski initially seized on the devices of emotional memory and authentic emotion as a way of helping his actors escape the clichés of presentational acting. But once the new idea of playing actions had replaced that of playing the symptoms of happiness, grief, horror, and so on, Stanislavski (as he told Stella Adler in 1934) searched for the emotion "in terms of the action, not in feeling." In life as on the stage, the emotion we are showing may not be something we are feeling if our involuntary partners choose not to cooperate, but that fact alone does not necessarily mean that we are not convincing.

What matters for the audience is not whether the actor feels the emotions or not. What matters is that the *audience* feels the emotions. What matters is that the context is properly established through the appropriate illusion of natural behavior and that the actor's external indicators seem authentic within that context. When those two factors are present, the audience should have the appropriate empathic response—how the actor brought about those factors is really irrelevant. Of course, when the illusion of natural behavior is convincing and when the external indicators are authentic within the context, the actor should feel the emotions being portrayed—particularly if the actor is playing the objectives properly. In other words, going through the motions of the feeling within the context of the scene should be sufficient to cause the actor to feel the emotions that are being portrayed. But the absence of feeling in the playing is not in itself a sign that the acting is not convincing or affecting. At best, feeling is an extremely unreliable indicator that the actor's behavior is authentic. At worst, the absence of feeling may be a sign to the actor of some specific fault (such as those previously described). And the opposite proposition is equally true: The fact that an actor feels a particular emotion is no guarantee that the audience is going to have the appropriate empathic response. If the external indicators are not properly controlled by the conscious mind or if the context of the emotion has not been properly established, the feeling will not be shared by the audience.

Or, let me say all of that another way: I have known actors to be intimidated by having to play certain extremely emotional moments. The emotional expression required by the scene may be so intense that actors sometimes become afraid of looking foolish, particularly in rehearsal. As a result, they will announce that they are going to hold back their playing of the emotional climaxes until they feel they have established a foundation for the emotional release in the previous moments of the scene. I firmly believe that actors in such situations are making a serious mistake. The better approach is to attack such scenes head-on from the first rehearsal. Actors should let themselves play the emotional extremes even before they feel they established the foundation for those emotions. If they wait to feel it before they do it, they may never feel it at all. If they do it without restraints—no matter how silly or foolish they may feel at first—they should be able stimulate the desired feelings (as long as they are still truly playing their objectives) just by physical means alone. Once the full intensity of the feelings has been generated in this way, then actors will know what kind of a foundation to build to support the feelings to come. And even if the feelings never come, at least the outer show of the emotion—if properly grounded in the context of the scene—should be sufficient to stimulate the audience's empathic response anyway. But if actors wait for the foundation before letting themselves go, there is a great risk that the actors will never be able to let themselves go, and the audience will have nothing with which to empathize.

In conclusion, it can be said that feeling *should* be a part of good acting. However, the desire for feeling should never be placed above the two principles of emotional expression we have been discussing. One is the principle of empathy, the way in which emotion is communicated to the audience by recognition of the external indicators of emotion in an appropriate context. The other is the principle that shows the true relationship between emotion and its external expression: They are connected, but the connection is under the control of the conscious mind. And that principle dictates that we must initiate the external (voluntary) indicators of emotion before the internal (involuntary) indicators can be properly stimulated to create the inner sensation of feeling. Therefore, feeling is something that has to come after (and as a result of) playing the situation, playing the relationships, and playing the objectives.

Emotion is the frosting on the actor's cake—the final element of the performance that comes about when everything else is right. It is not the cake itself.

SUMMARY

Before the nineteenth century, the scientific understanding of the emotions had not progressed much further than Aristotle's four biles. Somewhat as a consequence, the profession of acting had evolved along certain lines of business, which defined the conventional manner of emotional expression for various types of characters. Eventually, a more scientific basis of understanding the emotions was to evolve. Among others who contributed to this process were François Delsarte (who first proposed that emotions were the result of organic processes and not fluid imbalances), George Henry Lewes (who published important early ideas about emotional memory and acting), Theodule Ribot (who contributed an important work on the psychology of the emotions), and William James and Carl Georg Lange (who formulated the so-called "fright/flight" theory of the emotions).

Constantin Stanislavski used an approach to emotional expression onstage that was derived in part from Ribot. Emphasizing authentic emotion stimulated through affective memory, Stanislavski made his actors abandon the conventionalized emotional expressions of presentational acting. The use of affective memory for this purpose was brought to the United States by Richard Boleslavsky and Maria Ouspenskaya, who instructed Lee Strasberg. Through Strasberg's work with the Group Theatre and the Actors Studio, remembered emotion became identified as an important element of so-called "Method" acting.

Dissenters to the Method approach included Stella Adler, who learned firsthand from Stanislavski that in the years following 1924, his work had developed a new emphasis on action. This subsequent approach, now known as the "method of physical actions," has been taught in America by Sonia Moore. Important clinical justification for this approach has been provided by Paul Ekman, who has demonstrated how the experience of emotion and its expression on the face are linked. Ekman's findings lend further support to the principle of empathy (the tendency in all people to assume that other people's feelings are like their own).

In the end, two principles of the emotions are known and can be demonstrated with some certainty: The first is empathy, which shows that actors do not have to feel the emotions they portray in order to generate an empathic response in the audience. The second is the connection between emotions and their expression, which shows that emotions that are expressed are felt more deeply than those that are not expressed. From these two principles it can be demonstrated that the physical performance should receive an actor's primary attention; if the physical performance has been structured correctly, the actor should be able to feel the desired emotions naturally.

EXERCISES FOR CHAPTER NINE

The focus in this chapter has been on the proper function of emotion in the work of the actor. The most important principle is that the actor must set the external details of the role as a precondition for feeling the appropriate emotions during the actual playing of the scene. The following exercises are intended to help students perceive this relationship for themselves.

1. The principle that James and Lange articulated is that we feel emotion as a consequence of our actions. Try performing the following pantomimes:

    Assume that you have to sneak into a room in a house late at night. Your goal is to retrieve some object of tremendous importance to you without being discovered. Build the circumstances in your own mind; work out specific details of the room, the object, your need for it, and why stealth is required to recover it. Be sure that you construct the situation in your own mind in such a way that this particular action is your only recourse. Then rehearse the pantomime several times slowly and carefully. Observe all possible details of how you will get into the room, how you will move so as not to be heard or observed, and how you will search for the object without being discovered. Use the "If-I-Were" formula to be sure that all choices reflect absolute conviction. (Even if you personally feel that you would never do such a thing, try to build the circumstances in your own mind so that the action is justified.) When all the details have been carefully worked out consciously and deliberately, perform the action. Afterward, observe your emotional responses to the actions you played. Did you feel fear? If not, why?

    Assume that you are waiting in a bus terminal or an airport or some other waiting area to meet someone who is arriving from a great distance. Decide on a relationship with that person that is terribly important but required a long period of separation. Do not try to imagine someone you actually know; try to invent the existence of another character. Rehearse all the details of waiting carefully; pay particular attention to how your character would be allowed to behave in such a place. Have another actor play the returning person, and have that person walk onto the stage at the climax of your scene. When you have worked out all the details carefully, perform the pantomime. Afterward, observe your emotional response to the actions you played. Did you feel anxiety, followed by joy at the reunion? If not, why not? Work through the scene again if necessary until the actions create the desired response. Check the list of problems to be sure you are not creating any blocks for your own real emotions.

    Assume that you have been away from your home for many years. Try to build the circumstances of an imaginary home, an imaginary relationship with your parents, and the details of an imaginary living room. Try to imagine that your parents are gone and that you are returning to look around the home where you grew up one last time before the building is to be torn down. (Again, do not use images of your own home or your own real parents for this scene; the exercise should be purely theatrical.) Try to imagine that you are looking for a particular object that you are expecting to find there, such as an old photograph or knickknack or other similar item. Plan the details of your pantomime search very carefully; use the "If-I-Were" formula to plan how you would search the room thoroughly if you were really that person in that position. Then try performing the search; the scene ends when you give up trying to find the missing object. Afterward, observe your own emotional responses to the scene. Did you feel sorrow? If not, why not?

In each case, remember to play your objectives with conviction. Your purpose is to perform the actions described, not to try deliberately to stimulate your own emotions through the pantomimes.

2. Memorize a short speech from a play or a few lines of poetry. Use the words to express each of Ekman's fundamental emotions (happiness, sadness, surprise, fear, anger, and disgust). In each case, imagine you are speaking to another person. Develop the details in your own mind about the nature of whom you are speaking to, under what circumstances, and to what purpose. Be certain that your objective conforms to one of the six primary objectives as well. Try to avoid using any specific memories of your own experiences with these emotions before performing the actions. Build the circumstances with vividness in your mind so that the actions you play are at very high costs. Afterward, analyze your own response to the situations. Were you able to stimulate your emotions through the actions? If not, why not? Which ones worked better than others?

NOTES

1. Constantin Stanislavski, *My Life in Art* trans. J. J. Robbins (New York: Theatre Arts Books, 1924), pp. 377-78.

2. Oscar Brockett, *History of the Theatre, 3rd ed.* (New York: Allyn and Bacon, Inc., 1977), p. 320.

3. Brockett, pp. 380-81.

4. *The History of the English Stage* quoted in *A Source Book in Theatrical History*, ed. A. M. Nagler (New York: Dover Publications, Inc., 1952), p. 221.

5. Denis Diderot, "The Paradox of Acting" in *The Paradox of Acting and Masks or Faces?*, trans. Walter Herries Pollock (New York: Hill and Wang, 1957), p. 221.

6. Diderot, p. 20.

7. Brockett, p. 397.

8. Garff B. Wilson, *A History of American Acting*, (Bloomington: Indiana University Press, 1966), p. 110.

9. E. T. Kirby, "Delsarte: Three Frontiers," *The Drama Review*, vol. 16, no. 1 (March 1972), p. 62.

10. Joseph R. Roach, Jr., "G. H. Lewes and Performance Theory: Towards a 'Science of Acting,'" *Theatre Journal*, vol. 32, no. 3 (October 1980), p. 317.

11. Constantin Stanislavski, *An Actor Prepares*, trans. Elizabeth Reynolds Hapgood (New York: Theatre Arts Books, 1936), p. 167.

12. Stanislavski, p. 167.

13. Carl Georg Lange and William James, *The Emotions* (New York: Hafner Publishing Company, 1967), a facsimile of the 1922 edition, ed. Knight Dunlap, p. 13.

14. Constantin Stanislavski, *My Life in Art*, p. 465-66.

15. David Garfield, *A Player's Place: The Story of the Actors Studio* (New York: MacMillan Publishing Co., Inc., 1980), p. 13.

16. Lee Strasberg, "Acting and Actor Training," in *Producing the Play*, ed. John Gassner (New York: Holt, Rinehart and Winston, Inc., 1953), p. 140.

17. Strasberg, p. 140.

18. Harold Clurman, *The Fervent Years* (New York: Harcourt Brace Jovanovich, 1945), pp. 44-45.

19. Garfield, p. 33.

20. Sonia Moore, *The Stanislavski System: The Professional Training of an Actor* (New York: Penguin Books, 1965), pp. 52–53.

21. Paul Ekman and Wallace V. Friesen. *Unmasking the Face: A Guide to Recognizing Emotions from Facial Clues* (Englewood Cliffs, N. J.: Prentice-Hall, Inc., 1975), pp. 23–24.

22. Paul Ekman, Robert W. Levenson, and Walter V. Friesen, "Autonomic Nervous System Activity Distinguishes Among Emotions," in *Science*, V221, no. 4616 (September 16, 1983), p. 1208.

23. Ekman et al., p. 1210.

Lesson Ten

Conclusion

Realistic acting requires actors to create the illusion that they are in another place from the place where they really are, that they are people other than who they really are, and that they are doing something other than what they really are doing. Creating this kind of illusion successfully is the result of three different processes:

> Playing the Situation: communicating the character's passive and active relationship to the setting.
>
> Playing the Relationships: communicating the character's identity primarily in terms of the relationships among the other characters in the play.
>
> Playing the Objectives: communicating the character's motivation in terms of the desired result, the obstacle, the strategy, and the cost.

By focusing on these three processes, actors also communicate a lot of other information that the actor cannot play directly, including all of the various levels of motivation, personality, and emotions.

Taken all together, playing the situation, playing the relationships, and playing the objectives define the process of realistic acting.

Chapter Ten

What Is Good Realistic Acting?

Acting is not a mysterious business made up of alchemy, witchcraft, free-masonry, and voodoo. Acting is a craft. And like any other craft, there are logical, definable processes at work.

Also, like any other craft, acting can be done well or it can be done poorly. And since the process of realistic acting in particular can be defined logically, there are certain standards by which any piece of realistic acting can be evaluated. Some of these standards pertain to matters of pure technique, including the use of the voice, the ability to speak well, and the ability to move. In other words, many factors have to be present in the work of a realistic actor if that work is to be judged successful. A list of these factors forms a virtual checklist of the information that must be communicated to the audience in a piece of effective realistic acting. And these factors are all functions of the goals of realistic acting, which were explained at the beginning of this book.

The primary goal is the creation of the illusion of natural behavior. In other words, the audience should not see actors on a stage but *characters in a play*. The audience should not see scenery and props and costumes and lighting but *the place where the play is supposed to take place*. And most important, the audience should not see a group of people reciting the lines of a play and walking through the movements that were determined in advance with the help of a director, but *characters performing the actions that those lines represent.* The highest and most important goal of realistic acting—the sum total effect of all the parts of the illusion of natural behavior—is that an audience should not have to understand the language the actors are speaking in order to follow the essential action of the play. To achieve that goal, actors must communicate the following pieces of information to the audience primarily through movement.

The actor's general relationship to the space. The actor's movements, gestures, and business must all be appropriate to the setting of the play. An audience should be able to perceive choices in the actor's behavior that reflect whether the character is in a public, private, or personal space. How the character uses the furniture, how the character dresses (or undresses) in this space, how the character responds to the other actors in the same setting—all these factors must reflect the character's general relationship to the setting. The illusion of natural behavior demands that the actor deliberately make choices to communicate this information to the audience. In the scene from *Harvey*, we observed how Veta might choose to remove a shoe and rub her foot—an action that character would feel free to perform only in her own personal space. An audience would see the presence of that kind of detail in the actor's work as the actor's attempt to portray the character's relationship to the space.

The actor's specific relationship to the space. The actor must always have a clear idea of the character's specific reason for being in the place where the scene takes place. To that end, all blocking must appear to be motivated. There must be enough movement to keep the audience's interest in the scene, and there must be specific motivations for that blocking that make it clear to the audience why that character has not decided to go to some other place. Again, in the scene from *Harvey*, we observed that the script did not provide a specific reason for Veta and Myrtle to remain in the Dowd library once the phone call that brought them into that room originally had been completed. The decision on the part of the actor playing Veta to use the interruption of the phone call to give the character a moment to sit and rest would be a detail that the audience would recognize as the character's specific reason for remaining in that place. Actors must remember that simply because the script calls for a character to make an entrance is not a good enough reason to do so. The actor must determine a strong specific reason for why the character enters the place and remains in it until directed by the script to exit.

The character's identity. All the details of the actor's physical appearance must be carefully chosen to communicate the right information about the character's age, background, physical condition, economic circumstances, level of education, and so forth. Actors must not allow any details of their own personal appearance to become part of the characterization unless those details match exactly what that character might really look like. Any and all inappropriate details must be eliminated. If changes can be made in the actor's own appearance for the sake of communicating an appropriate character identity (or *Who*), those changes must be made.

The character's relationship to the other characters.   The proper distances between the various characters in the play must be maintained according to their relationships to each other. Two issues are of particular importance in this matter: One actor may be a personal friend of another in the company, but if their roles in the play call for a more distant relationship, they must not habitually maintain an inappropriately familiar distance. Also, and more important, characters who have an intimate relationship to each other must habitually use intimate distances. Also, there must be some degree of casual touching that is characteristic of such relationships. When actors play characters who are supposed to be in an intimate relationship and they do not use intimate distances and never touch, the illusion is not going to be effective.

The character's need *relationship to the other characters.*   Each character in a play must clearly be seen as having a need for each of the other characters with whom there is interaction. This factor is particularly important in the case of an intimate relationship in which there is any conflict. Characters who yell and scream at each other frequently do so because they care intensely about each other. Actors must not make choices in such situations that leave the audience wondering why the characters don't simply stay away from each other. In the scene from *The Circle*, Elizabeth's *Need* relationship to Arnold colors all the criticisms that she makes of him; if she didn't need him in some way, there would be no reason for her to be having that conversation with him in the first place.

The character's purpose.   For every moment that an actor is onstage, there must appear to be a clear and obvious purpose behind that character's behavior. To that end, there must always be three observable qualities of the character's behavior:

> *Point of focus:* The actor's behavior and dialogue must always be clearly directed toward another person who is the obstacle that the objectives are intended to overcome.
> *Activity:* The audience must be able to perceive the nature of the strategy the character is using to overcome each obstacle in turn.
> *Cost:* The intensity with which the character pursues the objectives must always be proportional to the degree of importance of those objectives to that

character. Also, repeated objectives must always be played with increasing intensity to reflect why the objectives are being pursued again.

The character's desired result.   From the point of focus, activity, and cost, the audience must be able to infer what the specific desired result is that the character is trying to bring about. There should never be a moment in the actor's performance at which the director could not stop the action and ask, "Why did you say that?" and not get an answer corresponding to one of the six fundamental objectives. The objectives must always be real objectives from the character's point of view. All nonobjectives such as result playing, playing the character, playing the emotion, playing the style, and so on, must be avoided.

The character's beat changes.   The moments at which the character's purpose changes must be clear as well. Furthermore, the actor should play an appropriately large number of beats in performance to create varying rhythms and tempos. The beat changes should be made whenever there is a change in the desired result, strategy, obstacle, or cost.

The character's personality.   Choices should be made in the interpretation of the character's objectives that create a sense of unity within complex characters and a sense of complexity within simple characters. The audience should be able to form specific expectations of how the actor's character might behave in future circumstances. Stereotypes should be avoided, except when roles are written to be played that way. There should be some characteristic behavior that seems appropriate and familiar and is reinforced to make the audience aware of it.

The character's emotions.   The audience should be permitted to have an empathic response to the character. Actors should modulate their portrayal of their characters' emotional states to be consistent with the context of the scene as a whole. Any emotional excesses for their own sake should be avoided. The effectiveness of the performance as a whole is to be judged on what the audience is made to feel, not on what the actors themselves feel.

Index

A

Acting:
    areas, 58
    conventionalized, 2–4, 8
    difference between film and stage, 16,
        65–66, 68
    in everyday life, 30–33, 232–33
    film, 12–17
    goal of realistic acting, 11, 17, 242
    "heroic," 216
    and magic, 29–30
    and omissions, 26–27, 30, 35
    presentational, 4–5, 8, 11–12, 212, 214,
        217, 220–21, 237
    processes, 9, 12, 33–34, 241
    realistic acting defined, 1, 8, 38, 241
    Romantic, 212, 216–17
    "school of emotionalism," 216
    styles of acting, 11
    stylized acting, 4, 8
Acting: The First Six Lessons, 222
Actions, playing, 7, 11, 17, 112–13, 163, 193,
        198, 235
Activities, 97–99, 117, 121, 126–28, 130, 137,
        181, 244–45
An Actor Prepares, 26, 152, 220, 225
Actors Studio, 224, 237

Adler, Stella, 225, 235, 237
"Affective memory" (*see* "Emotional mem-
        ory")
Alice Doesn't Live Here Anymore, 16
Allen, Woody, 15
All My Children, 8
All My Sons, 44
American Center for Stanislavski Theater
        Art, 226
American Laboratory Theatre, 221–22
American Theatre Association, 224, 226
Anglim, Philip, 65, 71
Antigone (Anouilh), 33
Antoine, Andre, 6
Aristotle, 27, 212–13
    theory of the emotions, 216, 231, 237
Arms and the Man, 45, 199
Astor Place Theatre (riot), 216
Audition (Shurtleff), 82
Auntie Mame, 204
Awake and Sing!, 45

B

Balinese temple dancers, 3
Ballet, 4
Barefoot in the Park, 42